The Lost Days
of Summer

Katie Flynn

The Lost Days of Summer

arrow books

Published by Arrow Books in 2011

2 4 6 8 10 9 7 5 3 1

Copyright © Katie Flynn 2011

Katie Flynn has asserted her right under the Copyright, Designs
and Patents Act, 1988, to be identified as the author of this work.

First published in Great Britain in 2011 by
Arrow Books
The Random House Group Limited
20 Vauxhall Bridge Road, London SW1V 2SA

www.rbooks.co.uk

Addresses for companies within The Random House Group Limited can be
found at: www.randomhouse.co.uk/offices.htm

The Random House Group Limited Reg. No. 954009

A CIP catalogue record for this book
is available from the British Library

ISBN 9780099550495

The Random House Group Limited supports The Forest Stewardship Council
(FSC), the leading international forest certification organisation. All our titles that
are printed on Greenpeace approved FSC certified paper carry the FSC logo. Our
paper procurement policy can be found at www.rbooks.co.uk/environment

Mixed Sources

Product group from well-managed
forests and other controlled sources
www.fsc.org Cert no. TT-COC-2139
© 1996 Forest Stewardship Council

Typeset in Palatino by Palimpsest Book Production Limited,
Falkirk, Stirlingshire

Printed and bound in Great Britain by
CPI Mackays, Chatham ME5 8TD

For Heather Chorlton of Holyhead who first
drew my attention to the Swtan cottage;
thank you, Heather!

Acknowledgements

Firstly, I'd like to thank Eric Anthony of the Holyhead Maritime Museum for allowing Brian to photograph his grandfather's 'death penny', thus opening up a whole new chapter of my book. He also guided us through the museum – which is wonderful – and directed me to books and First World War photographs and memorabilia, especially *Master Mariner*, the biography of the late Captain William Henry Hughes, DSC, written by Dewi Francis; an exellent and amusing work dealing with both world wars.

I also spent a good deal of time at the Swtan cottage, which has been beautifully restored by local volunteers and proved irresistible as a setting for my story so my thanks to them.

Last but not least my sincere thanks go to Nancy Webber, who untangled tangles, righted wrongs and generally kept me on the straight and narrow.

Chapter One

September 1939

Nell Whitaker sat scrunched up in the corner seat of the train which was taking her where she had no desire to go, and looked at her reflection in the dirt-smeared window pane. The compartment was full, and she hoped the other passengers thought that she was watching the passing scene and did not realise that she was balefully examining her own face.

In the window glass she saw a thin fifteen-year-old with a tumbled mass of dark hair, large dark eyes and, she had to admit, a mouth which drooped with bitterness and disappointment. And no wonder! Her mam had promised – absolutely promised – that she should not be sent away, evacuated as they called it. Yet here she was, on a train, heading for heaven knew where.

When war had been declared three weeks previously, her younger cousins had been sent with the rest of their schoolmates to a small village on the Wirral, where they had felt out of place and unwanted. There had been no question of evacuation so far as Nell herself was concerned; she had started at secretarial college within days of war being declared and her mother had promised that the two of them would continue to live their lives as they had in peacetime. 'If you do well at college I might be able to get you a job with me,' she had said. 'They know I'm hard-working and reliable, and they'll guess that you're the same. But even if not, secretarial jobs should be easier to find now that so many employees have either volunteered for the services or been called up.' She had sighed wistfully. 'I'd love to join the WAAF and do my bit for the war effort, but that's impossible whilst you're still in college. If only you'd taken a job in a factory – factory workers get awfully well paid . . . but that's not what you wanted, and I'm the last person to push you into a job you'd dislike. So if you work very hard and gain the qualifications you've talked about, I suppose I must put up with it.'

Nell had promised to do her best, secretly surprised that her flighty, fun-loving mother had even considered joining up and wearing a uniform, but she had worked hard and passed the weekly tests with flying colours. And Mum had been pleased and proud, Nell thought miserably now, staring out at the countryside trundling past. There had been no question of sending her away then.

Meanwhile, the cousins had stayed where they were, though Matty, the closest to Nell in age, had told her before they left that they didn't want to go, had no desire to leave Liverpool, no matter what. 'They say there'll be bombin', or paratroopers dressed as nuns descendin' from the skies,' she had pointed out. 'I reckon it's all talk, meself, and we'll be as safe here as anywhere.'

2

'But won't you like living in the country?' Nell had asked. 'I've always imagined life on a farm must be great fun.'

Matty had snorted. 'Fun?' she had said witheringly. 'It's bleedin' hard work, from wharr I've heared tell, an' no shops nor cinemas for miles. An' country schools is horrible, wi' outside privies and mud everywhere. Give me good old Bootle any day.'

Now, Nell looked round the crowded, stuffy compartment; it was a cold and windy day and no one wanted to open the window. The train which was to take her right across Wales and on to an island she had never even heard of seemed to be constantly held up, which meant that the journey, which someone had told her normally took two or three hours, might easily last all day.

Nell sighed and returned to the contemplation of her miserable reflection. She told herself that she and her mother loved each other dearly and had been very close – as close as sisters, her mother always claimed somewhat coyly – since her father, Tom Whitaker, had died. And now she felt that her mother had turned against her, reneging on her promise. She said she was sending Nell away because her sister, Nell's aunt Kath, had written suggesting that Trixie might send her eldest daughter to Ty Hen, her farm on Anglesey, where she would be safe, well looked after and a great help.

Nell had looked at her mother, almost unable to believe her ears. 'I didn't even know I had an aunt Kath, and I don't want to leave Liverpool,' she had

3

said. 'Besides, you're staying here, so why shouldn't I? If it's safe for you, it's safe for me.'

She had watched her mother's face flush and seen her eyes sparkle without understanding the cause, but presently she had learned the reason for her mother's excitement and also, in a way, for her own banishment. 'I'm going to join the WAAF, queen, along with your Auntie Lou,' her mother had said. 'They won't accept anyone with a dependent child, so when your Auntie Kath wrote offering to have you I was delighted.' She must have seen her daughter's horrified expression, for she had added hastily: 'Oh, queen, don't look like that! Don't you see? You'd be doing your bit for our country too, because growing food is much more important than being someone's secretary.'

'But Mam, I'm doing so well,' Nell had wailed. 'Is there a secretarial college near this woman's farm? Might I go to it to finish my course?'

Her mother had looked uneasy. 'It might be possible,' she had said. 'If you could continue your training, you'd be killing two birds with one stone. You'd be helping your aunt whilst planning for your own future. As soon as you arrive at the farm you can make enquiries; there's no harm in that.'

'Right. And now you can jolly well tell me why I've never heard of this Auntie Kath before,' Nell had said firmly. 'I know you've got a lot of relatives, and some of them I've never met, but I've never even heard of a Kath!'

Trixie Whitaker had looked rather guilty. 'Oh, Kath and I fell out. She was set to marry a feller I – I didn't approve of. There was a big age gap . . . in fact the whole family disapproved, so when Kath wouldn't take no notice, but married and went off to Anglesey, we lost touch. You could have knocked me down with a feather when I got her letter. She said that Owain – that's the name of the feller she married – had died, and she was finding the farm too much for herself and the one worker left to her. I wrote back explaining I'd been widowed myself and saying I'd be glad to entrust my eldest girl to her care.' She had chuckled, seeing her daughter's puzzled expression. 'Kath didn't even know your name, lerralone that you were an only child. Still an' all, it were a generous offer and I'm sure you and Kath will take to one another. She's not a bad old stick; in fact she and I were close until the quarrel. Why, I reckon she'll even pay you, 'cos she'd have to pay a land girl, only it seems she prefers family.'

'If she pays me, then even if there was a secretarial college two minutes' walk away I wouldn't be able to attend it,' Nell had said gloomily. 'And why didn't you tell me when my aunt's letter arrived? You did promise you'd never send me away, you know, or have you forgotten?'

'War changes things,' her mother had said vaguely. 'Just be grateful that I'm sending you somewhere safe, and to a blood relation.'

'What if I hate it?' Nell had asked suspiciously. 'Suppose Auntie Kath hates me, for that matter? Would one of the other aunts take me in?' She had pulled a face at the thought, for fond though she was of her mother's many sisters and cousins, their small houses

5

were already horribly overcrowded. She got on well with Auntie Lou, but she was going away with her mother and Nell had no particular desire to live with any of the others.

Trixie, however, had shaken her head decisively. 'I'd never forgive myself if you came back to Liverpool and got injured, or even killed, when the Germans start their bombing offensive,' she had said, and for the first time Nell had thought her mother sounded serious. 'If you are truly unhappy, then you must write and tell me and I'll try to find you another billet, but not in a big city. Promise me you'll stay with your aunt for at least six months. And remember the old saying: Out of the frying pan, into the fire. There are many worse places than a farm in the heart of the country, so please, queen, make the best of it. If I hate the WAAF, there's no way out for me until the war's over; why should it be different for you?'

After that, events had moved so fast that Nell and her mother had been too busy to discuss the matter further. Trixie's papers had arrived, telling her to report to Bridgnorth in Shropshire the following Monday, and detailing the personal possessions she was allowed to take with her. Auntie Lou's daughters were already employed by the munitions factory in Long Lane, Aintree, and had taken digs to be near their work, so Lou and Trixie sold the contents of their houses and left it to the landlord to find new tenants, thus making it impossible for Nell to run home, even if she wished to do so.

But I wouldn't, Nell told her reflection bitterly now,

because I keep *my* promises, which is more than Mam does. It had been no use arguing, however, when her mother and her aunt were so frantically busy and so very happy. Instead, she reminded herself, she had sulked. Drowning in misery, she had even refused her mother's offer to make her a packed lunch, in case the journey to Valley – that was the name of the station at which Nell was to alight – took longer than they thought. However, Nell had grudgingly accepted money to buy herself a drink and a sandwich when she changed trains, which had happened three times already. Not that she had bought food; she had simply changed miserably on to the next train, bagging a corner seat wherever possible.

So now here she was, sitting in the stuffy yet cold compartment, with her coat buttoned up to the throat and a dull ache in her heart, heading for an unknown aunt and an unknown destination. It was late September, and for the first time in her life, she realised suddenly, she would be celebrating Christmas in about twelve weeks without a soul she knew.

She had just turned back to the window to hide the tears which were forming in her eyes when she was startled by a voice speaking in her ear. 'You's very quiet, alanna. How about you havin' one o' me sandwiches? They's cheese and pickle, and it's me own bread, baked fresh yesterday. I reckon we'll be on this train till midnight if the driver don't get a move on, and you'll be pretty peckish by then . . . unless you've got some grub in that there bag slung on the rack.'

Nell turned towards the woman sitting next to her.

She was immensely fat and her round rosy face was pinched with cold, though she was smiling broadly. Nell looked longingly at the sandwich the woman was holding out. Looking round the compartment, she realised that everyone else was eating. A young couple, both in the uniform of the Royal Air Force, were sharing a packet of sandwiches and a bottle of Corona, and a thin, agitated-looking woman was handing round food to three boys, probably her sons, Nell thought. Hastily, she made up her mind; eating on a train must come under the heading of a picnic and anyway, what did it matter? Wartime changed everything, including manners. So she accepted the sandwich, saying as she did so: 'Thank you very much, it's awfully kind of you. I haven't any food with me because my mother gave me money to buy myself some, but I didn't have time to do so before the train left and though we've stopped ever so often I was scared of being left behind if I got down.'

The old woman agreed that the train had certainly stopped frequently and Nell, finishing the sandwich and accepting a second, admitted that she had not dared to so much as leave her seat even when the train was in motion, fearing that her place would be immediately taken by one of the many passengers standing crammed together in the corridor.

'You're right, alanna, but now you and me's acquainted I'll mek sure no one steals your seat,' her companion said comfortably. 'How's about you havin' a drop of me tay to wash that food down?'

'I'd love a drink; I'm dry as a desert but I don't think

8

I'd better,' Nell owned. She dropped her voice to a whisper. 'The truth is, I need to spend a penny, and if I have a drink of your tea it'll make it worse.' For the first time that day, she giggled. 'I've kept imagining myself leaping off the train and running across to the Ladies and hearing the train pulling out while I was still at it. So you see . . .'

The fat woman beamed at her, fished out a very large Thermos flask from her basket, unscrewed the cap and poured a generous amount of tea into it. ''Tis plain you don't travel much by rail,' she commented. 'This here's a corridor train, with a lavvy at either end.' She thrust the flask cap at Nell. 'Drink up; I'll guard your seat like the dragon they'll think me while you make your way to the WC.'

'Well I never; a toilet on a train!' Nell breathed. She drank the tea eagerly, then handed the cap back and got to her feet. 'I'll be as quick as I can. Don't let anyone snitch my haversack, though there's precious little in it. All my tickets and money and so on are in this' – she patted the small brown leather handbag her mother had given her as a farewell present – 'and I won't be parted from it no matter what.'

Presently, she returned to her seat, relieved in every sense of the word. Despite the crowds standing in the corridor, everyone seemed helpful and good-natured and had squeezed up to let her pass. There had been a queue for the lavatory – ever since the war started there was a queue for every perishing thing, Nell thought – and when she reached the head of it there had been no toilet paper in the tiny compartment

9

and the flush had not been working properly. However, there had been a tap over the hand basin, so she had been able to wash her hands and thought that, had the train been less crowded, visiting the WC would have been quite an interesting experience.

Back in her seat once more, she thanked her companion and promised that the next time the train stopped at a station she would jump down and buy a snack from the buffet, if there was one. Her companion smiled, but told her to save her money. 'I always pack enough food for an army, so I do,' she said. 'Mind, I've a long journey ahead of me. Where's you goin', alanna? All the way, like? This here's known as the boat train 'cos it's the one what connects up wit' the Irish ferry. I'm going to Ireland . . . and you?'

All Nell's misery returned abruptly. 'I'm going to stay with an aunt, to give her a hand on her farm,' she mumbled. 'I gerroff the train at somewhere called Valley. My mam came with me as far as Birkenhead and saw me off, but she couldn't come any further because she's joined the WAAF and had to be at some-where called Bridgnorth training centre by Monday morning. But I got on all right, though I were in a fair tizzy when we changed trains at Chester. I asked a porter where I should go and he said to follow everyone else, so I did and here I am.'

The fat woman nodded sympathetically. 'Awful, ain't it? But we don't have no more changes now, t'ank the good Lord. And you'll be gettin' off before I do, though only by a few minutes. Someone meetin' you, are they?' She delved into her basket once more, produced two slices of fruit cake and offered one to her companion. 'Or would you rather have an apple? I allus pack a few apples 'cos they don't dry up like sandwiches and cake, and since me darter lives in Connemara, I've the whole of Ireland to cross afore me next proper meal.'

Nell accepted an apple gladly and began to crunch. 'I'm being met, though I don't know whether my aunt will come herself or send someone else.' She looked at her companion's friendly, smiling face and decided to share her troubles. 'The truth is, my Auntie Kath and I have never even met before; there was a quarrel, long ago. I think my mother disapproved because my aunt's husband, Owain Jones, was very much older than my aunt. I think Mam tried to dissuade her from marrying him because of the age difference, but I suppose Auntie Kath must have loved him because she went ahead anyway. Then they moved to this Welsh island and she and Mam simply lost touch. Why, when she wrote to Mam to suggest that I might go and help on the farm, she didn't even know my name. She said "your eldest", so, as I said to Mam, she probably thinks I'm one of half a dozen!'

'And you ain't?' her new acquaintance said. 'Well, I reckon I should have guessed, 'cos you're very independent, like most only children. What's your name, by the way? I'm Mrs McFarlane, goin' to see me darter Siobhan, her husband Padraig and their new little baby what they're goin' to christen Albert, after my husband, 'cos I married an Englishman for me sins.'

Nell giggled. 'Albert's a very English name,' she

agreed. 'I'm Helen Whitaker, only everyone calls me Nell.' She held out her hand. 'Nice to meet you, Mrs McFarlane.' She got carefully to her feet as the train clattered to a halt. 'Guard my place while I see what's for sale in the buffet.'

Nell was fortunate; as she climbed down from the train, a man in a blue and white striped apron and checked cap came along the platform, trundling a makeshift trolley laden with sausage rolls, Cornish pasties and sandwiches. They looked good, and smelt better, and Nell was happy to part with a couple of shillings in return for two large pasties. She walked quickly as far as the engine and back to stretch her legs, then got back into the train and collapsed into her seat once more, handing over the larger of the two pasties to Mrs McFarlane, who tutted and told her she should not waste her money, but thanked her anyway and stowed the pastie away in her capacious basket, assuring Nell that she would save it until she boarded the ferry. 'Though I'm beginning to fear this perishin' train won't reach Holyhead in time for me to catch the night boat,' she told Nell. 'Still, there's always somewhere a well-cushioned woman can doze for an hour or two. But what about you? We ain't even reached the island yet. Suppose your aunt gives up on you and goes home?' She chortled, then gave Nell's shoulder a reassuring pat. 'Don't you worry, alanna, she'll wait. The stationmaster at Valley will tell her the train's been held up and you won't be arriving on time. I were only coddin' you when I said that.'

Nell smiled. 'I may not be as well cushioned as you, but I reckon by the time we do arrive I'll be so tired I could sleep on a clothes line. I wonder if there are taxis lined up outside Valley station, like there are in Lime Street at home?'

Her companion snorted. 'It'll be donkey carts more like; I were born and raised in Anglesey and only moved to Ireland when I were first wed, and Anglesey's rare like Ireland in some ways. I can tell you've never lived in the country, have you? You'll find it's very different; better in some ways, worse in others. But you'll see for yourself soon enough.' She settled herself more comfortably in her seat and lowered her voice. 'Anglesey is a queer place, not at all like the rest of Wales. You know the Welsh call it Mam Cymru? That means Mother of Wales. They say it's an enchanted island and it was from there that the Druids ruled in the ancient days. Wicked, they were.' She lowered her voice still further. 'They believed in human sacrifice; their whole religion was based on blood. Ever heard of the Wicker Man?'

Nell shook her head. 'No. I know nothing about the island at all,' she admitted. 'And I've never heard of the Wicker Man. Tell me about it; it sounds exciting.'

'Well it ain't, and you don't want to know about the Wicker Man,' her companion said firmly. 'It's all different now, of course, but I reckon, though the Druids is long gone, there's still a sort of magic about the place.' She smiled at Nell and nudged her in the ribs. 'Only it's a nice sort of magic now. Where's you going when you leave Valley?'

'I can't pronounce it,' Nell admitted, hanging her head. 'Well, part of it I can. It's Llan . . .' she spelt it out carefully, 'fwrog.'

Mrs McFarlane chuckled. 'An f is pronounced v in Welsh, and w is oo, so it's pronounced Llanvoorog,' she explained. 'Lucky for you you ain't headin' for the village I were born in, which is called Llanfairpwllgwyngyllgogerychwyrndrobwll llantysiliogogogoch.' She grinned at Nell's expression. 'Longest name in the world, they say, and the first railway station on the island, so when you reach it you'll know you've crossed the Menai Straits and are in Anglesey at last.'

'But surely I'll know when we cross the Menai Straits,' Nell objected. 'I thought that since Anglesey is an island we'd have to take a ferry. It would take an awfully long bridge to get the train from the main-land to the island, wouldn't it?'

'It is an awfully long bridge, but since it's completely enclosed it's more like going through a tunnel,' her companion explained. 'And in fact Anglesey is really two islands because Holy Island used to be cut off from Anglesey itself by an arm of the sea, but now there's a road and of course the railway across so it don't seem like two islands no more.'

'Well I never did,' Nell breathed, fascinated by Mrs McFarlane's revelations. 'Is the village I'm going to on Holy Island?'

Disappointingly, Mrs McFarlane shook her head. 'No, m'dear. The port of Holyhead is on Holy Island, and I've heard tell there's a lighthouse called South

14

Stack below the cliffs, which are mortal high. I dare say your aunt and uncle will take you for a trip around, show you the sights, such as they are.'

Nell opened her mouth to say that her uncle was dead, then closed it again. She had never known Owain Jones and guessed that Mrs McFarlane would want to know details, which she would have to invent since she had no idea what had caused his death. If it was simply old age . . . but best to say nothing. Instead, as the train began to slow, she turned towards the window and peered out. 'Is this the beginning of the tunnel?' she asked. 'Goodness, surely we must be nearly there? It's growing dark already.'

Her companion leaned across her to peer out of the window. 'I dunno where the devil we are,' she said doubtfully, 'except that we're nowhere near the Menai Straits yet. This perishin' train ain't goin' much faster than walkin' pace. Oh, drat it. I'm bound to miss the night ferry at this rate.' She sat back in her seat and closed her eyes. 'How I do run on! But now I'll make up for it and try to have forty winks. Just you do the same, m'dear. The train makes a hellish clatter going through the tunnel, so you ain't likely to miss your stop.'

Nell did not think she could possibly fall asleep. For one thing, her feet were numb with cold, and within seconds of closing her eyes her companion began to snore so loudly that other passengers turned their faces away to hide their grins. However, despite the rattle of the train, the subdued chatter and her companion's deafening snores, Nell did fall asleep. It was not, however, a very restful slumber. Visions of the island which was to be her home entered her dreams. Tall, long-haired Druids in blood-bespattered white robes pursued her along high cliffs and long, pale beaches. Lambs bleated, seagulls mewed and babies were carried away in monstrous wicker baskets, whilst Nell chased after them, bearing in her arms for some strange reason a large bucket of seawater. She knew that if she hurled the seawater at the Druid, it would save the life of the baby in the basket.

But presently the scene changed and she was having a polite cup of tea and sandwich with her aunt Kath, who was the image of her mother . . . who was her mother . . . come to take her away from this extraordinary land and back to her own dear place, which was the corner house in Kingfisher Court, just off the Scotland Road, where her mother had grown up. She could even hear the traffic going past on the road outside. Only suddenly the noise grew louder and louder and a huge train, its firebox spitting red-hot sparks, burst into the room. Nell and her mother both screamed and Nell awoke, shaking, to find Mrs McFarlane smiling down upon her.

'Told you the tunnel would wake you up,' her companion said triumphantly. 'It's enough to waken the dead, ain't it?' She had had to bawl to be heard above the roar of the engine. But then the train left the tunnel – Nell could see the stars sparkling in the dark night sky and knew her companion had been right; they had reached the island at last.

* * *

16

Darkness had fallen when the train finally drew in to a small station and a porter came along the platform shouting, 'Valley, Valley,' in a cracked and weary voice. Because of the blackout it was almost impossible to pick out any details, but Nell, with her haversack slung on one shoulder and her precious handbag clutched close to her chest, simply jumped down as soon as the train stopped and turned to look back at Mrs McFarlane. She could see the older woman's face only dimly in the faint blue light, which was all that was allowed.

'Goodbye, and thank you very much,' she shouted above the noise of the engine, preparing to start off on its final leg. 'Good luck for the rest of your journey!'

Mrs McFarlane shouted thanks back and then withdrew her head as the train began to move, and the last Nell saw of her was a large white hand, waving rhythmically.

Nell stood on the platform, watching the train until she could see it no longer. Despite the fact that it was very late indeed the moon and stars shone brightly, illumining the little station and the gleaming rail tracks. For a moment, panic seized her. She had never felt so alone, so totally friendless. Where was her aunt? The little railway station might have been put down in the middle of nowhere, for she could see no dwelling of any description. Despite her resolve, tears came to her eyes and trickled down her cold cheeks. In this alien landscape she simply longed for the sights and sounds with which she had grown up: the rattle of trams as they careered along on their shiny rails, the voices of passers-by, even the now hooded lights, blue-grey and ghostly, of cars and lorries as they traversed the streets of Liverpool. Although she considered herself to be an adult, Nell had never been out by herself since the war started, and now she was not only alone but also frightened, sure that the arrangements her mother had so hastily made had gone awry, that she would be forced to wait until it grew light and she could summon aid.

No one else had alighted from the train, but the porter was closing the big white gates so Nell turned and followed him, crossing the track as he did and finding herself in what must be the main village street, with the dark shapes of houses on either side. There was a signal box to her left and she guessed that it must be manned; should she appeal to the signaller or to the porter? But when she glanced round, the porter had disappeared.

She was turning back towards the signal box when she heard a soft clopping sound and saw a large horse and cart drawing up alongside her. Relief flooded her; even if it was not her aunt driving the equipage it was another human being, someone to whom she could explain her predicament. Uncertainly, she moved towards it just as a figure – she could not see whether it was a man or a woman – leaned down and addressed her. 'You a young person by the name of Whitaker?' it said.

Nell's heart lifted a little; it was a woman's voice, which meant, she imagined, that her aunt had come to meet her in person. 'Yes, I'm Helen Whitaker,' she said rather breathlessly. 'And you must be my

Auntie Kath, Mrs Kath Jones.' She held out a hand. 'How do you do? I'm sorry the train was so late, but the guard said it's quite usual.' Since the woman made no reply but simply stared down at her, she added uneasily: 'Mam said you'd probably come and meet the train, so . . .'

The woman didn't seem to have noticed Nell's outstretched hand, but this was not surprising since the moon had slid behind a cloud and for a moment the darkness was total. 'Ellen, did you say?' the woman asked in a lilting Welsh accent, and her voice sounded doubtful. 'I misremember what your ma called you in her letter, but it wasn't Ellen . . .' She gave an impatient sigh, then indicated the cart with a jerk of her head. 'Jump up; I had to fetch some cattle cake so I brought the cart rather than harnessing up the pony and trap. You can tell me what your name is as we go. Your ma did rattle on a bit; might have muddled you wi' one of your sisters, I suppose.'

Nell scrambled into the cart, but as soon as she was settled on the hard wooden seat she said what was uppermost in her mind. 'I don't know what my mam said in her letter to you, Auntie, but my name's Helen, with an h, and I'm usually called Nell. As for the names of my sisters, I've not got any, nor brothers neither. I'm an only child.'

Her aunt gathered up the reins and clicked her tongue. 'Not got brothers or sisters?' she said incredulously as they moved forward. 'But your ma's letter went on about Cissie and Molly, or some such names, anyway. When I answered her, I just said send the eldest. Truth to tell I read the letter that quick – it was the only letter she ever sent me – I can't say I took much heed of it; why should I?'

Nell was silent for a few moments, puzzled. Surely . . . 'Mam does run on sometimes and I suppose she said something about Auntie Lou's kids and you thought they were hers – my mam's, I mean – and got confused. The fact is that when Mam and Auntie Lou joined the WAAF the landlord didn't fancy my cousins living in his house with no mother to keep an eye on them, so Marilyn and Milly – that's their names – got lodgings out near Long Lane. That's where they're working, making munitions I think. They're a lot older than me; Marilyn's twenty and Milly's going on for nineteen. Were you expecting one of them? If so, perhaps I'll be no use to you. I'm only fifteen, and small for my age. Oh dear, I'm so sorry for the muddle.'

The older woman grunted. 'I did expect someone older, but I don't know as it matters,' she said gruffly. 'We'll have to see how you get on.'

Nell felt her cheeks grow hot. She was horrified by the misunderstanding and unable to clear her mother of blame. Trixie would have rambled on, forgetting the main purpose of the letter, and now here was Nell, miles and miles from the city that had been her home, with an aunt who had thought the girl with whom she had agreed to share her house was a big strong eighteen- or twenty-year-old, not a skinny kid. Nell cleared her throat. 'I know I'm not very old, but if you wanted one of my cousins . . .'

The moon reappeared at this moment and in its light

she saw her aunt frown and shoot her a quick glance. 'I can't say I wanted anyone,' she said gruffly. 'Oh, I don't deny there's work enough, but manage we could. The truth is I don't want no more evacuees dumped on me. I had 'em earlier; two limbs of Satan they were. I was that relieved when they went home and never came back. So when your ma's letter arrived I thought better the devil you know than the devil you don't. And here you are.'

'But you don't know me at all,' Nell pointed out, after a short pause. 'However, I'm quite strong, even though I'm small for my age. Still, if I'm no use, I can go back to Liverpool; though Mam isn't there any more, I've a heap of relatives living in Bootle and Everton, and I'm sure one of them would take me in. In fact I could go home tomorrow if you'd give me my fare. But it does seem a long way to come for nothing, and at school they said I was a quick learner. If – if you'd like to give me a try I would do my best for you, really I would.'

Even as she spoke, Nell wondered what on earth had got into her. She didn't want to stay here; she longed for the hustle and bustle of Liverpool. But rejecting her aunt and the island was one thing; being rejected was quite another. Besides, Liverpool without her beloved mam, she realised, lacked a good deal of its appeal. And if she were honest, she doubted that any of the aunts would want to take her in. They would say it must be her mother's decision, and Mam would ask her why she had not lived up to her promise to stay with her aunt for at least six months. So now she waited anxiously for Kath to reply.

The horse had been proceeding at a shambling trot, but in response to the hand on the reins it slowed to a walk. As the moon emerged from behind a bank of cloud her aunt turned to look searchingly at her, then gave a short bark of laughter. 'Right, we'll give it a try,' she said brusquely. 'We'll mebbe get on. And now you can tell me just what Trixie is up to.'

'Up to?' Nell asked blankly. 'I don't know what you mean.' She shuffled her cold feet and dug her hands into her coat pockets. The journey in the train had seemed interminable, and she was sure the horse had been ambling along for hours without indicating by so much as pricked ears or turned head that they were nearing their destination. The moon dodged in and out of the clouds, the harness creaked, her aunt slapped the reins impatiently on the animal's neck, and still there was no sign that they were about to turn off the road and make for human habitation.

'I mean what was your ma up to when she got in touch. Trixie wouldn't have writ to me without a good reason,' Auntie Kath replied gruffly. 'She said something about "essential war work".' She snorted. 'A right little good time girl your ma was; it's to be hoped you're different.'

'People say I take after my father,' Nell said rather grudgingly. 'But as I've already said, if I'm no use to you I'm sure I can go back to Liverpool. And – and I'd rather you didn't think of Mam as a good time girl, because she isn't, not a bit. She's had to bring me up alone since Dad died and she's got – or rather she had – a very important job with a big insurance company.

I don't know what she was like when she was young, but—'

'All right, all right, forget I mentioned it,' her aunt said impatiently. 'We'll give it a try. But you can still tell me what your mother's up to when she can't look after her own flesh and blood.'

'I told you she's joined the WAAF,' Nell said shortly. 'Is there anything wrong with that?'

Her aunt tutted. 'Don't be cheeky,' she said sharply. She clicked to the horse and it broke into a trot once more, turning into a narrow lane with tall banks on either side and stumpy trees almost meeting overhead. Nell gave a little shiver. The moon shone on large puddles and on branches already bare of leaves, yet still not on houses or farm buildings. But she took a deep breath and prepared to apologise for defending her parent.

'Sorry, Auntie Kath,' she mumbled. 'And I know what you mean; that she could join the WAAF without sending me to you. Only she couldn't if she had what they call a dependent child. She wants to do her bit for the war effort, so she had to send me away before the WAAF would let her join up.'

'I see,' Auntie Kath said drily. 'Convenient I am, then. What would Trixie have done if she'd not remembered her oldest sister?'

By now Nell had realised that her mother had deceived her daughter as well as her elder sister, pretending that Auntie Kath had written to her first, instead of the other way round. But there was no point in making a fuss – crying over spilt milk, as the saying went – and it had been a long day. Presently, despite herself, she found that she was nodding and had hard work to keep her eyes open. Even in her drowsy and exhausted state, however, she was aware of the horse's hoofbeats and the creaking of the harness, the rumbling of the wheels on the rough track, and the swaying of the vehicle in which they travelled. Soon be there, she told herself, soon be there . . . and could no longer resist the desire to tumble thankfully into sleep.

Chapter Two

'Wake up, girl, we've arrived. Come along now, stir yourself! Got to be up early tomorrow, I have.'

Nell was dragged out of a deep sleep by her aunt's peremptory tone as much as by the hand shaking her shoulder. She sat up groggily, rubbing her eyes and staring around her, not knowing for a moment where she was or how she had got there. She expected to see the whitewashed walls and the pretty floral curtains of her room in Liverpool, but instead she saw a series of gaunt grey buildings, and in place of her bedroom ceiling the dark night sky arching above her and blazing with stars.

'My goodness, if you're that difficult to wake as a rule, I'll keep a wet flannel by your bed I will, and slap it round your chops to get you goin' of a morning,' the voice said, bringing Nell abruptly to a realisation of her surroundings. She was in the cart, which was drawn up in the farmyard of what must be her aunt's home. Muttering an apology and assuring her aunt in a sleep-blurred voice that she normally woke at the first ting of the alarm, she picked up her handbag and looked round wildly for her haversack, but could see no sign of it.

She was beginning to ask her aunt the whereabouts

of her luggage when she saw, in the moonlight, that Kath had slung the haversack round her own shoulder and was holding out a hand to assist her niece to alight. Nell stood up, grabbed the proffered hand, jumped down on to the cobbles and followed her aunt towards a lighted doorway. 'You're showing a light, Auntie Kath!' she squeaked. 'You'll be in trouble if the warden spots it.'

Auntie Kath slowed her pace. 'There's no warden round here. This is the back of beyond, this is,' she said, her tone almost contemptuous. She pushed open the door, ushered Nell inside and pointed. 'This here's the kitchen; put the kettle over the fire and we'll have a hot drink when I've seen to the horse.'

She left the room on the words, shutting the door firmly behind her, and Nell began to take off her coat, scarf and gloves, hanging them on one of the hooks beside the door. It was lovely and warm after the cold outside – Nell rubbed her nose at the memory, amazed that no icicle hung there – and approached the range, holding out her hands to its warmth. It was good to be indoors, she told herself, and looked wistfully at a couple of comfortable basket chairs, but remembering her aunt's instructions she picked up the kettle, made sure it was full, and put it over the flame. Then she began to glance around her in the light of the old-fashioned lamp which hung from the ceiling.

She was glad of this opportunity to satisfy her curiosity, for had her aunt been present she would have felt it rude to stare. The kitchen was enormous, its floor covered in red quarry tiles, its walls whitewashed and the curtains at what must be a large window shabby and faded from their original bright floral print. There was a scrubbed wooden table, half a dozen sturdy ladder-backed chairs and the two comfortable-looking basket ones, each filled with cushions whose floral chintz echoed that of the window curtains. Against one wall was a vast Welsh dresser upon which a variety of china was stacked, as well as an untidy heap of pans. Nell saw that there was a proper rack upon which the pans should have been hung, but someone, presumably her aunt, had not bothered with such niceties, no doubt thinking that it was better to have them within easy reach.

Above the range, the mantelpiece supported a biscuit barrel, a clock whose fingers pointed to midnight, and an old photograph, browned and curled with age, showing a smiling man with one arm slung round the neck of a very large horse. Nell was wondering whether the man was her aunt's late husband and whether the horse in the photograph was the one which had brought her from the station when the door opened and her aunt reappeared, struggling out of a much patched overcoat.

Nell now saw the older woman properly for the first time. She was tall and angular, her face tanned and her mouth set in a firm line. Nell's mother and her Auntie Lou, as well as several other relatives, were blondes, but Auntie Kath's abundant hair was white as snow and, Nell thought, could be described as her one beauty. But as her aunt kicked off her gumboots and turned towards her niece, Nell saw that she had been mistaken, for Auntie Kath also had beautiful eyes, large and heavy-lidded and fringed with black lashes, echoing the shade of her eyebrows. Nell would have liked to ask her if her hair had been dark before turning white but did not quite dare to do so, knowing Mam and Auntie Lou cursed their fair lashes and brows and would not have dreamed of leaving the house before applying eyebrow pencil and mascara. Of course it was possible that Auntie Kath, too, darkened brows and lashes, but after a quick glance at her aunt's grim face Nell dismissed the idea. She did not think that her aunt would have cared if they had been bright blue. Instead, she said tentatively: 'If you'll sit down, Auntie, and tell me where you keep your tea caddy and your milk, I'll make the tea for both of us.'

Her aunt gave her a searching look. 'Getting your feet under the table, are you?' she asked disagreeably. 'You'll need to do more than make a cup of tea to get round me.'

Nell opened her mouth to reply hotly that she had no such intention, then changed her mind. 'Do you want me to waste my time searching for the tea caddy?' she asked, her tone every bit as cold as her aunt's had been. 'Naturally, if you want to make the tea yourself, you have only to say.'

She half expected her aunt to snap her head off, but instead the older woman gave her a grudging smile and Nell saw that there was a strong family likeness between Kath and the other Ripley sisters. Auntie Kath's hair grew in a widow's peak just like Trixie's and Lou's, her nose was straight, and she had a determined mouth, right now set once more in a tight line. Her skin was good, her ears were small and flat to her head, and somehow, Nell thought apprehensively, you could see she was used to being in command and would brook no interference from anyone.

But her aunt was speaking again. 'No need to lose your rag, girl. See that door over there? It's the pantry; the milk's on the cold slab under the window and the tea caddy's on the dresser. Sugar's beside it; I take two heaped teaspoons.'

Nell went to the pantry and fetched out a blue and white jug half full of milk. She reached for the tea caddy and the sugar, put tea leaves into a brown pot, added water from the hissing kettle and, whilst it brewed, poured milk into two enamel mugs. Then, as much to make conversation as anything else, she turned to her aunt. 'Sugar's going to be rationed in the New Year, they say, and probably other things as well. I like sugar in my tea, but then I like it on my cornflakes and porridge as well.' She laughed, picking up the teapot and beginning to pour. 'It'll be strange having to choose between sugar on my porridge or in my tea, but I suppose it will be the same for everyone, so I mustn't grumble.'

Auntie Kath sniffed. 'I keep bees; honey's good on porridge. Like it, do you? Besides, Ireland isn't at war with anyone and Eifion – my farmhand – has a younger brother on the ferries. Shan't be short of much we won't, wi' Merion to help out.'

Nell thought that this was cheating but said nothing. After all, there was no rationing of anything as yet, though her mother had warned her it was bound to come. 'I remember your gran saying that most nice things were rationed during the last war,' she had told her daughter. 'It'll happen in this one, you mark my words. I'm going to buy loads of dry goods and tinned stuff, enough to see us through for a good while.'

Nell had thought this an excellent idea and knew that her mother's hoarding, as the newspapers called it, had started almost before Mr Chamberlain's declaration that the country was at war. But now, of course, the tins, packets and bottles had had to be relinquished to other members of the family, since Mam was not allowed to take them with her to the training centre. 'Kath lives on a farm, so she should be pretty self-sufficient,' Trixie had said, busy packing a box of mixed groceries to sell to her sister Susan. 'But I've got you two pounds of sweets from Kettles on the Scottie, so you'll have something to suck on your journey.' As if I were still a kid, Nell had thought crossly, and had told her mother loftily to divide the sweets amongst her sisters. Mam had pouted and said Nell was ungrateful, but had done as she asked.

Thinking back to her rejection of the sweets, Nell grimaced to herself now, regretting her high-handed reaction. It would have been nice to offer a bag of humbugs or toffees to the other passengers in her compartment. She could have given some to her aunt as well, since that lady clearly had a sweet tooth. I wanted to make Mam unhappy because she had made me pretty miserable, and I don't believe I succeeded. In fact it was what's called cutting off your nose to spite your face, so I'll be well served if there's no sweet shop in the village.

'Well, miss? Are you goin' to hand over that paned – tea, I mean – or am I to go to bed dry as a desert?' Her aunt's words were accompanied by an impatient tapping of her fingers on the wooden table. 'And you never said if you liked honey. Rude you are.'

'Sorry,' Nell said hastily, feeling her cheeks grow hot. It seemed that she must watch her tongue constantly until she grew accustomed to her aunt's ways. 'Of course I like honey; doesn't everyone?' She poured the tea, added sugar to her aunt's mug and pushed it across to her. 'I'm afraid I was dreaming; it's been a long day. I was up before six, and to tell you the truth all I'm really fit for is me bed.'

Her aunt grunted. 'I hope you're not a dreamer,' she said censoriously, 'but it'll be a miracle if you ain't. Dreamin' runs in families, and it don't go with farm work. You have to keep your mind on your job when there's stock involved.'

'Stock?' Nell said. She wished she could tell her aunt how hungry she was and ask for a biscuit or some bread and cheese before bed, but before she could frame a request her aunt was speaking once more.

'Stock is what we call the beasts: cows, pigs, poultry and sheep.' She picked up her mug of tea and took a long drink, then glared at Nell over the rim of the mug. 'Drink up, and no more dreaming. Not here for a rest cure you are. Finished? Right, I'll take you to your room.'

Following her meekly, Nell hoped that her aunt

would not expect her to learn Welsh, for it was obvious that English no longer came readily to the older woman's tongue. But no doubt she'll find it easier once we've spent time together, Nell told herself optimistically as she climbed the stairs in her aunt's wake. And you never know; maybe I'll pick up the Welsh language quickly too. On that thought she followed her aunt into the room which was to be hers whilst she lived at Ty Hen.

Having seen her niece off to bed Kath went quietly down the stairs again, put on her thick winter coat, wrapped a scarf round her head and a muffler round her neck and headed for the back door. She was hot and bothered simply by another's presence in her house; now she needed the cold freshness of the farmyard to recapture the peace which had gone with the wind when Trixie's daughter had stepped into the cart.

Cautiously, Kath opened the back door. The cold rushed to meet her, so she went right into the yard, shutting the door behind her. After the comparative warmth of the house the air actually stung her nostrils, squeezed her lungs, but she told herself that a little cold never hurt anyone and pulled her muffler over her mouth to dull the chill. Then for a moment she just stood there, getting acclimatised, looking up at the arc of the dark sky, at the twinkling stars and the moon, whose light cast half the yard into brilliance, the other half into velvet shadow. Kath sighed with pleasure, and it was only then that she began to think. What had she done? She, who had for so long been sensible, had cast sense aside and agreed that Trixie's wretched brat might come to Ty Hen. She, who had deliberately cut the bonds between herself and her family and even friends who lived in the crowded courts off the Scotland Road, had not only opened and read the letter from her youngest sister, but had agreed to that sister's request, which was to take in her daughter for the duration of a war that was already complicating Kath's life quite enough.

It was all very well telling herself that it was not the girl's fault – Kath knew that. A girl of fifteen did as she was told and must damned well continue to do so, Kath thought with more than a trace of spite, no matter what Nell might think. I can cope with her, she told the unheeding stars above her. It's Trixie who might cause trouble. Her sister might think having her daughter actually living at Ty Hen was the thin edge of the wedge, might start insinuating herself into Kath's quiet but busy life. Kath could just imagine Trixie turning up at Ty Hen one day, all smiles and apologies, saying she simply had to see Helen, or Nell, or whatever the girl called herself. Blood was thicker than water Trixie would say, with the sweet, crooked smile which had made her so popular with the boys two decades ago. And then, because she was Trixie, and leopards, as is well known, do not change their spots, she would start interfering, making suggestions, charming people. And pushing Kath aside.

Well, I shan't have it, not this time, Kath told the indifferent moon. This is *my* house and *my* business and no one tells me what to do or how to do it. The thought gave her a pang; Owain had not been grudging with his knowledge when first she had come to Ty Hen. He had taught her everything she needed to know with all his usual generosity, insisting that his workers treated her as the boss when he was not available, never instructing or contradicting her when others were present. He had taken her side when the Jones family had shown their disapproval of this strange English girl he had foisted upon them, never blamed her when she had refused, at first, to learn Welsh, had finally taught her the rudiments of the language in the long winter evenings and as they worked around the farm.

But Owain was dead and his family had disowned her long ago, and now all the responsibility was hers. She had managed well enough when she had had the young men working for her, but now she and old Eifion often found they had to be in two places at once . . . not easy. She had heard talk of land girls but did not relish the prospect, so when Trixie had written, fairly begging her to let young what's-her-name come to Ty Hen, she had agreed to it. Now, she wondered whether she had made the biggest mistake of her life or whether the kid would really put her back into the work. After all, she's my niece, so she may have it in her to work like a slave on the land – I did, Kath reminded herself. Oh well, the die is cast; I told Trixie I'd keep her girl for six months and then make up my mind, and I'll do just that. Six months isn't a lifetime, after all.

For a moment longer she stood in the yard, no longer thinking but just enjoying the quiet, even the cold.

Then she turned decisively back towards the kitchen. Time would tell, she told herself, opening the back door and going into the warmth. Time would tell.

With quiet contentment she moved about the room, doing the small tasks she did every night before bed. She always left the kitchen ready for the following morning, with the breakfast things set out, the table laid, the kettle filled. Tomorrow, however, it would not be just herself and Eifion who would sit down to breakfast, but her niece and her worker's grandson; she must remember to lay the extra places.

Presently, satisfied that all was in order, she made up the fire in the range and damped it down so that it would be easy to get it going again in the morning. Then she headed for her bedroom, which was opposite her niece's. She just hoped the kid wouldn't have nightmares, or hear something frightening and come through to her room to wake her up. I need my sleep, she told herself grimly. I shan't be best pleased if she interferes with that.

It was not until she was in bed and drifting towards slumber that she remembered she had not told Nell which door led to her own room. She smiled to herself. It had been a mistake, but at least it should ensure her a good night. No young woman was likely to go knocking on strange doors in the wee small hours to complain that she was cold or wanted a hot drink.

Soon, Kath slept. And, immediately, dreamed.

The dream began as her dreams so often did: she was a girl again, her night shift at the hospital just finishing.

35

She came out on to the pavement to find the sky still dark, though the eastern horizon was streaked with flame and gold, the promise, she hoped, of a fine day to come. It had been stuffy on the ward but out here it was pleasantly cool, the breeze from the Mersey salt-laden and fresh. Kath breathed it in deeply, then set off towards home and the bed which she had longed for ten minutes earlier but which now lacked a certain appeal. The day ahead looked like being a fine one, and despite the earliness of the hour Liverpool was already humming with girls going to work in the factories which had sprung up when the war started back in 1914, men off to their jobs in the shipyards, streaming down to catch the ferry which would carry them to Birkenhead and Laird's, others off to queue for the trams which were going to Tate's, the sugar manufactory, or to a hundred different workplaces.

Tired though she was, Kath kept a lookout for friends and family and presently fell in with cousin Lottie, who worked at the Bryant and May match factory. Lottie, too, had been on a night shift and the two young girls greeted one another gleefully.

'I gorra night off tomorrer – today, I should say,' Lottie squeaked as soon as the two met. 'So after I've had me head down for a bit I'm off on the razzle-dazzle. Wharrabout you, queen? There's a good few of us goin' to New Brighton; fancy comin' along?'

'I'd love to, but I'm bleedin' exhausted,' Kath confessed. Her mother forbade swearing in the house and tried to persuade her girls not to speak with the nasal Liverpool accent, and for the most part they complied, but not when they were with friends, or with other young people who might accuse them of snobbery. 'If I could gerra couple of hours' kip first . . .'

'Oh aye, why not? You might bring your Lou along an' all . . . bring the lot, if you want! Well, perhaps not young Trixie – fellers steer clear of gals wi' kids in tow – but t'others. I mean to get me a feller to buy me dinner, seein' as I've spent me pocket money this week. How's you off for spondulicks?'

Kath smiled ruefully. 'I've not had a chance to buy so much as a length of ribbon for me hair,' she admitted. 'I'm flush, I am. Oh, here comes a tram. Is it . . .'

But before she could so much as examine the tram's destination board the scene changed, as scenes in dreams do, and Kath found herself at home, ascending the wooden stairs and heading for her bedroom door. It was not her bedroom, exactly, since she shared it with Lou, Carrie and young Trixie, but it was the nearest thing to a room of her own she would possess until she moved out. She slid round the door, closing it quietly behind her. Even in her dream she remembered that Lou and Carrie both had jobs; Lou worked in Woolworth's as a counter hand and Carrie was a conductress on the buses, so it would not be fair to wake either of them before their alarm went off.

Kath was beginning to undress when Trixie sat up in bed, rubbing her eyes. She began to speak and then, to Kath's horror, her youngest sister's bright little face began to turn green and grow a covering of scales. Her mouth stretched and stretched, teeth fairly sprouting from it, and smoke curled from her wide nostrils. The

Trixie-beast uttered a horrible sound – something between a shriek and a moan – and began to struggle out of her bed, showing short, curved legs with wicked claws, and a green and scaly body. She was a dragon! Kath tried to run, tried to scream . . . and woke, bathed in sweat. She mopped her brow on the sheet and swung her legs shakily out of bed. What a nightmare! It was all the fault of her niece, for the moment Kath had heard that Liverpool accent it had taken her back – oh, back more than twenty years, to the corner house where first her parents and then her mother alone had brought up her daughters.

Still trembling, she went over to the washstand and would have poured water into the basin, except that it was iced over and she simply did not fancy plunging her hands and face into it. Instead, carrying the jug, she stole quietly out of the room and descended the stairs. In the kitchen, she stirred up the fire and pulled the kettle over it. When it was hot enough she poured some of the water into her jug and returned to her bedroom to wash and dress. Only when she was entering the kitchen a second time and beginning to make breakfast for Eifion did she manage to shake off the memory of that horrible dream and begin to plan the day ahead.

Earlier on the same night, Nell lay in the thick darkness and shivered at the empty space around her. It was a feather bed, the only one she had ever encountered, and though it had seemed wonderfully warm and comfortable after the first few chilly minutes, now it simply felt alien, as did the huge room. Somehow, she had expected a bedroom on a farm to be small and cosy, but this one was very different from her imaginings. Like the kitchen it was extremely large, with uneven floorboards, whitewashed walls and a long window, curtained in some musty velvety material which might be black, navy blue or blood red for all she could tell by the light of the candle her aunt had handed her.

Auntie Kath had led her up a steep, uncarpeted staircase whilst explaining that she had not shown her the privy since it was what she described as 'a fair walk from the house' and a bitter wind was blowing. 'But there's a chamber pot in the cabinet by your bed, and a jug of water and a piece of soap on the washstand,' she had said, opening the door before them. 'I won't rouse you early, not on your first day.'

Nell had begun to thank her aunt and found she was speaking to empty air. Her aunt had disappeared, closing the door softly behind her.

Nell had begun to undress in the flickering candlelight, trying not to be afraid of the long shadows which chased across the walls as she moved. At home, in her small room, candlelight had seemed friendly, familiar. Here, where so much was strange – she doused the candle with relief and climbed into bed – candlelight only served to exaggerate the differences.

She was beginning to settle down when the night sounds began. A dreadful scream made her sit bolt upright. Who in God's name – or rather the devil's – was being murdered out there? Then a dog barked and the sound was swiftly followed by an eldritch shriek, then another, and another! By now, Nell was kneeling at the window, peering into the moonlight and sobbing beneath her breath. They said the country was quiet – well this country certainly wasn't; it was noisier and more terrifying than anything to be heard on the Scottie of a night-time. As Nell watched, she saw a great white bird float on silent wings across the yard, emitting a soft whoo-whoo as it went. An owl! And then another bird, darker and swifter, but still she imagined an owl, plunged down on something below and the harsh shriek she had heard earlier emerged from its beak.

Nell had been holding the curtain back as she stared, fascinated, at the moonlit scene, but now sheer exhaustion made her drop the heavy fabric and lie back down on the big brass bedstead. She burrowed under the blankets and heaved the pillow after her. It were only birds and that, nothing to be afraid of, she told herself firmly. Nell Whitaker, you are fifteen years old, not a scaredy cat of ten or so. Go to sleep or it will be morning before you know it.

Despite her brave words, however, sleep refused to come. At home, with Mam only a thin wall away, she knew she only had to call out and her parent would come running. Here, she had no idea which of the several doors on this landing hid her aunt. And even if I knew, I'd never dare disturb her, she told herself sadly. She doesn't like me or want me, and would love it if I ran away. But how can I? I've nowhere to run to, and no one either.

Full of self-pity she began to sob, burying her face in the pillow and soaking it with her tears, and presently she fell asleep, though her dreams were frightening and uneasy, causing her to weep and cry out. Twice she awoke from dreams in which she was in a great wicker cage whilst an evil-looking man, his long white robe bloodstained, walked round and round it, brandishing a great curved sickle and leering at her tears.

She awoke properly at last and saw with breathless relief that morning had come, or at least the window showed grey instead of black. Lying very still and straight in the big old feather bed, Nell willed herself to go back to sleep, but her mind was too active for slumber. Auntie Kath was so strange! Nell had realised the previous evening that her aunt was not at ease in the English tongue, having spoken Welsh for a great many years, but that did not quite explain her brusqueness. Now Nell thought that the older woman must have been constantly translating from English to Welsh and from Welsh to English. Thank God Auntie Kath still remembers English, she told herself. What would I have done if she could only talk to me in Welsh? As time goes on I'll learn some words, I expect, but for the time being I suppose we would have had to resort to sign language, and a fat lot of good that would have been! I want to ask her about the noises in the night, but if I were to go down to the kitchen now and start screaming and barking and flapping my arms like an owl, the poor woman would think I was off me bleedin' rocker.

Nell smiled at the sheer absurdity of it, but she knew it would be hard work to learn and the knowledge caused her to pull a face. It would be school all over again, and she thought she had done with that. Trixie had tried to learn French a year ago, since her boss had said that a second language would mean an increase in her salary, so Nell had signed up for a night school French class with her mam and Auntie Lou. She had found it uphill work, mostly because her mother had simply refused to try. She would not do her homework, learn her verbs or concentrate in class, and after six or eight lessons had simply stopped attending classes.

Remembering Trixie's many excuses for homework undone and verbs unlearned, Nell began to smile, and the memory of her mother's blandishments – *do let me copy your stuff, queen, just this once, and you shall have a box of chocolates all to yourself* – came to her mind, bringing with it a feeling of homesickness so acute that tears rose to her eyes. Don't be a fool, Nell, she told herself; you did let Mam copy your homework, and the box of chocolates never arrived. But that was typical of Trixie. She meant well, but forgot easily. Auntie Lou was better and so was Auntie Carrie, but judging by what she had seen of Auntie Kath so far, the oldest sister was a very different kettle of fish.

The sound of footsteps quietly descending the stairs brought Nell back to the present. She blotted her tears and wriggled down the bed; her aunt had said she might lie in today. But after ten minutes of trying to woo sleep, the memory of her nightmares caused her

42

to push back the covers and swing her feet out of bed. It was no use: she might as well wash and get dressed and go downstairs as soon as she could, and share her aunt's breakfast. She had gone to bed hungry, and woken hungry too. In her mind's eye, creamy porridge sprinkled lavishly with sugar and a plate laden with crisp rashers of bacon and a couple of golden-yolked eggs swam enticingly before her. Last night she had pulled on her winceyette nightdress over her under-clothes so now all she had to do was strip off the nightie, rifle through her haversack to find her flannel and toothbrush and set about her ablutions.

Ten minutes later she was washed, dressed and ready to go. She made her bed, shaking and punching the huge feather mattress before smoothing the sheet and tucking it in neatly. After that, she looked round for somewhere to hang the few garments she had brought with her, but there was nowhere suitable. Shrugging, Nell shook the contents of her haversack out on to the bed. She would ask her aunt for some hooks or clothes hangers when she got downstairs, or perhaps there might be a wardrobe in another room which she could use.

She cast a valedictory glance around the room, picked up her slop bucket and descended the stairs, looking curiously around her when she reached the ground floor, for she had seen very little the previous night. Now she saw that the stairs ended in a large square hall. Directly in front of her was the front door, with a coloured window light above it. To her right was the kitchen, she was pretty sure of that, and to her left two other doors. One will be a parlour, she told herself, but I wonder what the other is? She would doubtless find out soon enough, so, repressing an urge to take a peep, she opened the kitchen door and stepped inside.

For one moment she wondered if she had made a mistake, for seated at the scrubbed wooden table was an elderly man in a cloth cap, a faded tweed jacket and rough serge trousers. He was in his stockinged feet, and she saw two extremely muddy wellington boots and a pair of overalls by the back door. She guessed that this must be Eifion, the farmhand; good manners had caused him to remove his rubber boots and overalls before seating himself at the table. Nell crossed the room and stood her slop bucket down by the wellingtons, then glanced up at the clock on the mantel. Its hands pointed to half past six.

Her aunt had turned from the stove to stare at her as she entered the room, her eyes flickering over Nell's thick grey jumper and droopy brown woollen skirt with what seemed like disparagement. Nell, eyeing her aunt, thought indignantly that she must look downright well dressed beside the older woman, who was wearing a dowdy black dress and a calico apron, liberally stained with food. She appeared to be frying a quantity of cold potatoes, thinly sliced, in a large black pan, and the smell of them made Nell's mouth water. She looked enquiringly from her aunt to the farmhand, wondering why they were about to sit down to what looked like their dinner before the sun had risen, and saw a tall, thin boy of about her own age, or maybe a year or two older, with crisply curling

44

fair hair and round hazel eyes that just now were fixed unwaveringly on her face sitting beside the old man. As her eyes met his he grinned, obviously amused by her puzzlement. Nell thought he was the handsomest boy she had ever seen and his smile enhanced this impression.

'Good morning,' she said politely, and all three answered her at once. The boy would have said more but Auntie Kath forestalled him. 'Just in time for breakfast, you are, Nell,' she said stiffly. 'We always have a good meal before doing the early milking and mucking out. Oh . . .' she gestured at the old man, 'this here's Eifion Hughes, what I told you about; the lad's his grandson, Bryn.' As she spoke, she was sliding piles of golden potato discs on to three plates and now she reached over to the dresser and took down a fourth, then began to fry bacon. 'Eifion, this is my niece; her name's Nell Whitaker. She's come to help us . . . oh, drat it,' and she broke into Welsh, not one word of which could Nell understand, save for her own name.

The old man grinned at her, his eyes twinkling. He nudged the boy and spoke to him in rapid Welsh. The boy nodded, then turned to her. 'My taid says glad to meet you,' he said in excellent but strongly accented English. 'Mrs Jones wants me to help you to learn the Welsh, just while I'm staying wi' my nain and taid – that's grandmother and grandfather, you know.' He addressed Auntie Kath. 'Do I have that right, Mrs J?'

Auntie Kath nodded. 'Aye, you're a bright lad,' she said. 'I don't have the time to keep thinkin' in two languages and it's mostly Welsh as is spoken round

45

here, which me niece hasn't a word of.' She turned to Nell. 'Bryn will help you whilst he's here. A young thing like yourself will pick it up quick enough.'

'He'll be an interpreter,' Nell said, much amused. She giggled at the look on her aunt's face. 'I do hope he's getting paid for this work?'

Nell had been joking, but her aunt shook a reproving head. 'Not in money, no, but in . . . oh, what d'you call it?'

'I think you mean in kind,' Nell suggested, 'if you're going to give him his meals, and perhaps some farm produce to take home when his work is over.'

'That's right,' her aunt said. 'I'll be feeding him three good meals a day, and giving him a small wage as well.'

'But how long is he here for?' Nell asked. 'Does he live nearby? Only he won't be able to teach me much in a few days.'

Bryn tutted. 'Speak for myself, I can,' he said reprovingly. 'I've put in for a berth on one of the Irish ferries – I'd like to sail on the *Scotia*, because I've an uncle who's a steward aboard her and I've met many members of the crew. It would be nice to sail with fellers I know.'

'But hasn't the *Scotia* gone off somewhere?' Eifion said, knife and fork poised. 'As I recall . . .'

'Aye, that's right,' Bryn said at once. 'She's been taken off the Ireland run for the time being and sent to Southampton to carry troops to France. That means her home port will be down south, but I dare say by the time I get aboard she'll be berthing in Holyhead again. But I've agreed to work at Ty Hen until my papers come through.'

Nell found herself hoping that Bryn's papers would be long delayed. If she had to learn to speak Welsh – shades of her classroom back in Liverpool came into her head – then she would rather have a handsome young man as teacher than a fusty old schoolmaster.

However, it would never do to say so, so she turned to the old man. 'Does Bryn live with you, or is he like me, just staying with a relative because of the war?' she asked. She was pretty sure, by the look on the old fellow's face and by the fact that his mouth began to open, that he had understood at least some of her question, but Bryn answered for him.

'Taid's English is a bit slow to come; he prefers the Welsh,' he explained. 'As for me, I live with my mam in Holyhead, but she's joined the WRNS and is away on a training course, so I'm staying with Nain and Taid. He turned to Auntie Kath. 'But until my papers come through you're going to feed me, which will be grand 'cos you're the best cook on the island, and in return I'll talk in Welsh to your niece as we muck out and milk and see to the stock.' He turned back to Nell, grinning. 'Don't you fear; I may not be an old greybeard but I'm good at languages and I reckon you and me will get on.'

'I believe you,' Nell said fervently, looking at the well-piled plate which had just been placed before her. At a word in Welsh from her aunt, the boy said grace and the four of them settled down to eat, Bryn clearly relishing every mouthful. When they had finished, he

47

and Eifion returned to the yard whilst the women cleared away and washed up. Rather to Nell's dismay this was done in silence, but when her aunt emptied the dirty water into a bucket which stood below the sink she spoke at last.

'Follow me,' she said. 'Bring your slops.' As she spoke she thrust her feet into a pair of wellingtons, similar to those owned by Eifion but not nearly so muddy. Nell was about to point out that she had no boots when the back door was thrown open by her aunt's impatient hand and a gust of wind blew into the kitchen. Lacking boots, she tried to grab her coat, but Kath was striding across the yard and Nell did not wish to be left behind. Shuddering, she clanked along in her wake, the bucket seeming to grow heavier with every step. As they reached the corner of what must be a stable or cart shed, her aunt turned to her. Most of what she said was lost as the wind whipped the words from her lips, but Nell caught 'muck heap' and saw what she was supposed to do with the contents of the slop bucket as her aunt approached a huge and very smelly mountain which was roughly fenced in on three sides with ancient, rotting planks. Nell stood back as her aunt went round to the side and hurled the slops at the top of the muck heap. Then she gestured to Nell to follow her example, saying something to the effect that the wind was strong and spiteful so Nell should look out.

'I'll do my best but I don't have any boots,' Nell began, but she realised that if she had been unable to hear her aunt's voice, her aunt would be unable to hear hers. Instead, she took a couple of steps nearer the muck heap and followed her aunt's example . . . only to find herself soaked as the wind caught the slops and hurled them straight back at her.

'Oh . . . ugh . . . how horrible!' poor Nell stammered, pushing wet hands through her wet hair and trying to squeeze some of the water out of her thick, much worn jersey and skirt. Too late she realised that her aunt had been trying to warn her not to throw the contents of her bucket straight at her objective because of the wind. She turned to the older woman, but before she could speak a new sound came to her ears. Her aunt, empty bucket in hand, coat still not buttoned, was laughing; laughing as if she would never stop. She pointed a trembling finger at her niece and went off into another burst of merriment, then seized Nell's arm and began to hurry her back to the house.

'Move yourself!' she bawled above the wind. 'You've a great many things to learn, and you've just had your first lesson: chucking pee into the wind is definitely one way of gettin' your own back!'

Nell was so angry that she threw caution to the winds. As they slogged side by side across the yard, heading for the back door, she gave vent to her feelings. 'Really, Auntie! I notice you can speak bloody good English when you want to say something nasty; it's just polite conversation that you can't manage!'

They had reached the back door and as she flounced in ahead of the older woman she received a ringing slap round the ear. Too startled for a moment to do anything but regain her balance, for the slap had nearly

49

knocked her to the ground, Nell gave a stifled sob. 'What was that for? Speaking the truth?' she asked breathlessly. 'Don't you ever hit me again or – or . . .'

'If you're rude to me again you'll get another clack, harder too!' her aunt said between gritted teeth. 'You're just like your ma was when we were girls together. Hot to handle and ungrateful, always wanting what wasn't hers . . .' She had thrust her niece into the kitchen and now she followed, slamming the door behind her. 'As I've already said, you've a lot to learn, Helen Whitaker!'

Nell spun round, feeling the hot blood of fury suffuse her cheeks. 'How dare you hit me! You called my mam names, but I know better than to hit you. Come to that, Mam's never hit me in my life, or not without reason at any rate. Well, that's it; I'm going home on the first train and you can empty your own damned slops!'

'You'll do nothing of the sort, since I don't mean to lend you a penny and you told me last night you'd no money for the fare,' Aunt Kath said, her voice thin with spite. 'You're here to work and to do as I say, so put that in your pipe and smoke it!'

Nell gave an angry sob. It was so unfair! Just because she was only fifteen and her aunt many years older, she would have to put up with whatever dreadful treatment the older woman handed out until she could beg, borrow or steal enough money for the fare back to Liverpool. And when she got there, what could she do? Auntie Carrie had not suggested that she stay with her whilst her mother went off to join the WAAF. What would she say if she turned up on her doorstep, penniless and weeping, having flouted her mother's plans for her and run away from her sister Kath? The aunts might not have much time for their eldest sister, but in her heart Nell knew that they would fight shy of taking her in. They would say that the only person who could make arrangements for her was her mother, and she had sent her to Kath, who lived in the country on a lovely farm, where Trixie's precious one and only child could be safe for as long as the war lasted. And there she must stay, Carrie would say, and Mam's cousins in Bootle would agree, Nell concluded sadly, heaving a deep sigh.

Better get it over with then; eat humble pie and promise to be good and await my chance to . . . to what? Run? Go to the nearest town and find work? But the humble pie bit must come first. Or I could try the only other option . . . you never know, Auntie Kath's harsh exterior might, just might, hide a soft centre, like the chocolates Mam likes so much.

Without saying another word, she ran out of the kitchen and up the stairs. In her room she took off her dirty things, rinsed hands and face in the water left over from her earlier ablutions, and put on clean clothing. Then, without giving herself time to reflect, she went back to the kitchen and put her wet clothing on the draining board before addressing her aunt in a small voice.

'Auntie? I'm sorry I was rude, but you laughed . . . and I know you're right, really. I can't possibly go back to Liverpool now Mam's not there any longer, nor Auntie Lou. The other relatives might take me in, but

I just know they'd tell me to return to you and thank my lucky stars I wasn't living down by the docks, like they are. Will . . . will you forgive me? Can we start again?' She let water collect in her eyes and then squeezed her lids tight shut for a moment so that the tears ran slowly down her cheeks. 'Auntie? I'm sorry, honest to God I am.' She had been watching her aunt's face, which seemed to be made of granite, but suddenly it changed. What have I said *now*, Nell asked herself despairingly; she soon found out.

'Take not the name of the Lord in vain,' Auntie Kath said angrily. 'I'm a God-fearing woman I'll have you know, so don't blaspheme in my house. Your ma never went to church if she could get out of it, but whilst you're under my roof you'll do as I do and act godly. Understand me?'

'Sorry, but honest to God is just an expression, not a – a blasphemy,' Nell said quickly. 'All Liverpudlians use it. And Mam does go to church sometimes, only she's often too busy. But I'll do as you say, of course . . .'

'I'm always busy, but that don't stop me from churchgoing,' her aunt snapped, but her mouth was no longer so grimly set. 'Oh, get on with you! The lad will be in in a minute – he can show you round the farm. I've better things to do.' She picked up Nell's dirty clothes. 'I'll run these through the wash and dry 'em on the clothes horse in front of the fire. You've not got many clothes, so best get these ready for the next time you need a change.' She cocked a dark eyebrow at her niece. 'A decent dress for Sunday, do you have?'

Nell nodded. 'Yes; and white stockings and button shoes. I've only got one coat – coats are expensive – but Mam put in a couple of thick jumpers. I suppose I could wear them one on top of the other . . .'

'No, no, that will never do,' her aunt interrupted. 'But I've an old coat which will keep you dry. I'm no hand with a needle, but I can turn up a hem and shorten sleeves. I'll do that tonight, but in the meantime . . .' She crossed the room to the pegs by the door and took down a waterproof cape. 'Wear this for today.' She heaved a sigh. 'There's a market held in Llangefni a couple of times a week. When I've time we'll take the pony trap and see what's available in your size.'

'Oh, but I don't want to put you to any expense,' Nell said hastily. She could have said, with more truth, that she did not wish to be beholden to her aunt, but though she said nothing Kath must have read her thoughts, for she looked knowing.

'Actually, your ma sent me a bit of money because she guessed you'd need working gear,' she said. She went over to the back door and flung it open, shouted, then closed it hastily, for the wind was strong, and blew a scattering of leaves into the kitchen. 'The lad won't be far away . . .' Aunt Kath glanced at the clock, 'you'll have time for a tour before we have our elevenses. You'd best borrow my boots for now.'

Nell was promising to take great care of both the boots and the waterproof cape when the back door opened a crack and Bryn sidled into the room, clad in his own well-weathered garments. He gave a snort of laughter at the sight of Nell in the huge cape and equally large boots, then led her out into the yard where the force of the wind seemed strong enough to blow both of them off their feet. Despite his appearance, however, Bryn was sinewy and stronger than he looked and together they stumbled towards the nearest doorway, which proved to be the stable. Once in its warm interior, with its comforting smells of horses and hay, Bryn introduced her to the animal which had drawn the cart the previous night. The great creature turned dark, enquiring eyes on the two young people and accepted, with gentle eagerness, the carrot which Bryn offered him. 'Hal, his name is,' Bryn told her. 'He does everything that needs strength; he ploughs the fields, fetches and carries, spreads the manure in the autumn and carts the crops as they come ripe.' Bryn gestured to the stall next to Hal's, in which stood a very much smaller animal. 'She's Feather; she pulls the pony trap, takes the missus and her produce to market, does all the light jobs.' Bryn produced another carrot, hesitated, then snapped it in two. 'Give this bit to Feather, but keep your hand flat so she don't mistake your fingers for food,' he instructed.

Nell took the carrot, but shook a reproving head at her companion. 'What sort of an idiot do you think I am? Liverpool's full of horses pulling milk carts or coal wagons or brewery drays, and we always give 'em sugar lumps or bits of carrot. If we didn't know to keep our hands flat, there wouldn't be a kid in Liverpool with a full set of fingers.'

Bryn smirked. 'Sorry,' he said, leading her out of the

stable and across the yard. He lowered his head protectively but raised his voice above the howl of the wind. 'Pigs next . . . see 'em? Us don't name pigs – not the baconers – but the sows are Polly and Princess; they're the huge critters in the big sty at the end.'

After the pigs Bryn took her to the big, roomy hen house, taking her right inside and pointing out the nesting boxes and the long perches. 'You'll be collecting the eggs when I goes away, so you might as well start now,' he said, and showed her how to move an indignant hen from her comfortable straw-lined box and take the eggs thus revealed, which he put carefully into his mackintosh pocket.

After that they fought their way over to the pond where in better weather, Bryn told Nell, a number of ducks and geese disported themselves, though today nothing disturbed the dark waters save for the wind. 'Mrs J uses goose and duck eggs when she makes lardy cakes and that,' he shouted. 'She sells the hens' eggs at market in Llangefni, along with her butter and cheese.' He smacked his lips. 'Oh aye, a grand cook is Mrs J.'

Next came the cattle shed and shippon, but the cows were all out despite the horrible weather, so Nell just took a cursory look round and then followed Bryn to what he told her was the big barn where, as the weather worsened, the sheep would be brought in to give birth to their lambs.

'A great many sheep your aunt do keep,' Bryn said, then grinned. 'That was a poem, wasn't it? But as I was saying before I broke into verse, if we have a mild winter the sheep will be turned out to graze when the lambs are only a few days old. I reckon it'll be our job – yours and mine – to give an eye to the littl'uns. There's plenty foxes on Anglesey, on the lookout for a nice lamb dinner.'

Nell shuddered. 'That's horrible,' she protested. 'But how could I stop a fox grabbing a lamb and running off with it? I'm sure a fox could run twice as fast as me. Why, it might even attack me if it thought I was after its dinner.'

Bryn's hazel eyes slit with amusement. 'You're a real townie, aren't you? I bet you've never seen a fox, have you? They're not like wolves; most of them are no bigger than a farmyard cat, though the dog foxes can be about the same size as Fly, your aunt's collie bitch. You've not met the dogs yet 'cos they're out wi' Taid, checking the sheep in the far pastures. There's two of them; Fly is the bitch and Whisky the dog. But we'd best get on; we don't want to miss your aunt's elevenses.'

He led the way out of the shelter of the barn, securing the door by dropping a wooden beam across it. Immediately, the wind attacked them, but Bryn caught Nell's arm when she would have headed for the next building. 'That there's where your aunt keeps the carts, the pony trap and all the farm implements,' he shouted. 'Nothing much to see there, so we'd best get back to the house. Mrs J's makin' butter in the dairy today; she may need a hand.'

Back in the empty kitchen, they both shed their outer clothing and Nell filled the kettle; then she carried it across to the range and stood it over the heat whilst Bryn fetched out a tin of scones and began to butter them. Only then did Nell turn to her companion. 'Thanks, Bryn, for the tour,' she said gratefully. 'But there's one thing I really don't understand. My aunt used to employ two farmhands as well as your taid; what on earth did they find to do with themselves? Collecting eggs, feeding the pigs and chasing off foxes doesn't seem particularly hard work to me.'

Bryn gave a crow of amusement. 'Just you wait, girl,' he said, his eyes sparkling with mischief. 'Just you damned well wait!'

Chapter Three

When 23 December arrived, Nell had been at the farm for about three months and no longer wondered what her aunt's farmhands found to do with themselves. It seemed to her that she and Bryn worked all out from sunrise to sunset, and it was not merely a matter of feeding pigs or collecting eggs. It was tough, physical work, of a sort she had never experienced before. To be sure her aunt and Eifion worked hard as well, especially when you considered that Auntie Kath cooked, washed, cleaned and made good anything which was broken in the long evenings. But Nell, unused to hard physical labour, was often so tired that it was all she could do to climb the stairs and fall into bed.

Kath had given her niece an alarm clock, and its strident ring was the signal for Nell to tumble out of bed, wash and dress – sometimes, she thought, in her sleep – and be at the kitchen table in time to eat a hearty breakfast before going with Bryn to milk the cows and muck out. Washing was a skimpy affair in the icy water, though her aunt had unbent a little and now provided Nell with a stone hot water bottle, the contents of which were still pleasantly warm next morning. Nell emptied it into her basin and washed in that, which was considerably better than using the water which had usually frozen in her ewer.

But when the alarm clock rang on this Saturday morning, Nell found herself wide awake and looking forward to the day ahead because it was to be a day off. Auntie Kath meant to drive to the Christmas market at Llangefni in the pony trap. She had said, rather evasively, that she needed to buy a few things for the holiday, and had actually suggested that the young ones might like to accompany her.

'Your taid says he can manage the milking, and your uncle Merion will be in port for a week since the ferry's engine is in urgent need of an overhaul, so he's agreed to give a hand,' she had said, shooting a quick, wary glance at her niece. 'You've not worked badly, the pair of you . . . that's to say I suppose you've done your best, so I reckon you deserve a day off. I'll give you both some money to spend, but don't you go wasting it. Despite what you may think I don't have money to burn; it's hard earned.' She had looked at them consideringly. 'I've put in a bit extra which will serve as my Christmas present to you.'

Nell clattered down the stairs and crossed the hall, heading for the kitchen. Her initial shyness had long fled, though she still treated her aunt with a good deal of caution; Auntie Kath was so strange! Sometimes she could be nice as pie and at others as disagreeable as a dog whose bone had been snatched away, and there was no way of guessing in advance which her mood would be. Nell had realised, though, that the mere thought of her sister Trixie could change Auntie Kath from a reasonable human being to a bitter, bad-tempered woman who would find fault with everything her niece did. As far as Nell could discover her aunt appeared to have got on quite well with her other sisters, though they had grown apart. She knew it happened in most families; cards were exchanged at Christmas and birthdays, but members of the family who had moved away seldom returned except perhaps for a family wedding or a funeral. Nell knew that neither Trixie and Auntie Lou nor their other relatives had ever considered visiting the farm, and Kath had never dreamed of returning to the city of her birth.

At this point in her musings Nell entered the kitchen and went immediately to the table, where she began to slice and butter the loaf. She glanced at her aunt under her lashes, hoping to see some sign of approval, but Auntie Kath, wielding the big black frying pan with expert nonchalance, did not so much as glance up. Eifion and Bryn were busy with their usual breakfast, only today bacon had been replaced by sausages, and instead of potatoes each plate held a slice of golden fried bread.

They both smiled at Nell as she went past them into the pantry, returning with a jar of marmalade and another of honey. 'Morning, Auntie Kath; morning Eifion, Bryn,' she said cheerfully, putting the jars down in the middle of the table. If only her aunt were in a good mood, how pleasant the day ahead of them might be!

'Morning,' Auntie Kath said gruffly, a moment after Eifion and Bryn had greeted Nell. 'Get that plateful down you, girl, while I set out a dinner for Eifion and Merion; then we'll be off.'

'Is there anything I can do to help?' Nell asked, though her heart had sunk at her aunt's tone. Clearly, despite the day's holiday, Kath was not in a sunny mood. 'I could harness Feather to the trap . . .'

'No need; Eifion done it before breakfast,' Aunt Kath snapped. 'Just put on your thick coat and muffler; mortal cold it is out there.'

Nell gobbled her food, determined not to keep her aunt waiting, which would certainly get the day off to a bad start. As it was, she was struggling into her outdoor clothing and Bryn was putting on his own coat and wrapping a huge scarf round his neck by the time Aunt Kath had arranged a large meat pie, a plateful of bread and butter and a jar of pickled onions on the kitchen table.

'Keep the wolf from the door that will,' she told Eifion, who was eyeing her preparations with interest. 'Put the pie in the oven thirty minutes before you cut it . . .' Remembering that he much preferred his own language she broke into Welsh whilst Bryn translated beneath his breath for Nell's benefit.

'She's tellin' Taid there's some home brewed in the pantry, on the very top shelf,' he explained. 'She says he's not to go takin' too much, 'cos she doesn't want to find the farm work only half done and him flat on his back on the kitchen floor when she comes home. And now Taid is telling her he's never cheated on her yet . . . and now . . .'

'I know; now they're laughing,' Nell said, smiling

to herself. How rare it was to hear her aunt laugh, but how pleasant! 'Ready, Bryn? Come on then, boyo, let's fetch Feather out of the stable.'

It was the work of a moment to bring the pony and trap round to the back door, and though Aunt Kath did not thank them, unless you could count a grunt as she climbed rather stiffly into the equipage, Nell thought that she did not look displeased. It was no longer pitch dark, but the sun had not yet risen and, as her aunt had warned, it was very cold indeed. Without waiting to be told, she and Bryn climbed aboard and wrapped themselves in the rugs which were folded up on the rear seat of the trap, exchanging delighted smiles as they began to warm up. Indeed Bryn, apparently impervious to atmosphere, asked if he might drive, vowing that though his hands were cold they were no longer numb. Auntie Kath told him rather sourly that he would be better occupied in teaching Nell more Welsh but added that he might drive on the way home if she was too tired to take the reins herself.

Once they were on the move and away from the farm and the fields she was beginning to know so well, Nell began to look about her. There were pink and gold streaks on the eastern horizon which promised fine weather later on, though at the moment the banks and hedges were white with frost and the sheep in the meadows steamed gently as they cropped the crisp grass and waited, Nell imagined, for the birth of their lambs, for all the ewes were big-bellied and heavily fleeced.

She commented on this to Bryn, who nodded wisely. 'Most beasts have their littl'uns in the spring,' he told her. 'I expect it's because the spring grass is so sweet and rich. But it means the babies are often born into wicked cold, of course, and some of them die of it. Still, soon we'll be bottle-feeding if a ewe has twins or triplets and can't manage all of them. When I were a kid I loved bottle-feeding the little lambs, feeling them tug on the teat as if them an' me were havin' a wrestling match.'

Nell laughed, and saw out of the corner of her eye a hastily suppressed smile cross her aunt's grim visage. She did not comment on it, however, knowing that if she did so it would bring her aunt's wrath down upon her head. 'I'm sure I shall love feeding the lambs, but I didn't know folk kept sheep in Holyhead,' she said demurely. 'I thought it was a port, like Liverpool. So how, Mr Clever Clogs, do you know so much about bottle-feeding lambs?'

'Because I've always spent a fair amount of time either with my nain and taid or with my cousins, the ones who live at Beaumaris. And I've a pal who lives near the Welsh longhouse on the cliffs above Church Bay; Hywel, he's called.' He looked rather apprehensively towards Auntie Kath, but she was singing a song beneath her breath and concentrating on her driving. Bryn lowered his voice. 'But don't mention that in front of your aunt; I'll tell you why when we're alone.'

'Okay, I can wait,' Nell said breezily, then changed the subject. 'I'm really looking forward to doing some shopping. I mean to get a little something for your nain and taid. What do you think they would like?'

'Nain would like a china ornament,' Bryn said definitely. 'She likes pretty things, does my nain.'

Auntie Kath snorted. 'You won't get a thank you from Eifion, not if you buy the prettiest china shepherdess you see,' she said roundly. 'Baccy or beer for the fellers, that's what I always get 'em. They can't ever have too much baccy and beer.'

Bryn nodded reluctantly. 'Yes, I guess you're right, Mrs J. I'm getting Taid some metheglin; he likes a drop in his tea as a special treat.'

'What on earth's that?' Nell asked, intrigued. 'It sounds like cough medicine.'

Auntie Kath's tight little smile appeared and Bryn gave his most superior smirk. 'Townie, townie,' he jeered. 'It's a sort of mead, made with honey. I've never tasted it, nor want to, but I believe it's very strong.'

'Right, then I'll buy him tobacco . . . and the same for yourself, of course,' Nell said, grinning. She knew very well that Bryn had never smoked a cigarette and thought the habit disgusting. He maintained that he could not remain in a room where people were smoking, so now he leaned over and tried to box Nell's ears.

'And I shall buy you a set of curlers for your hair and a nice bright lipstick,' he said tauntingly. 'We've got to find some way of making you look like a woman instead of a scruffy kid.'

'You mochin ddrwg!' Nell said furiously, aiming a blow at her companion's head. 'Nice women don't bother with curlers or lipsticks, they just use plenty of soap and water, and brush their hair a hundred times each night. If anyone's a dirty pig it's you.'

A nasty disagreement might have ensued had Kath not turned to glare at them. 'That's enough,' she said brusquely. 'You're too old for squabbling, unless you want me to believe you really are only a couple of kids.'

Hastily, the two drew apart and Nell changed the subject, speaking rather breathlessly. 'Pax, pax, Bryn! Only I hate the feel of makeup on my face, and don't intend to wear it ever. Let's talk about something really important. Your taid was telling me that four of the cows are in calf. He says they have their mother's milk for a few weeks, then they have to be weaned.'

'Yes, that's true,' Bryn agreed. 'But I doubt if I'll still be at Ty Hen when the cows drop their calves. Still, whenever my ship's in port, I'll pay you a visit, see how you're getting on.'

'Your ship,' Nell said scornfully. 'That's all we've heard lately. But I suppose it's possible that someone in the Navy might need a cabin boy . . .'

'Merchant Navy you mean,' Bryn corrected, apparently not one whit offended by the remark. 'They need every man they can get, and I can turn my hand to most things. But as for cabin boys . . .' He dug a sharp elbow into his companion's ribs and another quarrel might have started, except that Auntie Kath turned a furious glance upon them which effectively shut them up. Grinning, Bryn began to discourse on the duties of a deck hand aboard one of the naval fleet and harmony was restored.

As they talked, the light had been gradually strengthening, and Nell gasped as the sun rose, round and red and glorious, casting long beams of golden light across the frosted landscape and causing her to clutch Bryn's arm. 'Dear God, isn't that the most beautiful thing you've ever seen!' she said, her tone awestruck. 'Every twig is as white as though it had been dusted with icing sugar, and those cows over there are outlined in gold!'

For a moment she had forgotten her aunt's strictures against the sin of taking the Lord's name in vain, and was about to apologise abjectly when her aunt spoke. 'Glad I am to see you appreciate this place, even if you are city reared,' the older woman said quietly. 'I remember when I first came here and Owain tried to make me see the beauty of it, how I fought against admitting its loveliness because I was so homesick. I come round in the end, but glad I am that you've more sense.'

Nell was so flabbergasted that she did not reply, but Bryn immediately burst into speech. 'You wait till you see Llangefni, Nell. It's the county town, with huge buildings and heaps of shops. Holyhead got nowhere near the same sort of shops and market stalls as you'll see today. Love it you will; I do, and even my mam likes to go to Llangefni on market day, especially at Christmas.' He looked down at her and in the strengthening light she could see the anticipation of the treat to come in his glowing eyes. 'Mam's English, you know; she comes from Shrewsbury. I've never been there, but she says it's a grand town, even bigger than

Llangefni. All my family love Holyhead, but Llangefni . . . well, wait and see.'

Nell smiled to herself. She had never visited Shrewsbury either, but guessed that it would seem very small compared with Liverpool. 'Yes, I believe Shrewsbury is a very nice town,' she said tactfully, however. 'I suppose it's because of having a Welsh father and an English mother that you speak both languages so well.'

Bryn nodded, grinning. 'You're getting the hang of Welsh yourself,' he said generously. 'When I come back after Christmas you'll be chatting away like a native, because you won't have me to interpret for at least a week, maybe longer, and scarcely at all when I get my papers through telling me where to join my ship.'

Nell had heard that recruiting had slowed down due to a lack of uniforms and weapons, but she did not want to upset her companion so pretended to agree with him. She realised that she would miss him. Ty Hen was some way from the nearest village, so she knew no one else of her own age, which meant that she relied heavily on Bryn's companionship as well as on his ability as a teacher. He had insisted that they speak nothing but Welsh on the farm, so whilst they worked she strove to copy his words and to learn their meanings. In turn, he had explained that his spelling of English was poor, so Nell had begun to compile a dictionary of the most frequently used English words and Bryn pored over them when-ever he could. In the weeks which had elapsed since Nell's arrival, Bryn's reading and spelling of English had improved, and Nell's Welsh was coming on apace.

At that moment Auntie Kath turned and addressed a remark to Bryn in Welsh, and to Nell's astonishment she understood at least the gist of it. Her aunt was asking Bryn to take care of Nell whilst she herself sold the eggs, butter and cheese which were stowed away in a box beneath the back seat. She turned to Nell and began to translate what she had just said, but her niece broke in, too excited and pleased with herself to remember how her aunt disliked being interrupted. 'It's all right, I understood!' she said proudly. 'But how will you sell the stuff, Auntie? You're not taking a stall today, are you?'

Kath shook her head. 'Not today, but I've a friend who comes in from Amlwch, a Mrs Williams, who'll let me sell from her stall. I'll stable Feather behind the Bull Hotel and meet you there when it's time to go home. We'll have to leave well before dark since I don't intend to risk an accident.'

'What time shall we see you at the Bull?' Nell asked timidly. She half expected her aunt to snap a disagreeable reply, but instead the older woman suggested that they should meet around one o'clock. 'Wicked cold it is,' she observed. 'I'll treat the three of us to something hot before we set off for the farm.'

Bryn nudged Nell in the ribs. 'On market days, the Bull does a steak and kidney pie which is almost as good as the one Mrs J makes,' he whispered. 'And since it's Christmas, maybe the cook will have made a plum pudding. Love plum pudding I do.'

Nell was about to say that she too loved plum pudding when her aunt spoke once more, pointing ahead of her with the whip which she had assured Nell she would never use on Feather, save to guide the pony when they reached a junction. 'See them houses do you? The ones all crowded close at the bottom of the hill? That's where we're bound. Now, I mean to drop my dairy produce off before I stable Feather, so you two can give me a hand at unloading and then go on your way.'

Nell sat back in her seat and gazed around her as they drove into the small town, where the strengthening sunlight shone on glittering frosted slates, houses and shops. After the Liverpool street markets, this one might have seemed small and insignificant to some, but to Nell it was delightful. The brilliant colours of the goods on display and the joviality of the traders warmed her heart and made her realise how very cut off from the rest of humanity she had felt on the farm. The fact that her aunt and Eifion, the only adults with whom she came in contact, always spoke to one another in Welsh had increased her feeling of isolation, and though she and Bryn chatted away in a mixture of the two languages when they were not working she still needed to have a great many words and phrases explained, making her feel foolish and inferior.

Now, as she descended from the trap and began to help her aunt to carry her boxes of produce to her friend's stall, she heard English being spoken in a variety of accents all around. Auntie Kath introduced Nell to her friend, explaining that Mrs Williams was as English as Nell herself, but had married a Welshman and now spoke both languages with equal ease. She also explained in a whispered aside that Mrs Williams was a widow.

Nell smiled at the spry little woman and guessed that Mrs Williams and her aunt had been drawn together when they had first come to the island because they were both foreigners. She would have liked to ask Mrs Williams how long it had taken her to learn to speak Welsh, but she and Bryn were soon busy erecting the stall and setting out Auntie Kath's wares, and the two older women – Mrs Williams must be in her sixties, Nell supposed – were deep in conversation and it would have been rude, Nell told herself, to interrupt.

As soon as the trap was emptied Auntie Kath drove off, manoeuvring skilfully through the crowds, for though it was early the market was in full swing. Gypsies, their dark eyes bright with excitement, were selling great swags of holly, ivy and mistletoe, no doubt cut from someone else's property before the day had so much as dawned. But it was Christmas, so nobody was likely to object, Nell thought, though when she saw others selling eggs, butter and fowls trussed and ready for roasting she whispered to Bryn that such things must surely be stolen, since gypsies had no dairies in which to turn milk into butter, nor farm-yards full of hens.

Bryn raised his eyebrows. 'They aren't idiots, you know,' he said reprovingly. 'They don't go round thievin' and then march into the market where they could be took off to prison as soon as a farmer recognised his butter pat mark. No, they buy the stuff off a farmer's wife who's either too busy to come to market or has too little to sell to make a visit worthwhile. Then they add a few pence for their trouble, and there you are. Of course, everyone knows the gyppos steal, but not at the Christmas market.'

'Oh, I *see*,' Nell said. 'I never thought . . . of course, Auntie Kath's butter has a picture of a cow with the letters 'OJ' under it, so whoever buys it knows it's hers. I call that clever. By the way, what was it you were going to tell me about Auntie Kath and your pal Hywel?'

'It's not about Hywel exactly, it's more about the Swtan, which is the Welsh longhouse I mentioned. The thing is, it belonged to your uncle, and it's your aunt who owns it now, but years ago, when she first came to the island, there was bad blood between the Swtan and Ty Hen. I don't know much about it, it was before I was born, but even now it don't do to mention the Swtan to your aunt.' He gave Nell a broad grin, his blue eyes dancing with mischief. 'Wish I hadn't told you; it 'ud be interesting to watch you put your foot in it.'

'How charming you are. I find it all too easy to say the wrong thing and get into trouble, without any help from anyone,' Nell said gloomily; then she brightened. 'But she's been really nice to me today; perhaps things are looking up at last.'

For a while the two wandered amongst the stalls, arguing over what gift would be most suitable for

Bryn's taid and for Auntie Kath; Nell would have been ashamed to go downstairs on Christmas morning without a gift for her aunt, even though she sometimes resented the older woman and longed for her own home and her laughing, heedless mother.

Finally, they settled on pipe tobacco for Eifion, a china figurine for his wife and a box of homemade fudge for Auntie Kath. Nell bought a tiny enamelled pansy brooch for her mother – it had to be small since it would go by post that very day – and another for her Auntie Lou. Then she and Bryn spent a few pence on a bag of toffee apples and finally, when she saw by the clock tower that it was past noon, she shooed Bryn off, telling him sternly that she would see him in twenty minutes since she wished to take a look round without him hanging on her arm.

Bryn gave her a knowing grin. 'So do I too,' he said ungrammatically. 'See you in twenty minutes by the clock tower, then.'

Relieved of his presence, Nell began to search the stalls for something the young man would like. Auntie Kath's Christmas gift of money had been generous, but she had no idea how much it would cost to send the brooches to her mother's present RAF station, so felt she must hold back a reasonable sum whilst still wanting to buy something nice for Bryn.

As she searched, she kept glancing about her, fearing that he might be hanging around, watching to see what she bought. Sure enough, she suddenly became aware that someone was following her; spying on her in fact. She thought at first it must be Bryn, though like most people at the market the watcher was wrapped in warm clothing and had a cap jammed well down on his head, making identification difficult. Nell took a couple of steps towards him, but he dodged out of sight. She continued to search the stalls, and was soon able to assure herself that the spy was not Bryn, for she had seen his face for a fleeting moment. He was as dark as Bryn was fair, and when he realised he had been spotted he grinned and gave her a wave before disappearing into the crowd once more.

As soon as she was sure she was unobserved, she turned up her coat collar, pulled her scarf up round her mouth and nose, and scuttled for the river which tumbled and foamed on the far side of the market. She began to study the goods on the stalls there, seeing several things which she thought Bryn would like – a fishing rod, a canvas holdall, a large torch – and presently, when she reached the last row nearest the water, she slowed and crouched over a display of clasp knives. She picked one out at random and caught the seller's eye. 'How much?' she hissed.

The elderly man behind the counter grinned tooth-lessly and told her the price, which was within her range, so Nell dug into her handbag, found the correct money and grabbed the knife, shoving it deep into her coat pocket. She would find some nice paper later, she decided, since it did not matter if Bryn saw the wrapping for his present.

The watcher seemed to have disappeared; certainly he had not followed her to the outer stalls, so if, as she suspected, Bryn had set a friend to watch her on his behalf, he would still not know what she had bought him.

But now, glancing up at the clock tower, she realised she should be making her way back there, so that they could meet Auntie Kath at the Bull Hotel. She had barely reached the tower when she was joined by Bryn, grinning all over his face and carrying a bag bulging with interesting-looking objects. 'You'll never guess what I've bought you . . .' he was beginning, when Nell interrupted him.

'It's a bleeding miracle I managed to get you anything at all,' she said sharply. 'Every time I so much as began to ask a price, I saw some feller hiding away nearby, watching me like a hawk. If I could have caught him, I'd have boxed his perishin' ears. Honestly, Bryn, a Christmas present is supposed to be a secret until Christmas Day. Were you trying to find out what I was buying? Why get someone to follow me from stall to stall? In the end, I had to buy your present in a real hurry.'

Bryn stared at her, his eyes rounding. 'I don't know what you mean,' he said. 'Anyway, I was far too busy searching for something which you'd like to worry about what you were getting me. In fact I wasn't even in the market. I remembered seeing something in a shop on Stryd Fawr as we drove into town, so I went up there.' He guffawed loudly. 'Why on earth would I ask someone to follow you? And who would waste their time doing so, even if I had asked someone? The Christmas market only happens once a year, you know!'

'I don't believe you,' Nell said indignantly. 'The feller followed me from stall to stall, but though he kept dodging out of sight I was too quick for him. When I managed to catch his eye, he had the nerve to grin and wave, as though we were old pals. He *must* be a friend of yours, Bryn, and you *must* have set him on to follow me. I'm disgusted with you, really I am.'

'And I'm disgusted with you,' Bryn said, his cheeks flushing. 'You've known me for weeks and weeks and actually think I could play a mean trick like that. The fact is, you're a stranger and there aren't many of them at the Christmas market, so I expect the lad wondered who you were and what you were doing on the island.'

'Oh,' Nell said slowly. 'Yes, I suppose that's quite possible. I'm really sorry if I misjudged you, Bryn, but it did seem so strange. If he hadn't kept dodging out of sight, I wouldn't have thought twice about it, but . . . if I was wrong, I'm really sorry. As you say, I've known you for quite a while now and you've never played a mean trick on anyone to my knowledge. But I can't help wondering who he was and why he followed me.'

'I've *told* you,' Bryn said impatiently. 'Country folk are curious, but you wouldn't know that, of course. Or mebbe it was a sneak thief, after your purse. There's always warnings to women to keep a hand on their cash when there's gypsies about.'

'If he was a thief . . . oh, what's the point of arguing?' Nell said dismissively. 'I've said I'm sorry and now I'm sick of the whole subject. Let's go and meet Auntie Kath, because if we're late . . .'

She left the sentence unfinished but it galvanised the pair of them into action and they sprinted for the Bull and the hot meal which Kath had promised them. Nell, hurtling in Bryn's wake, knew her aunt well enough by now to realise that punctuality was almost as important to her as godliness. 'Wait for me, Bryn, and don't you mention that I was followed – all right, all right, don't mention that I thought I was followed, then. Just remember that if we're not back at the Bull in the next five minutes we'll be in big trouble.'

'Aye, you're right there; your aunt is always on time herself, so we'd best get a move on,' Bryn agreed.

They reached the inn yard just moments ahead of Auntie Kath, who was also laden with parcels and packages, though when Nell offered to give her a hand she was told severely that her aunt could manage perfectly well, thanks very much.

'We'll go into the bar parlour and have a hot meal, then get off home,' she said. 'I know you're spending Christmas Day and Boxing Day with your family in Newry Street, Bryn, so I thought we'd have a bit of a do tomorrow, to exchange our presents before you leave. Is that in order?'

Bryn said it was and Nell, who had not realised her friend would not be spending Christmas at Ty Hen, was a little dismayed and knew she would miss him sadly. However, she did not intend to give him the satisfaction of saying so and merely agreed with her aunt that she would pack up her presents in good time.

'I've got some little things – brooches, actually – to send by post, so I'll write out the envelopes whilst we have our food,' she said. 'They're for Mam and Auntie Lou, and though I don't suppose they'll receive them until after the holiday, I'd like to get them off today.'

'Good,' Auntie Kath said absently. 'I'll put a line in your envelope, just saying you're doing well enough and – and wishing Trixie and Lou the compliments of the season.'

Nell's mouth dropped open but she hastily shut it when her aunt turned in her direction. Fancy Auntie Kath actually volunteering to correspond with her younger sisters! But by now they had reached the bar parlour and the elderly waiter was coming towards them, pad in hand.

'Steak and kidney pudding do you?' her aunt asked. 'Same for you, Bryn? Then that's three steak and kidneys and we'll order our dessert later on.'

The meal was excellent, and, putting their argument behind them, Nell and Bryn kept up a constant flow of chatter. Auntie Kath put in an occasional word, and when the meal was over they returned to the pony trap, all pleased with their day. 'If it's the war which got all my goods sold, then I suppose I should be thanking Herr Hitler,' Auntie Kath said as she drove the pony out of the inn yard. 'Every pat of butter, every piece of shortbread went . . . I've made a tidy sum today.' She smiled at Nell. 'We're going to have a good Christmas!'

Nell woke on Christmas morning knowing that this would be a very different day from those she had enjoyed in the past. At home all the aunts, uncles and cousins gathered at one or other of the larger houses, often at the Whitakers', since their old corner house had a large kitchen and an even larger parlour, quite big enough to hold the whole family, if one was not fussy about sitting on the floor on cushions, or sharing chairs.

Everyone contributed to the Christmas dinner and from an early hour the chosen kitchen buzzed with aunts and older cousins. First they made a huge cooked breakfast, and when those dishes had been cleared away they began preparations for their Christmas dinner, which was usually eaten at around five in the evening. Each aunt would undertake to roast potatoes, prepare sprouts, leeks or carrots, or make bread sauce, to say nothing of a gallon of gravy; Trixie and Lou cooked the birds – the family usually consumed four large capons – and the other aunts, having helped with the breakfast, went back to their own homes and returned later, staggering under the weight of the pans and dishes which contained their contributions to the feast.

Whilst all this activity was going on the children played various games, and it was only after the last morsel of Christmas pudding had been joyfully dispatched that presents were exchanged. No one spent a great deal of money on the gifts they gave, but Nell appreciated that a lot of thought went into their choice.

She had never been disappointed when she unwrapped her own presents and now, sitting up in her bed and contemplating the day ahead, she told herself that if she were lonely and miserable it would be her own fault. She had meant to suggest to Auntie Kath that they might both go back to Liverpool for the festivities, but as they had driven back to the farm after their trip to Llangefni Auntie Kath had said casually that her niece would be meeting some strangers on Christmas Day. 'I always invite Mr Bellis and Mr Waters; they're both in their eighties and used to work for us in years gone by,' she had explained The old men were widowers, eking out a precarious living in two tiny cottages, and did odd jobs from time to time to make ends meet. During lambing they came up to the farm to help out, and then Auntie Kath paid them and gave them all their meals. 'But Owain always insisted that we should invite them for Christmas Day,' she finished.

Hearing this, Nell had abruptly changed her mind. In her heart, she had known that it would not be a good idea to try to prise her aunt away from Ty Hen until she knew her a good deal better. Furthermore, now that she knew about the elderly farmhands, she could scarcely suggest that her aunt should accompany her, leaving her invited guests to fend for themselves. Nor could she abandon Auntie Kath to a couple of ancient farm workers and go off to relatives who would probably simply regard her as another mouth to feed. No, she would have to make the best of Christmas at the farm, so, telling herself that the festivities in Liverpool would not be the same with Trixie and Lou both missing, she had decided to do her very best to make this particular Christmas a special one for her aunt.

Now, Nell flipped the curtain back, made a port-
hole on the icy pane with her breath, and peered out.
She could see the yard from her window, though day
had not yet dawned properly, and for a moment she
contemplated snuggling under her covers once more.
When she had complained to Auntie Kath that sometimes she could not sleep for the cold her aunt had
fetched extra blankets from somewhere, and now Nell
was as snug as a dormouse in its nest and always got
up reluctantly. She was about to lie down again when
she changed her mind. She would get up as usual,
help her aunt to get breakfast – for there were cows
to be milked and Eifion would expect a cooked meal
as he did every day – and then accompany her to early
service. Auntie Kath had told her she always attended
early service on Christmas Day as well as midnight
communion, and though she had not precisely ordered
her niece to follow suit, Nell had gone to the midnight
service and had loved it, and felt sure she would enjoy
the early service as well, for the church was decked
with greenery and such flowers as had withstood the
fierce frosts, and everyone was cheerful and jolly.
Indeed, the previous evening was the first time that
Nell had felt at home, a part of the community, instead
of an outsider.

So now she jumped out of bed, flew across the icy
floor to the washstand, and began to prepare for the
day ahead.

When she climbed the stairs again at the end of the
day, Nell realised that though it had indeed been

the quietest Christmas she had ever known, she had still enjoyed it. The food had been even better than what her aunts and cousins would have enjoyed, she told herself as she undressed. They had had a turkey – she had never even tasted turkey before – and delights such as roasted parsnips and a dish called ponch mipe, which was swede, carrot, butter and a great deal of black pepper, vigorously mashed until you could not tell one vegetable from the other. Nell knew her aunt had been busy baking for days, and today she had sampled mince pies, the mincemeat soaked in brandy, the pastry enriched with butter and egg yolk. The Christmas cake had not been iced – icing sugar had been banned, and it was one thing Auntie Kath did not keep in her pantry as a matter of course – but it had been rich with fruit, once more soaked in brandy.

Nell, no backslider when it came to eating, had opened her eyes at the amounts the old men had put away. She had whispered as much to her aunt, who had said it was a well-known fact that all Anglesey men had hollow legs. 'You should have met young Adam, one of the farm workers,' she had confided. Aloud, she said: 'Eat for Wales he could! Why, I doubt even the army can cope with the lad's appetite. Someone told me that on Christmas the officers serve the other ranks, and a good deal of food will get chucked around.' She had chuckled. 'If Adam chucks any food, down his perishin' throat it will go.'

Mr Bellis, who had been listening, had given Nell a tolerant smile. 'Hard work it is, farming, so we need plenty of good food,' he had observed. 'How does it suit you, missy?'

Nell had stared, suddenly aware that despite the cold and the long hours she was beginning to enjoy it. Surely it was better to help a ewe to give birth to her lamb than to work on a factory bench making munitions; better working to encourage life than to end it. But Mr Bellis had been gazing at her, one grizzled eyebrow raised, so Nell had hurried into speech. 'I hated it at first, hated the cold and the dirt and the hard work,' she had told the old man. 'There are still lots of things I don't like, but I'm beginning to see that there are nastier ways of doing one's bit for the war effort. I really love the animals, and the sheepdogs are a bleedin' miracle . . .'

Mr Bellis had tutted and Nell, who had temporarily forgotten where she was, had apologised at once. 'Sorry. I do know how folk hereabouts feel about bad language, especially my aunt,' she had admitted. 'I forgot myself, I suppose, it being Christmas.'

Mr Bellis had glanced quickly round the table, and had then addressed Nell in a whisper. 'You'll grow accustomed, lass. Just you think before you speak, and you'll soon learn our ways. But it don't do to offend folk.'

Nell had agreed to take his advice and now, curling up in her dormouse nest, she reflected that it had been a far nicer Christmas than she had anticipated. She had missed Bryn, of course, for despite their quarrel he was still her only true friend on the island, but nevertheless she had had a lovely day. Her aunt had accepted the fudge, flushing with pleasure, although she must have known it had been bought with the money she had given her niece as a Christmas box. Then she had handed over a small parcel which proved to contain a dear little brooch, similar to the ones Nell had bought for Trixie and Lou, save that this one was primroses, not pansies.

Over steak and kidney pudding at the Bull Hotel, she had informed her niece that she had taken the liberty of buying a few small presents for Nell to pass on to their guests. Nell had already followed Bryn's example and bought pipe tobacco for Eifion, and her aunt had bought the same for the ancient farmhands, knowing that Nell had never met them and might buy something altogether unsuitable. Nell had not imagined that the two old men would buy her anything, however, and had been thrilled when they had given her a small diary.

'Me daughter-in-law give it me to give to you; I paid her for it, of course, sharing the price wi' me pal here,' Mr Bellis had said bashfully. 'We thought it might be useful for you to jot down important events and that.' He had grinned shyly. 'There's a little pencil what goes with it and me daughter-in-law says the binding's real leather.'

Nell had thanked the old men from the heart and said she would start writing in it as soon as the New Year arrived. By then she hoped that Bryn would be back, for they had planned expeditions to various places which he wanted her to see. Undoubtedly, they would visit the market again and perhaps go to one of the cinemas in the town.

Thinking of Llangefni made her remember the stranger's odd behaviour, popping up whenever she looked round. With hindsight, she was beginning to believe that he had not been spying on her at Bryn's request. She knew her friend well enough to know he was no liar and in fact on Christmas Eve, before going off to Holyhead, he had given her a small parcel containing a wristwatch which, he told her drily, he had most certainly not bought on the market.

Nell had felt rather guilty, for the watch must have cost considerably more than the clasp knife, and she determined to be extra nice to Bryn when he returned after his holiday.

But a week later, when Auntie Kath was commenting that it was about time Bryn came back to them, they heard bad news: Bryn had gone to a party given by an old school friend and had developed measles. 'He won't be back until his quarantine is up,' Auntie Kath told her niece, for Eifion's explanation, in Welsh, was a little too much for Nell to understand. 'A shame it is, but we know he'll be off anyway as soon as the *Scotia* has a berth for him, so we might as well get used to doing without him.'

Nell, agreeing rather dolefully, wrote him a letter apologising for calling him a liar over what she referred to as 'the Llangefni market affair', and thanked him all over again for her lovely wristwatch. Then she settled down to do twice as much work as the snow started to fall and the gales to blow.

'It looks like being a hard winter,' Auntie Kath told her niece. 'But at least it's good news for the air force, according to what I've heard. Bad weather will keep the Luftwaffe grounded; give us a breathing space. And Bryn will be back with us as soon as he's well enough, you mark my words. He needs to earn a bit of money until they find him a berth.'

Chapter Four

Exactly two weeks after Christmas Day, the first spots appeared. Nell was woken as usual by the alarm and swung her feet out of bed to pad over to the washstand, or start to do so at any rate. Halfway there she stumbled, swayed and fell to the floor, realising suddenly that she felt very odd indeed, not at all like her usual self.

Groggily, she got to her feet, reached the washstand and saw her reflection in the mirror. She was as red as a tomato, and realised suddenly that she was shivering with cold, despite feeling hot – very hot. She continued to peer for a moment, puzzled. Why had she fallen over? She had thought she must have tripped on the edge of the rug, but now she was not so sure. The rug lay flat on the boards, and would not have been on the path she habitually took from bed to washstand in any case. After a moment she gave up the puzzle, shrugged, and heaved her nightgown over her head – then gasped. In the small mirror she saw that her chest and neck were covered with a fine web of small red spots . . . and now that she could see them, as if they had just been awaiting their opportunity, they began to itch.

'Damn!' Nell said. She struggled back into her

nightgown, added a thick woollen dressing gown which had once belonged to the uncle she had never met, and headed for the stairs, jug in hand. She would ask Auntie Kath for some hot water and might mention the spots or might not, depending on her aunt's mood, she decided.

However, the choice was not to be hers. She entered the kitchen, began to speak, and walked slap bang into the table, banging her hip so hard that she cried out. Auntie Kath turned from the pot she was stirring and frowned, then put her spoon down and approached her niece. She seized Nell under the chin and stared hard into her hot face, then ran a hand across her spotty forehead.

'Measles!' she cried triumphantly. 'I guessed how it would be when Eifion told us Bryn had contracted them at that confounded party. It's gone through the schools like wildfire; both Mr Bellis's grandchildren are full of them, and I said to myself it'll be Nell next, and wasn't I right? Don't tell me you've had the measles already, because you can't get 'em twice and if ever I saw a case of it, I see it before me now!'

Nell's eyes filled with tears which trickled down her hot cheeks. 'No, I've not had measles, and I'm sure I wish I hadn't got them now,' she protested, scrubbing the tears away with the heels of her hands. 'Have you had them, Auntie? And what about Eifion? If old Mr Bellis gave them to me, I suppose I might give them to you.'

Her aunt pulled a chair out from beneath the table and pushed Nell into it, then gave a derogatory sniff.

'Course I've had measles; so has everyone with any sense,' she said crossly. 'My mother made sure I had all them infectious diseases whilst I was still a child. Oh aye, I had measles, mumps and chickenpox, all of 'em. So did Trixie, as I recall. You'd have thought she'd have had the sense to make sure her daughter had 'em before landing you on someone else, but that's just like your ma. I dare say she never gave it a thought.'

Nell began to try to defend her mother, but the sheer misery of the situation overcame her and she threw herself down on the table, buried her head in her arms and began to cry again. 'How could my mother have made sure I caught all the infectious diseases?' she asked in a muffled voice. 'She did her best, I'm sure, and I have had chickenpox and that other one you mentioned. It's just that when some of my cousins had measles, which was a good five years ago, Auntie Carrie took me and my other cousins into the country for a bit of a holiday. We went down to Herefordshire for the hop-picking.' Nell gulped and raised a tear-stained face, glaring up at her aunt. 'It were lovely, honest to— I mean truly it was, so if you want to blame anyone, you'd best blame your sister Carrie.'

Auntie Kath, ladling porridge into a bowl and setting it down in front of her niece, had the grace to look a little ashamed, Nell thought. 'All right, all right, so it weren't your ma's fault, but a fat lot of use you'll be to me while you're covered in spots,' she said gruffly. Then, to Nell's astonishment, she gave her shoulder a comforting squeeze. 'Never you mind me; I'm just disappointed to be losing my new worker just when she's learned to milk.' She reached for the sugar bowl, handed it to her niece and then returned to the range to heat the big frying pan. 'Reckon it'll take a good fortnight, maybe three weeks, before you're out of quarantine. Then you can start work again.'

Nell sprinkled sugar sparingly over her porridge, knowing that it was now on ration. Usually, she helped herself from the big honey jar, but today, because of the measles, she felt justified in having some sugar. 'But Auntie, if you and Eifion and Bryn have all had the measles, why can't I carry on as usual,' she asked plaintively. 'Or are you afraid I'll give it to the cows?'

Her aunt actually chuckled, but shook her head chidingly. 'You can't give it to the animals, thank the Lord,' she said piously. 'But you're not going to feel like milking the cows or mucking out the beasts yet awhile; you've got to resign yourself to some time in bed. When Bryn's better and comes back to work, I dare say he'll carry up some food for you a couple of times a day. If not, I suppose I'll have to do it myself. Now finish that porridge and then go back upstairs, for I'll warrant you don't feel like a cooked breakfast this morning.'

Nell opened her mouth to say that, on the contrary, she felt very hungry indeed, then realised that her aunt was right; she could not even finish the porridge. She laid her spoon down and got carefully to her feet. 'I'm sorry about the porridge, Auntie, but I think you're right and I'll be best in bed,' she said meekly. 'Oh dear, I feel ever so odd . . .'

She swayed and might have fallen, but her aunt

looped a strong arm round her waist. 'I'll help you upstairs,' she said curtly, and presently Nell found herself glad to be back in her bed, though she wished she had thought to bring up with her the mug of tea her aunt had just poured.

Auntie Kath went out of the room, closing the door firmly behind her, and Nell was just wondering whether she might return to the kitchen and beg for a drink when the door reopened and her aunt came in. 'Had a good sleep?' she asked and Nell, casting a startled glance at the alarm clock on her bedside table, realised that she must have slept for several hours. She sat up and her aunt placed a tray containing a large mug of weak tea and a bowl of what looked like rice pudding across her knees. 'You won't be wanting meat and veg for a while yet,' she said, and her tone was almost kindly. 'When you begin to feel better you can come downstairs and lie on the couch in the parlour. But right now bed's the place for you.'

Nell did her best, over the next week, to put up with the isolation, for it turned out that Bryn had been very ill indeed once the measles took hold. Auntie Kath tutted and said it just proved that he should never have been accepted for the RNVR. Nell had hoped that he would return to stay with his grand-parents once more so that he could visit her as she got better, but Eifion's wife had decided that he should remain in Holyhead where his mother, who had finished her training with the WRNS and was at home awaiting her first posting, could nurse him herself. The doctor had applauded this decision, insisting that

Bryn should be kept indoors and carefully watched for a good three weeks. Auntie Kath, hearing this, had decided to follow the doctor's advice too, though she did allow her niece to come down to the kitchen at teatime and stay downstairs until seven or eight o'clock in the evening.

Poor Nell speedily grew to hate the four walls of her bedroom. She had brought no books with her to the farm, expecting that there would be a library within walking distance or that her aunt would be able to supply her with reading matter. Whilst she was working on the farm she had not missed it, but now, spending most of the day in her bedroom, she simply longed for a book – any book – with which to while away the long hours. Auntie Kath, when appealed to, had said that Owain had been a great reader, but she rather thought that after his death the rector, the schoolmaster and several fellow farmers had asked for permission to take his books, and had done so. Nell had asked her aunt for a writing pad, and as soon as her eyes had stopped hurting she had written long letters to her mother and all the aunts, explaining about the measles and begging them to post off to her any old magazines, newspapers or books which they happened to have about them.

Meanwhile, she asked whether it might be possible for her to search the attic, since she remembered her aunt once saying that it was full of all manner of rubbish, no longer wanted in the house itself. But it seemed that the idea of Nell climbing up the ladder-like stair did not appeal to Auntie Kath. 'Don't you go poking around in all that dust and muck,' she said crossly. 'There's nothing up there which isn't broken or useless. If it's books you want, there's a good library in Llangefni, and though I'm too busy to go there while the snow's making so much extra work – trust you to get ill in the worst winter for a hundred years – I'll try to find you something to read next time I'm in town.' And with that, Nell had to be content.

However, the winter which Auntie Kath had described as the worst for a hundred years showed no sign of letting up and Auntie Kath's temper was not improved when tremendous snowstorms and the resultant drifts cut the farm off from the outside world and for several days the milk lorry did not call. She fed them on junkets, custards and delicious savoury onion sauces; then she made butter, cottage cheese and anything else which would stop her having to waste the milk.

Nell, who had suffered her three weeks' quarantine with as good a grace as she could manage, rebelled against yet more incarceration. As she pointed out, she was over the measles and, if she wrapped up warmly, could reach the shippon to help milk the cows, cart the heavy buckets of swill to the pigs, collect the eggs, feed the poultry, give an eye to the ewes now shut up in the big barn . . .

Auntie Kath reluctantly agreed that her niece might as well be useful. 'You've learned to milk all right, and I don't mean you to forget the knack,' she snapped. 'So you can begin this afternoon by eating your tea and then giving Eifion a hand with the evening milking. You can start with Dora and Daisy; they're patient creatures and won't mind if you're a bit slow and fumblesome at first.'

Nell was only too eager to comply, because whilst the lanes were blocked and the churns could not be collected Auntie Kath seemed to be perpetually finding fault. She tried to teach Nell some simple cookery, but after a couple of unsuccessful attempts she refused Nell's request to be taught to make more interesting things such as cakes and puddings. 'I've got enough to do without you ruining good food,' she said shortly. 'Though you can give a hand with the butter and cheese making, since I don't mean to see all this good milk go down the drain.'

Churning milk into butter was both boring and extremely hard work, but Nell stuck at it and earned grudging praise from Auntie Kath. Then one icy morning she entered the kitchen to find her aunt wrestling with what appeared to be a couple of elongated tennis rackets but which, her aunt told her brusquely, were snow shoes.

'I'm not going to let all this good food go to waste,' she said, jerking a thumb at a large cardboard box piled with packs of butter, cheese, clotted cream and a tray of eggs, 'so I'm taking this little lot over to Valley on the sledge. After all, there's a war on, as they keep telling us, and the country needs feeding. Besides, I'll likely get a tidy sum for all this grub if I put it on a train for London. You'll have to make do with porridge this morning, since I'll be off as soon as I get these dratted things attached to my boots.'

'Oh, Auntie, are you taking it to London yourself?'
Nell asked, dismayed. 'Will you be gone many days?
I know I can milk now, but suppose a ewe drops her
lamb early, or one of the cows begins to calf after
Eifion's gone home . . .?'

Her aunt gave a short bark of laughter. 'As if I'd
bobby off and leave you in charge!' she said derisively.
'Oh, I know you've more sense than your ma, but even
so . . .'

'All right, all right; sorry I spoke,' Nell said huffily.
'I only asked. You know I want to be useful, but . . .'

Auntie Kath tutted and shook a reproving head. 'Oh
well, you're not a bad kid when all's said and done.
And of course I'm not going to London; Tommy Evans,
or his brother Jack, whichever one is guard on the train
today, will sell it for me – they've done it before when
folks have had a glut. I've made out a list of prices,
so Tommy or Jack will collect the money for me and
bring it back.'

'Oh, I see,' Nell said blankly. It all sounded rather
hit and miss to her, particularly considering the
weather. 'But suppose the trains aren't running?
Because of the snow, I mean.'

'Then I'll have to leave it at the station and hope
the line clears tomorrow,' Auntie Kath said briskly.
'There's a meat pie for your dinner, and I used the
trimmings to make an apple flan for afters; I reckon
I'll be home in time to make us a nice high tea.'

'If I put on my boots and my thick coat, wouldn't
it be better if I came with you?' Nell asked. 'Suppose
you fell and broke your leg, or suppose you got lost?

Everywhere looks very different when snow is on the ground.'

Her aunt, struggling into her own thick overcoat, shook her head. 'I'm taking Fly and Whisky with me; if anything unfortunate were to happen to me, I'd keep Whisky with me and send Fly for help.' She eyed her niece rather sourly. 'You might not know what to do if you heard Fly barking and leaping around outside the back door, but Eifion would.'

'That's all right then. But if you do reach Valley, could you buy me something to read? I'm that desperate, even *Farmers Weekly* would be welcome.'

Her aunt sniffed. 'I'll maybe bring back a pile of newspapers, if nothing else,' she said rather grudgingly. 'Tell you what though, I've been meaning to buy a wireless set, ever since the war started. I'll see if I can get one sent over from Llangefni, 'cos I don't think Valley would run to such things. How would that suit you?'

'Oh, Auntie, that would be wonderful,' Nell said happily. 'And whilst you're gone, I'll help Eifion as much as I can. Off you go then, and if I hear so much as a squeak out of Fly, I'll come running, only I don't suppose I'll be able to find my way to Valley in all this snow.'

Her aunt was knotting a head square under her chin and bending to fasten the snowshoes so her reply, when it came, was interspersed with grunts. 'My dear Nell, of course you wouldn't be able to find me. That's why you must tie a piece of rope through Fly's collar and hang on to the other end. And even if I did fall – not that I shall, of course, I've got more sense – someone would come across me sooner or later.'

'And find a stiff and frozen corpse, I dare say,' Nell said sarcastically. 'Oh, go by yourself then, but if you aren't home by five o'clock, I warn you I shall panic.'

Her aunt laughed and stood up, having strapped the snowshoes on to her sturdy boots. 'Now eat up that porridge before it goes cold.' She picked up the box of food, not without difficulty, and carried it out to the yard just as Eifion appeared outside the back door, towing the sledge. 'Goodbye for now, the pair of you. See you later.'

As soon as her aunt had disappeared, Eifion came clumping into the kitchen, knocking the snow off his boots and rubbing his cold hands vigorously together. Nell had learned some time previously that Eifion understood English as well as she did herself, though he was shy of trying to speak it to someone he did not know well. To her own secret astonishment Nell realised that she now understood a great deal of Welsh, thanks largely to Bryn, so it was no longer difficult for herself and the farm worker to converse, even though both were careful to pick their words and to speak slowly.

Nell took the porridge saucepan from the range and smiled at Eifion as he unbuttoned his coat and sat down at the table with a sigh of relief. 'Only porridge today, and as much bread and butter as you can eat, as well as a good mug of hot tea,' she said cheerfully. 'Then we'll do the milking. After that I've got to cook our dinner and prepare the high tea, so you'll have to manage without me then, I'm afraid.'

'That'll suit,' Eifion said briefly. 'I reckon the missus will be back afore dark, or soon after.' He scraped his spoon round his porridge dish and pulled his mug of tea towards him. 'Grand it is to have a paned on a cold morning,' he said. 'Did I tell you young Bryn won't be coming back no more? His mam don't want him missing out on a berth aboard the *Scotia* because he's still not fit, so she's keeping him at home and seeing that he don't overdo himself.'

Nell had already been told it was unlikely that Bryn would be returning, and, though she had been dismayed at first, the knowledge that she and Eifion now understood one another pretty well had lessened her disappointment. She really liked Bryn and would miss him, but she thought him young for his age and often rather silly. She also knew in her heart that she would probably learn Welsh more quickly when it was a case of necessity.

She murmured that she hoped Bryn would return for a few days when he got leave from his ship, and sought for a new subject of conversation. She had long wanted to know for certain the identity of the man in the photograph on the mantel and addressed her companion casually. 'Eifion, you know that photograph on the mantel, the one with the man and— Oh!' She had turned towards the range as she spoke and to her surprise realised that the old brown photograph was no longer there. Instead, a bright calendar advertising a certain brand of cattle cake was in its place. Eifion, however, did not so much as glance at the mantel.

'What about it?' he asked, shovelling porridge, and

Nell realised that he was so accustomed to the photograph that it had not occurred to him to turn and examine it. 'That's Mr Owain, that is.' He gave her a searching look from under his thick, grizzled brows. 'Who did you think it were?'

Nell shrugged. She had thought it must be Owain Jones, but when she had asked Auntie Kath, shortly after arriving at the farmhouse, she had received no proper sort of answer. 'Why do you want to know?' her aunt had said belligerently, and before Nell could explain that it was simple curiosity her aunt had changed the subject with sufficient finality to make it plain that Nell would not be told anything about it – or not by Auntie Kath, at any rate. Naturally, this made Nell even more curious, and more determined than ever to discover the identity of the man in the photograph.

But now Eifion was looking at her enquiringly, so Nell rushed into speech. 'Oh, I just wondered who it was,' she said vaguely. 'I was pretty sure it must be him.' She finished off her porridge, drained her mug of tea, and got to her feet. 'It wasn't important. My aunt's husband was a handsome chap, wasn't he?'

Eifion snorted and got up. 'Handsome is as handsome does,' he said sententiously, grinning gummily at her. He switched to Welsh. 'You might say I were handsome, in my day, like. You might say you was handsome . . .'

Nell laughed. 'Thanks very much,' she said sarcastically, taking down her coat and putting it on. 'You certainly know how to turn a compliment!' She pushed her feet into her rubber boots and cuddled her hands into the thick mittens her aunt had knitted for her. 'Come on then; let's get the cows milked and the shippon mucked out. Then I'll come back indoors and start on the dinner.' As the two of them, heads bent, let themselves out of the door and into the blizzard, she raised her voice. 'I wonder where that old photograph went, though? Any ideas, Eifion?'

'Dresser drawer,' Eifion bawled above the howl of the wind. The two of them burst into the shippon, grateful to be out of the whirling snow which, in the short distance across the yard, had clung to their clothing and stung their cheeks. 'She said something about a new frame . . . it'll be in the dresser drawer.'

Nell nodded and picked up her milk pail and stool, then went across to Dora, her favourite cow. 'Here I am, lass,' she said cheerfully, arranging her stool by Dora's side and taking a length of twine out of her pocket so that she might tie Dora's tail to her hind leg whilst she was being milked. Nell did not much like to have a cow's tail, coated with dung, lashed across her face every time Dora turned round to see how she was getting on.

As the milk began to hiss into the pail, she thought how luck had smiled on her. Under normal circumstances, Auntie Kath would have been in and out of the kitchen all day, making it impossible for her niece to search the dresser drawers and take a good look at the photograph, and to see for herself whether there were books in the forbidden attic. As it was, when Nell went in to cook the dinner, she would have every opportunity both to find the photograph and to search the attic. The man in the photograph appeared to be in his early twenties, yet Trixie had insinuated that there had been a considerable age difference between Owain and his bride. Presumably this must mean that the photograph had been taken a long while before the marriage.

Thinking it over, Nell could not imagine why her aunt had hidden it away in the dresser drawer. So far as she could see, it made no sense. Burying her head in the cow's warm side, she thought smugly that Auntie Kath could do her best to keep her niece in the dark, but by hook or by crook she, Nell, would find out all she wanted to know. Smiling to herself, she drained Dora's udder and moved to the next cow. At least she knew for certain now that the man in the photograph was Owain Jones. It's a start, she told herself.

As soon as the milking was finished she and Eifion mucked out the cows, who could not be turned out in such conditions. Then Nell hurried across the snowy yard to get dinner, leaving Eifion to collect the eggs and check on the sheep.

Back in the warmth of the kitchen, she put potatoes into the sink to be peeled and chose a large cabbage from the vegetable rack. Then she succumbed to temptation and attacked the dresser drawers. The first one was full of papers – bills, receipts, letters and so on – and the second held a variety of tablecloths, napkins and similar tableware. The third, however, proved to contain the photograph, as well as a broken silver frame. So Eifion had been right. The photograph must have been in the frame once, though not in her time.

Nell looked guiltily round her, then picked up the photograph, turned it over and saw, to her disappointment, that there was nothing written on it. It was a pity, but at least she knew for certain now that this was indeed Owain Jones, who would have been her uncle had he not died long ago.

She peeled the potatoes in record time, then chopped the cabbage into a steamer which she balanced on top of the pan of potatoes. She would pop the apple flan into the oven as soon as they sat down to eat their main course, and there was a big jug of milk and some Bird's custard powder awaiting her attention. Nell smiled wryly. Her aunt had clearly not forgotten the horrible results of her attempt to teach her niece to make a proper egg custard, not to mention the sinful waste of her precious sugar in the process.

As soon as she had got the dinner on the go, Nell went over to the kitchen window and peered out into the snowy yard. There was no sign of Eifion. Nothing moved in the silent scene, apart from the snowflakes drifting lazily down, indicating that the wind had eased. At least Auntie Kath won't have to tackle fresh snowdrifts on her way home, Nell told herself. She moved away from the window and crossed to the door leading to the hall, glancing up at the clock as she did so. Good! Auntie Kath always served dinner at one o'clock and it was only a quarter past twelve. Eifion was a creature of habit and needed no watch to tell him the time; he would be scraping the snow off his boots at five to one, hanging his coat on the clothes horse to dry at three minutes to one, scrubbing his hands at the sink at a minute to one, and sitting down at the table at exactly one o'clock. Smiling to herself at the mental picture, Nell wondered whether Eifion would retain his greasy tweed cap. He always grumbled if Auntie Kath tried to make him take it off, saying that more heat escaped through the top of a man's head than by any other route. Nell absolved Eifion of vanity and thought he genuinely believed that his cap should remain on his head for all his waking hours. In fact she had once asked Bryn if his grandfather wore the cap at night, expecting him to laugh and deny it. But Bryn had looked at her owlishly. 'I dunno; likely he does though . . . keep it on all night, I mean,' he had said, his mouth quirking into a grin so that Nell was not sure whether he was teasing her. 'Nain once told me she bought him a nightcap one Christmas. It were wool and a lovely red colour, but he said folk would confuse him wi' Santy Claus and he weren't having that.'

'You're kidding me,' Nell had said uncertainly, but he had assured her it was the gospel truth he was telling her, then changed the subject.

Now Nell, ascending the stairs, suddenly got a mental picture of Eifion in a pointed red woollen hat and choked on a laugh, then dismissed the thought and began to run up the flight. She knew it was silly to hurry, because her aunt could not possibly get back from Valley station until four or five that afternoon, and if the unheard-of happened and Eifion came in earlier than usual, there were a thousand reasons why she might have gone up to her room in the middle of the day. There was no reason why she should feel guilty, imagining that any moment a voice would hail her, demanding to know what she was up to.

Ever since she had arrived at the farm, she had longed to explore it properly, for despite having been there for many weeks she had still never visited some areas of the huge house. The parlour, with its stiff brocade curtains, cabinets full of rare and beautiful china, elegant furniture and huge oil paintings, held no interest for her, nor did the still room with its shelves packed with bottled fruit, pickles, chutneys and salted beans and peas. The bedrooms other than her own and her aunt's were of course plainly furnished and boringly like one another.

No, it was the attic which interested her. If Auntie Kath had not more or less forbidden her to mount the ladder-like stairs and look round the attic she might never have thought of going up there, but forbidden fruit is always the more tempting – Auntie Kath should have remembered Eve in the Garden of Eden, Nell thought – so she had long ago made up her mind that as soon as her aunt left the house for a long period she would take advantage of her absence to climb the narrow stair, push open the trapdoor and see for herself just what the attic contained.

The fact that her aunt had done her best to discourage exploration by saying that the attic was dangerous had not had the desired effect. Nell had listened to Auntie Kath's description of woodworm, death watch beetle, rats, giant spider webs and inch-thick dust without emotion; truth to tell, she had not believed a word of it. But she had known better than to show disbelief. She had giggled, then shivered. 'It sounds like the Sleeping Beauty's palace,' she had observed. 'Perhaps there's an old woman up there, spinning away and turning the cobwebs into magical garments. Perhaps I ought to take a look.'

'Perhaps you ought not to go poking your nose into what don't concern you,' her aunt had snapped. 'Sleeping Beauty indeed! You'd be well served if you found yourself in trouble, 'cos my Owain told me years ago that the floor was rotten. He always reckoned that anyone who didn't know the worst patches might get a broken leg, or worse.'

So which of Auntie's horror stories am I to believe, Nell asked herself now as she approached the narrow wooden stair which led to the attic. I can't say I believe in rats because I'm sure I would have heard them scuttling, and as for death watch beetle, someone once told me that the reason they're called that is because of the constant tick, tick, tick they make whilst nibbling rotten wood. And if there are woodworm chewing away at the beams and boards there soon won't be any house left anyway, because most of it is wood.

So I shall go on regardless, Nell told herself, and so saying she mounted the rest of the stairs and pushed open the heavy trapdoor, revealing a huge room which, contrary to her fears, was anything but bare and empty. It was simply crammed with every unwanted item which had been too good to throw away, yet was no longer wanted in the house below. Furthermore, she could see that the floor was sound. In fact, when she sniffed the air, a familiar odour came to her nostrils. She looked around and saw that mothballs had been scattered pretty freely, whilst even the most cursory glance convinced her that the great beams supporting the slate roof were as sound as the boards of the floor.

Nell took a deep breath; someone, and it must be her Auntie Kath, had been up here within the past few months to spread the mothballs, so she must be well aware that the floor was safe and the beams untouched by either woodworm or death watch beetle. So why, for heaven's sake, had she told . . . well, fibs to dissuade her niece from exploring the attic? And it was obvious now where Owain Jones's books had gone. Not to the rector, or the schoolmaster; in fact, they were here. Big and little piles, they called to Nell as though they had voices of their own, entreating her to pick them up, dust them off, and read them.

Nell scrambled right into the room. She saw that a huge old sofa with horsehair stuffing leaking from one of its cushions stood against one wall, and to Nell's joy there were four windows, so the torch which she had pushed into the pocket of her overalls would not be necessary. She gave a quick look round, then crouched to peer out of the windows, which were at knee level. The two nearest her overlooked the farm-yard and the other two, which she could not approach directly without first clearing a path through the attic's myriad contents, must look out over the snowy countryside.

Nell plumped herself down on the sofa and regarded the contents of the room with delight. She would have a grand time exploring up here! She reached for the nearest books, banged them together to get rid of the dust, and examined the titles. The two largest were leather-covered editions of *Bleak House* and *David Copperfield*, the second of which she happened to have read at school, so she guessed that the other too would be exciting and enjoyable. Unfortunately it was also rather large, which meant it would be difficult to hide from her aunt's inquisitive eye, and Nell had no intention of letting the older woman know that she had visited the attic.

A little further down the pile she discovered two slimmer volumes: *The Farming Year* by Harold Ewart and *A Shepherd's Calendar* by J. K. Ross. Flicking through the dusty pages, she realised that both volumes were crammed with fascinating information for anyone eager to learn about farming. Smiling to herself, she tucked both slim volumes inside her sensible woollen vest, a garment her aunt had handed on to her and which she had regarded with scorn until she came to appreciate its unglamorous but delightful warmth. Now, turning back to the rest of the room, she thought smugly how surprised Auntie Kath would be when she began to air the knowledge culled from the two books.

Having selected reading matter sufficient for at least the next few days, Nell returned to the sofa, placed both volumes of Dickens on the cushion beside her, and examined the rest of the room. Broken chairs, cushions worn threadbare, an ancient sewing machine, cracked crockery and an enormous number of boxes filled to overflowing with old clothes and other such things met her interested gaze. There were tennis rackets with broken strings and cricket bats with their handles un-ravelling. Children's picture books rubbed shoulders with farm ledgers so old that they had all but disinte-grated. With a wriggle of sheer excitement, Nell pulled one of the big wooden tea chests towards her, and soon discovered that there were a great many toys up here, boxes of them, as though each generation, having tired of their playthings, had banished them to the attic without apparently considering that younger members of the family might enjoy them. There were dolls with perfect porcelain faces, teddies so worn and patched that Nell could see how dearly they had once been loved, train sets, model cars, picture books, paint boxes, coloured crayons – oh, all sorts.

Rummaging through one box, Nell unearthed a doll's china tea set so delicately lovely that she gasped, remembering the cheap celluloid ones sold by the stall-holders on the Scottie. Owain and his sisters – or perhaps she should have said ancestors, Nell thought – had indeed been fortunate. There was a doll's house too, but it was empty, and Nell was rifling through a large box which seemed to contain all manner of things – lead soldiers, chess men, playing cards – when she came across more books. She opened the first one and it proved to be a photograph album. Dull stuff, Nell thought to herself, flicking over the pages. Old men and women in the clothes of a bygone era; occasional portraits, very stiff and formal, of young men or women in uniform, standing self-consciously before potted plants, or with one hand resting on the head of an embarrassed-looking dog.

Nell laid the album down and fished out a brightly decorated object which she could see further down the box. It appeared to be a telescope and was very heavy, so she carried it across to the nearest window, knelt down, and pointed it at the distant white-covered meadows.

Immediately, a picture formed, though not the one she expected to see. Strange geometrical shapes, brilliant colours which reminded her of the stained glass she had sometimes seen in church windows, red, green, yellow, blue . . . every time she moved the telescope even a little, the colours and shapes changed.

Nell took the telescope away from her eye and stared at it. It was very heavy, and very brightly coloured on the outside as well as inside. She jiggled it thoughtfully in her palm, and then the penny dropped. It was a kaleidoscope! One of the cousins had had one; she had played with it when she was six or seven and had been intrigued by the variety of tiny pictures it could make. Even when one of the older boys had explained about mirrors and reflected light, she had been intrigued, and always dived on the toy to have first go when she visited the cousins' house.

She turned back to the window once more and this time saw something she had missed on first examining the view. Very distant, but clearly defined against the white of the snow and the dullness of the sky, was a line of dark slate blue, fading to grey. It was the sea! Staring, she remembered the plans she and Bryn had made to visit the coast when summer came. Knowing that he was likely to be aboard ship when the fine weather arrived, he had promised to tell her the best and quickest way from Ty Hen to Church Bay, which was his favourite beach. Nell drew in an ecstatic breath. Bryn's descriptions had made her long to know the bay as he did, but of course it would be far more fun if they could go there together. Putting the kaleidoscope down, she told herself that ships go to and from their home ports pretty regularly; surely Bryn would be given enough leave to enable them to spend time together? It would be rather mean to visit the bay without him when he had so patently longed to show it to her.

She had not yet investigated even a tenth of the boxes awaiting her attention, but some slight sound from downstairs came to her ears and she rose hastily from her knees, prepared to run like a rabbit if it was her aunt returning. However, a little thought convinced her that Auntie Kath could not possibly be back already. Listening hard, she realised that there had been no noise of any sort save for the creaking of the floorboards when she moved in order to see more clearly through the low window. It was my imagination, she told herself. I knew I shouldn't be up here, so guilt made me believe I was about to be discovered. But why should I worry, anyway? Auntie Kath told proper lies about the attic when she said first that it was full of rubbish, and next that it was riddled with woodworm and death watch beetles. They were real untruths, not just little white lies. Still, it's probably about time I went down and got dinner on the go. I've not even peeled the spuds yet!

She thought she would take one last look at the kaleidoscope before leaving. She picked it up and turned the eyepiece. It was rather stiff, as though it did not want to be turned to its full extent, but she persevered and suddenly it moved, and she was looking, not at geometrical shapes or brilliant colours, but at a photograph, brown with age, a photograph of a young man!

Nell was so surprised that she nearly dropped the kaleidoscope; what on earth had happened? But now that she thought back, she remembered that it was possible to insert something other than coloured glass into the instrument. She and Benny, one of her cousins, had unscrewed the end piece of their kaleidoscope and tipped out some of the contents, replacing them with flower petals and small leaves to create their own pictures. Presumably, whoever had owned this toy had done the same. Only whoever had done it had made a far better job of it than she and Benny had managed, for the coloured glass did not intrude upon the photograph, and vice versa.

Thoughtfully, Nell gave the kaleidoscope a shake, twisted the eyepiece to the left and saw once more the glittering glass. Then she twisted it to the right, but for some reason the photograph of the young man would not appear again, and after a couple more unsuccessful tries Nell replaced the kaleidoscope in its box, covered it with the photograph album and pulled up the sleeve of her jersey to examine Bryn's watch. Heavens, she had better get back to the kitchen or Eifion's dinner would be late indeed.

She was about to leave the attic when the movement of the two slim volumes hidden in her underwear reminded her that she could take something else with her provided it was small enough to be easily hidden. She would have liked the kaleidoscope, but it was a bit too big. She gazed round her, spoilt for choice as her mother would have said. What should it be? Oh, what should it be? Her chances of revisiting the attic were ruled by her aunt's absence . . . she might not be able to climb that narrow, ladder-like stair again until summer came and her aunt visited friends or went into the village or did whatever else she did when the weather became clement. Should she take another book, or one of the games? Too big, impossible to hide. She could not play chess, but she could play snap, or gin rummy, so the cards . . . but to play rummy, or even snap, one needed an opponent. She dithered, eyeing the books wistfully. If only *Bleak House* were not so big! But perhaps she could sneak up here at night when her aunt was asleep, and have a crafty read, or look for the photograph in the kaleidoscope again; or even risk taking the Dickens and hide it deep in her feather bed during daylight hours.

Abruptly, however, her mind decided for her. Her hand shot out and she grabbed a pack of miniature cards. She could play patience without involving anyone else and she was sure that other card games would occur to her once she had had time to think. Nell stuffed the cards down to join the farming books hidden in her vest and set off down the steps, closing the trapdoor behind her. On the landing, she nipped into her bedroom and hid the books and cards in her underwear drawer, telling herself that her aunt was unlikely to so much as enter the room. In one of her more relaxed moments, she had told Nell that everyone needed a place of their own where they would not be disturbed, and Nell appreciated her aunt's thoughtfulness. Having disposed of her booty, she went down to the kitchen where she began preparations for dinner with an unpleasantly thumping heart.

Eventually, however, her heart resumed its usual steady beat and she laid the table before popping the meat pie into the oven. She lifted the hob and pulled the potato pan over the flame, but she still felt as though she had escaped from something unpleasant; from what, exactly? Was there a horrid secret waiting to be discovered, such as had confronted Bluebeard's sixth wife – or was it his tenth? – when she entered the forbidden room? If her aunt found she had been in the attic she would think that her niece was a nosy, ungrateful girl and probably tell her off, but she would come round, particularly if Nell spun her a yarn about a bird's being trapped. She could even say she had released a starling, which had fallen down the chimney, no doubt addle-witted by the terrible cold. No, not the chimney; there was no fireplace in the attic so far as she could remember. She would have to invent a broken slate, or a window not properly closed. Either would do at a pinch. Nell told herself that it was all very well to say that her aunt had lied – she had – but in going directly against her aunt's wishes she had done wrong, and done it knowingly, furthermore. But if Ty Hen was to be her home until the war was over, then she should be able to explore it without guilt.

She stuck a fork into a potato, then checked that the meat pie was warming through. She made some gravy and brought the milk and the Bird's custard powder from their place in the pantry, then fetched a bottle of her aunt's home brew for Eifion and a glass of lemonade for herself. Do stop nagging me, Nell Whitaker, she told herself as she checked that she had done all that was necessary. Remember, Auntie Kath knew there were books in the attic, because who else but she would have sown the place with mothballs? I shouldn't have *had* to trespass if she'd popped up there and brought me a couple of books to read, or even some of those old farming magazines. I don't intend to let her know that I've been in the attic, though, and I mean to go there again whenever I've a mind, she concluded as the back door creaked open and Eifion's ruddy face appeared round it. He grinned at her, displaying bare gums.

'Dinner ready yet, Miss Nell? It's desperate cold out here.'

'It'll be ready by the time you've shed your coat and cleaned up,' Nell said cheerfully. She glanced at the clock on the mantel. 'Honest to God, Eifion, I don't know how you do it! You must have a clock in your inside!' She repeated aloud the words she had thought earlier that day. 'I've noticed that at five to one you're scraping the snow off your boots, at three to you're hanging your coat to dry in front of the range, at one to you're washing—'

'That's enough, you cheeky young varmint,' Eifion said, but Nell saw he was grinning. 'At one o'clock you should be dishin' up, not argufying wi' your betters.'

'I am, I am,' Nell said, draining the vegetables over the sink. 'My, doesn't that meat pie smell good? One of these days I'm going to persuade my aunt to give me more cookery lessons. My mam was always too busy; we had shop stuff as a rule.'

Eifion sat himself down at the table and, when his full plate was before him, began to eat, not fast but with obvious pleasure. 'Shop grub is rubbish,' he said when he had swallowed his first mouthful. 'If you can get your aunt to show you how to cook like her, your husband will be a lucky man.'

'First catch your hare,' Nell said, grinning. 'Some chance I have of meeting a husband, stuck away out here.'

'Oh, there's fellers not that far away, as you'll discover when summer comes,' Eifion said. He took a long draught of his beer. 'Any one of 'em would be pleased to wed a cook like your aunt, even if she was ugly as a pan o' worms.'

'Thank you, you are too kind,' Nell said sarcastically, helping herself to another potato. 'I've a good mind not to tell you what's for afters.'

Auntie Kath returned safely from her trip to Valley, though she was rather later than she had intended, and despite telling herself over and over that her aunt was a very independent woman and would not do anything so foolish as to fall into a snowdrift or break her leg Nell had got rather worried as it began to grow dark. However, her aunt came breezily into the kitchen just as she and Eifion were sitting down to a cup of tea and an enormous pile of bread and butter, and pooh-poohed any suggestion that she might have run into trouble.

'It all went just as I hoped, and Tommy reckons the stuff will sell like hot cakes,' she said complacently, taking off her coat and boots and sinking into a chair. 'Ah, you're a good girl, our Nell; a nice cuppa is just what the doctor ordered.'

The next day she did the rounds of the farm and pronounced herself well satisfied with her niece's work, agreeing that she was now fit and able to take up her usual tasks. Nell was delighted, and set about doing her best to save Eifion some of the harder work, for he was finding the weather made even the simplest task more difficult, chiefly because his rheumatism became worse as the cold deepened. Unfortunately, the winter still showed no signs of letting up, though things were not as bad as they might have been for Nell now that she had some reading matter. She took her bedtime candle upstairs each evening at around nine o'clock and studied her farming books assiduously, and her aunt, who had been true to her promise to try to find Nell something to read, thought that she was gleaning her information from the copies of *Farmers Weekly* which she had brought back from Valley, and congratulated her niece on her intelligent use of the information.

Nell was delighted with her aunt's interest and praise, but very nearly fell from grace one dark morning when her aunt had been suffering from a head cold and was consequently later up than usual. Nell took her a cup of tea and a couple of rounds of buttered toast and told her not to hurry down, since she and Eifion could manage all the yard work between them, even if they were somewhat slow.

'You're not a bad girl,' her aunt said thickly, taking the tea and holding the mug cradled in both hands. 'I'll just drink this and eat the toast, then I'll dress warmly and come down to help with the milking.'

Nell protested that there was no need and left the room, feeling that she and her aunt were making progress; they were almost friends. But on her return to the house for the customary mug of hot cocoa and couple of Welsh cakes, she found her aunt sitting at the table and staring at a small playing card, which Nell recognised with a sinking heart as one of the pack she had taken from the attic. She thought she had hidden everything well, but she took her place at the table as nonchalantly as possible, and helped herself to a Welsh cake just as Eifion came shuffling in, complaining loudly that the cold seemed to be getting worse, not better. He began to drink the tea Nell had poured ready for him, whilst selecting the largest of the Welsh cakes and winking at her. 'Bitter cold out,' he said. 'Glad of hot tea I am.'

'Yes, it's bitter today,' Nell agreed, then leaned forward and took the card gently out of her aunt's hand. 'I found that behind one of the drawers in the chest you gave me for my clothes,' she said with all the casualness she could muster. 'Do you know where the rest of the pack is, Auntie? If we had the whole set, we could play whist or something when it's too dark to do outdoor work.'

Her aunt grunted. 'Last time I saw a card like this, it were with a lot of old rubbish in the attic,' she said rather coldly. 'But of course you wouldn't dream of going up there when my back was turned, I dare say?'

'But Auntie, you said the floor was unsafe and there were rats,' Nell said, opening her eyes very wide. 'Can you play cards? I seem to remember you mentioning village whist drives and saying that chapel people thought they were wicked 'cos it was gambling, but that the rector organised drives when the weather permitted, to raise money for the church.' She handed the card back to her aunt and raised her brows. 'Where did you find it, anyway?'

'It was lying on the floor, just in front of your chest of drawers,' her aunt said. 'I don't usually go into your room, but seeing as how you've got all my work to do as well as your own I thought I'd give you a hand by making your bed. As for the cards, they aren't an English pack. My – my husband brought them back from France and we used to play cards together when we were first married.' To Nell's surprise, her aunt gave a grim chuckle. 'At first, I never won – we played for matchsticks – but after a bit I learned how to cheat. We both cheated, of course, and how we laughed over it! Eh, we had some grand times, so we did. We taught each other every card game we knew, and since the fellers' only amusement in the trenches was playing cards we soon knew the lot – gin rummy, whist, cribbage, anything and everything. Of course the soldiers didn't gamble for money any more than we did, because they didn't have much . . . eh, even talking about it takes me back. And that's not a bad idea of yours – to have a game or two of an evening – so I'll look out a full pack when I've a moment. And now you can pour me another cup of tea before you and Eifion start on the day's work.'

Kath had enjoyed her trip to Valley, cold, snow and all. It had been satisfying to chat to the people she had met, to exchange horror stories about the weather, and the waste of their produce when they could not reach their customers.

'But at least the weather's kept Hitler's planes on the ground, the same as it has ours,' the postmaster remarked, as he dispensed stamps. 'There's been no flying from Valley airfield since the bad weather set in, and that's meant lives saved, if you ask me. I was talking to one of the young fellers who services the planes and he says it's the sand; it blows into the engines and clogs them up . . .' He looked at his audience, one brow rising quizzically. 'What the devil did they expect? The day the wind don't blow a perishin' hurricane on the island will be a cold day in hell!'

Kath grinned and saw others doing the same, though guiltily. Mr Mason was an Englishman and allowed a good deal of licence, being regarded by the older inhabitants as a poor savage who knew no better. The younger ones admired his frankness, copied his slang, and kept their opinions to themselves.

But though her legs had remained unbroken and her spirits high, it had been on that trip that she had contracted the heavy head cold which had laid her low for a couple of days, and the cold had been the cause of her going into Nell's bedroom, not to see what the girl was up to, but simply to make her bed for her, since Nell would be busy all day doing her aunt's chores as well as her own.

Her discovery of the card had been a shock, and one from which she had not fully recovered, despite Nell's perfectly plausible explanation. Kath had pretended to accept it, but now, in the privacy of her own bedroom, she could not help wondering. When she had first come to Ty Hen as a bride she had put all her personal possessions in a large, old-fashioned trunk and stowed it away in the attic. In those days she had regarded the attic as her own special place and had spent a good deal of time up there when she was not working on the farm. She had loved the distant view of the sea, the peace and quiet of the place, and of course, being young and therefore inquisitive, she had enjoyed sorting through the fascinating jumble of stuff – the rubbish of ages, Owain called it – which generations of her husband's family had abandoned in the large room. Only the swallows, nesting in the eaves, looked in on her, for Owain respected her desperate longing for a place of her own, and would not let anyone disturb her when she climbed the steep stair to her refuge.

She climbed into bed, pulled the covers up to her

chin, and gave the matter of the playing card some thought. She remembered how lost and lonely, how far from friends and family, she had felt when Owain had brought her to Ty Hen. She supposed, grudgingly it must be admitted, that her niece, too, must have felt lost and lonely, far from everything she knew and loved. At least I had Owain, she reminded herself. A good, kind man who taught me the language, tried very hard to make his family accept me, and let me have the attic for somewhere to be alone. Is it possible that Trixie's daughter might have found her way into the attic when I was away from the house that day, the day I managed to reach Valley with my dairy products? Oh, dear God, suppose she finds . . . but I'm being downright stupid. Even if she found something I'd put up there to be out of sight, it would mean nothing to her. And anyway, it's all my own fault for making it so obvious that I didn't want her to go up there. Anyone with an ounce of grit would decide to take a look . . . and whatever I may think of Trixie, her daughter has her fair share of spunk. But what made her take the cards – if she did, of course.

At this stage in her musings, however, sheer weariness overcame her and Kath Jones, who had once been Kath Ripley, the prettiest as well as the oldest of all the Ripley girls, fell deeply asleep.

And dreamed.

The dream began innocently enough as a tiny, bright picture a long distance off. Despite herself, Kath was fascinated, though somewhere in the back of her conscious mind a little voice was warning her that if she went nearer she might regret it. But this was a dream, wasn't it? She went nearer and saw the little picture grow in size, until it was like a picture show at the cinema, only in glorious colour, not black and white.

A step nearer and she could hear as well as see, though she could not make out a single word. But now there were voices, girlish, excited . . . and suddenly the scene began to blur and sway as though she was seeing it through water. She grew frightened, wanted to withdraw, was suddenly unable to do so. Like a swimmer caught in a strong current she was helpless to change direction, felt herself sucked into the scene before her, could hear the voices properly now, could feel the bedroom floor beneath her feet, could smell the scent – Californian Poppy – with which her sister Lou was anointing herself . . .

It was real, her sisters were real, she must go through with it – whatever 'it' was, she had no choice.

'Kath, oh, darlin' Kathy, say I can come with you! I'm old enough to go to dances, I'm sure I am, so why shouldn't I go with you? You'd take care of me, best of me sisters, and I'd be good, good as gold, good as . . .'

'But I've told you, queen, that I'm going with a friend – a young man – and so I wouldn't be able to look after you properly,' Kath said patiently. She, her sister Lou and the baby of the family, Trixie, were in their bedroom in the house on the corner of Kingfisher Court, just off the Scotland Road. Now, Kath smiled at Trixie through the mirror and pulled open the little drawer in their big, old-fashioned dressing table. She extracted her box of face powder, her small pink stick of lip rouge and the little pot of Vaseline which she brushed on to her lashes; dark lashes, the envy of all the other Ripley women, who were blessed with richly curling blonde locks and, alas, the white brows and lashes that go with such colouring.

Trixie, who was watching every move from her perch on the foot of the bed she shared with Kath, sighed enviously. 'Why can't I have black lashes and eyebrows like you, Kathy? Everyone says you're the prettiest of the Ripley girls and it's because you don't have horrid white eyelashes. I'm sure my complexion is roses and cream, and—'

She was interrupted by a loud laugh and then by a raspberry, blown by Louisa, who was vigorously brushing her yellow curls into a fashionable bob. 'Roses and cream! Honest to God, kid, the things you say! And as for white lashes, what's mascara for if not to darken 'em?' She snorted. 'And there's no way Mam would lerrus take you to the Grafton, so you'd best make up your mind to waiting a few years.'

Kath, who had been carefully dusting her nose with powder whilst her two sisters argued the toss, interrupted. 'Don't tease her, Lou,' she said good-naturedly. 'You were young once; you must remember how horrid it was to be left out of things just because you're the baby of the family.'

'Oh, darling Kathy; then you will take me!' Trixie squeaked, bouncing up and down on the bed and seriously crushing the patchwork quilt the girls had made the previous winter out of scraps of material discarded by an aunt, who had a second-hand clothing stall on Paddy's Market. 'I *knew* you would, best of me sisters!'

Kath put her makeup away in its little drawer, then turned to Trixie, shaking her head sorrowfully. 'Not this time, queen. And just you tidy that bed before you go down for your tea or you'll be in big trouble.'

The two older girls made for the door, ignoring Trixie's shriek of protest and her threat that not only would she make the bed, but she would conceal a spider in Kath's side of it, and how would dear, clever Kath like that when she returned, worn out, from dancing all night. Or whatever else she did that meant she could not give an eye to her youngest sister and which she clearly preferred that Mam should not know about, Trixie added threateningly.

Receiving only mocking laughter from her elders, Trixie pursued them down the stairs, alternately pleading and threatening, until she reached the kitchen where Mrs Ripley quickly put a stop to such behaviour. 'I don't care what your sisters may or may not have promised; you aren't going dancing, at the Grafton or anywhere else, until you're sixteen and have developed some manners,' she said severely. 'I've worked hard all my life to bring you up nice and what thanks do I get? To hear you shrieking like a fishwife and calling names gives me more pain than – than a knife in my heart.'

Kath was about to tell her mother that she and Lou

had teased Trixie, letting the child think she might accompany them, when the scene changed and without so much as heading for the door she found herself on the dance floor, and in the arms of a handsome young man. He was telling her some story, but she was only half listening, for as she twirled around she saw, to her astonishment, Trixie . . . not the child who had begged to be allowed to go to the dance but an older and very much more sophisticated Trixie, smiling up into the eyes . . . oh, God, into the eyes of the young man whom Kath had already decided she liked more than anyone else she had yet met.

Hastily, she tried to break free from her partner, but he hung on to her, laughing at her efforts, and then he was no longer a handsome young soldier but an elderly man, grey-haired, pot-bellied, who spoke to her in Welsh, sweaty hands clutching her waist even as he whispered into her ear that she might as well make the best of him, for her lover had returned to France, was even now plodding through the thick, slimy mud, heading back to the trenches.

'I'll show you where he is . . .' he said, and taking her face between his hands he forced her to gaze into his eyes. To her horror, reflected in their rheumy depths she saw, for one terrifying instant, the trenches, the mud, the relentless rain . . . and the despairing face of the man she had agreed to meet that evening.

Kath gave a choking cry, and woke. Her sensible nightgown was damp with sweat; her heart thumped out an uneven rhythm, and when she touched her face she found her cheeks were wet with tears. For a moment she lay very still, willing her heart to behave, her fear to recede, then she glanced at her small alarm clock and realised that she had barely been in bed twenty minutes. She half sat up; what on earth had her nightmare been about? Something pretty horrible, that was for sure. But she should go back to sleep, for morning was a long way off and tomorrow she would have a great deal to do, as indeed she had every day.

Outside her window an owl hooted; a comforting sound. Presently, she lay back down, her thoughts wandering to her preparations for the next day's dinner. She had cut a couple of sticks of sprouts and there were enough onions – and milk in plenty of course – to make onion sauce . . .

Soon she grew cool and comfortable, the dream forgotten. She pulled the blankets up round her ears and began to count her blessings, even better for wooing sleep than counting sheep. She had a good worker in Eifion, and Nell was more of a help than she had believed possible. Thinking it over, Kath decided that her niece was not a bad girl, even if she had visited the attic on the sly; she certainly worked hard, so could be counted as a blessing, if not an un-alloyed one. The fact that every time she opened her mouth Kath was reminded of the long-ago past was no fault of the girl's. Her occasional lapses into a broad Scouse dialect were unintentional, and Kath did not like to correct her; it made her sound too much like the elderly, fault-finding relative she knew herself to be.

We've managed pretty well, despite the war, Kath thought drowsily, already more asleep than awake. I never thought to see a winter like this one, yet we've coped . . . we've coped . . .

And Kath plunged into slumber, dreamless slumber, and slept soundly until the alarm shrilled at six o'clock.

The weather continued so foul that it was a positively Herculean task just to get the full milk churns up on the sledge and thence to the main road, with Nell, her aunt and old Eifion all putting every ounce of strength they possessed into the task. Nell made it a rule, furthermore, to slog her way into the village at least once a week to collect the post. She blamed the weather for the fact that letters from her mother were the rarity rather than the rule and ignored the sceptical look in her aunt's eyes. Once, she had actually managed to get into Holyhead to visit Bryn, who was much better but still not sufficiently fit to join his ship.

The first time she had seen him, Nell had been shocked by his appearance. He was lying on the sofa in the front room of the small house in Stryt Newry, looking white as a ghost and thin as a lath. When his mother had thrown open the door and ushered Nell inside, he had been reading and had glanced up incuriously. As soon as he saw who his visitor was, however, his eyes had lit up and he had beamed with pleasure.

'Nell! Oh, grand to see you it is,' he had said. 'The perishin' doctor thinks I'm made of sugar and will melt if I go out into the cold, and my mam's just as bad, ain't you, Mam?'

Mrs Hughes was a tall, buxom woman with dark hair cut in a bob and bright pink cheeks, and reminded Nell of a Dutch doll she had once possessed. She had smiled at Nell and gone over to the sofa to give her son's shoulder an affectionate pat. 'Just you get yourself well, boy, then you and your young lady can enjoy the summer, because it's bound to be a hot one after such a dreadful winter,' she had observed. 'Bryn's been drawing maps and writing plans for what he means to do when he's better, but he'll tell you all about it while I go and brew the tea and butter some scones.'

Nell had approached the sofa rather cautiously, but relaxed when Bryn had seized her hand and pulled her down to sit beside him. 'I've got my berth aboard the HMT *Scotia*,' he had told her proudly. 'If it hadn't been for the perishin' measles, and then a thing called a quinsy, which grew in my throat and stopped me eating for the best part of a week, I'd have been aboard her now.'

'You poor old thing; no wonder you're so skinny,' Nell had said, deciding, tactfully, to ignore his mother's remark about 'your young lady', though she wondered what Bryn had said to give his mother such a wrong impression. Instead, she had murmured that it was a good job the measles had struck when it did, since he would not have been popular had he infected the whole crew.

'Oh, I expect they've all had them,' Bryn had said airily. He had reached out to a small table beside them and spread out a number of papers. 'Mam told you I've been drawing maps and writing descriptions. Of course I hope I'll be able to take you down to the shore myself when summer comes, but in case I can't get leave, I've drawn the way on these sheets of paper.' He had grinned at her, his eyes sparkling. 'My writing's not very good and my spelling's appalling, or so you used to say, but I hope you can make it out. Here, take a look.'

Nell had examined the three sheets of paper he had handed her and had told him, in all honesty, that they were works of art. Every tiny track or lane, every gate or stile, every rock or patch of gorse was beautifully drawn, and she had been able to assure her friend that if the need arose she would be able to find her way to Church Bay without a second's hesitation. 'But I'd much rather go with you, honestly I would, Bryn,' she had told him. 'Everything's more fun if there are two of you. Oh, you don't know how I've missed you these past weeks. Auntie Kath is getting used to me – she doesn't bite my head off every time I make a remark – but I've still not dared to let her know much Welsh I understand. You see, when she's out of temper, she says some really horrid things, either to Eifion or under her breath to herself, and think how embarrassed she'd be if she realised I understand!'

The pair of them had laughed together and Bryn had just been beginning to say that he was glad his teaching had come in useful when the door opened and Mrs Hughes, with a heavily laden tray in her arms, came back into the room.

The trip to Holyhead had been a wonderful interlude and for some days after it Nell had plotted to go back and see how Bryn was getting on, but somehow there was always too much work and incredibly enough the weather actually worsened.

'If this doesn't let up soon, I'll go mad with boredom,' she told Eifion as they milked, fed and watered, mucked out and even watched one or two early lambs come into the world. 'I'm sure the weather's not nearly as bad as this in Liverpool!'

''Tis nationwide, so they say,' Eifion assured her. 'The Thames is fruz, I've heard tell. You'd be just as badly off in the city, and you wouldn't eat so well neither.'

'It wouldn't be so bad if I could go into Llangefni; there are cinemas there,' Nell said longingly as the pair of them moved from cow to cow in the warmth of the shippon. 'I want to see someone who isn't you or my aunt. I want to gossip with a girl of my own age, or read the hints in one of the women's magazines, or listen to a comedy on the wireless . . .'

'Your aunt's ordered one of they from a feller in Llangefni,' Eifion reminded her. 'When the weather clears . . .'

'I don't want to wait all the time! I want things to happen *now*, not next week or next year! Oh, Eifion, I want to – oh, how I want to go home, if only for a little while,' Nell said. She spoke passionately, not far from tears, yet even in her distress she continued with her job, stripping Dora's udder and moving on to her last cow.

Eifion tutted sympathetically and stood up slowly and carefully, for his rheumatism was bad today. Auntie Kath had suggested that he might take a few days off and stay in his warm bed, but this Eifion refused to do, saying that if he once gave way he'd probably never move again. Now, having straightened painfully, he picked up the two full pails and headed for the dairy. Nell heard him emptying them into the cooler, then carrying the churn of now cold milk out into the yard. As the milk began to hiss into Nell's pail, she heard him call: 'Never you fear, maid; this weather won't last for ever. I met old Waters in the village yesterday and he's a good weather prophet so he is. He reckons the thaw will start in a couple of days and then it's all downhill to summer.'

'I'll believe it when it happens,' Nell said gloomily. She finished milking and carried her full pail into the yard, where Eifion took it from her. 'If you ask me, it always snows and blows on Anglesey, like the Snow Queen's realm in that story where it was always winter and never spring. And there was something about an icicle in the little boy's heart . . .' She reached up and snapped a long icicle off the gutter as she accompanied Eifion into the dairy. 'I've got an icicle in my heart,' she concluded crossly. 'And it won't melt until the snow and ice does, so there!'

Chapter Five

Despite Nell's fears, the thaw began as old Mr Waters had said it would, though because of the depth of the snow and the hold the ice had on the land it was a slow business. Nell had not once revisited the attic all through that long and dreadful winter and now, waking in the night to the slow drip, drip of melting snow, she found that her interest in the place had all but disappeared. This was fortunate since her hands and feet were covered with burning, itchy chilblains – although she piled on every warm garment she possessed, she was always cold – and with Auntie Kath never far from the house, it was too risky to climb the ladder-like stair.

To sneak up to the attic at midnight and look at the kaleidoscope again had been a daft idea, Nell concluded. It was asking for trouble, and she was getting on much better with the older woman, though her aunt had never produced the pack of cards she had promised. After her aunt's discovery of the miniature card Nell, forewarned, had actually prised up a floorboard in her room and hidden the farming books and the miniature card pack in the space beneath, though to be fair she did not think her aunt was the snooping kind. Secretive, yes, a woman of few words, certainly; but not a snooper. She leaves that to me, Nell told herself with grim humour. And I seem to have gone off the idea of late. No doubt the attic is still fascinating, but for the time being at least I'm too busy – and too cold – to go ferreting about up there.

So now she waited with recently learned patience for the thaw and at the end of March, when all the snow had disappeared, she and her aunt decided to go for walks together, though they never strayed far from Auntie Kath's property, which was considerable; thirty acres or more, Eifion had told her. On these walks the older woman pointed out and named the wonders which were appearing in every lane and coppice. Snowdrops came first, closely followed by the brilliant yellow gorse blossom smelling of roasted chestnuts, and then golden celandines. Later on, her aunt told her, the banks would be covered with sweetly scented violets and shy primroses, and when May arrived the woods would be carpeted with wild white anemones. Later still, bluebells would scent the air.

Nell's obvious delight in such things made a bond with her older aunt and Nell realised, almost guiltily, that she no longer fretted for her old home in Liverpool. In fact, she would not have changed places with her older cousins, despite their well-paid jobs and fascinating social lives. Her mother's letters were short and rare, but Marilyn and Milly took it in turns to write, keeping her up to date with life in Liverpool. To be sure, they were mostly concerned with the conquest of young men, but the shortage of food was mentioned occasionally, as were such things as the scarcity of makeup and the nastiness of shopkeepers who, according to Marilyn, seemed to positively enjoy disappointing would-be customers.

I were after some silk stockins, but Mr Timmins, what owns that cheap clothing store on Vauxy, looked me in the eye and said he'd not had so much as a glimpse of silk stockins since the war started. 'What's them?' I screeched, pointing at the shelf behind him, where I could see two or three pairs, plain as the nose on his nasty old face. He gave a wicked grin and met me eyes, bold as brass. 'Them?' he says, 'them ain't silk; it's the way the light's falling on them.'

I were that mad I would of jumped over the counter and grabbed a pair, only before I could so much as open me gob he'd turned, swept them into a drawer, locked it and put the key into his kecks pocket.

I don't know if things is different in the country, but if you could lay hands on some silk stockins I'd pay you back double, as well as postage. Me only pair is more ladder than stockin, and I'm a poor hand at darning.

Nell had grinned to herself and handed the letter over to Auntie Kath; they were having breakfast at the time. 'Some chance,' her aunt had said briefly, having perused the badly written sheet. 'But best not to blight her hopes; just tell her the next time you're in town you'll take a look around.'

Nell had not yet revisited Llangefni, though she had been into Holyhead a couple of times. The main road

133

had had to be kept as clear as possible so that folk could reach the ferries and other shipping, and the town teemed with sailors, seamen from the merchant shipping, Wrens and the like. It was a busy shopping centre as well as a port, and Nell had been able to buy not only a writing pad but a couple of sturdy notebooks as well, and one of these she decided should be her countryside book. In it she faithfully put down the names of the flowers she had seen and when they had first appeared, and got real pleasure from the gradual acquisition of such knowledge.

Now, she realised, life on the farm fascinated her as much as the life burgeoning in the surrounding countryside. When her chores were finished for the day she searched for birds' nests, never interfering with the tiny eggs or the gaping fledglings, but simply noting in her book every detail she had observed. At night, when she heard the vixen yell, she imagined the pretty little cubs curled up in their den and was no longer nervous when the dog fox barked, or the tawny owl shrieked. Now such things were a part of her life, understood and appreciated, never feared.

Yet despite her increasing knowledge and pleasure, Nell was lonely. Her aunt talked of other farmers helping with the barley harvest, everyone going from farm to farm at haymaking time. She had explained that farm machinery was too expensive for farmers to purchase their own, so they had formed a co-operative, each man – or woman – paying a percentage of the cost. Then, when harvest time came, the men as well as the machinery moved from farm to farm until, as Auntie Kath put it, 'all be safely gathered in'.

It sounded good to Nell; surely she could manage, amongst the motley throng of farm workers and their families, to find someone who would be happy to befriend her. She missed Bryn far more than she would have believed possible, for he had come to the farm some weeks ago, full of excitement, to tell her that he was joining his ship the following day. 'But I'll be back home on leave every so often. Then you and me will get plenty of chances to visit my favourite place together.' He smiled winningly at her, cocking his head to one side. 'Goin' to give me a kiss goodbye, like? Because I've decided that one of these days you're goin' to be my girl.'

But Nell had punched his shoulder and told him to get along with him; then she had agreed that she would not visit Church Bay until Bryn could accompany her. Privately, she did not intend to wait for Bryn before she began to explore the rest of the countryside, hopefully with someone her own age whom she would meet when the farm workers converged on each other's property to help with haymaking. Of course she longed to go down to the shore, but thought she really would have to wait for Bryn to get leave before doing so. He was really keen to show her the place he loved most, so how could she deny him the pleasure? As for his announcement that she would be his girl one day, she took that with a pinch of salt. Sailors, it was well known, had a girl in every port, and Nell did not mean to be Bryn's Holyhead lover.

So Nell, missing both Bryn and the companionship of the cousins whom she had known almost from birth, began to count the days until haymaking was upon them.

Nell awoke to find sunshine streaming in through her bedroom window and sat up, rubbing her eyes and wondering why she felt no exhilaration at another day of glorious weather. Then she remembered: Auntie Kath's wireless set had arrived three weeks earlier, at the beginning of May, and last night the announcer had talked of the evacuation of allied troops from Dunkirk, which was taking place even as he spoke.

She scrambled hastily out of bed, grabbed her dressing gown from the hook on the door and pushed her feet into her slippers. Then she began to descend the stairs, donning the dressing gown as she did so, unable to suppress a huge yawn. She and Auntie Kath had sat up until almost midnight, hoping for good news, but though the announcer had said that the evacuation was under way, there had been no more details.

Hurrying down to the kitchen, Nell wondered if the fact that the troops were being brought home meant that the war was over and Germany had won. She went cold at the thought and pushed open the door to find the wireless already switched on and her aunt placidly stirring the porridge pan, whilst eggs, bacon and sliced potatoes stood on the side, awaiting her attention. Upon hearing the door open, Kath turned and raised her eyebrows. 'What's got into you?' she said rather disagreeably. 'Why aren't you dressed? D'you know what the time is?'

'Oh!' Nell glanced at the clock on the mantelpiece, realising she must have slept straight through the alarm. 'Sorry, Auntie, only we were so late to bed last night . . .'

'It wouldn't matter, but Eifion will be in any moment,' her aunt said. 'We don't want to shock the old feller, so you'd best get back up them stairs and dress yourself.'

'Right,' Nell said. The wireless was playing music so she must have just missed the news. 'I came down to hear how the evacuation was getting on. Have they said anything about it this morning?'

'Yes, but we won't discuss it whilst you're flaunting yourself in that flimsy dressing gown,' her aunt said disapprovingly. 'Get a move on, girl. The porridge only needs another couple of minutes—'

She stopped speaking as the back door opened, and Nell fled, taking the stairs two at a time and hurling her clothes on after a wash and brush up which her aunt would have described as 'a cat's lick and a promise'. Tying her hair back into a ponytail and checking her appearance in the mirror, she thought sadly that the war news could not have been good if her aunt's temper was anything to go by. 'Flaunting myself in a flimsy dressing gown indeed,' she informed her reflection. 'The darn thing is made of wool and covers me from my neck to my ankles; what more does she want? Come to think, it was her dressing gown before she passed it on to me and took back the one her husband had owned.' She chuckled. 'And I can't imagine Auntie Kath flaunting herself, no matter how flimsy the dressing gown.'

Having checked her appearance, Nell straightened her bed and set off down the stairs once more. When she reached the kitchen, Eifion and her aunt were already seated at the table, eating their porridge, so Nell sat down and pulled her full bowl towards her. Knowing her aunt's dislike of being rushed, she bade Eifion good morning, but did not again raise the question of the evacuation, waiting until her aunt had replaced her spoon in her empty dish and was rising to begin frying the rest of their breakfast. Then she cleared her throat.

'Is there any more news of the evacuation, Auntie?' she asked bluntly. 'I was too late to hear the wireless announcements, so—'

Kath cut across her. 'The War Cabinet, or whatever they call themselves, have appealed for anyone who owns a boat to cross the Channel and pick up some of the troops waiting on the beaches,' she said. 'Eifion here tells me the Irish ferries have already left to do their bit; isn't that so, Eifion?'

Eifion nodded, his eyes bright with excitement. 'Aye, that's right. My daughter-in-law tells me the port's pretty well empty of shipping, 'cos they've all answered the call.' He sighed wistfully. 'Wish I could have gone along to help, because every fishing boat has up-anchored and left, some of 'em without half their crew; but I know I'd be more of a hindrance really.' He grinned ruefully at Nell. 'And who would do the milkin' while I were off savin' me country?'

'Me,' Nell said promptly. 'And Auntie Kath might lend a hand, isn't that so, Auntie?'

Her aunt snorted and began to put bacon, cold potatoes and eggs into the smoking frying pan. 'You're needed here, Eifion Hughes,' she said severely. 'One egg or two?'

Whilst Eifion was protesting that they were late this morning so he'd best make do with one egg, Nell was plucking up her courage to ask the question uppermost in her mind. 'Auntie Kath, are they bringing our troops home because we've lost the war?' she asked timidly. 'Is this what they call a retreat? Oh, I know in the past there have often been retreats in big battles, but this one . . . well, it does look as if our soldiers were running away . . .'

Her aunt slapped a second egg on to Eifion's plate and turned a furious face towards her niece. 'How dare you even think such a thing,' she said, her voice vibrant with rage. 'Don't you ever let me hear you say that British soldiers are cowards, you stupid, thoughtless, ignorant girl. Why, our soldiers are the best and bravest in the world . . . I should know! I was married to one and I knew a score of others who fought like tigers twenty years ago to rid the world of the Hun.'

Nell was shocked by her aunt's fury, but when she began to apologise she saw that her aunt's eyes were full of tears, saw them slowly trickling down her pale cheeks and realised, guiltily, that her thoughtless remark had stirred up memories best forgotten. So instead of continuing to speak she jumped to her feet and ran round the table, flinging both arms about the rigid figure and plonking a kiss on the tear-wet cheek, something she had never done, she realised, in all the time she had been at Ty Hen. 'I *am* a stupid, thoughtless, ignorant girl,' she said vehemently, still hugging her aunt's spare figure, and felt her relax for a moment. 'But I didn't call our soldiers cowards, you know, because that would be a wicked lie and I do try not to tell lies. So I suppose this must be what the Duke of Wellington called a "strategic retreat" when his men backed off from Napoleon's army in order to re-form on better ground. Have I got it right?'

Auntie Kath freed herself from Nell's arms, but she did so gently. 'Get along with you,' she said gruffly. 'I dare say you've guessed I'm not quite myself today.' She returned to her work of dishing up their breakfasts, pointing her big serving spoon at her niece's chair. 'Now sit down and eat your breakfast; Eifion, Fly and Whisky brought the cows in a good fifteen minutes ago.' She looked ruefully at Nell. 'I'm not a woman who wears her heart on her sleeve, but I reckon it was wrong of me to jump to conclusions; I should have known you better, girl.'

Nell smiled at her aunt and began to eat. She wanted to ask a favour and thought perhaps right now would be a good time to do so. 'I don't think anyone can be blamed for worrying, even if it is a strategic retreat, because such things can go wrong,' she observed. 'But I'm sure you're going to have the wireless playing for the one o'clock news. Can you call Eifion and me in

140

for dinner five minutes early, so we can hear what's happening in France?'

'I'll do that,' her aunt said. 'More bread and butter, anyone?'

'When you think of the winter we've had, isn't it a perishin' miracle that ever since we started evacuating the BEF it's been sunny and mild?' Nell's voice was a trifle muffled, due to the fact that her head was buried in Daisy's warm side. 'The man who drives the milk lorry has been giving soldiers who come from the island lifts back to their home villages. Everyone's doing their bit. Except me, of course,' she added bitterly. 'Only Auntie says with all the troops coming home we'll have to produce even more food; can't have our men starving.'

'Not the only one grumbling because you can't take part in bringing our fellers home you are,' Eifion said equally indistinctly, since he was also milking. 'Every feller I know has rushed into Holyhead, hoping to get a place on a fishing boat or one of the ferries. I bet our Bryn's gloating over other young men who wouldn't join the Navy but went for the army instead. And now they're having to be rescued by the very seamen they despised! Not that they did – despise 'em, I mean – but that's how the sailors see it.' He chuckled, hissed the last of his cow's milk into the pail, and stood up. 'Have you met Bryn's cousin Arfon? Very full of himself, very superior. I'm told that down in Southampton he and Bryn were strutting around the docks like a couple of turkeycocks, boasting of how they'd rescue the BEF single-handed; or that was how it sounded, any road.'

'So long as they come back safe that's all that matters,' Nell said fervently. 'Oh, Eifion, they're too young to throw their lives away!'

'War's like that,' Eifion said, standing creakily upright, a hand going to the small of his back. 'But young Bryn's always been like a perishin' cat, wi' nine lives to play around with. He – and Arfon too no doubt – will be back home in a couple of days, with tall stories about rescuin' the soldiers in the very teeth of the Huns, see if they ain't.'

'I hope you're right,' Nell said. She picked up her full pail and followed Eifion out to the yard. 'I'm glad Bryn isn't in the engine room, though. Auntie Kath said they'd keep him in the open air as much as possible because he'd been so ill with the measles and that. Apparently the crew are all Holyhead men and know Bryn well, so they'll keep an eye on him. Not that he's new to shipping, from what he told me, at any rate.

'That's right; he and Arfon have both worked aboard their uncle's fishing boat, sailing out of Amlwch, so they ain't inexperienced,' Eifion said. 'Come on now, girl; let's get this milk through the cooler and into the churns. Then we can start muckin' out.'

Throughout the evacuation Auntie Kath, Eifion and Nell worked from dawn till dusk, for as Kath kept reminding them food would be even more urgently needed now that the troops were coming home in such large numbers. Twice she took a cart loaded with supplies down to Holyhead, where the Women's Institute workers fell on it with cries of joy, for seeing that every man who stumbled from the trains, worn out, hungry and filthy, got a hot drink and something to eat was becoming more and more difficult.

Nell accompanied her on both these expeditions, and was cut to the quick by the sight of the soldiers, some of them jauntily stepping out with their guns on their shoulders, others barely able to walk, with wounds roughly bandaged with anything they could find. She gathered from what the men told her that all their equipment had been left behind and knew the soldiers were worried about their lack of weapons and vehicles, but, as several of them said, better live men than dead tanks with no one to man them. She and Auntie Kath joined the women handing out hot drinks and food, and tried to remain cheerful, though it was not easy. The troops were pathetically grateful for the food and drink supplied, some making light of their ordeal, others telling horrific tales of the suffering of the men waiting for rescue on the long, pale beaches.

'The Luftwaffe strafed us from the moment we came out of the sand dunes until we reached the water, and then they fired on the boats,' one man told Nell as he took the hot drink she offered. 'The naval shipping can't get in close to the shore because it's too shallow, so the little boats come right in and pick up the fellers and ferry 'em out to where the big ships can take them aboard. There have been heavy losses, among both the military and the rescuers, but they're getting us off; that's what matters. He who fights and runs away will live to fight another day,' he concluded. 'Except that we aren't running away.'

'That's not what the French and the Belgians think,' the man behind him said morosely. 'But it would have been suicide to try to fight on once the panzers came. Wish the Brylcreem boys had been more in evidence, though. Those bloody Huns had it all their own way.'

'I've got a pal aboard one of the ships,' Nell said timidly, when her aunt was out of hearing. 'He's only seventeen, but he knows boats and shipping like the back of his hand. His taid works for my aunt, and he says Bryn rows like a man twice his age and swims like a fish . . . I hope he'll be all right.'

'Sure to be,' the soldier said. 'Sure to be, missy.'

'Ye-es, but he's not been back to tell me how he got on,' Nell said uneasily. 'I hope he hasn't been wounded, or . . .'

'The ships scarce stop in port save to let the fellers get off; small chance the crew have got to go to their homes,' the next man said, taking the drink Nell offered. 'Your pal will be all right. What's the name of his ship?'

'It's one of the Irish ferries they've taken into service, the HMT *Scotia*, I think,' Nell said uneasily, and saw the soldiers to whom she was talking exchange a significant glance. They would have moved on but she grabbed one of them by his torn and filthy tunic sleeve. 'Have you heard anything? Anything bad, I mean?'

Neither man answered, but the next soldier in line, who had a blood-caked bandage round his head, spoke up. 'Did you say you knew someone aboard the

Scotia? I've heard the Luftwaffe dropped a bomb clean down her funnel and she sank within minutes. Lost wi' all hands, I reckon.'

Nell felt a terrible coldness creep over her, felt herself sway, and swiftly reached forward to take a drink from the trolley and hand it to the waiting boy, for he was little more. 'All hands?' she faltered. 'No one saved?'

The soldier whose tunic she had clutched frowned and patted her arm. 'The *Scotia* was hit all right, but there were fellows saved,' he assured her. 'Don't you start worrying yet, miss. Your sweetheart will be coming home to you, mark my words.'

'He's not my sweetheart; just a good pal who's worked with me and taught me a good deal,' Nell said, pulling herself together. 'Nevertheless, I hope you're right and he's been picked up.' The boy with the bandaged head was simply repeating gossip, she told herself, and making the most of it, what was more. He could not be aware that almost all the crew of the *Scotia* were Holyhead men, well known to everyone in the small port. She pushed her dread that she might never see Bryn again out of her mind and smiled brightly at the men as they filed past. 'Hot tea and a cheese ab-dab? Go on, take a couple; you look as if you could do with feeding up. How much longer will the evacuation last, do you think?'

But no one had a clue and once more Nell found herself playing the waiting game, though this time it was the same for everyone. Auntie Kath had only one meadow put down to grass, but because of the evacuation, though the hay was cut, it simply lay there in the brilliant sunshine waiting for the men and women with their pitchforks to turn it so that it could dry out on both sides. The friendly get-together, to which Nell had so much looked forward, did not happen. Indeed, she, Auntie Kath and Eifion had to do everything, starting when the sky was grey with dawn and finishing when they could no longer see to work, though a neighbour had come and built the stacks, since this was specialised work.

'It's true what you heard; that the *Scotia* was sunk, and lives were lost,' Auntie Kath said, when she returned from another visit to the port. 'I spoke to Arfon – he's come home uninjured and wasn't aboard the ship which sank, thank God – and asked after Bryn. He said he believed Bryn was on the *Scotia*, but he said a good number of the crew had been saved; fortunately she went down fairly near the shore so the little boats picked up the men in the water. And Bryn could swim like a fish, so he had a better chance than most.'

Then one morning Eifion came to work late, his face grey, his steps faltering. He told them that Bryn had indeed been aboard the *Scotia* when she was hit, and though a couple of his pals had asked every survivor they could find for news of Bryn, as yet there had been no word.

Nell wept unrestrainedly all through that dreadful day, though she and Eifion did their best to do their work. She told herself that although she could scarcely claim to have loved Bryn she had liked him very much, admired his courage and tenacity, and could not believe she would never see him again. 'He was so excited at the thought of being useful,' she told her aunt, seeing the tears in Auntie Kath's eyes and knowing that her own lids were puffy and red with weeping. 'He tried to kiss me goodbye, only I wouldn't let him, though I did wish him luck . . . oh, Auntie, life is too cruel. Is it – is it absolutely certain?'

'Nothing's certain in this life, cariad,' Eifion put in. 'I won't give up hope until the last man's ashore. I've not been to the Gors Hospital on Garreglwyd Road, but I've heard from my nephew Rhys that Bryn hasn't been taken in there.'

'Oh, really, you two,' Auntie Kath said crossly. 'Anyone would think Holyhead was the only place in the entire country to have men returning from Dunkirk, and the Gors the only hospital. Young Bryn probably arrived at one of the southern ports and likely he's tucked up in a hospital bed in . . . in Southampton or Portsmouth or even in Liverpool, telling all the nurses how he saved the world. So just get on with your work and look on the bright side. That way we stand a chance of winning this perishin' war.'

Nell did her best to believe her aunt was right, but she started to have nightmares in which she attended Bryn's funeral or came upon his body on a great white beach, and despite her resolve to remain cheerful and optimistic she began to feel sure her friend really had drowned when the *Scotia* went down. Nell threw herself into her work now with a sort of grim fury. The damned Jerries must be stopped, she thought, and she for one would do everything in her power to stop them. When she was old enough she would join one of the women's services, as her mother had, and help to win the war that way, though she knew that for the time being at least Auntie Kath needed her desperately. Bryn had been a good friend and she meant to avenge his death, though when she said this to her aunt that lady gave her a quizzical look and said she'd do it best by helping to produce as much food as was humanly possible. Nell had to smile; Auntie Kath was so sensible! She had loved Bryn in her way, but did not let her very real grief intrude into her working life.

Nell herself thought of Bryn often, talked to him in the quiet solitude of her bedroom before she slept at night, promised never to forget him. Not for the first time, she regretted that she had sometimes been abrupt with him, teased him, slapped him down when he had tried to kiss her goodbye. He had wanted her to pretend that she was his girl; why had she refused to do so? It would have hurt nobody and would have pleased her old pal.

She tried to tell herself that she must not brood, but it was no simple matter to put the only real friend she had made since arriving at Ty Hen out of her mind and she continued to grieve until Auntie Kath, who had caught her having a quiet little weep one evening, told her that life must go on and she should put Bryn's tragic death behind her. 'A great many others suffered the same fate,' she reminded her niece, 'and many more will die before this war is won. You feel Bryn's death personally because the two of you were good friends, but you mustn't dwell on it; that would be unhealthy as well as unhelpful. Instead, you must concentrate on doing everything you can to help the war effort. If everyone else does the same, we'll win all right, just like we did in the last lot.'

Then the letter from Trixie Whitaker arrived, and Nell felt that her cup of misery was overflowing. She read it at breakfast one morning, and could scarcely believe her eyes. When she had perused it twice she handed it to her aunt without comment, and saw Auntie Kath's brows almost disappear into her hair, though she showed no other sign either of surprise or of disapproval as she read. Eifion glanced at Nell, then got to his feet. 'Start the milking I will,' he said awkwardly. 'No need to hurry yourself, girl; join me when you've finished here.'

Nell thanked him and took the letter back from her aunt to read it again, still almost unable to believe it.

Dear Little Nell,

Well, I don't suppose it will surprise you when I tell you I've had enough of the WAAF. The way I've been treated is ridiculous, and me a grown woman with a daughter almost old enough to join up herself! Go here, go there, do this, do that, there was no standing it. Then I got punishment drill for something so small I can't even remember what it was, then I was a bit late – I missed the gharry which I should have caught – back at the airfield and they said I'd gone AWOL which means absent without leave. For a few hours – I ask you! They tried to say I couldn't leave the station but I wasn't standing for that, so I waited until the place was quiet and everyone had gone to bed and escaped. I guessed they'd search for me in Liverpool or even at Ty Hen, but in any case, darling, I've met the most wonderful man, quite as wonderful as your father. He's a Canadian, and he's just been sent up to Scotland on some sort of secret mission, and he insists that I should follow him there. You mustn't breathe a word of this, darling, so I won't tell you his name or anything else about him except that he means to marry me as soon as his divorce is absolute, and until then we're both keeping our heads low, but I'll write as often as I can. You must address your letters to your Auntie Susan in Bootle, because she has promised to act as post office between us and will forward your letters on to me at the address I've given her. Your Auntie Lou has been most unsympathetic and unkind. She thinks I ought to stay with the WAAF, as she is doing, and we had several quarrels. We are no longer speaking; I assume she must be jealous.

But to return to nicer things. After the war Gil — that's his first name, sweetheart — means to carry me off to Canada, the land of opportunity, he says. I told him I had a grown-up daughter and he said you were welcome to come with us, but as I said, by the time the war's over you'll be eighteen or nineteen, I suppose, and will want to fend for yourself.

I'm very sorry your friend was drowned when the Scotia *went down, Nell my dearest, but these things happen in war. Dear me, this letter is far too long; I must make my man his tea! How strange, but nice,*

that sounds after so long on my own.
  Take care of yourself and write often, chuck.
  Your loving mother xxx

'Well?' Nell said brusquely, as her aunt handed the letter back. 'I did know she wasn't happy in the WAAF, because she kept grumbling and saying they were treated like children, and told to obey ridiculous rules, but I never thought . . . never guessed . . . And of course Auntie Lou wouldn't throw in the towel, as my mother has. Well, for a start, she's still got a husband, though he's at sea. But she wouldn't let him down by chickening out.'

'Yes, you're right about Lou; she wouldn't let her family down. But I can't pretend I'm astonished at what your mother has done,' Auntie Kath said cautiously after a moment. 'You were cross with me when I said Trixie was a good time girl, or words to that effect, but this letter makes it clear that she's not changed all that much since we were young.'

'But to leave the WAAF just because they expected her to – to do as she was told and – and to play fair,' Nell muttered. 'And to dismiss Bryn's death as though – as though it were something of no particular importance, when I told her in my last letter how brave he was and how I missed him, how I . . . oh, Auntie Kath, how can I bear it?'

And on the words she burst into tears, crying as though her heart would break. She felt completely alone. Bryn, the only true friend she had made since coming to Ty Hen, had gone for ever and her mother, the woman she had thought so wonderful, had gone too, for Nell knew she could never regard Trixie with admiration again. To run away just because she couldn't – or more likely wouldn't – abide by rules which had been made for her own good and that of her fellow Waafs! And I bet that chap never marries her, Nell thought bitterly, scrubbing fiercely at her eyes with the backs of her hands. When his divorce becomes absolute, indeed! That's a grand excuse for not getting wed, that is. Why, for all she knows he might have half a dozen wives, and if he has, good luck to him! And as for writing to Mam care of Auntie Susan, I shall do no such thing. Why should I?

She said as much to Kath, who shook her head and wagged an admonitory finger. 'She's still your mother, even if she has behaved badly. Just write a reply, keeping it short and formal, telling her not to do anything foolish. The day will come when she'll need you, if I'm any judge of men. And in the meantime, get on with your life as though the news of her – her infatuation meant nothing to you. Knowing Trixie, her letters will get fewer as her interest in this chap becomes stronger. If it does, of course.' She smiled almost kindly at her niece. 'And she's right about one thing, you know. As you get older you and your ma will grow apart, and that's natural, and a good thing. So for now, just forget the whole matter and do everything you can to win the war.'

Nell decided this was good advice, but misery had her in its grip and when she and Eifion had finished the milking she told her aunt that she needed to be alone and would like to go off as soon as her chores were done, to get used to the horrible things that had happened.

She was surprised but pleased when Auntie Kath nodded approvingly. 'Go right now; take some food and a bottle of my raspberry cordial and stay away for the whole day, but be back before dark or I'll worry,' Kath said. 'And don't be too hard on your mother. After your father died I told anyone who would listen that Trixie was one of those women who needed a man, unlike myself.' She smiled ruefully at her niece. 'Well, it's taken a bit longer than I anticipated, but I've been proved right. Your mother is still quite young, and she used to be very pretty; I don't suppose that has changed, has it?'

Nell sniffed mournfully. 'No, she's still very pretty,' she admitted grudgingly. 'But that isn't an excuse for behaving badly; nor a reason, either.'

'No, but pretty women expect to be cosseted by men; courted by them, too. Look, queen, if we're being honest, it won't hurt you to admit that your ma has had admirers before. Isn't that so?'

Nell admitted that it was, and her aunt, who had been packing sandwiches, cake and biscuits into Nell's haversack, nodded. 'There you are, then! But once she was cut off from Liverpool, the Scottie, and the men who danced attendance on her – all the things she knew best, in fact – she must have been lonely, as I know you are. Now she won't be lonely ever again – or that's what she thinks – because she's found someone to take your dad's place; no harm in that.

And though I know it upset you when she said she'd told her Canadian that you wouldn't want to emigrate after the war was over, she was right, wasn't she? Do you want to set off into the unknown with only your ma and a strange man to keep you company?'

'No, I'm staying right here,' Nell said, beginning to smile, though her cheeks were still wet with tears. 'If you'll have me, that is.'

Her aunt, never demonstrative, put down the haversack and gave Nell a quick hug. 'I dare say I can put up wi' you for a while longer,' she said. 'Now just you go off and get yourself straightened out. And don't forget; be back before dark.'

The weather was far too warm for a coat so Nell slung her haversack across her shoulders and set off. She had studied Bryn's beautifully drawn maps of the area until she knew them by heart, but nevertheless she popped them into her haversack just in case she went astray. For the first five minutes she just walked, not even considering her eventual destination, but then she stopped short and began to think. Ever since arriving at Ty Hen she had longed to visit the sea, which she knew was not too far distant; had she not seen it through the attic window, looking enticing even on a freezing cold day? But she had promised Bryn that she would not go to Church Bay without him, and whenever she had thought she might make for some other part of the coast something had come up to prevent the expedition, generally the weather. Then spring had come, and she had been so enchanted by the flowers, the birds, even the beasts, that all thoughts of the sea had disappeared from her mind.

Now, however, it was summer and Bryn's death had made her promise to him null and void. Waiting for him was useless, but why should she not find the beautiful bay for herself? She knew roughly in which direction it lay, she had Bryn's map, and suddenly she realised that a wander along the beach, climbing the rocks Bryn had talked about, seeing the little pools and the strange sea creatures which inhabited them, would take her mind off her troubles more effectively than anything else. After all, she would be sixteen in a couple of weeks, and she had never actually waded through the waves, dug in the sand, or collected shells . . . oh, there were a thousand things she had never actually done!

Slowly, Nell turned to face Ty Hen, which she could see through the wind-bent trees on top of the banks that edged the lane. Yes, there it was; she could see the attic windows, but which ones were those through which she had seen the sea? A moment's thought, and she knew the answer. The windows she could see from here would overlook the farmyard; the windows on the far side, which she could not see, were the ones pointing in the right direction. Nell set off along the lane, and presently found the stile drawn in neatly on her map and took to open country. Here, sheep grazed on the short, sweet turf, moving slowly round the great grey rocks which reared up from the smooth green grass like leviathans from a silken sea, making it perilous country for those who walked in a dream.

The gorse, which was kept under control at Ty Hen, ran riot here and Nell was continually forced to leave the straight line she imagined would lead her to the sea in order to avoid huge areas of gorse, smelling sweetly in the hot sunshine. A bouncing lamb came round a big nose of rock and bleated with surprise when it saw Nell, then bounded away, its action more like that of a kangaroo, she imagined, than that of a three-month-old lamb searching for its dam. In one gorse bush a tiny bird she had never seen before made a curious noise not unlike that of a sewing machine, and in another a bird she did know, from its habit of always choosing the highest object around on which to perch, swayed on the topmost branch making the tac-tac call of the stonechat.

Suddenly, the sweet scents of summer and the beauty of the surroundings turned the day into a holiday, a day which, Nell knew, Bryn would have commanded her to enjoy to the full. She came across a great many rabbits, old ones, young ones, big and small ones, playing in the sunshine. Some were grazing, some running apparently at random, others bounding into cover, still others sitting back on their haunches and staring at Nell as though she were a great curiosity but known to be harmless.

Nell slowed and smiled with pleasure. She wondered if Auntie Kath might let her have a rabbit of her own, then decided against it, remembering the excellent roasted rabbit she had enjoyed only a few days earlier. Then there was rabbit stew, rabbit pie . . . oh dear, how awful that she could not vow never to eat the sweet little creatures again. Or not whilst the war – and meat shortages – lasted, at any rate.

Presently, she came to a stream bubbling along on its pebbled bed. It was overhung with mosses, its banks home to more wildlife as well as to stunted trees all bent in one direction by the almost never-ceasing wind. Nell saw a kingfisher, its colours so vivid that she recognised it at once from a picture in one of the children's books she had found in the attic. When she bent over the water she saw the flash of fins and tiny, incredibly fast-moving silver bodies. Baby fishes . . . fry, weren't they called? Oh dear, that conjured up more images of food, not that she had ever eaten fish so tiny. Nor wanted to do so, she reminded herself severely. Nature might be red in tooth and claw but she was not! And was that a frog, doing the breast stroke close to the overhanging bank? Oh, and a water vole, swimming unconcernedly along, totally fearless and uninterested in what must seem, to the vole, like a great giantess standing on the bank above him.

Nell watched the stream for a while, then took off her sandals and dabbled her toes in the water. Auntie Kath had once implied that only kids paddled and played on the sand, but she had probably been in a bad mood on that occasion. Indeed, thinking back, Nell realised that when she had first come to Ty Hen her aunt had almost always been in a bad mood. She was better now, but in any case, Nell reminded herself, this is *my* day, so if I want to paddle . . .

In seconds she was in the water, and it was delicious . . . she waded out into midstream, where it was still very shallow, scarcely reaching her knees. She bent to pick up a brightly coloured pebble, then stood very still and watched the little fishes, as curious in their own way as she, come cautiously approaching to investigate her toes.

It was thirst which drew her out of the stream in the end; thirst and the recollection that her aunt had included some of her delicious homemade ginger nuts in the packet of food she had given her. She clambered out on to the bank and sat down on a lichen-covered rock. There was no point in trying to dry her feet and legs on her small pocket handkerchief; the sun would dry them quickly enough. She produced her food and fished out the bottle of raspberry cordial. She pulled out the cork and took a hearty swig, then choked and pushed the cork firmly into place once more, returning the bottle to her haversack. She had quite forgotten that the cordial needed to be diluted with water; that was why her aunt had included a mug when packing up Nell's picnic. It would have been rather nice, she thought wistfully, to have used the clear and sparkling water swirling past her to dilute the cordial, but she was still too much a city girl to feel comfortable about doing so. Suppose sheep or cows piddled in streams? Reluctantly, she gave up the thought of having a drink. She ate two ginger nuts, but they only made her thirstier. Never mind; she was bound to come across a farmhouse sooner or later, and when she did so she would explain her predicament and beg some water from their well.

Two curious lambs, clearly indulging in a game of

chase, appeared round the nearest gorse patch, saw her sitting there and bleated, more than a little startled by her presence. She held out one of the ginger biscuits and the small, woolly creatures came a little closer, but as soon as she moved they turned tail and tumbled out of sight behind the gorse once more.

Nell looked up at the great golden disc of the sun and realised that it must be dinner time. I've wasted half the morning and I've still not reached the sea; I really meant to go down to Church Bay. She remembered Bryn saying that it was also called Porth Swtan, and wondered what the name meant. Porth was bay, clearly, but she knew very well that the Welsh for church was eglwys . . . she must ask someone to explain. In the meantime, Bryn had said it was a grand place and that she would love it, as he did. He also said he had learned to swim there. She looked up at the blue sky above her and wondered if he were watching from some remote heaven. If so, he wouldn't think much of her resolution. She could almost hear his mocking voice telling her to get a move on or she would have wasted her day's holiday.

Nell pushed the remaining biscuits back into her haversack, did up the straps and set off once more, grimly determined not to allow herself to be diverted from her main purpose, which was to reach the sea. As she walked, she thought back to the couple of times she had visited Seaforth Sands. Her mother had never taken her there, always pulling a face and saying she hated the sand, which got into everything, the wind which never seemed to stop blowing, and the oil deposits from the shipping heading up the Mersey. As she often said, Seaforth Sands was not truly the seaside, being on the estuary of the river.

Blinking in the sunshine and leaning back against a convenient rock, Nell remembered her first visit there, when she was four or five. On that occasion, her aunt Beatty had taken a group of them and Trixie had supplied her daughter with a fine bucket and spade and a shrimping net. When one dug in the sand, however, one reached horrid smelly oily stuff, and despite most diligent searching nothing alive was foolish enough to swim into her shrimping net. Still, she had enjoyed the trip and afterwards the fish and chip supper which Beatty and a couple of her sisters had provided.

She had been ten before she visited the Sands again and she chiefly remembered the occasion because cousin Alfie cut his foot on a broken bottle, half buried in the sand. The aunts had insisted upon taking him, with his shirt wrapped around his foot, back to the Stanley Hospital, where he had been haled off by a doctor and nurses to have the cut, which was both long and deep, cleaned and stitched. Unnerved by his shrieks of protest, Auntie Beatty had gathered up the children and taken them by tram back to Kingfisher Court, leaving Auntie Ethel in charge of Alfie. The young Nell had run home, eager to tell Trixie of Alfie's dramatic wound, only to find the house locked.

She had stood for a moment, baffled, but then her cousin Fanny had appeared. 'Oh, Nelly,' she had said breathlessly. 'Mrs Adenbrook from number nine just telled our mam that Uncle Tom's ship docked an hour ago. He's took your mam off on the razzle-dazzle. They didn't know you'd be back early.'

'Oh, Fanny, wharrever am I to do?' Nell had quavered. 'Mam hasn't left the spare key out or anything; I can't gerrin.'

Fanny had put a comforting arm round the younger girl and given her a squeeze. 'Our mam says I'm to bring you back to our place,' she had said. 'She's give me money to buy us all a fish supper later, and I'm sure Auntie Trixie and Uncle Tom will be back before your bedtime.'

Trixie and Tom, however, had not returned until the early hours, so Nell had been told to share Fanny's bed, where she had lain awake, miserably worried, until she heard her parents' noisy and probably drunken return. Then she would have turned over and slept at last save for the fact that her mother had loomed up over the bed, breathing alcoholic fumes and telling her in a slurred voice that they had come to take her home, so she'd best gerrup, purron some clobber, and accompany them back to No. 15.

I should have known then that Mam wasn't to be relied on . . . nor Dad neither, Nell thought sadly as she toiled up a grassy hummock and down the other side. I remember someone saying that a loving mother doesn't simply walk out and leave her child to another's care, but Mam did it often – well, whenever it suited her, I suppose – especially after Dad's death. Only this time she's done it in a more final sort of way. This time, whatever Auntie Kath may say, there'll be no going back. Do I care, though, in my heart? Or am I secretly relieved, just a little?

But before she could answer this question, she topped a rise and, for the first time, saw the Irish Sea at close quarters. But how different it looked from the sea she had glimpsed through the attic window! That sea had been the colour of slate, forbidding, unwelcoming. Nell could not imagine bathing, or even paddling, in that sea. This sea, however, sparkled blue and promising, reminding Nell of postcards, pictures in children's books and her own secret imaginings. From here she could not see white-topped waves, nor golden sands, but she was suddenly sure that when she got nearer such things would meet her gaze. Oh, the delights that she was about to encounter! Nell began to hurry.

Chapter Six

She had still not reached the sea, which proved to be a good deal further off than it had seemed, when she came across the cottage. It was down in a gentle dip, a sort of miniature valley, and had trees to one side of it, a couple of outbuildings, and a straggly sort of low stone wall round what she assumed to be a vegetable patch, since even from this distance she could recognise broad beans, peas and summer cabbage laid out in neat rows. It was a strange sort of cottage; Nell had never seen anything like it before. It was very long and had been whitewashed, only the last coat must have been applied some while ago for it was flaking off, showing the grey of stone beneath. Unlike the other cottages which she had seen on her way to and from Llangefni and Holyhead, this one was not roofed with slate, but was thatched. It also looked somewhat tumbledown, or at any rate in poor condition. The thatch needed repair, the entire cottage needed repainting, and somehow it had a sad and solitary air, as though it was abandoned to the wind and weather, and longed to be cherished as it had once been.

Nell, who was still extremely thirsty, saw that there was a well some way from the cottage and wondered why it had been built such a distance from its water supply. She supposed it could have something to do with the closeness of the sea – salt water would make well water brackish, she knew – and decided on impulse to ask at the cottage if she might take some water from their well. She would have to ask in Welsh, of course, but since she and Eifion almost always conversed in that language now it would be an easy matter for her to frame her request so that the inhabitants of the cottage would understand her.

Yet somehow Nell felt that she would like to know a little more about the people who lived in such a beautiful but remote spot before approaching them. From where she stood, she could see that the place was definitely occupied; the family kept poultry, a cow and possibly a pig. She thought she could just glimpse an old and rusty bicycle, leaning against the farther wall, but it might have been simply a pile of rusting metal; she would have to look more closely, though not right now. She supposed they almost certainly had a dog, and she knew from the way Fly and Whisky behaved when a stranger approached Ty Hen that dogs could become aggressive, could even attack, when someone they didn't know got too close to their domain, especially if they realised that the stranger was nervous.

Nell had been peering at the cottage from behind a large rock, and now she moved forward, dodging into the shelter of a gorse patch. Yes, there was at least one old dog; she could just see its head resting on its front paws, whilst the remainder of its body was hidden by a rough kennel. She sighed and drew back into the shelter of the gorse. She was not afraid of dogs – living closely with Fly and Whisky had put an end to any fear she might have felt – but the heavy afternoon hush was undisturbed even by birdsong and she knew what a cacophony of sound would erupt as soon as the dog realised she intended to approach the cottage. She willed someone to come out of the green-painted door; the dog would know better than to kick up a rumpus when its master or mistress could see the danger for themselves.

But no one emerged from the cottage. No one worked on the vegetable patch or was on his way to catch the cow, or feed the pig. No one was collecting eggs; no one even sat on the wooden bench by the door. No one came out of the door to fetch wood for the fire or water from the well. If they're old, perhaps they have a sleep in the afternoons, Nell thought, and was struck by an idea. There was plenty of cover here-abouts, provided she stayed away from the dip in which the cottage stood; she could keep out of sight – and scent – of the dog, and reach the well without let or hindrance. Water is free, she told herself defensively. Probably they'd prefer me to help myself rather than have the dog kicking up a din and disturbing everybody for miles around.

She reached the well and sat down upon the low stone wall which encircled it with a sigh of relief. The sun was very hot, so she moved until she was in the shade of the small pitched roof, then settled herself comfortably, feeling a cool breeze on her hot face with pleasure. She had managed to get here without alerting the dog, which was quite something for someone who had sometimes been accused of being a city girl. Proud of her achievement, she took out her mug, then leaned over and gazed down into the depths of the well. It was deep; she could just see the water sparkling below, reflecting a slice of blue sky. The bucket which the cottagers would use to bring the water, cold and sparkling, up from the depths hung on a stout rope over a beam. Nell unhooked it and lowered it into the water, then drew it up slowly and cautiously. Water, she knew, was heavy, so she had made sure the bucket was only half full before she began to haul it up. She nearly lost it when it came within reach as she released the rope for a second, but she managed to lodge the bucket on the wall and dipped her mug into it. She was so thirsty by now that she did not wait to uncork the cordial but drank the well water straight down. Only when her thirst was slaked did she uncork the cordial and add it to the last mug of water.

She sat on the wall with one arm round the bucket, making her think of Jack and Jill, and sipped the diluted cordial, looking casually around her. From here, probably because she was sitting down, she could not see the cottage at all, which meant of course that the owners could not see her, either. Thinking back, she realised that this must be the Swtan longhouse, the place Bryn had mentioned when telling her about Church Bay. He had said something else, but for the life of her she could not remember what it was, and after frowning over the problem she gave it up and turned her mind to another: whether to leave the bucket on the ground, for it was still almost half full, or to carry it down and stand it nearer the cottage door. But she knew it was usually children who fetched water, and though it might be exciting if they thought the fairies were using the well, on the other hand it might frighten them into refusing to collect water in future. No, it was better that no one should ever know she had drunk her fill here. Accordingly, she topped up the cordial bottle and then made a bowl of her hands and splashed her face and neck before reluctantly tipping the bucket and sending the water hurtling down into the depths, where it landed with a splash which seemed extremely loud in the hot stillness of the afternoon.

Nell smiled to herself and turned away to glance around her. Had anyone heard? But she doubted if a sound so much in tune with the countryside would bring even the dog running. However, she would just go and take a look at the cottage, make sure she had not disturbed these people by using their well.

Moving slowly, for the heat of the sun did not encourage haste, Nell returned to a point where she could look down on the cottage, then frowned and shielded her eyes with one hand. Odd! The dog had disappeared, and when she stared very hard indeed it seemed as though a slight mist lay between her and the Swtan longhouse. Then, even as she watched, the green-painted door was pushed slightly ajar and an old man, grey-haired and clad in shabby working clothes, came out. Behind him was a bent old woman, wearing a dark dress and a very large white pinafore, who hovered in the doorway for a moment, looking out towards the rise upon which Nell stood.

Nell rubbed her eyes, then looked again, and the door was closed; the slight mistiness which had accompanied the scene had disappeared and the afternoon was ordinary again. Even the old man had gone, either back into the house or into one of the outbuildings. Heat haze, Nell told herself firmly, returning to where she had dropped her haversack and settling it across her shoulders. Odd about the dog though; she was sure she had seen a border collie, yet now there was no sign of it. Nell was pretty sure that the dog would not have been allowed in the cottage, nor presumed to try to enter. I suppose it must have gone in search of shade, Nell told herself, and tried to forget the kennel she thought she had seen. It was certainly not visible now.

With her body leaning against the wall of the well and her head comfortably settled on the haversack, Nell hesitated. I wonder if I should go down after all, and explain that I've had a drink of water from their well, she thought, but even as she framed the explanation in her best Welsh she knew she would not. Instead, she relaxed and let her thoughts drift; away from the shade the sun burned down, but here, with the soft birdsong and the gentle breeze easing the heat from her tired limbs, she was so comfortable, so content, that she could easily sleep . . . easily sleep . . . sleep . . .

Nell dreamed. She was curled up by the well, on

the soft grass, but instead of the midday sun the moon beamed down on her and a voice was speaking.

'Said you'd like it, didn't I? But it's the beach, the sea, that I meant, not the perishin' Swtan. That's just a house, a house for old men and women when they can't do the work of a real farm no more. Get off your fat bum and explore, why don't you?'

Still in her dream, Nell's eyes shot indignantly open, and there was Bryn, grinning down at her, wearing nothing but a pair of much patched trousers and a cap pushed to the back of his head. He looked about ten years old, and the grin he gave her was taunting. 'Don't you start ordering me about,' Nell shouted at him. 'Nor don't you say my bum's fat, because it isn't! And anyway, you're dead!'

'Do I look dead? I'm bleedin' well nothin' of the sort,' Bryn said, and now he no longer sounded Welsh but had the genuine Scouse accent with which Nell had been surrounded all her life until she had come to the island. He looked at her critically as she jumped to her feet. 'All right, all right, don't get all uppity wi' me, cariad. One of these fine days you and me's goin' to get wed, ain't that so?'

'No it is not,' raged Nell, and realised suddenly that in the way of dreams the dark and the moonlight had gone and it was a hot and sunny day once more. 'And you *are* dead, even though you don't want to admit it. I wish you weren't, because you were my pal and I liked you, but facts is facts, Bryn. Your ship blew up.'

Bryn pulled a disdainful face. 'Girls don't know nothin',' he announced. 'Particularly English girls. I

169

can swim like a fish so I can, and I'm tough as old boots . . . old boots . . . old boots . . .'

His voice faded, and Nell found herself lying on the soft grass which surrounded the Swtan's well, with her head pillowed comfortably on her haversack and her limbs sprawled in considerable abandonment. Hastily, she sat up. She had dreamed that Bryn was alive, and had had the cheek to insult her, call her fat . . . Slowly, Nell got to her feet. She supposed that it was natural to dream of her old pal when she had come to this very spot because he had wanted her to do so, had followed his instructions on how to get here, using the very map he had made for her. And it had been a pleasant enough dream, because Bryn had been alive and on dry land, for a start. So often, since the sinking of the *Scotia*, her dreams had been of Bryn being dragged down by the undertow of the great ship, going deeper and deeper into blackness, unable to help himself . . .

Shuddering, Nell picked up her haversack once more and slipped her arms into the straps, then adjusted the weight of it until it rested comfortably between her shoulder blades. The sun was already past its zenith and she had come here, after all, to visit the seaside, and to remember Bryn, which she had already done if you could count the dream; best get on or she would still be trudging back to Ty Hen when the sun had gone and the moon ruled the sky. As for the dream, it had been just that. Now she must tackle real life again.

She turned away from the cottage and began to descend the long hill up which she had climbed earlier, and as soon as she left the hollow a delightful salt breeze lifted the hair from her hot forehead and sent the delicious smell of the gorse blossoms wafting towards her. She began to walk faster, then turned for a last look round and saw . . . someone . . . behind a large rock.

For a moment her heart missed a beat; was it Bryn's ghost, come to haunt her? 'Bryn!' She thought she had shouted it, but a moment later realised she had scarcely spoken above a whisper, and what a good thing that was. She would have made the most awful fool of herself, for this youth was most definitely not her pal. This was a young man, maybe as old as twenty, at any rate a good deal older than her friend, and whereas Bryn was angelically fair this young man was dark-haired and dark-eyed, with very short black hair, and was trying not to be seen. But even so, though she only caught a glimpse of a narrow face whose mouth tilted at the corners with secret amusement, her heart gave a great, uneven thump. She was almost sure she recognised him, and, far from being Bryn, it was the person who had been spying on her at Llangefni market before Christmas! And it looked as though he was still anxious not to be seen, for he had dodged behind a rock as soon as she had turned towards him. Well, if he did not wish to be seen she would pretend to have noticed nothing, then would suddenly turn when he least expected it and confront him. And not only with spying on her now, she thought with satisfaction, but also with his behaviour at Llangefni market.

Only what was he doing here? The only dwelling she had passed as she made her way seawards was the thatched cottage in the hollow, so she supposed he must have come from there. Suddenly she remembered what it was that Bryn had told her – hadn't he said that a friend of his lived hereabouts? She tried to remember whether he had mentioned a name, but after all that had happened the trip to Llangefni seemed a lifetime ago, and she couldn't recall any more details of their conversation. Whatever he was called, the boy must have seen her snooping and followed her silently, no doubt using the gorse and the rocks as cover; in fact he had probably behaved just as she had.

Remembering Llangefni market, she concluded that he had decided to take a good look at her before accusing her of trespass. But why should she think ill of him, or he of her for that matter? He was probably shy. She decided that the next time he appeared she would wave, shout, ask him how she might get down to the beach, explain about her visit to his well.

Nell settled her haversack more comfortably upon her shoulders and set off in the direction she thought the watcher had taken. But though she searched for a good half-hour, examining every gorse bush, every rock, every stand of the little, wind-stunted trees, she saw no more of him that hot afternoon.

Nell told herself not to waste such a perfect day and set out to find her way down to the shore, for she had a great longing to eat her picnic on the beach, with the smell of the salt sea all around and the sea itself, always moving, to watch her. Sighing, she started to walk towards the cliffs Bryn had mentioned, and as she went she looked about her at the close-cropped, sheep-nibbled grass, at the great gorse patches and the rocks; not easy land to cultivate, she concluded, with the knowledge she had gained both from her aunt and from her hidden farming books. The dwellers in the cottage must work very hard indeed to make a living, and it would be a pretty poor living at that. She would ask Auntie Kath about it when she got back to the farm.

Soon she reached the cliffs and saw below her the enchanting little bay with its bite of golden sand and dozens of sky-reflecting rock pools. To her right stretched a much bigger bay, with what looked like caves in the cliff face. How right Bryn had been to enthuse over this place! But to her disappointment it seemed impossible to descend from the cliffs here and reach sea level. She had almost turned away when she saw that what at first she had taken to be a peculiarly shaped rock was in fact a boat. It had been turned upside down, but even so she could glimpse both oars and a stumpy mast; clearly it was very much in use. Fishing! That was one means of making a living for which, no doubt, the cottagers were grateful, because fish would be a very nice addition to their diet, unless they chose to sell their catch to neighbours who had no boat. To Auntie Kath, for instance.

As she moved along the cliff, searching for a route down, Nell saw what looked like a couple of baskets in the boat's shadow and remembered her aunt saying that the rocky coast was the haunt of crabs and lobsters, both of which could be sold for a good profit in towns. So it was not just the sale of fish which would increase the cottagers' meagre income.

Auntie Kath had asked her if she liked crab and Nell had said truthfully that she had no idea since she had never tasted it. 'Never tasted crab? Well, we'll remedy that when summer arrives,' Auntie Kath had said briskly, and explained how the creatures were caught by local fishermen who baited basket-like traps with rotten fish and then harvested the crabs and lobsters who got into the traps and could not get out.

Nell had thought this sounded unsporting to say the least, but had not said so; at that stage she had only known her aunt for a short while and already knew better than to cavil, especially about something she did not really understand.

Even thinking about crabs and lobsters made Nell remember how hungry she was; should she sit down here, on the cliff top, and eat the picnic her aunt had made for her? But even as she looked around her for a likely spot she saw the top of a narrow, winding path which looked as though it would take her safely down to the beach, provided she was careful. Before she started down it, however, she took another long look round, wondering if the young man would reappear. But he did not do so, and Nell descended to the beach alone.

As soon as she reached the shore she went over to the boat hoping to find some clue as to its owner, but there was nothing, though she saw the name *Maud* painted on the stern. She tried to peer beneath the boat but could see nothing, and, shrugging, she went over to the cluster of rocks and tiny pools which she had seen from the cliff top.

She chose a dry ledge of rock, sat down upon it and opened her haversack; her mouth watered at the sight of the hard-boiled egg, the thick cheese sandwiches and the apples, to say nothing of the ginger nuts, and the slice of rich fruit cake. Nell gave no more thought to the watcher who had hidden himself away so successfully, and began to eat.

Replete at last, she gave a satisfied sigh, packed the remainder of the food and cordial into her haversack and looked appreciatively around her. The beach was every bit as beautiful as she had imagined from Bryn's description, the little rock pools as fascinating. She began to explore the nearest, discovering creatures like living flowers which she knew must be anemones. She poked at them and gave a squeak of delight when their tentacles closed around her finger, then spat it out and curled in on themselves until they were no longer clusters of flowers, but small cushions of scarlet jelly. When she had teased the anemones for long enough – they refused her offering of cake crumbs as disgustedly as they had rejected her finger – she moved on to another pool, shaggy with seaweed, and found that it, too, teemed with life. There were tiny crabs no bigger than house spiders, brilliant shells – orange, yellow and purple – and of course little fish. When she lifted a heavy curtain of dark green kelp, quite a sizeable crab emerged indignantly from its shelter and dug itself into the sand so rapidly that within seconds it had disappeared.

Other pools offered further distractions. Two sea urchins, looking like miniature hedgehogs, swayed to and fro with the movement of the ripples and Nell realised with a start that the tide had turned; very soon these rock pools, the rocks themselves and quite a bit of the beach would probably be under water. She must make her way back up the cliff path, for she knew it had taken her a good while to get from the farm to the bay and even as she began to head for the cliff she saw that the sun was setting, streaking the sky with crimson and gold. She quickened her pace, remembering her promise to her aunt, and also realising that she was not sufficiently familiar with this part of the country to find her way back to Ty Hen in the dark. She reached the top of the cliff breathless and a little worried. She really must not allow herself to be distracted; she must concentrate on getting home. Nevertheless, she could not resist a slight detour in order to see whether anyone was working outside the long white cottage. By the time she reached her former vantage point the light was beginning to fade, so she just took a hasty look, saw that nothing was moving, except for a curl of smoke coming up from the chimney, and turned her face towards Ty Hen, albeit reluctantly. How like a feller, she thought crossly, to spy on you one minute and disappear the next! But I'll come back one day soon and ask the old man if there's a boy living there. It would be nice to know someone a bit younger than Auntie Kath. And if he is – was – a friend of Bryn's, we could talk about him as well.

But now was not the time to linger. She set out for

home, finishing off the food her aunt had given her and beginning to sing to herself as she walked. 'Pack up your troubles in your old kitbag and smile, smile, smile,' she warbled. She had had a lovely day and she realised, almost guiltily, that for several hours she had forgotten her sadness over Bryn's death, and her misery over her mother's defection. But hadn't that been the reason Auntie Kath had given her a day's holiday? So there was no need to feel guilty. Her happy day had got things in perspective and she knew she would be better for it.

It was a long walk, but at last she crossed the farm-yard and burst into the kitchen, still singing. Auntie Kath was removing something from the bake oven, something which smelled delicious. She turned as her niece entered the kitchen and her eyebrows shot up. 'So you're back. I reckon you must have smelled the rabbit pie and it brought you home like reeling in a fish on a line. But why were you singing that old song?'

'What old song?' Nell asked, genuinely bewildered. Once she had reached the lane leading to Ty Hen she had sung all sorts of things simply because the rhythm kept her striding out. 'I didn't know I was singing an old song.'

Aunt Kath sniffed. 'If "Keep the home fires burning" isn't an old song, I don't know what is,' she declared. 'Where have you been, then?' She pointed to the sink. 'Wash your hands while I dish up. Since everything's ready, we'll eat at once.'

It was the work of a moment to wash and dry her hands and take her place at the table, where she discovered that despite having devoured every crumb her aunt had supplied for her picnic she was still hungry. She began to eat, but her aunt tutted. 'I asked you a question, young lady! Where have you been, and did you have a good day?'

Nell put down her knife and fork and beamed at her aunt. 'I had a fantastic day,' she said. 'Of course nothing could stop me being unhappy about Bryn, and the way my mother has behaved, but I suppose you could say I've come to terms with what's happened.'

'What can't be cured must be endured,' her aunt said, nodding sagely. 'When you first lose someone you love you think the pain will never grow less, but it does. Time heals isn't just a saying, it's true. With every day that passes, the pain of loss eases; I know it. I still miss – miss Owain, but now I remember the good times and am grateful for them. Now tell me about your day.'

Nell complied, thinking that this was the first time her aunt had actually shown real interest in her doings. She told her story right from the moment she had left the farmhouse that morning to the time when she had crested the hill and seen the cottage in the hollow below. 'I'd love to know the people who live there,' she finished. She suddenly remembered something. 'Bryn said it belongs to you, so I suppose you know them, even though they're a long way from Ty Hen. Have they got a son of about nineteen or twenty? Bryn talked about a friend and I think I caught sight of him for a moment, but when I tried to catch him up he'd disappeared. I suppose he went into the cottage.'

Auntie Kath shook her head. 'I doubt it. That long-house has been empty for the best part of twenty years. Nobody's lived there since it got too much for the old folk. Though I did have trouble with a gypsy at one time. He moved in . . . but that was years ago. I hope he hasn't had the cheek to return. I wonder who the young man was? Probably someone like yourself, come down from one of the nearby villages to fish from the rocks, or check his lobster pots. But do satisfy my curiosity. Why did you go all the way to Church Bay – Porth Swtan, the locals call it – when there are many beautiful beaches and bays much nearer to Ty Hen?'

'Because Bryn loved it there, and I honestly can't imagine anywhere more beautiful,' Nell said rather impatiently. Why did her aunt always have to put her on the defensive? 'But why do you say it's empty, Auntie Kath? The longhouse, I mean. There was smoke coming from the chimney, and there was a dog, a border collie. I haven't told you yet, but I was dread-fully thirsty so I had meant to ask the folk living there if they could spare me a mug of water. Only when I saw the dog I remembered the row Fly and Whisky kick up if someone they don't know comes to the farm. It was such a hot afternoon that I thought the people in the cottage might be snoozing, so I didn't go down after all. Instead, I went to the well and pulled up a bucket of water to dilute the raspberry cordial. It was while I was sitting by the well that I saw the young man.'

'Dog? You think there was a dog?' her aunt said incredulously, ignoring the mention of the young man.

'And it didn't bark?' She gave Nell a pitying glance. 'Farm dogs always bark, always give warning of a stranger's approach. Well, I'll say one thing for you, young lady, you've got a great deal of imagination. Unless you're going to tell me that the dog was deaf and blind.'

Nell smiled perfunctorily. 'I didn't imagine it, honest to G— I mean honestly I didn't, Auntie Kath,' she protested. 'Next you'll be saying I imagined the young man. But actually, I've seen him before; he was at the Llangefni Christmas market. I noticed him especially because I'd asked Bryn not to follow me since I would be buying his present, and when I saw him I thought at first Bryn had told him to follow me, so I kept my eye on him. I knew it wasn't Bryn, of course; this chap was older and quite a bit taller. And Bryn was fair; the man at the market had black hair and sallow skin. Do you know him, Auntie?'

Kath shook her head. 'I can't say I do, but then why should I notice one young man more than another? If he was at the Christmas market then I reckon he'd have been wearing a cap, so I wouldn't have seen his hair. In fact I'm surprised that you did; are you sure it was the same fellow, Nell? Are you sure it wasn't Bryn at Llangefni, dodging about to tease you? How good a look did you get at him?'

'Pretty good, and I know it wasn't Bryn,' Nell said guardedly. Perhaps because of her aunt's disbelief, she was reluctant to lay herself open to another charge of imagining things. Abruptly, she changed the subject. 'Oh, and there was a boat on the beach, with a pair of oars and a couple of lobster pots . . . or did I imagine that as well?' she added sarcastically.

Her aunt shook her head. 'No, of course you didn't. Lots of local people fish from that bay, particularly now, with so many of the other beaches sown with land mines to discourage an invasion fleet. The boat could have been used by anyone who wanted to put down pots for crab or lobster. Come to that, someone might have been net fishing. Did you see a net?'

Nell thought back. 'No, I didn't see one, but the boat was upside down, so it might have been underneath. What does Swtan mean, Auntie? I know Porth means bay . . .'

'It doesn't have a meaning exactly; it's the name of a small fish – I think the English call it whiting – which is abundant along the coast round here. It's good to eat, as you'll find out now that summer has come. But I'm intrigued that you should have thought the Swtan longhouse was occupied. Are you planning to go down to the coast again? If so, I think you should brave the mythical dog and see for yourself that the cottage is deserted. I'd be interested to know just what made you think it was still lived in.'

'Well, the garden's tidy and there are vegetables, and I thought I saw a very old-fashioned, rusty sort of bicycle . . .' Nell began, then gave an impatient sigh. 'If you don't believe me, Auntie, then I could go there a hundred times and come back with my story and you'd still think I was either daydreaming or making it up. So why don't you go and take a look for yourself? If it's too far for you to walk, I suppose you could go in the pony and trap.' She stared defiantly at her aunt, knowing she sounded offended, but not caring; it was always infuriating to be disbelieved, thought either an idiot or a liar. It had been on the tip of her tongue to say that she had seen not only a dog but an old man, and had caught a glimpse of a woman as well, but she had stopped herself in time. It had been the heat haze, she told herself, just the heat haze. Her aunt would simply jeer if she mentioned those barely glimpsed figures.

So it was no surprise to Nell when she saw Kath shaking her head. 'What, waste my time on a wild goose chase?' she said mockingly. 'I'm a very busy woman, as you know, and anyway reaching Church Bay by road is three times as long as cutting across the fields. Incidentally, if you had gone down to the Swtan and offered the cottager five bob for his old bicycle, you could have gone over to Church Bay whenever you had any free time. But as for confirming your story, you'll have to be my deputy, for I've no doubt that having discovered the beach you'll want to go back, hoping to prove me wrong.'

'What's the point of me going back to confirm what I already know to be true, when you'll only say I'm imagining things?' Nell repeated, grinning at the older woman. 'You can't have it both ways, Auntie Kath.'

Her aunt gave a reluctant chuckle. 'You're right there, queen. And of course when I think about it, I've not visited the Swtan longhouse for more years than I care to remember, so trespassers might have moved in. But it's not important. Now, let's clear away and get to our beds. I'm sure you'll sleep like a top after your adventurous day; I certainly shall, having had all your work to do as well as my own.'

Nell's cheeks grew hot. 'You said I could have the day off—' she began, but was swiftly interrupted.

'Of course I let you have the day off; I'm not denying it,' Kath snapped. 'Now get off up to bed, do, because I'm worn out and you'll be pretty tired as well. Goodnight.'

'Goodnight,' Nell mumbled, making for the stairs. 'See you in the morning.'

As soon as she reached her own room, Kath got herself ready for bed, blew out the candle and pulled back the blackout curtains. She was growing almost fond of her niece, but she knew that after their conversation she would probably dream tonight of the Swtan longhouse and days long past. In the beginning she had tried to fight the dreams that came because of Nell's dreaded but still familiar Scouse accent, but she had come to accept that no one, no matter how fiercely determined, could control their thoughts in sleep. And sometimes there were times when she woke with tears on her cheeks but absolutely no recollection of what her dream had been about.

So now she gazed out into the moonlit yard, still reflecting back the heat of midday from its cobbles, and thought about the Swtan. Suppose Nell was right and someone had moved in there once more? Come to that, it might be the gypsy she had mentioned to Nell. Or one of Owain's vast family, in which case she would be the last person to hear of it.

But I really shouldn't have attacked the kid because she's interested in her surroundings, Kath told herself. At first I didn't care what she thought, but now that I know her better I suppose I want her to understand, to be on my side. It's just unfortunate that she so often pokes her nose into something I'd rather forget. I suppose it would be a good deal more sensible if I told her how things are – or how they were, perhaps – and then she can decide for herself who was in the wrong and who in the right.

Moodily, she almost wished she had tried to propitiate her husband's family after his death – would it have been so hard? – but their freely expressed resentment that Owain had left her Ty Hen had been more than she could cope with at the time. Now that she was older and wiser, perhaps she could understand their jealousy and annoyance. But Owain had bitterly resented the way they had treated his bride, just because she was English and spoke no Welsh, and had retaliated by leaving her Ty Hen and the Swtan, and making it very plain in his will that the property was hers and hers alone.

The family had expected her to crawl to them for help, not realising that Owain had found in her a willing pupil, so that when he died after a mere five years of marriage – but what happy years, she reflected now – she was almost as capable of running the farm as he.

She knew there had been a good deal of local disapproval when the family had put it about that Owain had left everything to a green girl, not yet thirty, but it had all been done legally and hard though they had tried – and try they most certainly did – they could not force her to hand over a single acre of land or one brick of the farmhouse.

They should have tried cajolery, or pleading, or perhaps offers of help when times were hard, even a nice 'would it be possible . . .' Kath told herself now, but that was not their way. Bludgeoning, ganging up on her at cattle sales, whispering behind their hands: they thought such tactics were bound to work, to drive her back to Liverpool, and had been surprised and indignant when they had not.

She knew now, of course, that her own attitude had not helped, but she had been so intent upon making sure that the farm was run as efficiently as it had been in Owain's time that she had scarcely heeded the family's animosity. Not at first. Only after they pointedly ignored her when they met at market, or deliberately outbid her when they saw her hand go up at an auction, did she realise that she had made implacable enemies. And she had been too young – and too proud – to try to put things right.

And now in a way I'm doing it all over again, she told herself ruefully, gazing out through her window at the stars twinkling in the dark sky. If only I'd told Nell why I tend to keep myself to myself, why Owain's family will have nothing to do with me, then it would be easier for her to appreciate the way things are. I expect her to be on my side, when she has no idea that sides have been taken. Were taken long ago, in fact. Yes, in fairness I'll explain things the next time Nell and I find ourselves alone.

For a little while longer Kath sat on the wide window seat, gazing out. Then she sighed, pulled the sash down to let in the mild night air, and got into bed. She snuggled down, then sat up crossly, for the night was still warm, and threw off the patchwork quilt and the thin blanket, so that she was covered only by the sheet. The pillow was cool against her hot cheek, the night wind smelled of new-mown grass, and from outside came the sound of a fox barking at the moon. Kath saw in her mind's eye the fox's earth, the vixen curled up in the dark with her cubs close and safe. She felt her lids begin to droop and told herself firmly that she would not dream, she would not . . .

She was twenty-six and walking along a path through a beautiful garden, and she was not alone; John Williams had his arm about her waist. He was telling her that he had carved her a love spoon, which was the way the Welsh plighted their troth.

'But a real ring, an engagement ring, I'll buy for you . . .' he was saying earnestly, and when Kath looked at the third finger of her left hand she saw that a beautiful ring sparkled there. She gasped, turned to face him . . . and woke.

She lay very still, staring at the dark ceiling above her head. What a wonderful, lovely dream! And though she had dreamed it, it was more like a memory, for she had recognised the scene. Now that she was awake, she remembered the incident perfectly. It had taken place in Prince's Park, where a small party of them had gone for a picnic. Kath smiled to herself. It had not taken her lover long to detach her from the others, though Trixie had made a spirited attempt to follow them when they had moved away from the group. In fact she would have done so had not Lou, dear Lou, called her back. Trixie had been sulky, had pointed out in a voice deliberately loud enough to be heard by the departing couple that John was *her* friend, that he had come to the house to see *her* and was not interested – not truly interested – in anyone else.

But Louisa had told her sharply not to make a fool of herself. 'It's your birthday quite soon; how do you know they aren't discussing what they should buy you?'

Kath had risked a quick glance over her shoulder and had seen that Trixie was smiling once more, which had made her smile too, because though Trixie had been eighteen years old and thought herself sophisticated and grown up, she was really just a child still. She had been like a little butterfly, fluttering from one flower to another, spreading her wings for the admiration of all and sundry and believing herself to be loved by anyone who looked at her twice or paid her the least attention.

As they had walked rapidly away from the picnicking party, Kath and her companion had exchanged rather guilty smiles because they both knew that it had indeed been Trixie who had first got to know the young gunner and had introduced him to the rest of her family. Kath had smiled at him and had felt her heart beat faster as their eyes met. Working as a staff nurse on a ward full of wounded soldiers, she had met a great many young men. Many of these, when they were discharged from hospital, had invited her to go dancing, or to the seaside, or to see a play or a film at the picture palace. She had liked most of them and enjoyed their company, and when they realised she did not intend to become serious, having never felt a decided partiality for any of them, they had moved on, leaving Kath to do the same.

Kath had thought herself cold, a spinster in the making, but had never regretted it. After meeting John, however, she had known this was not so; she was the same as any other girl. One glance from his dark eyes, one touch of his hand on hers, and she had fallen in love for the very first time in her life. It was embarrassing but true that Trixie had brought him home, rather as a young dog brings in a rabbit after a successful hunt. But within moments of their meeting, Kath had seen her own feelings reflected in his eyes and had understood the misery and despair which other girls felt when their men left them to return to the horrors of the trenches. As for Trixie's affections, she had not believed then and did not believe now that they had been seriously engaged. It was just that Trixie wanted all the admiration, all the attention, and could not bear to see her elder sister admired above herself.

But there had been other young men around, a great many of them, Kath reminded herself now, lying in her bed and gazing up at the ceiling. With hindsight, she wished that she and John had not let their feelings show so plainly, but would things have been better had they pretended indifference? Remembering Trixie's attitude, she thought not.

The odd thing was that of all the young men who danced attendance upon the Ripley sisters, 'Welsh' John had been easily the plainest. He had been stockily built, scarcely more than a couple of inches taller than Kath herself, with straight, almost black hair which flopped forward across a broad, tanned forehead. His face had been thin and his chin determined, but his dark eyes twinkled with humour, and when he gave his lopsided smile, Kath knew that hers was not the only heart that had melted. Her wretched little sister had fallen prey to that smile before Kath had even met him. But Trixie had been too young to stick to any one fellow for very long, and had John not made it clear that his relationship with Kath was serious the younger girl would probably hardly have noticed his defection. For Trixie, at that stage in her life at any rate, had had no thoughts of permanence, or marriage. She moved from one man to the next with a sunny smile, and had even seemed to forgive Kath for so clearly preferring John to any of the other young men who came to the house.

It had been just a coincidence, though a strange one, that the next man to take Trixie's fancy had also been Welsh. John Williams returned to his regiment and along came Owain Jones, much more physically attractive than his countryman – tall, slim-waisted, with richly curling brown hair and beautifully white teeth – to be introduced to the Ripley household. He had been immediately annexed by Trixie, who had been very proud of her conquest.

The tinkle of the alarm bell brought Kath to the

startled realisation that dawn now streaked the sky and the sun was edging up from behind the nearest hill. Obedient always to the alarm clock's call, she got out of bed and crossed to her washstand, pulling her long cotton nightdress over her head and beginning the all-over wash with which she started each day.

She tried to banish all thoughts of the past from her mind, but the dream refused to be sent packing. She had only known John for a few months and though they had indeed become serious, had talked of marriage, she had no idea where his home had been, though she had assumed it must have been somewhere in North Wales since his accent was similar to Owain's. So why, in the name of all that was wonderful, had she dreamed of that trip to Prince's Park?

Kath finished washing and drying herself, dressed briskly, and left her bedroom. On reaching the kitchen, she opened the base of the range and pulled out the ash can, which she carried across the yard and emptied on the cinder path which led to the WC at the end of the garden. Then she returned to the house, made up the fire and wielded the bellows until the flames began to crackle. As she began to prepare breakfast, she reminded herself that she meant to explain to Nell why she had refused to visit the Swtan. Not that she had refused exactly, but it must have been plain that she had no intention of going to the longhouse herself. Sighing, she began to measure milk, water and oats into the big black saucepan, hearing her niece descending the stairs as she did so. Remember, she told herself severely, that your habit of never explaining hasn't done you much good in the past. You've promised yourself that you'll explain things to Nell and it's about time you started. Why, you've not even told her . . . but I swear I'll do it today.

Nell came into the kitchen and went straight to the pantry to get out the eggs and bacon and the big loaf of homemade bread. As she passed, she turned and grinned at Kath.

'Morning, Auntie,' she said cheerfully. 'It's going to be another hot one, by the look of it.'

Immensely relieved that her niece had apparently decided to forget the sharp words they had exchanged the previous evening, Kath agreed that the weather looked set fair and began to stir the porridge.

Another day had begun.

Chapter Seven

A couple of days after Nell's trip to Church Bay, she was woken from a pleasant dream in which she had somehow learned to fly by a great deal of noise coming from downstairs. She shot up in bed and stared at her alarm clock, but it would not ring for another ten minutes, so the row from the kitchen was definitely not because she had overslept.

Sensing excitement of some sort, Nell dressed in record time and thundered down the stairs, bursting into the kitchen to find her aunt, Eifion and his wife, and another elderly man whom she knew to be Eifion's brother Merion, all talking excitedly and with many gestures. When old Mrs Hughes saw her she came rushing across the room to clasp an astonished Nell in her plump old arms. 'He's fit and well, not dead at all,' she said in a rush. 'Oh, the dear Lord be thanked for his mercy; my favourite grandson's coming home to us!'

'Bryn? Do you mean Bryn's alive?' Nell squeaked, extricating herself with some difficulty from the old woman's embrace. 'Where is he? Why isn't he here?'

'In hospital he is; in Liverpool, though he'll be sent home as soon as he's fit enough,' Eifion said. He pulled out a vast khaki handkerchief and blew his nose resoundingly. 'It's like a miracle so it is!'

Auntie Kath was pouring out mugs of tea which she pushed across the table, eyeing her niece thoughtfully. 'I'll make a big pan of porridge,' she said. 'And you, Nell, can start on the toast. Now sit yourselves down, everyone, and we'll hear just what happened.'

Eifion finished blowing his nose and transferred the handkerchief to his eyes, which were running with what Nell guessed to be emotion. He took a drink of his tea, began to speak, choked, and gestured to his brother. 'Best if you tell the tale,' he said unsteadily. 'Still too shocked – happy – I am. Go you on, Merion, you'll tell it better than meself, being less involved.'

Merion grinned, and began to speak. 'A lot of what we heard was right,' he said. 'The bomb which went down the funnel of the good old *Scotia* blew her up all right, with great loss of life. We'll maybe never know how many, for the ship had just picked up between four and five hundred French soldiers, and of course when the ship went down . . . but enough of that. Bryn was on deck and managed to dive clear of the undertow, but then he was knocked on the head by a chunk of the ship and lost consciousness for a few moments. When he came round again, he was in the water, sick and dizzy, but alive.

'He can't remember much after that, save for being picked up by what he now thinks was a fishing boat. They took him to France, where he was treated in a field hospital and then put aboard a ship heading for England. He did try to tell folk he was from Anglesey and that his name was Bryn Hughes, but it wasn't until they got him into a hospital in Liverpool that they realised his people had not been informed that he had survived. They sent a telegram . . . his mother got it yesterday . . . and of course the news went round like wildfire.'

'That's just wonderful,' Nell said warmly. 'I expect Mrs Hughes is already on her way to Liverpool. Oh, it will be marvellous to see Bryn alive and well once more!'

'Yes, indeed,' Merion Hughes said. 'And of course it has given hope, where none existed before, that others may yet be found alive.' Rather to Nell's surprise, he then cast an anxious glance first at her aunt and then at herself. 'But you've not heard the rest of my news. Bryn's mother has been posted to Scotland, and though she rushed down to Liverpool she could only stay a couple of hours as her job is an important one and Bryn's injuries are not life-threatening. So I rang the Stanley Hospital and the sister on Wellington ward said the lad might begin to pick up if he had a visitor who could speak Welsh, and some of his own things.' He looked apologetically from Kath's face to Nell's. 'And of course none of us Hugheses family know Liverpool, so we put our heads together and we thought . . .'

'I suppose you're going to suggest that my niece goes traipsing off to Liverpool to see the young fellow,' Kath said bluntly. 'Leaving me and Eifion here to manage as best we can. Well, I know Bryn and Nell are good friends . . .'

Nell sighed. She was delighted that Bryn was alive, pleased to think he would soon be home, but realised that if she agreed to go to Liverpool and take with her some of his personal possessions folk would draw conclusions she had no wish to see drawn. Friendship was all very well; friendship was grand in fact, but she was too young, she told herself, for any deeper involvement. So she looked hopefully at Auntie Kath, expecting that hard taskmistress to point out that she needed all the help she could get on the farm. However, such hopes were soon dashed.

Auntie Kath caught Nell's eye, but failed to read the message there. 'I suppose I shall just have to manage for a couple of days,' she said. 'After all, Eifion and myself got by before young Nell here came to live at Ty Hen.' She smiled at Nell. 'I expect you're longing to see your old pal again and to have a day or two in Liverpool, so I'll have to agree to your going off. But don't imagine you can stretch a couple of days into a couple of weeks; if you do I'll dock your wages, see if I don't!'

Despite herself, Nell giggled. For a couple of months now her aunt had been giving her money from time to time, but she had never received a regular wage and indeed had not wanted one, for what would she spend money on? Her aunt provided bed, board and working clothes, paid her library subscription, and bought stamps, writing paper and envelopes, which were kept on the dresser for anyone to use. But this was scarcely the time to remark on it and Nell merely said, in a subdued voice, that of course, if there was no one else free to go, she would be happy to visit her old friend. 'I promise not to be away for more than a couple of days; three at the most,' she said earnestly. 'I can pack my haversack with anything I shall need in two minutes flat, so if someone can meet me on Holyhead railway station with a bag full of Bryn's stuff, then I can be in Liverpool the same day.'

Old Mrs Hughes cleared her throat and cast a deprecating glance at Nell. 'If you would agree, miss, I'd like to accompany you to this hospital, whatever it's called,' she said timidly. 'Never crossed the water, me, but with you beside me I'd not be afraid to be blown up by a bomb or smothered in my bed by some foreign seaman. Bryn thought a lot of you; I'm sure he would say you'd look after me.'

'Gladly,' Nell said, though she felt secretly dismayed. The old lady would complicate things, for she could not possibly expect her relatives to take in not only herself but a total stranger as well. However, there were cheap boarding houses along the Stanley Road; she and Bryn's grandmother could doubtless take a room in one of them. But Nell did not mean to give up without a struggle. 'Don't you think it might be better if I stayed here and your husband accompanied you to Liverpool?' she asked. 'I'm awfully fond of Bryn, but I'm sure he'd far rather see his taid than me.'

'You're wrong there,' Eifion said at once. 'He's spoke to the sister on his ward and said to ask if you'd come in particular.' He gave poor Nell a coy look from under his thick and grizzled brows. 'Rare fond of you is our Bryn.'

Nell felt uncomfortable. 'I'm sure he'd much rather see you, Eifion.'

'No, I'd be lost in a big city,' Eifion said quickly, and Nell realised that he was actually frightened by the mere idea of a visit to Liverpool. 'I rode in a tram once. Didn't care for it. No, Nell, you'll take care of my old lady a lot better'n I could. And the young cleave to the young, as you doubtless know.' He chuckled, then leaned across the table and patted Nell's hand. 'You needn't be shy. He speaks of you as his girl; we've heard him say so often, haven't we, Mother?'

Mrs Hughes gave a little bleat of agreement, but Nell cut in at once. 'I shan't be sixteen for another week, and that's too young to be anyone's girl,' she said firmly. She turned back to Mrs Hughes and, seeing the anxious look on the older woman's face, smiled warmly. 'But of course I'll be happy to take care of you if you really mean to come with me to Liverpool,' she added reassuringly, and was glad she had done so when she saw the anxiety leave the other's eyes.

'There; Bryn said you was a good girl,' the old lady said with considerable satisfaction. She pushed her empty porridge bowl away from her and began to sip her tea with obvious pleasure. She beamed at her hostess. 'Thank you, Mrs Jones dear; this is good.'

Merion Hughes smiled at Nell and thanked Kath for the tea she had just placed in front of him, announcing that he meant to move into Eifion's cottage whilst Mrs Hughes was away, in order to help out at Ty Hen. 'As you know, I'm a good stockman and can milk a cow in half the time it would take young Nell here. So if you're willing, Mrs Jones . . .'

* * *

Nell sat scrunched up in the corner seat of the train which was taking her where she had no desire to go, looked at her reflection in the dirt-smeared window pane and wished herself anywhere but here. How odd it was, she thought, remembering her previous train journey. How very differently she felt about both Ty Hen and Liverpool now. She had never expected to fall in love with the farm, but now that she was leaving it, albeit only for a short time, she realised that her heart was in Anglesey, and she would never, of her own free will, live in the big city again.

'Sandwich, Miss Nell?'

Nell was abruptly jerked back to the present and to the little old woman sitting on the seat beside her, holding out a greaseproof paper parcel which contained several delicious looking cheese and onion sandwiches. 'Sorry, Mrs Hughes; I was dreaming. Yes please, I'd love one. It seems ages since breakfast.' She helped herself to a sandwich, then turned a reproachful gaze on her companion. 'But didn't we agree that you would call me Nell, as everyone else does? It feels very odd when you call me Miss.'

'So we did, so we did,' Mrs Hughes said placidly. 'And I'll try to remember so I will. Where are we now?'

'Almost there,' Nell said, peering out of the window at the countryside, dotted now with houses. 'By the time I've eaten this sandwich we'll be coming in to Lime Street station, so I'd better get our bags down from the rack.'

Ten minutes later, her prophesy was proved correct; the train drew up with much hissing of steam and shrill whistling and Nell donned her trusty haversack, picked up the bag of Bryn's belongings, and disembarked, turning to help her companion step down on to the platform. To her secret surprise, Mrs Hughes, though her eyes rounded with astonishment, did not seem frightened by the crowds, though she clung on to Nell's sleeve until they emerged on to the pavement. Then she pointed to a tram. 'Can we ride on one of them, cariad?' she asked eagerly. 'I know my Eifion don't care for 'em, but I's different. They's only big charabancs on a long bit of stick, like.'

'Well, I was going to suggest that we should hail a taxi, but if you'd really rather take a tram, I'm willing,' Nell said readily. 'It's a good deal cheaper for a start, and if we catch a number 23 or 24 it will take us all the way to the Stanley Hospital. But we'll get off one stop earlier, so we can book ourselves into a lodging house before we go to see Bryn.'

They joined the queue and Nell had to strain her ears to catch what her companion was saying, for she had quite forgotten how noisy the city was. Everyone in front of them seemed to be shouting. Despite the restriction on petrol, the streets were full of vans, lorries and even a few cars, though the brewers' drays, the milk carts and several other vehicles were still horse-drawn. Nell found herself longing to stuff her fingers into her ears, but Mrs Hughes's eyes sparkled with excitement and once they were aboard the tram she demanded to know the name and purpose of every big building. St George's Hall impressed her mightily with its recumbent lions, statue of Queen Victoria and plateau, and when she glimpsed the rounded dome which housed the Picton Library she announced that she would visit it before returning home.

'And I mean to see a theatre, and the museum, and that there art gallery,' she shouted above the rattles and squeaks of the tram's onward progress and the constant ringing of its bell. 'Because I don't reckon I'll ever get to visit the city again, so I've got make the most of it.'

'Well, I don't know . . .' Nell was beginning doubtfully, when the tram drew in at the stop she wanted, and the two of them joined the rush of passengers descending.

It was quieter here, though the pavement was lined with shops and small houses. Mrs Hughes gazed into every window they passed, admiring everything, saying she was sure Liverpool must be even bigger than London, and a great deal smarter.

Nell agreed, more for the sake of peace than anything, since she had never been to any other city. But she did say, quietly, that they were here to see Bryn and not to enjoy themselves, which made her companion go very red about the gills and mutter something which, perhaps fortunately, Nell did not catch. Then she saw a side street where she remembered, in the past, seeing signs in front windows indicating that the occupants took in paying guests, so she steered her garrulous companion into Easby Road and presently found a house displaying a vacancy sign.

She rang the doorbell, which was almost immediately answered by a short, fat woman whose light-coloured hair was pulled into a neat bun on the nape of her neck. She was clad in a cotton frock covered by a large calico apron, and she grinned at her visitors, revealing the fact that she had a fine set of pink gums but no teeth. 'Mornin'!' she said cheerfully. Her small grey eyes flickered over them shrewdly, taking in their clothing and their luggage. 'Wantin' a room, are you? Aye, I guessed as much.' Once again her glance swept them, then she jabbed a plump pink forefinger at Nell. 'Come to visit a sweetheart what's been wounded at Dunkirk? Or mebbe a brother, seein' as you're a bit young to go gettin' yourself a feller.' She shot a penetrating glance at Nell's companion. 'Mebbe it's your son you've come avisitin', I'd guess. Aye, there's folk pourin' into the Pool these days to visit fellers what's been brought home wounded. But why am I runnin' on like as if you were a guessing game? I've the first floor front vacant, with the grandest double bed you ever did see, modern mattress an' all. And it's right next door to the lavvy, so if you're caught short in the middle of the night you can nip in there in a trice.' She drew herself up. 'No need for a po under the bed in *this* house, I'm tellin' you. Want to see it?' She gave a snort of laughter, shaking her head at herself. 'The room, I mean, not the lavvy! Oh, and I forgot to tell you I provide breakfast – porridge, tea and toast – and I can do an evenin' meal for an extra half-crown a head. But what am I thinkin' of? I'm Mrs Trelawney and I've not told you I charge ten bob a room, bed and breakfast, that's for the pair of you. Does it suit?'

Stunned by this gentle eloquence, Nell was speech-less for a moment, but Mrs Hughes seemed unruffled. 'See the room first we will, before we make up our minds,' she said decidedly. 'Then we can talk terms.'

'That's wharr I like; someone who knows what they want,' the landlady said, beaming once more. She began to usher them inside, then suddenly clapped a hand to her mouth. 'I forgot to put me fangs in afore I come to the door,' she said, her voice muffled. 'Wharrever will you think of me?' She delved in the pocket of her apron, turned away from them for a moment, then turned back and grinned once more, showing an excellent set of dentures. 'There now. Come along in; straight up the stairs and first door on the right. I doesn't climb the stairs 'cept when I goes to bed or cleans me rooms, but when you come down I'll have a pot o' char and some of me homemade shortbread all ready.'

Thirty minutes later Nell and her companion left the house in Easby Road, exchanging meaning glances as they turned in the direction of the hospital. They had booked the room and left their luggage locked inside it, and now Nell put the key carefully in her coat pocket and turned to Mrs Hughes, blowing out her cheeks in an expressive whistle. 'Phew! You mustn't think all Liverpudlians never stop talking. I rather liked her, though, and I'm sure she's as honest as the day and will do everything she promised, though when you tried to beat her down from ten bob I was quite frightened in case she wouldn't let us have the room.'

Mrs Hughes chuckled. 'Well, she might not have accepted less money, but we're getting a boiled egg with our breakfast.' She smacked her lips. 'There's nothing I like better than an egg to my breakfast.'

As they walked slowly along the pavement – for Mrs Hughes was still examining every window they passed – Nell tried to break it to her friend that the theatre trips and visits to museums and galleries she had planned were scarcely possible in the time at their disposal. 'We are supposed to be visiting Bryn, don't forget,' she pointed out. 'You wouldn't want to upset him by gadding off to the theatre when you could be by his bedside, would you?'

Mrs Hughes glanced up at Nell with a little smile, but all she said was: 'We'll see. It wouldn't surprise me if we were here for a while longer than we'd planned.'

'Not me; if you stay, you stay alone,' Nell said as they reached the hospital and turned into the foyer. A passing nurse directed them to Wellington ward and told them that she rather thought the patient they were seeking was in a bed on the left as you went down the room.

'It's a long room,' she warned them, 'all young men who have come back from Dunkirk. Some of them . . . but you will see for yourselves soon enough.'

They did. They entered the ward, glancing rather uneasily about them, for everywhere men were in plaster casts, on traction, or heavily bandaged. There was some talk, some laughter, but for the most part the patients were quiet, and this affected both Nell and

Mrs Hughes, who found themselves whispering as they trod quietly between the double row of beds.

They were almost at the end of the ward when Nell gave a frightened gasp and turned back to a patient she had just passed: a young man, his entire head swathed in bandages and a pink celluloid shield over one eye. His left arm and shoulder were plastered and his eyes were tightly closed. She grabbed Mrs Hughes's hand. 'Is that – can that be Bryn, the feller in the bed we've just passed?' she asked tremulously. 'I – I didn't recognise him, probably because I was looking for his yellow curls and big grin, but there's something . . . let's go back.'

They retraced their steps. The young man lay on his back, very still, his face as white as the bandages which covered his head. The eye they could see was closed, his mouth a little open, but even as they stared, incredulous, the uncovered eyelid flickered, rose, drooped . . . rose again, and the boy's tongue moistened his pale lips, which twitched suddenly into a brief, painful smile.

'Nell?' he whispered huskily. 'Oh, I've prayed you'd come! When they sent the telegram I begged them to ask if you could come instead of my mam . . . oh, Nain, I didn't see you there. I didn't ask Mam to send you . . . how on earth . . .?'

'We came together,' Nell broke in, guessing that Bryn's remark had sounded like rejection and wanting to spare Mrs Hughes's feelings, though she thought that the older woman might not have heard the words, for she was a little deaf and Bryn's voice had been faint. 'We've booked a room not far from here. We brought your stuff; your taid packed the bag . . .'

'Good,' Bryn murmured. He moved a little, then winced and stayed very still for several moments, saying nothing, but Nell guessed, by the strained look on his face, that every movement was painful. When he spoke again his voice was even fainter than before, so that Nell had to bend over the bed to hear. 'I'm so thirsty! I had a cup of tea yesterday but then I vomited . . . I'd love some of Mrs Jones's lemonade . . . but my head thumps so! If I move even a little . . . being sick was agony . . . what's that noise? Oh, if only someone could make them stop! Why would they let a band play in a hospital? I'm sure my head will split in two.'

Nell assured him that there was no band playing anywhere in the vicinity and put a gentle hand on his; it was hot and damp and he grasped her fingers tightly for a moment, then tried to lift her hand to his cheek, but let it drop back on the coverlet with a tiny sigh. 'Too heavy,' he moaned. 'I can't . . .'

Their conversation had been in Welsh and now Nell turned to stare at Mrs Hughes with frightened eyes, addressing her in the same language. 'He's most awfully ill,' she murmured. 'I think we ought to get a nurse . . . ah, here comes someone, thank God!'

A nurse in a dark blue dress with a crisp white apron over it and a starched cap on her smooth hair came rustling up the ward and frowned reprovingly when she reached Nell and her companion. 'Are you related to this young man?' she asked, her voice low. 'He's very ill and shouldn't be having visitors, unless you are family, of course.'

Nell began to speak, but Mrs Hughes cut across her. 'We're family,' she said firmly. 'I'm the lad's nain – grandmother, that is. But mebbe we'd best come back later . . . we can see he's ill.'

The nurse nodded. 'Very well. As you're family I've a deal to say to you, but we'd best go to my office; we can talk there without fear of disturbing him.'

She led them out of the ward and into a small, functional room containing only a desk, filing cabinets and three chairs, two obviously for visitors and one behind the desk for the nurse herself. As soon as they were in the room the nurse shut the door firmly and held out her hand.

'I'm Sister Bailey, in charge of Wellington ward. And you are . . .?'

Nell introduced Mrs Hughes and then began to explain that she was an old friend, but the sister cut her short. 'The whole ward has heard of you, Miss Whitaker,' she said, smiling for the first time. 'When he was delirious young Bryn talked of nothing but his Nell, saying that if she came to see him he knew he would get better. Well, stranger things have happened, and now that you are here I hope there'll be an improvement.'

'I don't know what difference my presence will make,' Nell began, then said what was in the forefront of her mind. 'Only could you tell us please, Sister, just what is the matter with Bryn? We heard he was hit over the head and nearly drowned . . .'

'He has a head wound,' the sister acknowledged. 'It

runs diagonally across his crown and halfway down his cheek. Unfortunately it has done some damage to his right eye, but the doctor thinks he'll recover completely. He has a broken shoulder and a couple of cracked ribs as well, but he's young and those will also mend, leaving little or no trace. When he was admitted he was in a poor way, and within a day or so he began to run a very high fever. He was talking wildly, but since he did so in Welsh there was little we could do to help him save telegraph his mother, asking that she visit. She couldn't stay very long, but promised that someone else would come as soon as it could be arranged.' She smiled brightly at them. 'And now you are here and very soon, I feel sure, the young man will turn the corner to recovery.'

After Nell had asked and received permission to come back later armed with the lemonade the patient craved, the two women left the hospital, but as soon as they were back on Stanley Road Mrs Hughes burst into floods of tears, making a great deal of noise and causing folk to stare. Since she seemed unable to stem the flow, Nell steered her into the nearest café, ordered tea and buns for two, and asked her, somewhat impatiently, just what was the matter. 'I know Bryn's ill, but crying isn't going to help him,' she said, as gently as she could. 'When we go back to the ward this evening I shall take a fan with me as well as a large bottle of lemonade, and sit there fanning his poor hot face and talking quietly of the good times we've known. Perhaps that will help.'

Mrs Hughes sniffed and nodded, then began to cry

again, though more quietly this time, letting the tears form in her eyes and trickle down her cheeks without the wailing which had accompanied her first transports of misery.

Nell waited until the tea and buns had been delivered, then poured two cups and pushed one across to her companion. 'Drink that and tell me what's wrong,' she said. 'Remember, Bryn's alive, and that's what matters most.'

'Yes . . . but it's all my fault, all my fault,' Mrs Hughes said, folding her hands round the cup but not attempting to drink the tea. 'I kept saying I wanted to stay here longer, so we could go to the theatre and see the museums and that. I never give our Bryn bein' poorly a thought, 'cos I were sure he'd come up smilin', like what he always does. I brung it on him, that's what I done, wi' me talk of enjoying a visit to a big city . . . oh, Nell, a wicked old woman I am!'

'Well, you can make up for your wickedness, if you want to call it that, by spending every spare moment by Bryn's bed until he's better,' Nell said. 'We'll walk down the road until we find a shop that sells books, and I'll buy one or two and we can take it in turns to read to him. Nothing too exciting, just quiet country tales, I think.'

Mrs Hughes gulped, took a drink of tea, and shook her head. 'I can't read English and I don't suppose they'll have books writ in God's own language,' she said sadly. She brightened. 'I could tell him Bible stories, though – the Prodigal Son what was cast off by his wicked brothers and Samson pulling down the pillars, and the dogs eating the unrighteous when the wall of Jericho came tumblin' down . . .'

Nell bit back the words *Oh yes, just the sort of thing to cheer up an invalid*, and said they would have to see how Bryn went on. 'Once he comes out of the fever he'll probably want to read for himself,' she said tactfully. 'In fact, when I leave he could read to you whilst you sit by his bed and knit, or sew, or just hold his hand.'

Mrs Hughes, however, looked thoroughly alarmed by this suggestion. 'But where would you be?' she quavered. 'I thought it would be you sittin' by his bed. I'm sure he'd sooner have a pretty young girl beside him than his old nain!'

'I've got to go back; I promised Auntie Kath,' Nell said at once. 'You'll be all right. You like the city, you've been saying so ever since we arrived.'

'I like it when you're wi' me to keep me safe; I wouldn't like it at all by meself,' the old woman insisted. 'And it's you, cariad, what our Bryn wants, not me. Say you'll stay. Promise me you won't leave my poor boy!'

'I'm not promising anyone anything,' Nell said, trying to sound both determined and kind, not an easy combination. 'Remember, he's your favourite grandson. Surely you can stay with him until he's well enough to go home? You really can't expect me to abandon Auntie Kath when she needs me so badly!'

Despite Nell's hopes, it was a full week before Bryn came out of the fever and became rational once more, though at first he was peevish, demanding her constant presence, being off-hand to the point of rudeness with his grandmother, and telling the staff he wanted a private room so that he and his girl might be alone.

Nell had to speak sternly to him – which reduced him to tears – but in the end her firmness paid off. 'It's not your friend speaking, it's the weakness, as well as the blow to his masculine pride when you refused to drop into his arms,' Sister told Nell. 'Give him another day or so and he'll begin to cheer up.'

She was right. After they had been two and a half weeks in the city, Bryn actually came down the ward to meet them, grinning, and catching first his grand-mother and then Nell in an exuberant hug. 'Where's me kecks?' he said in a mock Liverpudlian accent, releasing Nell with one last squeeze. 'Sister says I can dress tomorrow, though the cast on my arm means I'll not get into a shirt for a while.'

'We brought your stuff when we first arrived, but the staff took the clothing away,' Nell said. 'Ask them. If it's all right for you to dress, they'll doubtless hand it over.'

She and Mrs Hughes had been taking it in turns to stay with Bryn, though he made no secret of the fact that he would have preferred to have Nell's undivided attention at all times. However, she did not intend to let Bryn monopolise her and told him severely that since she was in the city of her birth she must visit her many relatives, for once they knew she was back in Liverpool everyone would want to see her, from the oldest to the youngest. Furthermore, she needed time away from Bryn and the hospital, and knew it would do Bryn good to be with his nain for a bit, chattering away in Welsh.

This afternoon it was Nell's turn to spend time with Bryn, so the old lady gave her grandson one last hug and left, saying she would go back to their lodgings. 'Mrs Trelawney and me are going to take a look at this Paddy's Market I've heard so much about,' she said. 'See you later, Nell.'

'Oh, Bryn, you look almost like your old self,' Nell said as the two of them went along to the day room, deserted at this hour, and settled in two comfortable chairs. 'Thank goodness, because I really must go back to Auntie Kath, you know, and I couldn't possibly have left you the way you were when we first arrived in Liverpool.'

'If you leave me now I shall stop getting better and go back to being really ill again, I know I will,' Bryn said at once. 'Please stay until I'm well enough to leave this horrible place, cariad! It's you who've made me well, and if you go—'

'Nonsense,' Nell said briskly. 'It would be just as good if your nain was here. The pair of you chatter away in Welsh as it is, and sometimes you speak so fast that I can't follow what's being said.'

'She's my gran, not my girlfriend,' Bryn said un-answerably. He smiled sweetly at Nell, and then his expression grew crafty. 'I know you want to go back to Ty Hen before I'm well enough to go as well, so if you'll promise me that you'll marry me when I come home . . .'

'Oh, Bryn, don't be so daft,' Nell said, giggling. 'I'm only just sixteen and you're seventeen; much too young for marriage.'

'All right, then promise me we'll get engaged; I've not spent any money whilst I've been cooped up here, so I can afford to buy you a ring,' Bryn said. 'Go on, be kind to me! All the fellows on the good old *Scotia* had girlfriends; some of them were younger than me even. Go on, promise!'

'I won't,' Nell said stoutly. 'Think about it, Bryn. You're the only feller I know at all well on the island, and you know scarcely any girls . . .'

'I do know girls then, lots and lots,' Bryn insisted. 'I've lived in Holyhead all my life, just about, so I know everyone and some of the girls are crackers, pretty as pictures. But I've never met a girl I liked the way I like you. Say you'll be my – my – what's the word? Oh yes, fiancée. And if you change your mind – or I change mine, only I won't – then that will be all right, too.'

'Ask me again when we're back on the island and don't try to blackmail me,' Nell said severely. 'Now settle down, because I want to tell you about my trip to Church Bay. Auntie gave me a day off, so I went the way you said and saw the Swtan—'

'Church Bay? You went there without me?' Bryn looked outraged. 'I thought we'd arranged that I'd take you there when I got leave from my ship.'

Nell opened her mouth to say that he had been presumed drowned, then closed it again. How tactless could one get! Instead, she said: 'Yes, I know, but you weren't around and, as I said, Auntie had given me a day off, so I thought I'd follow that marvellous map you made for me and explore.'

'Oh yes, I forgot the map,' Bryn said, clearly mollified, for he could scarcely claim that she had promised not to go to the Bay without him when he had actually mapped out a path for her. 'Like it, did you? I knew you would. When I get home—'

'Yes, I loved it. And I went to the longhouse you told me about – the Swtan. It's pretty run down now, isn't it? I thought I saw an old man coming out of the door, but Auntie Kath said it was just my imagination and I suppose she might be right.' She had already decided that the old woman she had half glimpsed really was just a figment of her imagination.

'Perhaps it was a ghost,' Bryn said. 'No one lives in the Swtan, for a very good reason: they say the place is haunted by an old woman, a witch, who puts spells on those who treaspass or spy on her.'

'Oh, very funny,' Nell scoffed. 'What a good thing I'm not superstitious.' But even as she spoke, a little chill ran along her spine as she remembered that faint, wavery figure which had hovered in the cottage doorway. Had it been the witch? But she certainly did not mean to let Bryn know he had shaken her. She moistened her lips and spoke steadily. 'And you're certain there isn't anyone living in the longhouse? I was pretty sure I saw an old man . . .'

'I tell you no one lives there. If you really did see someone, then he was probably looking for something to steal,' Bryn said. 'And now let's talk about something more interesting – me!'

Nell laughed, but at that moment the door of the day room opened and a man came in. He was the occupant of the bed next to Bryn's and was known as Curly, which Nell thought was a splendid nickname because he was as bald as a coot. He grinned at the pair of them and sketched a salute. 'Mornin', young lovers! Awright if I has a crafty fag while there's no nurses about?'

Nell said that was all right by them; they would be glad of his company since the conversation was becoming boring, she said, adding rather frostily that she could see no young lovers in the room, only Bryn and herself. At this, Bryn jumped to his feet with an exclamation of annoyance and marched out, saying over his shoulder that he was going to fetch the bag of peppermints his grandmother had left for him and would be back in a trice.

Curly lit up, then raised a brow. 'In a perishin' rage again? That young feller of yours is always either up in the clouds or down in the dumps, though he's a deal better than he was. Before you come he used to have awful nightmares; woke the lot of us up shrieking that the water was comin' in, or the sharks was circlin', or someone was beatin' a drum close agin his lughole. But there's not been a sound out of him since you and the old lady arrived, so we oughter thank you on our bended knees, I reckon.'

Nell smiled. 'That's very kind of you. But I really do think I shall have to go home now that he's so much better. If only I could make him see how unfair he was being . . .'

'Oh, he's not a bad lad,' her companion said laconically. 'Tell him that at his age he's a man, not a perishin' kid, and a man doesn't hang on to a woman against her will. He'll see reason in the end, see if it ain't so.'

And a couple of days later, Curly was proved right. Nell pounced on the young doctor as he finished his ward round and explained that she was needed at home but that Bryn was desperate for her to stay with him until he, too, could leave the hospital. Dr Graham grinned at her and ran a hand through his thatch of dark hair.

'He's exceeded all our expectations,' he admitted. 'His broken shoulder is healing at a far faster rate than is usual, and though it will never be perfect the sight in his right eye is beginning to improve as well. That's what bothers him most, I'm afraid – he tells me that he wanted to train to be a signaller and of course the RNVR insists upon twenty-twenty eyesight in that job. But there are many other openings for a young man such as himself.'

'What will happen to him next?' Nell asked anxiously. 'He was hoping to get a transfer to the Gors Hospital on Anglesey . . .'

The doctor grinned and raised his eyebrows. 'The Gors? Afraid not. He's to have a month in Blackpool at a rehabilitation centre, learning to use his arm again and to get fit generally. Then he'll be sent home and no doubt his company will get in touch with him.' He cocked his head on one side. 'He's very keen on you, young lady, but you mustn't let him use his injuries as blackmail to get his own way. He's young for his age, but war matures us all.'

'I know he's young for his age,' Nell said gloomily, 'but he likes to think that he and I are sweethearts, which is ridiculous. We're both far too young.'

Dr Graham cleared his throat and looked guilty. 'Mrs Graham and I were childhood sweethearts, as it happens. We met at Sunday school when we were both seven and we've neither of us ever looked at another.' He grinned sheepishly at Nell's expression. 'Don't look so horrified. I promise I won't tell your young man.'

Later, when she returned to the house in Easby Street, Nell told Mrs Hughes that she meant to accompany her when she want home in two days' time. 'I know I was a help to Bryn at first, just by talking Welsh to him and interpreting for the nurses and doctors,' she said. 'But now he really doesn't need me, so I'm simply wasting my time hanging about the ward.'

Mrs Trelawney, who was dishing up supper in her large, well-fitted kitchen, nodded. 'I shall miss you, but as they keep sayin', there's a war on and we've all got to do our bit,' she said. 'If you tell your young man that gettin' himself fit again is his war work, like, then he oughter agree to you leavin', and no more fuss and high-strikes.'

Nell laughed. 'I'm sure you're right, and I'll do as you say,' she promised. 'But oh, how I long to be back at Ty Hen!'

Despite her hopes, however, it was another week before she was able to bid goodbye to Mrs Trelawney, pack her haversack, and shake the dust of the city from her heels. This was because she had visited Kingfisher Court, meaning to tell her relatives that she was going back to Anglesey in a couple of days, and had learned that her aunt Lou was coming home on leave. Lou was returning, Auntie Carrie informed her niece, for two reasons. One was to accompany Grandma Ripley on a search for a quiet country lodging. The other was because Nell herself had written to her, saying that she would be in Liverpool for a few days, and would very much like to know just what her mother was doing.

Auntie Lou had come to the house in Easby Street the day after old Mrs Hughes, after a tearful parting with her grandson, had left for home. On hearing the front door knocker, Nell had jumped to her feet, meaning to answer it, but before she could do so the landlady had risen, gestured to her guest to remain seated, and disappeared into the hall. There had been a murmur of voices, then the swift patter of footsteps, and Auntie Lou, looking very smart indeed in her uniform, had come breezing into the room, given her niece a hug and then stepped back, holding Nell by the shoulders and fairly beaming at her.

'Well, well, well! You've growed like a perishin' beanpole,' she had said cheerfully. 'I got your letter and I were due for some leave so I spoke to the wing officer, explained a thing or two, and she give me a whole three days off.' She had grinned across at Mrs Trelawney, taken off her cap and put her kitbag down on the dresser. 'Ooh, a hot cup of tea! That's just the ticket . . . did I say ticket? I don't mind if I do!'

Mrs Trelawney and Nell had chuckled at this

reminder of a popular wireless programme, and then the landlady had got another plate from the sideboard and without a word put a generous helping of meat pie on it, added potatoes and peas, and gestured to a chair. 'Sit down, my dear,' she had said. 'I've always got grub to spare for a member of our services, rationing or no rationing, especially when she's also our Nell's aunt.' She had turned to Nell. 'We introduced ourselves on the doorstep. Now there's plums and custard for afters, and though the custard's made wi' dried milk it's none the worse for that. We'll round the meal off wi' a cuppa, and then the two of you can go into me parlour and have a crack.'

Half an hour later, Nell and her aunt were seated in the parlour with a large mug of tea apiece, and Nell was asking her first question.

'Auntie Lou, is Mam really going to marry that feller? And where is she now? I worried at first, but Auntie Kath told me I should remember that Mam's never been particularly reliable, and that like as not she'll chuck this chap and everything will go back to normal. She also said that by the time the war is over I'd be looking to live away from Mam anyway . . .'

'Aye, she's right there,' Auntie Lou had agreed. She had taken a long drink of her tea, then wiped her mouth with the back of her hand. 'My, I needed that! Your mother is still in Scotland, I believe. I've not had a letter for ages, but Kath is right. Trixie's always been – well, I'd best say a bit of a goer – and she don't change. She's got this feller, half her age he is, under her spell, though, and I reckon he'll do right by her, in the finish. Just you stay with our Kath and bide your time and one of these fine days your mam will turn up on the doorstep full of apologies for not writing and give you a great big hug . . . and you'll forgive her, same as we've always done.'

'Ye-es, but I wish she'd write, just to let me know she's well and happy,' Nell had said. 'And of course I'll stay with Auntie Kath; I'm planning to go back to the island now that I've seen you. You see, the boy I worked with when I first went to Ty Hen . . .'

She had told the story quickly, but at the finish her aunt had looked worried. 'I'm rare glad you're happy, chuck, but I've a favour to ask you. I'm trying to get Grandma Ripley to move away from the court into the country, and she's finally agreed to go, if I can find a pal to go with her. I've kept suggesting various relatives, but she doesn't like any of 'em. And tomorrow's my last full day.'

'How about Great-aunt Vera?' Nell had suggested. 'And have you thought of that little village – I can't remember the name – where Uncle Matt went when he retired from being a coal heaver?'

Her aunt had stared at her, speechless for a moment. Then she had slapped her knee and begun to laugh. 'But Grandma and Auntie Vera hate each other, queen! They spend more time proving each other wrong . . .'

'Yes, but it gives them an interest,' Nell had pointed out. 'If the two of us tell Grandma Ripley that it's Great-aunt Vera and Uncle Matt or nothing . . .'

'Right, we'll give it a go,' her aunt had said. 'And do you know, I wouldn't be surprised if you've hit on the solution! You come to the court at eight tomorrow morning and we'll go straight round and put it to Gran, and Aunt Vera too.'

'I'm on,' Nell had said briefly. 'I shan't have time to go to the hospital and tell Bryn what we're doing, but I dare say he'll just think I'm shopping. You'd better go back to the court, though, Auntie, and get some rest. Tomorrow may be a trifle difficult!'

In fact, however, the day had gone extraordinarily well. Uncle Matt, who lived alone in a tiny house in Parkgate, had said the two old ladies could lodge with him if they agreed to cook his meals as well as their own, and help him keep his house and garden tidy. Grandma Ripley had sniffed but having examined the house minutely said that it would do for now, and Great-aunt Vera, eyeing the neat rows of vegetables in the small back garden, had said she had always wanted to grow things and would be happy to help her nephew with his digging, weeding and planting.

But what had been even more satisfactory than having sorted out the two old ladies had been the fact that Bryn had thought Nell had gone home and far from pining or fretting himself into a fever, as he had threatened, had been found later that evening playing cards in the day room and laughing uproariously over something one of the other men had said.

Nell had taken Auntie Lou to see Bryn and explained where she had been all day, and had then reminded Bryn that she would be leaving Liverpool the next afternoon. 'So I popped in to say goodbye,' she had told him, half expecting a scene. When none followed, she thought Auntie Lou's presence was probably responsible for Bryn's polite, unemotional farewell.

'Your young man's a charmer,' her aunt had said as they left the ward, and raised her eyes heavenward when Nell had almost shouted her reply.

'He's bloody well *not* my young man, Auntie Lou, he's just a perishin' friend, and I'm beginning to think he's not even a friend, because he keeps pestering me to marry him as soon as we're old enough.'

'Sorry, sorry,' Auntie Lou had said, but a smile had lurked. 'You aren't a bit like our Trixie, young woman. She would have taken one look at his blond curls and blue eyes and agreed to every word he said, so it's probably a good thing that you're different. Now, are you sure you'll be all right seeing Gran and Auntie Vera to Uncle Matt's tomorrow before you go? I'd stay to help if I could, but I have to catch the early train or I'll never get back in time. So I'll say goodbye now, queen – and good luck!'

Chapter Eight

Kath was sitting at the kitchen table, frowning over government forms, when she heard the bus grinding slowly along the main road, if you could call the winding lane a main road. For a moment she stopped her work and listened, head cocked. Would it stop at the end of their lane or would it go chug-chugging on to the next village? She had listened for it so often, and it had not stopped . . .

Now, it drew to a halt with a grinding and squeal of brakes and Kath got to her feet and hurried over to the kitchen window, which overlooked the yard. Then she sighed and returned to her place. She was being ridiculous; Nell would have written, or sent a telegram even, had she been able to leave Liverpool, so that someone could meet the train. She would not simply leap aboard it on the off-chance that the bus might be passing, so to speak.

Sighing, she applied her mind to the forms spread out on the table before her. It was evening, and presently she would have to join Eifion at the milking, but she reckoned the cows could wait an extra five minutes whilst she filled in the sheet before her. She did not immediately begin to write but sat, chin in hand, thinking how strange it was that she had missed

Nell's company as much as the work the girl under-took. I was unfair to her when she first came, Kath told herself, thinking of the skinny, wide-eyed kid who hadn't understood farming, or the Welsh tongue, or her aunt's inexplicable dislike. I wasn't fair to her, even after I realised that she was doing her best, and Eifion and Bryn both liked her. I thought she would be like her mother, light-minded, fickle, man-mad, and even when I realised she was nothing of the sort I couldn't let her alone. I nagged and criticised and felt I was punishing Trixie . . . but for what? Being right? And even now, though I've missed her sorely and know very well she would have come back sooner if she could, I'm blaming her for not doing so.

Then there were her letters; in all of them Nell had said how she longed to be back at Ty Hen, how noisy the city was, how grim, what with the blackout, the dimmed headlights of vehicular traffic and the wailing of the sirens whenever enemy aircraft were in the vicinity. But suppose this had been said merely to comfort Kath? In the city there were dozens of picture palaces, theatres, museums, galleries . . . and no doubt there were friends from Nell's schooldays, young men coming off the ships being unloaded in the docks . . .

Kath finished filling in the form before her and got to her feet. Suppose Nell decided to stay in the city, forget her brief sojourn with her aunt? If she never came back, life, Kath knew, would lose a good deal of its savour. If she does come back, Kath told herself, I'll show her I value her, show her that it was my dislike of her mother which made me so crotchety, so difficult.

Satisfied that this was the right way to behave, Kath headed for the back door. It had been another hot day and the sooner she joined Eifion in the shippon the sooner she would be able to relax. She actually had her hand on the latch when it was pushed violently from outside and someone – someone small and skinny, with a good deal of untidy brown hair and a pair of golden hazel eyes – bounded into the room, gave a squeak of delight, and cast herself into Kath's surprised embrace.

'Oh, Auntie, Auntie, Auntie, it's grand to see you so it is,' Nell burbled. 'I'm sorry I couldn't let you know when I was arriving, but it was a last minute thing . . . I was taking Grandma Ripley and Great-aunt Vera to Uncle Matt's and just as we were all set to leave Auntie Vera opened the lid of her cat box to make sure Sir Galahad was all right and out he leapt, and Grandma Ripley swore she wouldn't share a house with anyone stupid enough to open a cat box in the street and Auntie Vera wailed and wept, and I had to stay an extra day – a whole day, Auntie Kath – and he's such a bleedin' ordinary . . . sorry, sorry, but he's a black cat with a white weskit, and of course I brought back the wrong perishin' cat half a dozen times before I bagged the right moggy. So anyway, I settled 'em in and sneaked out of the house in the early hours, caught a bus into the city, gorroff at Pier Head, gorra ferry across to Woodside, climbed aboard a train and here I am . . . oh, it's so good to be home! Are you glad I'm back, Auntie?' She grinned, a look of pure mischief on her small, pointy-chinned face. 'You seemed pretty glad, or was that just surprise?'

'I've missed you,' Kath said gruffly, 'especially evenings and mornings. It's strange, because before you came I looked forward to a nice quiet evening with only myself to please. I knitted or sewed, or read a book . . .' She sniffed and then, unable to prevent herself, gave her niece a huge smile. 'The truth is, I've got kind of used to your chatter. Before, I never noticed how quiet the house was . . . but I dare say now you're back I'll miss my nice quiet evenings, 'cos there's no power on earth which will stop you jabbering away!'

Nell returned the smile with one equally broad. 'I missed you too,' she said. 'Oh, Auntie, I'm so glad to be home!'

In her own, dear, familiar bed that night, Nell thought she had never been happier. Her aunt might pretend that she only missed Nell's company in the evenings, but she had been unable to hide the pleasure which had lit up her eyes whenever they had rested on her niece.

'You're not a bad girl, when all's said and done,' she had said gruffly as they had made their way up the stairs to bed. She had shot a quick, almost guilty glance at Nell as they reached the landing. 'Sometimes we have to lose something before we appreciate it; I hope you get my meaning.'

Nell had been unable to resist grinning. 'I do,' she

had said gravely, however. 'Another way of putting it would be absence makes the heart grow fonder, only I expect you think that's a bit too flowery.'

Aunt Kath had smiled reluctantly as she opened her bedroom door. 'If you want to talk in quotations, then I'll cap yours – all work and no play makes Jack a dull boy – because I mean to even the score. I've put in a request . . . but no point talking about it until I see what comes of it. Goodnight, Nell; sweet dreams.'

Snuggling beneath the covers, Nell wondered just what her aunt had meant by that enigmatic remark. 'I've put in a request . . .' Well, it could mean anything. Only I fancy Auntie's more likely to demand than request, Nell thought. She wrestled with the puzzle for another five minutes, then gave it up and was very soon sound asleep.

A couple of weeks later Nell came down to breakfast stifling a yawn. She was relieved to find that her aunt seemed to be in a good mood this morning; she returned both Nell's greeting and her smile, and this was not always the case. However, she made no comment, but began to cut slices off the loaf for toasting and was shielding her face from the heat of the fire whilst holding out the toasting fork with a round of bread impaled upon it when the back door opened and Eifion came into the room. 'Met Evans the Post as I was coming up the lane,' he said, dropping a number of official-looking envelopes on to the table. 'There's one what you might call ordinary, but mostly they'll be these dratted government forms, I reckon . . .'

'Bore da, Eifion,' Auntie Kath said reprovingly, 'and how are you today?'

'Bore da,' Eifion and Nell chorused, and Nell giggled as she always did because it reminded her of school. 'Good morning, Miss Rachel,' the convent girls used to say, standing up as their teacher entered the room. She had asked Bryn once how the children in the local school greeted their teacher each morning, so she had learned the meaning of the greeting Eifion and her aunt exchanged before any other phrase. Now, of course, she understood practically everything the two older people said, though it took her rather longer to frame the words in what she still regarded as a foreign language.

The toast began to smoke and Nell snatched it hastily off the fork, propped it against the marmalade pot, and impaled the next slice. She had usually toasted six rounds of bread by the time Auntie Kath served the porridge, but today it seemed things were going to be different. Her aunt had snatched up one of the brown envelopes and opened it, and now she smiled with evident pleasure before she spoke. 'Leave the toast, Nell. We'll have to make do with bread this morning, because I've something to say to the pair of you.' Her tone was brisk but not unfriendly, so Nell took her place at the table, spooned honey on to her porridge, and looked expectantly at her aunt.

'What's up?' she said baldly. 'It's the first time you've ever agreed to forgo your slice of toast!'

Her aunt raised her brows. 'Who said I was going to forgo my toast? There's two slices ready and waiting, even if one of 'em's a trifle on the black side,' she said, and there was actually a touch of humour in her tone. 'You two can manage perfectly well with bread, but I've got news to impart which will affect all of us.' She looked from face to face as though expecting one of them to question her, but neither did so. 'Well? Aren't you going to ask me what's it all about?'

Eifion and Nell exchanged a quick glance, then Eifion spoke for both of them. 'You're going to tell us, missus, even if we goes down on our knees and begs you not to, so why should we pretend different?' he said. 'Fire ahead.'

Kath gave a reluctant laugh and Nell thought, not for the first time, how laughter peeled the years from her aunt's rather serious face and turned her into a pretty woman again. 'Well, well, there's telling me you are, Eifion Hughes! And you're right, of course. Did I tell you that I'd applied for a land girl?'

Two heads shook, as her aunt must have known they would, Nell thought. 'No, you never said a word,' she admitted. 'In fact you got cross whenever anyone suggested it.'

Her aunt smiled rather self-consciously. 'Yes, well . . . I'd not really given the matter much thought until you went off to Liverpool, Nell.' She glanced at Eifion. 'But we're none of us getting any younger . . . and as I said, all work and no play makes Jack a dull boy.' She grimaced. 'Anyway, I applied for the forms and I've been filling them in whenever I had a spare moment. I sent the whole lot off a few weeks back, and today I've had a letter from the Min. of Ag. telling me that we've been allotted one – a land girl, I mean.

They've given me her name and address and told me to write to her explaining how to reach the farm. Well, I'll write the letter and put it in an envelope, but I've run out of stamps so I'll have to ask you, Nell, to go into the village later and post it off for me. According to the Min. of Ag. she'll set out, trains permitting, as soon as she is able.' Once more she glanced from face to face. 'Well? Don't say you two chatterboxes have been struck dumb! If so, I'll apply for a land girl twice a week!'

'Us needs time to take it in,' Eifion said slowly. 'Does she speak Welsh, this girl? Does she know the first thing about farming?' He gave a martyred sigh. 'Oh well, young Nell here has managed to pick up enough know-how to be useful, so maybe this new lass will be the same.'

'My goodness, your enthusiasm is amazing,' Auntie Kath said sarcastically. 'I don't suppose she'll speak Welsh, nor know anything about farming.' She turned to Nell. 'And what have you got to say for yourself, young woman?'

'I think it's great news,' Nell said excitedly. 'What's her name? Where does she come from? Gosh, she'll be here the day after tomorrow, if I can get the letter in the post in time. She'll live on the farm, of course?'

Auntie Kath nodded. 'She's called Margaret Smith, and she'll have the bedroom next to yours; that was one reason why we were allotted someone so quickly. Apparently, according to Mr Mason at the post office, a great many farms need extra help but cannot offer the girls accommodation.'

She produced an envelope from her pinafore pocket and handed it to Nell, who read the address aloud.

'Brompton Avenue, Toxteth Park, Liverpool.' Her eyes widened. 'I say, that's an awfully posh area! Do you know how old she is?'

Auntie Kath had turned away and was beginning to fry the bacon, but she glanced across at Nell and shrugged. 'I've no idea, but we shall find out soon enough.' She slid the bacon on to three warmed plates and began to crack eggs into the sizzling frying pan, remarking as she did so that she hoped her listeners knew how lucky they were. 'For most folk, bacon's been rationed since January; you two eat a whole week's ration every morning. And they tell me if people want eggs, they've got to keep hens.' She pointed at the letter Nell had propped against the marmalade pot. 'As I remember, the houses in Brompton Avenue had decent gardens, so likely Miss Smith won't have been short of an egg or two, but I doubt her mam and dad keep pigs.'

Nell smiled. 'Just about every household with a back yard keeps a couple of hens,' she reminded her aunt. 'We didn't bother, though, because Mam didn't want the extra work. Did Gran keep hens when you lived at home, Auntie Kath?'

Immediately she regretted the question, for her aunt's expression changed at once from interest to wariness. 'Not as far as I remember,' she said. 'Eat your breakfast, and as soon as you've finished milking you can take my letter down to the village. And while you're there, you might write out one of Mr Mason's cards to put in his window, asking if anyone has a bicycle for sale.'

Nell, delighted, asked if such a bicycle would be for her, causing her aunt to give her a sharp glance. 'Planning to get your leg loose, are you?' she asked disagreeably. 'I'm not getting a land girl so you can have a holiday, but I don't see why we shouldn't all take a day off, when we aren't extra busy, that is . . . which is when a bike will come in useful.'

'I know that,' Nell cut in, feeling the hot blood rush to her cheeks. 'But if it isn't for me . . .'

'It's for anyone who needs transport,' her aunt said curtly. 'And now get on with your breakfast or you'll miss the midday post.'

As soon as the milking was finished, Nell returned to the farmhouse for her jacket and to tell her aunt that she was off. She was promptly handed a large marketing bag and told to buy porridge oats and several pounds of self-raising flour. 'And don't forget to put the card in the post office window,' her aunt admonished, handing over the housekeeping purse. 'You'd better buy me half a dozen stamps while you're about it.' Nell agreed to do so and was halfway out of the door when her aunt stopped her. 'I didn't like to say this in front of Eifion,' she said quietly, 'but his arthritis is getting worse every day. I told the Min. of Ag. that it wouldn't be long before I'd have to replace him and suggested I'd appreciate having a second land girl by the time next winter comes; and I mean to offer you his job when he goes. Don't say anything to him, but I'm sure you agree with me that he's earned his retirement.'

'I'm surprised he's gone on so long,' Nell said frankly. She smiled quizzically at her aunt. 'As for being your official farmhand, I'd love it. But poor Eifion; the land is his life. I'm glad you'll have to be the one to tell him and not me.'

Her aunt smiled too, but did not reply directly. 'We'll see, when the time comes,' she said vaguely. 'Try not to be late for dinner.'

Nell walked briskly along the lane which led from the farm to the village. They seemed to be having an Indian summer in mid-September, and before she had gone half a mile perspiration was running down her back. Trust Auntie Kath to send me on an errand when it's hot enough to bake bread, she thought ruefully. And coming home would be worse, because the marketing bag would hold not only the housekeeping purse but the big sacks of porridge oats and flour which her aunt needed. If I had a bicycle, I could be there and back in a quarter of the time it takes me to walk, she thought wistfully. Wouldn't it be lovely if someone came forward with one for sale, just as I was pinning my notice to the board in the post office window!

This made her think of the rusty bicycle she had seen leaning against the wall of the Swtan, and the price Auntie Kath had suggested she might offer. Five shillings seemed very little; she was almost sure she had seen a bicycle advertised for sale in the *Liverpool Echo* before she left home priced at ten shillings. But then the seller had had to pay for the advertisement, which she guessed must cost a good deal more than the tuppence Mr Mason charged. However, she already knew that the housekeeping purse would only contain sufficient money to buy the goods her aunt required. No doubt Auntie Kath would part with a larger sum when, and if, someone came forward. Until then, Nell thought, wiping beads of sweat from her forehead, she would have to be content with Shanks's pony.

And that was an odd term when you thought about it: Shanks's pony. It made her think of Feather, for at one time she had suggested that she might learn to ride her, but Auntie Kath had vetoed the idea. 'She's never been broke to riding,' she had explained. 'She'd likely buck you off the moment she felt you on her back. No, that would never do. But I'll teach you to drive the pony and trap when I've a spare moment . . . if I ever have a spare moment, that is.'

At this point in her reflections, Nell reached the post office and joined the queue which had formed. Despite the heat, the village street was busy, with women bustling in and out of the shops and children playing what looked like relievio. Nell knew a good few of the villagers by now and they exchanged greetings. Several people asked after her aunt and one tall, heavily built woman with a booming voice demanded to know whether Mrs Kath Jones intended to join other WI members on an outing to Wrexham, as she usually did. 'We'll be going next Monday, because that's the day they hold the beast market on Eagle's Meadow,' she said persuasively. 'You can come an' all, young 'un, though I take it you're not yet a member of the Women's Institute.'

'No I'm not,' Nell said. 'We've been terribly busy,

like all the other farmers, but I'm sure if she feels she can get away, Auntie Kath will join you. Only I'm afraid Ty Hen couldn't manage without both of us, so . . .'

She stopped short. She had been shuffling slowly up the queue, looking forward to the moment when she actually got inside the post office and out of the direct rays of the midday sun, but now a movement ahead of her caught her attention. Someone was putting a card up in the window, a tall, thin fellow in RAF uniform, who looked vaguely familiar. He wore a forage cap, set at a jaunty angle on his curly black hair, and his skin was deeply tanned. Nell was frowning over his identity when light dawned; it was the fellow she had seen at the Swtan!

'Oh, very well, me love, we'll not expect yourself; but remind Mrs Kath, would you? She can let me know by the milk lorry if she's not coming into the village for the next few days. We've already got a good crowd . . .'

But Nell was no longer attending. She was watching the card going up in the window and wondering whether she should leave her place in the queue and grab the fellow as he came out of the post office, tell him she had recognised him as the watcher at both Llangefni and the Swtan. But if she did that she would have an audience of half the village, and if she missed the post . . . she shuddered at the thought. Auntie Kath had made such a point of getting the letter to the land girl – Margaret Smith – as soon as she possibly could; if Nell had to admit failure she could imagine all too well her aunt's chilly annoyance. And we do seem to be getting on much better, Nell reminded herself. No, I dare not leave the queue, not even to satisfy my almost unbearable curiosity!

So she remained where she was and watched, still not sure whether to draw attention to herself when the chap came to pass her. The queue shuffled forward once more and Nell reached the doorway, passed it, and saw him grin at the postmaster, raise a hand in farewell, and leave. He had not so much as glanced in her direction and, convinced that she had missed her only chance of confronting him, Nell turned eagerly to the woman behind her. It was Mrs Blue-door Jones, so called to distinguish her from the many other Joneses living in the village. She smiled comfortably as her eyes met Nell's.

'Well I never did, it's the little gal from Ty Hen,' she said affably. 'Come to shop for your auntie, ducks? It's pension day, that's why there's such a queue, and by the same token that's why there's queues at most of the other shops. Come in for one thing, most of us does, and end up doin' the week's shop.'

'That's right,' Nell said breathlessly. 'Mrs Blue-door, who was that young man, the one with curly black hair, who just went out? I thought . . . oh, but it's my turn next and I've got to write out a card to put in the window . . . oh dear, I wanted a word wi' that young feller, but me aunt'll have me guts for garters if I don't get her letter in the post double quick!'

She turned to look anxiously after the boy and saw him look round, then join the queue outside the baker's shop. She smiled at Mrs Blue-door. 'It's all right. I reckon he'll be here for a while yet; he's going into the bakery so he's probably doing his mam's messages – shopping, I mean. But who is he? I've not seen him in the village before.'

The plump little woman tried to see where Nell was pointing, but her view was obscured by others in the queue, all a good deal taller than herself. She strained her neck, then gave it up, shaking her head sadly. 'I can't help you, my dear, though I know every mortal soul hereabouts. Never mind; as you say, the young feller will probably be around for a while yet. Now tell me, how's my old friend Mrs Kath?'

By the time Nell had answered Mrs Blue-door and hastily written out the card and bought her stamps, she had almost given up hope of seeing the boy from the Swtan again. She stuck one of the stamps on the letter to the land girl and went outside to post it. Then she turned towards the grocer's shop and just as she did so the boy emerged from the baker's, carrying two large loaves beneath his arm. Nell saw he was heading towards a rusty bicycle and followed him; she could buy porridge oats and flour *after* she had spoken to this elusive young man!

The young man in question was settling the loaves in the large wicker basket on the front of the bicycle. When he had done so, he produced a list from his pocket and was scanning it when Nell addressed him. 'Hey! You're the feller from the Swtan, aren't you?' she asked, grabbing hold of the bicycle by its handlebars in case he simply leapt aboard and pedalled away from her. 'I saw you spying on me when I was there a while back, and I saw you at Llangefni market before Christmas. You were dodging in and out of the stalls, watching everything I did. What's your game, wack? And don't go trying to pretend it weren't you because I know better.'

The young man grinned. 'Wack indeed! I'm a member of the Royal Air Force, young woman, so don't think yourself so mighty important! Why should I want to spy on a scruffy kid? I've better things to do with my time.'

'Huh! That's a loud one,' Nell said. 'I'm not asking *if* it was you; I bleedin' well know it was! You weren't in uniform then, I admit, but for one thing there aren't many fellers with hair that black and for another I've a good memory for faces, so stop fooling around. Why were you spying on me? C'mon, you must have a reason.'

The chap grinned again. 'You say I was spying on you, but I could say you were spying on me. You were dodging round the rocks and gorse patches, looking down at the Swtan longhouse, but you never came down to ask if you could have a drink of water from the well; you just went and helped yourself.'

He had clearly meant to put Nell at a disadvantage, but though she felt warmth rise to her cheeks she continued to stare challengingly at him. 'I didn't want to disturb the dog and perhaps wake whoever lives down there,' she said defensively. 'Besides, it may be your well, but it's not your water. Water belongs to everyone.'

She expected the young man to start arguing over

this remark, but he was staring at her, his dark eyes holding an arrested expression. 'You saw a dog? The old feller who's moved in now doesn't have a dog.'

'I'm pretty sure I saw a dog, a black and white border collie,' Nell said obstinately. 'I saw the old feller for a moment, too. But you're trying to divert my attention, pretend that it's me who was spying and not yourself. Well it won't work, wack. Tell me why you were spying on me or I'll – I'll . . .'

The other laughed. 'All right, all right, I'll come clean,' he said. 'But not in the middle of the village street, if you don't mind. I don't suppose you've got a bike?'

'No, but Auntie Kath is going to buy us one. I've put a notice in the post office window . . . but there you go again, trying to avoid giving a straight answer!' The young man heaved a sigh and started to push the bicycle up the road so Nell released her grip on the handlebars and grabbed the saddle instead. 'I'm coming with you, whether you like it or not,' she said breathlessly.

'I suggested that you should, if you remember,' he said patiently. 'We'll go a little way out of the village while we talk. Then we'll come back and do the rest of our shopping. Will that suit your ladyship?'

Nell was beginning to say that she saw no reason for secrecy when she changed her mind. The chap was quite right; she did not want the entire village knowing her business. They walked on, and after a very few minutes there were no more houses, only gently sloping green fields, rocks and gorse. He leaned the bicycle against a crumbling stone wall, then seated himself on it and gestured to Nell to join him.

'Right,' he said. 'I'll start at the beginning, with the Christmas market at Llangefni. Bryn's my pal, you know. He and I have always been as thick as thieves – that's what his mam used to say – so naturally, when I saw him with a girl, I was intrigued. To the best of my knowledge, Bryn has never so much as glanced at a girl. I reckon he's young for his age because he was ill quite a lot as a child. Anyhow, I wanted to get a good look at you, see what the attraction was.'

His eyes scanned Nell from her shabby old sandals to the top of her head and she felt a blush warm her cheeks. She shifted uncomfortably on the old stone wall. 'Yes, well, you can leave out that side of it,' she said hastily. 'I take it you didn't know Bryn was staying with his taid and helping out at Ty Hen?'

'Of course I knew,' her companion said rather indignantly. 'I told you, we're pals; pals tell one another all sorts. But I'd not seen him for weeks, and though he mentioned that he was moving in with old Eifion he said nothing about no girl.'

'Thank you,' Nell said sarcastically. 'So you were spying on me at the market in order to see what sort of girl your pal was with. But that doesn't explain why you ran away from me at the Swtan.'

'I didn't run away; I hid,' the young man said, grinning sheepishly. 'By the way, my name's Hywel, Hywel Jones. To tell you the truth, I'm not at all sure why I did hide. When I saw you at the well, I meant to come up to you and ask you what you were doing, but I'd

239

promised to take one of our cows across to young Bleddyn Jones's bull. We live in Llanrhyddlad and I knew my uncle had already brought her in from the field, so I had to get a move on because Bleddyn would have brought his bull in as well. So because I didn't have time to talk to you, I thought it would be better if you didn't see me. Understand? By the way, what's your name? I told you mine.'

'I'm Nell Whitaker,' Nell said readily. 'Mrs Jones at Ty Hen is my Auntie Kath, and I'm staying with her and working on the farm. I understand now why you followed me at the market and kept dodging out of sight the other day. I suppose you thought it was an odd coincidence, me turning up at your place when you had connected me, in your mind, with Llangefni.'

Hywel shook his head. 'No, you've got it wrong. I didn't realise that you and Bryn's girl were one and the same person. What I did think was that you might have come down from one of the villages inland to steal a lobster or two. We've a sort of keep-net in one of the pools, which saves us having to take our catch of crabs and lobsters into Valley or Holyhead every day of the week. Provided no really violent weather blows up, and we put stout rubber bands round the lobsters' claws to stop them fighting and ripping each other to bits, the critters are safe enough in the pool until we need 'em.'

Nell began to say huffily that she was no thief, but Hywel shook his head and cut across her. 'Of course you ain't, but someone's been taking the odd lobster now and then, thinking we wouldn't notice, only we count 'em whenever we put them in the pool.'

'Well, whoever's stealing them, it's not me,' Nell said. She looked very hard at her companion. 'And now explain about the sheep dog I saw . . . or perhaps I should say the one I thought I saw.'

Hywel grinned. 'What d'you know about this island, Mam Cymru, Mother of Wales?' he asked. 'I don't know how much Bryn told you, but I know he'd agree with me when I say strange things happen here. D'you believe in magic?'

'No I do not. I'm not a child; I'm sixteen,' Nell informed him frostily. 'What's it got to do with seeing border collies anyway?'

'Maybe nothing, maybe everything,' Hywel said. 'I'm telling you, the whole island is steeped in mystery and – oh, and a sort of magic, and the Swtan, being so old, is steeped in it too. But perhaps I shouldn't call it magic. It's – it's as though the life that went on once is still here, but only certain people are aware of it. Can you be open-minded and not simply scoff if I try to explain about the dog?'

Nell sat very still, with the sun burning the back of her neck and the sweet scent of warm grass coming to her from the nearby meadow. She remembered the stories that the fat old Irishwoman in the train had told her, and the shimmering veil which had seemed to form about the Swtan when the old woman had popped her head out of the doorway. When she thought about it, there was something mysterious about the island, and if she wanted to understand she would have to listen to what Hywel had to say, and take it seriously, what was more. 'Yes, I'll be open-minded, and I promise I won't scoff because I agree the island has a sort of magic,' Nell said at last. 'Fire ahead!'

Hywel looked down at his strong, square hands, clasped about one blue-uniformed knee, and when he spoke it was slowly and thoughtfully. 'I've lived in the village above the bay all my life, first with my parents and then my grandparents. My da and taid were fisher-men. I won't go into details, but my mother died when I was two, and my father was lost at sea when the *Sea Sprite* went down in Dublin Bay with the loss of all hands. There was a terrible storm, the worst storm of the century; the fishermen still talk about it today. I was four then and remember the occasion perfectly.' He looked at Nell from under his thick, black lashes. 'You see, I knew my father had died before the news of the loss of the *Sea Sprite* reached us.'

He met Nell's eyes, clearly expecting her to make some disbelieving remark, but she said nothing, simply returning his look, so he began to speak once more. 'I'd been down on the beach that afternoon, digging for cockles, because Gran had promised me that if I got a whole bucketful we would have them with bread and butter for our tea, and when they were all eaten up I should have a chocolate biscuit. It may not sound much to you—'

'No, it's all right, I understand,' Nell put in quickly. 'I don't suppose you had many sweets, living so far from the village. Go on; what happened next?'

'Well, as I said I was digging for cockles and dropping each one into the old tin bucket with a most satisfying *clunk*. I never noticed the sky clouding over, never thought about the weather at all until the rain began to drive into my face. Then I looked at the sea, which had been blue, with tiny white-crested waves lapping at the shore, and it had turned grey as charcoal and the little waves had become huge, threatening rollers, charging up the beach as though they meant to reach the cliffs and beyond.

'I was scared, then. I grabbed my bucket and made for the little path which winds up the cliff and began to climb. When I reached the top I stopped for a moment and looked out to sea, for the thunder was rolling and the lightning jabbing at the water and dancing along its surface, rough though it was. It was a weird and terrible sight, and though I was still very frightened I couldn't tear myself away. And then, in my mind's eye, I saw my father's trawler suspended above the sea and outlined with a blue light. The *Sprite* wasn't really there, you understand; she was miles away, so I suppose it was what they call an illusion. But even as I stared, I saw a huge wave break over her, saw her turning turtle before my very eyes.'

Nell leaned forward, knowing her mouth was an O of astonishment. She saw how pale he had gone, and knew that whether she believed his story or not he believed it absolutely himself, had no doubt that what he had seen had been the death of the good ship *Sprite*. 'Go on,' she said breathlessly. 'You poor thing, though!

What did your grandparents say when you got back to the village?'

'Not a great deal, because by then I was running a fever and barely managed to tell my story before Nain had me wrapped in blankets and drinking some fever cure she'd invented. And when I kept repeating that the trawler had gone down and my da with it, she soothed me and said I was imagining things and should not talk about it. She stayed with me until I fell asleep, and by the time I woke she knew that I had been speaking the truth. The *Sprite* had indeed foundered, and all her crew were dead.'

'Gosh!' Nell said inadequately. 'What has this got to do with my seeing that dog, though?'

Hywel sighed. 'Might as well not have told you a thing,' he said resignedly. 'The old feller who lives in the Swtan doesn't have a dog. So once again, little unbeliever, your black and white border collie was not actually a living dog, but something – oh, something which happened in the past. That dog was probably owned by someone's great-great-grandfather, and what you saw wasn't real, but a – a sort of picture, left over from the past.' He must have seen her puzzlement, because he took her hand, wagging it up and down to emphasise what he was saying. 'I *told* you it was hard to understand! Some people believe they can see into the future, but you and myself, Miss Doubting Thomas, can see into the past. Oh, not always and not often, just occasionally. Can you understand?'

'Not really,' Nell said honestly. 'But I do believe you, because I take your word for it that there isn't a black and white collie, though I definitely saw one. And I'm pretty sure I caught a glimpse of an old man in working clothes, but when I thought I saw an old woman standing in the doorway . . . well, there was this dazzle for a moment, as though the sun was in my eyes, which it was not, and when it cleared the woman had gone. Have you ever heard of second sight? It sounds a bit like that.'

Hywel leaned back with a contented sigh. 'Thank the good Lord you didn't scoff,' he said devoutly. 'And yes, I suppose it is what they call second sight, but I've always thought of it as a sort of glimpse of something which happened long ago. I told Bryn about seeing the shipwreck years later, but Bryn is very down to earth and just laughed at me, so I've never told him about the other odd things I've seen. What would have been the use? But how I'll crow over him when I tell him you never doubted my story of the shipwreck for one moment!'

Nell stared at her companion. 'Is he back on the island?' she asked. 'I visited him when he was in hospital, but I've heard nothing since. They were sending him to a convalescent place in Blackpool . . .'

'So far as I know he's still on the mainland,' Hywel admitted. 'But we're not as close as we were. The idiot joined the Navy, when he could have done as I did, and got a posting to RAF Valley. We fell out, so now the position of best friend is vacant. Any takers?' Nell snorted but did not answer and Hywel slid off the wall and went over to his bicycle. 'Well, I suppose you don't know me well enough to realise what a splendid offer

I've just made you, so we'd better be getting back to the village. You know how folk in villages talk; I don't want to hear anyone say I'd stole my best pal's girl whilst he was out of the way.'

'You said he wasn't your bezzie any longer. And besides, I'm not anyone's girl,' Nell said indignantly.

Hywel shrugged. 'Oh well, if that's how you feel . . . and now let's talk about something different. Tell me how you like living at Ty Hen.'

'Oh, I love it,' Nell said eagerly. 'I don't miss Liverpool at all – or not the city itself, at any rate. What I miss most is people of my own age.'

'There's a fair number of people your age in Llanfwrog,' Hywel pointed out. 'But I'll grant you the girls are a silly lot. And the girls in my village aren't much better. They say the Swtan's haunted and steer clear of it, though of course they're all very eager to visit the well. When I saw you there, I did wonder if you'd been listening to gossip, but then I realised that if you had, you wouldn't have come calling at midday, with the sun cracking the paving stones the way it was.'

'Why not?' Nell said at once. She was trying to recall the details of the dream she had had beside the well, but they refused to be remembered, so she gave it up and turned to her companion once more. 'What difference does it make if you visit a well at noon or midnight?'

'None, of course,' Hywel said. 'But it's plain you've not been told that the Swtan well has magical powers! It's all nonsense, of course, but the girls believe that if you sleep in the shadow of the well on the night of the full moon, then you'll dream of the man you're going to marry.'

Nell chortled. 'Do they believe it? Aren't girls daft!'

Hywel laughed too. 'I don't know if they believe it or not, but to the best of my knowledge no one has actually put it to the test. Which is a good thing, since the old feller don't want giggling girls queuing up to sleep in the moon's shadow and shrieking the place down if an owl hoots or a fox barks.'

So there really was an old man living in the cottage, Nell thought. Now, however, remembering how frightened she had been at first every time an owl hooted or a fox barked, she cleared her throat. 'But you said earlier that they thought the Swtan was haunted; wouldn't that be enough to put them off?'

'Probably. But in fact it's a common superstition – that you dream of the man you're going to marry if you sleep at a particular spot on the night of the full moon,' Hywel assured her. 'Anglesey is full of such superstitions. One well on the other side of the island has a similar belief attached to it. They say that if you bend over the well on the night of the full moon you will see, appearing over the shoulder of your reflection, either the man you're going to marry or a skull. If you see the skull, it means you'll die unwed.'

Nell shuddered. 'Who would want to know the future so badly that they'd risk a heart attack, which is what I'd have if I saw a perishin' skull peeping over my shoulder?' she asked. 'The old man ought to invent a skeleton of his own; that would keep the girls away.'

By this time they were re-entering the village and Hywel produced his list and scanned it, frowning. 'I've already got the bread,' he said, indicating the large loaves in his bicycle basket. 'We grow most of our own vegetables, but fruit trees don't do well because of the strong winds, so Nain said to buy some apples for a pie and some dried fruit so she can bake bara brith.' He looked at Nell, raising an eyebrow. 'You've been to the post office. What else does Mrs Kath want?'

'Porridge oats and flour,' Nell said briefly. 'Like you, we grow most of our own vegetables, but Auntie Kath wants a packet of mixed spices.' She cast her companion a rueful glance. 'Thank God spices come in little light packets, because the flour and oats are a month's supply and weigh a ton.'

'Tell you what, we'll walk some of the way home together,' Hywel said. 'We'll meet back here in ten minutes; is that okay with you?'

Nell agreed that it was, and was doubly grateful when she re-joined Hywel to find him taking her heavy bag and resting it on the bicycle's carrier. Her attempts to take the bag back were half-hearted, particularly when Hywel pointed out that it was the bicycle and not himself doing all the work. Before they had gone more than a few yards, however, she asked the question uppermost in her mind. 'Are you part of a very large family, Hywel? You said your parents were dead . . .'

Hywel laughed. 'There's only me and Nain in our little house; Taid died two years ago,' he told her. 'Why do you ask?'

248

'Well, you've bought an awful lot of bread for two people,' Nell said, indicating the loaves. 'Most islanders bake their own bread; my aunt Kath certainly does. That's why she wants such quantities of flour.'

Hywel grinned. 'I shall have to call you Miss Sherlock Holmes,' he said mockingly. 'But you're right, of course; Nain bakes her own bread.' He jerked a thumb at the basket. 'These are for the old feller – Toddy, we call him – who moved into the Swtan a couple of months ago. He's pretty self-sufficient, but when I come into the village I do his shopping. As a rule, he bakes soda bread, because that doesn't need yeast, or proving, but it's a treat for him to have proper bread from time to time.'

'I see,' Nell said slowly. 'So who is this Toddy? And where does he get the money from to buy real bread?'

Hywel grinned. 'He has a pension from the last war, I believe, and sells fish when he's had a good catch, and crabs and lobsters, of course. That's about all I know, because he keeps himself to himself. He doesn't encourage visitors; he wouldn't be rude, but I believe if he sees someone approaching he simply shuts himself into the longhouse or makes off either down to the beach or over the hills. A shy sort of feller is Toddy.'

'Does he know the Swtan belongs to Auntie Kath?' Nell asked rather breathlessly. She was having to hurry to keep up with Hywel's longer legs. 'I'm sure she doesn't grudge him the use of it, but I suppose he really should be paying her rent of some sort.'

Hywel shrugged. 'Of course he knows your aunt

owns it,' he said. 'If she wants rent from him, I'm sure she only has to say.' He gave Nell a challenging look, his dark eyes, which had been warm and friendly, suddenly cool. 'From what I've heard, your aunt does pretty well without having to take money from someone who has scarcely any. And besides, if she wants rent, then she'd have to make good the thatch and do all the repairs that Toddy hasn't yet tackled.'

Nell felt the colour flame in her cheeks. 'I'm sorry, I spoke without thinking,' she said stiffly. 'I'm sure my aunt would say old Toddy could have it and welcome. Bryn told me before Christmas that even the mention of the Swtan makes her cross, but we don't know why.'

By this time they were in the lane which led to Ty Hen. Hywel smiled at her and reached out a hand to pat her flushed cheek. 'It's all right, I'm sure you won't tell on the old feller,' he said. 'I know your aunt, of course, but she's another one who keeps herself to herself, and she has the reputation of being a hard case. I remember when I was a lad and she first came into Ty Hen, folk didn't want to work for her, but it seems she really looked after her employees and managed to win almost everyone over. Now she's highly regarded, even though they say she's sharp-tongued and stands no nonsense from anyone.'

'She is rather sharp-tongued,' Nell admitted. 'But she's extremely kind, you know. None of her workers pay rent for their cottages, not even when they retire, and she pays a higher hourly rate than anyone else on the island. Well, you should know that, since you're such big friends with Bryn. Eifion – his taid, I mean –

wouldn't work for anyone else and says it's worth being ordered about by a woman when she's as generous and knowledgeable as my aunt.'

'Yes, I've heard my taid on the subject,' Hywel admitted. He put Nell's shopping carefully on the ground and remounted his bicycle. 'Nice to have met you, young Nell. See you again sometime.'

'TTFN,' Nell said. 'And thanks for your help, Hywel.'

Hywel cycled slowly along the winding lane which would take him, eventually, back to his village above Church Bay. Once there, he would share his grandmother's midday meal and then catch the local bus back to his airfield.

Right now, however, he had other things on his mind. That girl! Isn't it just my luck, he thought morosely, that the only lass I've ever taken a real shine to happens to be my old pal's girl. And I can't take advantage of the fact that he's still at that convalescent home in Blackpool, because that would be a dirty trick. So all I can do is wait for Bryn to return and then see how things go.

He had seen Nell first at the Christmas market, and had been intrigued by her elfin features and the mass of curling, chestnut-brown hair which she kept pushing impatiently back from her face. Also, of course, he had been struck by the fact that Bryn, who had never taken any interest in girls, seemed interested in this one. But when he mentioned her to Bryn – who was she, where did she come from, any chance of an introduction –

he had been left in no doubt that Bryn considered Nell his property. Naturally he had backed off, but once Bryn was home and back on board a ship wouldn't it be fair enough to offer to take the girl about when his pal was not in port, and thus get to know her better?

Cycling slowly along the summer lane, he thought how odd it was that out of all the many girls he knew this particular one had appealed so strongly to him. He had heard of love at first sight and never believed in it, did not believe in it still, but nevertheless even the thought of her sent a tingle along his spine. He visualised her small, elfin face, the way she compressed her lips when she was thinking, even the wrinkling of her straight little nose with its band of golden freckles when she disapproved of something he had said, and knew he would contrive to see her again as soon as he possibly could, Bryn or no Bryn.

The thought brought him up short as he realised that Bryn had one big advantage over himself. He had been at Dunkirk, was actually aboard the *Scotia* when she went down and had been romantically rescued, whereas Hywel, an aero engine mechanic, had had a far less dramatic and exciting war. On the other hand, he had what he considered a glamorous uniform, and was a good two years older than Bryn. He believed girls liked an experienced feller . . . he hoped they did, at any rate.

But it's early days yet, Hywel told himself. He might meet another girl tomorrow, a prettier girl . . . only it wasn't only her looks which had appealed to him, he was sure. She was . . . oh, she was a darling! He had not asked her age but guessed she was no more than fifteen or sixteen, and he was nearly twenty . . . not that age mattered, or not to him, at any rate.

Hywel bent to his pedals again and had slowed to round a sharp bend when he saw Muffy Evans and Rhodri Jones ahead of him. Hywel speeded up. Might as well have some company on the rest of the way to the village. 'Where have you two been?' he shouted. 'Nain sent me into Llanfwrog to get her rations . . . she's registered with Olly Jones and unless she can catch the bus it's a hell of a walk.'

'We've been to visit Muffy's nain and taid,' Rhodri said. 'Are you going to the dance, come Saturday?'

'Dunno; depends on whether I'm free,' Hywel said. 'I've got to be back on the airfield by six, though, so it's unlikely.' He bent to his pedals once more, easily overtaking the other two. 'Race you to the Cross Foxes,' he shouted.

Chapter Nine

Despite Nell's hopes that the land girl would arrive within a couple of days, it was a further week before they got a telegram saying that Miss Margaret Smith would be arriving at Valley station at around 1200 hours the next day and would be grateful if she could be met.

Remembering her own arrival at Ty Hen, Nell was determined to be especially friendly towards the land girl and had offered to accompany her aunt to the station, though she took it philosophically when her offer was refused. 'With me off half the day, because heaven alone knows what time her train will actually arrive, it 'ud be best if you and Eifion simply got on with the work,' she had said, and though her words might have seemed harsh her tone was quite kindly. 'You'll have plenty of time to get to know the girl over the next few weeks.'

So when her alarm clock rang that Friday morning, Nell bounced out of bed and rushed through her morning ritual of washing and dressing feeling a warm glow of excitement and elation. Bryn would be returning to the island any day now and Nell was looking forward to telling Hywel that his best friend would soon be home once more. Of course she would not see much of Bryn, because the RNVR intended to take him back as soon as he was fit again. No one knew yet whether he would be offered a shore job or would go to sea again, but Nell thought it would be grand to have Margaret Smith's company in her leisure activities as well as sharing the farm work. After all, the girl would have little choice but to go about with Nell, since she was unlikely to strike up a friendship with old Eifion.

Nell smiled to herself at the thought, for only the previous day Eifion had told her that he had never yet seen a 'talkie' at any of the cinemas in Llangefni or Holyhead, and did not intend to do so now. 'I don't see as how Charlie Chaplin or Buster Keaton can be any funnier talkin' than they are silent,' he had told her. 'Anyhow, them talkies won't last.' He had sniffed disparagingly. 'Why, they'll be talkin' about fillums in colour next!'

So now Nell hurried down the stairs and burst into the kitchen. The earliest Margaret Smith's train could arrive at Valley was around lunchtime, so Auntie Kath was placidly getting breakfast and Nell, sighing impatiently, flew across the room to collect the loaf, thinking how nice it would be to have four of them round the table once again. Discussing farming matters was all very well, but when Bryn had been with them the talk had ranged over a great many subjects: the news of the day, the doings of local people, the comings and goings in the port of Holyhead. Now they discussed sheep shearing, the dairy herd and even the new-fangled milking machines which were used in large farms on the mainland, but they did not often discuss current events because Eifion had young relatives in all the services and, though he would have denied it emphatically, both Kath and Nell were aware that he worried about them constantly. One of them, Gareth, was in the air force and stationed in North Africa, whilst another was a corporal with the British army in India, and several of his lads, as Eifion called them, were in either the Royal or the Wavy Navy. Eifion was proud of them all, but Nell knew he appreciated her aunt's efforts to cause him as little anxiety as possible; accordingly, the two women only discussed the war when Eifion was not around.

Nell began her daily task of slicing the loaf and making toast, and as she did so she glanced out of the window and saw that the fine day was changing; clouds were racing across the blue sky and her aunt, following her niece's gaze, gave a grunt of satisfaction. 'It looks like rain, which we could really do with,' she said. 'Of course we've needed the sun to ripen the grain, but we need the rain too. I was just telling myself we'd soon have to start feeding hay to the cattle and horses, but if we have a good soak it may not be necessary for several weeks yet.'

Nell was about to remind her aunt that in the next week or so they would be cutting their own corn and helping others with their crops, so rain would not be welcome, when the back door opened and Eifion came in, a sack draped over his head and shoulders. He hung the sack on the back of the door and approached the table, rubbing his hands. 'Nice spot of rain,' he said. 'My garden could do with it. The winter cabbage don't seem bothered by the drought, but the runners is lookin' droopy.' He sat himself down in his usual place as he spoke, and grinned at Nell as she piled the toast up beside the marmalade pot. 'What we want now is two full days and nights of steady rain, not hard enough to knock down the corn, but wet enough to nourish the root crops,' he remarked as Kath put a filled bowl of porridge before him. 'Thanks, missus. You'll be off soon, I dare say, seeing as you'll be picking up our new worker.' He tutted and smiled slyly at Nell. 'First you goes off, then the missus disappears for half the mornin' . . .'

Nell finished the last slice of toast, sat down in her chair and pulled the bowl of porridge towards her. 'Shove the honey this way, please, Eifion.'

Eifion did so and the three of them ate their breakfast and drank their tea almost in silence, though Nell noticed that they were all keeping an eye on the weather. As soon as the last piece of toast and marmalade had disappeared, she jumped to her feet and began to clear the table, causing her aunt's eyebrows to shoot up and Eifion to give a throaty chuckle. 'What's your hurry, cariad?' the old man asked. 'Goin' off somewhere when the milkin's done, are you?' He got to his feet and shuffled to the back door. 'I guessed as much.'

Nell felt the colour steal into her cheeks and reflected that Eifion was no fool, though on this occasion he had not precisely hit the nail on the head. She grinned at him sheepishly. 'Well I did think, if we finished the yard work early, I might be able to go to the station with Auntie. I could do the rest of my chores when we came back – feeding the pigs and poultry and so on.'

Eifion laughed and closed the back door behind him and Auntie Kath laughed too, but shook her head. 'Good try, Nell; but I'm afraid it really won't do,' she said. 'Once Eifion goes home, which he'll likely want to do early if the rain persists, then the farmhouse will be empty. That wouldn't matter in the usual way – you and I have both gone off to Llangefni or Holyhead occasionally, and left the house unoccupied – but today I want you to get a meal ready. The girl will want something to eat and drink when she arrives after a long, hot train journey.'

Nell pulled a face. Going over to the sink, she began to wash up. 'You didn't do that for me. I arrived after a long train journey, freezing cold and starving, and did you offer me a delicious hot meal? So far as I recall all I got was a cup of tea, and I had to make that myself!'

Auntie Kath laughed. 'Oh well, you're a relative; this girl's a stranger. But I suppose, if you're set on it, I could prepare something cold and leave it on the table, so we could eat as soon as we got back.'

Nell laughed too, but shook her head. 'All right, all right, I know my duties as a relative, and that includes making supper, or lunch, or whatever. What'll it be? I can scrub potatoes, pod peas, peel apples . . .'

'All right, you don't have to labour the point,' Auntie Kath said, grinning, and Nell reflected how delightful the older woman could be when she was in the right mood. It was a pity this happened so seldom, but now she came to think of it, Auntie Kath was a good deal happier these days than she had been when Nell had first moved in. Lucky Margaret Smith! Perhaps her aunt was just putting on an act for a new employee, but if so it wasn't like her. No, Auntie Kath was nothing if not straightforward. Perhaps in future life would be easier for everyone at Ty Hen.

But her aunt was looking at her enquiringly and Nell spoke hastily. 'Sorry, Auntie; I'll make the meal so long as you don't expect any fancy stuff. What do you suggest?'

Auntie Kath picked up a teacloth and began to dry the crocks her niece had just washed. 'I made a hunter's pie last night. It's in the meat safe in the pantry, so if you dig up a root of potatoes and pull a lettuce and some radishes – oh, and there are some tomatoes in the cold frame – that'll do nicely. Then you can employ your cooking genius by stewing some plums and making custard.'

'Ooh, I could make a plum cobbler; I'm good at them,' Nell said confidently. 'They're only scone mix made a bit thicker and balanced on top of the fruit.' She fished the cutlery out of the hot water, plonked it on the drainer, dried her water-wrinkled hands and headed for the back door. 'Milking now!' she shouted over her shoulder. 'See you for elevenses, Auntie!'

Out in the shippon, Eifion already had his head buried in the warm, fudge-coloured flank of Nell's favourite cow, but she picked up her milking stool and galvanised pail and moved along to the next stall. Pansy greeted her with a soft moo and Nell petted her before beginning to milk. She liked the fact that all her aunt's cows were well treated, for both Aunt Kath and Eifion talked to the animals as they were moved from one pasture to the next, praising them fervently when the milk yield was only average and even more extravagantly when it was good.

'Which it almost always is, if you gain the cow's trust,' her aunt had impressed upon Nell in the early days. 'A cow which is afraid of its milker tightens its bag and never really gives of its best. Remember that when you're dealing with my small dairy herd, if you please.'

Nell had remembered, and was glad when her aunt had said firmly that she would never bring a milking machine on to her property, far less allow any of her workers to use one on her animals. When they had been discussing modern farming methods Bryn had said that it was all very well, but progress was progress and though each cow's individual yield might be smaller if she were milked mechanically it would also be done in half the time. But he had not said this in her aunt's presence, only privately, to Nell, when they were mucking out. 'And anyway, it wouldn't be worth the cost of the machines for a small herd,' he had said. 'Mrs J keeps eight cows, four in calf and four in milk, and she only needs the produce from one or two of 'em for her own butter and milk, the rest she can sell.' He had grinned conspiratorially at Nell. 'I was just a kid when I first heard folk talking about your aunt and saying she'd never make a success of Ty Hen. She was English, and though she spoke Welsh pretty good by the time Owain cocked up his heels, everyone knew she was a city girl and green as grass; it was plain as the nose on your face, they said confidently, that she'd be cheated right, left and centre. But was she?' He had chuckled, his eyes sparkling. 'No she was not – quite the opposite. It was soon pretty plain that Owain had taught her well and in fact she drove an even harder bargain than he had done when it was necessary. Within two years she had the farmhands firmly on her side; she raised their wages and kept their cottages in good repair, but that wasn't the only reason. They respected her, and if she needed extra help at haymaking or harvest she either joined with other farmers or employed relatives of her own workers – kids, cousins, aunts and uncles – and of course that meant money in their pockets. Oh aye, she knew what she was doing, Mrs J.'

'It's been a real success story. But that reminds me – what happened to those cottages?' Nell had asked curiously. 'I know Eifion and your gran – I mean nain – live in one, but there's another, isn't there? Who lives in that?'

'That's right. The other one is occupied by old Mrs Dibble Davies, whose sons worked for Mrs J until they were called up,' Bryn said. He had grinned at Nell. 'I don't believe old Ma Dibble pays rent, any more than my taid does, so you can see why your aunt is well thought of locally.'

Now Nell chatted to Pansy as she milked, and

thought about Bryn and smiled with pleasure; she wished – how she wished – that he were here.

And when the land girl arrives she'll be another friend – if I'm lucky that is – Nell told herself, moving along to the next cow. I would have liked to go with Auntie to the station, but actually her going off at midday will be an ideal opportunity for a quick visit to the attic. Since the coming of the long light evenings Nell's interest in its treasures had revived, and she had been changing her books at regular intervals for ages, reading them in her room after her aunt had retired to bed. She smiled to herself, sitting down on her stool and beginning to milk Heather, murmuring soothingly all the while, for Heather was a tail-swisher when she was impatient to get out of the shippon and back to whatever pasture the cows had left.

By the time the milking was finished the rain had ceased. Nell and Eifion put the milk through the cooler and then into the big churns, setting aside some for Auntie Kath to make into butter. After that Nell mixed the pigswill, a messy but delightful job, and fed the two large sows, both with a dozen candy pink babies tugging at their teats. Not that they tugged for long once the swill was in the troughs; all the sows' maternal feelings went to the wall when it was a choice between suckling their young and feeding their own bellies, Nell thought with a grin, seeing piglets scattered ruthlessly as their mothers surged to their feet and charged across to the troughs. Nevertheless she leaned over the sty and scratched both pigs behind their large and flapping ears before returning to the kitchen to make up the poultry meal to feed the hens. Auntie Kath had already collected the eggs and gone out to the pond to feed the dozen geese who lived there with the gander, terrorising anyone who ventured too near.

Eifion had gone off to check on the sheep and Nell followed him, knowing how foolish sheep can be. He had told her how they would push their way through the thin part of the hedge and then try to get back a different way, tearing their long fleeces in winter and spring and sometimes doing themselves a far worse injury when they were shorn. On this occasion, however, all was well and the two returned to the kitchen just as Auntie Kath put mugs of tea on the big table beside a plate of buttered scones.

'All done?' she asked briskly. 'Then get the grub down you. The ministry vet is coming tomorrow to check the cows and heifers for TB, so we'll want to get all our yard work done early.'

'We'll have extra help tomorrow, though,' Nell said smugly. 'Has anyone answered our advert for a bicycle, Auntie?'

'Not so far as I know; and as for extra help, I don't suppose the land girl will be much use at first. I thought I'd show her round the place, explain about feeding and so on, then get her to do simple jobs for a day or so. I'll give you two a hand when I can, but if I supervise her for a couple of days we'll have a better idea of where she fits into the scheme of things.'

'I wish a bicycle would fit in,' Nell said longingly as Eifion left the kitchen. Ever since her trip to the Swtan she had wanted to go there again, to learn to swim in that crystal clear sea, to discover for herself what the longhouse was like inside as well as without. 'Will you have a chance to pop into the post office when you've got the land girl in the pony trap, Auntie?'

'You make it sound as though I'm going to put her between the shafts,' Auntie Kath said, smirking. 'But I might make time, I suppose.' She reached her coat down from its hook and slipped into it, then turned back to her niece. 'Get Feather tacked up and bring her round to the door, there's a good girl. You can start making that plum cobbler as soon as I leave.'

'Right,' Nell said briskly. She grinned wickedly at her aunt. 'Don't forget Margaret comes from a very posh area of Liverpool; remember to curtsy when she gets down from the train.'

Auntie Kath snorted, Nell laughed, and the back door banged as Nell hurried over to the stable. When she got there she found that Eifion had already tacked Feather up, so between them they backed the pony between the shafts and then Nell led her over to the door where her aunt was waiting.

'Don't forget to curtsy,' she called as the equipage moved off, and laughed as her aunt made a rude gesture. The older woman was becoming almost human, she thought.

Returning to the kitchen, she prepared the salad and made the plum cobbler. When it was cooked to a golden brown, she stood it on the windowsill to cool, laid the table for four and examined her handiwork. She thought that a few flowers would give the table a festive touch and hurried outside to the vegetable patch, which was divided from the rest of the garden by a thick hedge of Mrs Simkin's pinks. She picked a generous handful, then chose a pretty green glass vase and put the arrangement in the middle of the kitchen table.

Satisfied that she'd done all she could, Nell headed for the stairs, glancing at her wristwatch as she went. The train was supposed to get in at noon; if it really did arrive on time, then Feather could come trotting into the yard in another fifteen minutes or so. But when did a train ever get in on time whilst the excuse that there's a war on could be made, Nell told herself. Still, I'd better get a move on.

She raced up the stairs, paused on the first landing to nip into her room to fetch the books she had finished reading, then climbed quickly up to the attic. It was hot up there and as soon as she had scrambled out on to the dusty boards she went over to the sash window and pushed it up, letting in deliciously cool air. Then she approached the nearest pile of books, smiling to herself as she returned the two she had carried upstairs and selected two more for later perusal. She loved the feeling that she had her own private library in the attic and could change her books without all the fuss and botheration of tickets, dates in and out and other people snatching the book she wanted whilst she was still hesitating over which title to choose.

Having made her selection, she put them down by the trapdoor, went to the window – the one over-looking the approach to the farm – and checked that the lane was empty, then returned to find the kaleidoscope. She had not had a chance to examine the toy since her first visit to the attic because on previous occasions her aunt had never been sufficiently far away for Nell to take her time. She had simply climbed the stair, changed her books and descended rapidly. But now, with Auntie Kath in Valley, she did not need to hurry.

She took the kaleidoscope over to the horsehair sofa, sat down upon it, clapped it to her eye and trained it on the window. Then she began, with great care, to turn the lens, counting each complete revolution as she did so. For the first four, she saw only brilliant colours and different patterns, but on the fifth turn the photograph appeared and this time she was able to confirm that the young man in the picture was definitely not the young man in the photograph which her aunt had removed from its customary place on the mantelpiece. Nell frowned thoughtfully. Oh, how I wish I could take the kaleidoscope down to the kitchen and ask Auntie Kath to explain about the photograph. But for the time being it's impossible—

Nell jumped to her feet, a hand flying to her heart, as the hush was broken by the rhythmic tapping of what sounded like hooves. Unless Eifion had seen fit to move Hal, and it was the big carthorse she could hear clicking across the cobbles, it must be Feather returning! She shot across to the open window and peered down, just in time to see Feather's rump disappearing into the farmyard below. She gave a gasp of horror and withdrew from the window, closing it carefully, anxious not to draw attention to her presence.

Heart still thumping, she hurried down to her own room and threw the books on to her bed, then had to return to put them under her pillow, since she supposed it was quite possible that her aunt might take the land girl on a tour of the house, as she had done with Nell herself.

Trying to stay calm, though her heart was still leaping about all over the place, she left her bedroom, closing the door quite loudly behind her – I was in my room, changing my blouse . . . no, that wouldn't do . . . putting away some washing . . . hell and damnation, *what* washing! . . . I was having a rest on my bed . . .

For heaven's sake, Helen Mary Whitaker, get a hold of yourself, Nell commanded as she left her room and began to descend the stairs two at a time. Auntie Kath will be too busy chatting to the land girl to wonder what you've been up to, unless you give yourself away by rabbiting on. She hurled open the kitchen door and entered the room breathlessly, still trying to think up an excuse for obviously coming down the stairs when she should have been in the kitchen, attending to their cold dinner.

The kitchen was empty. Nell blinked, then thanked providence; Auntie Kath must be untacking Feather and rubbing her down, and the land girl must be watching. She grabbed the pan of potatoes which she had put on the back of the range to stay warm and tipped them into a tureen, added a large knob of butter and a sprig of mint, and stood the tureen on the table next to the pie. Then, her heart now beating at its normal rate, she crossed the kitchen and opened the back door just as her aunt and a stranger came towards her.

Nell smiled gaily. 'The train must have been on time – what a miracle!' she said. 'I've just put a knob of butter on the potatoes; they're still nice and hot.' She held out a hand to the stranger, a tall thin girl with wispy dark hair, clad in the land girl's No. 1 uniform, which did not suit her, since it appeared to have been made for someone a good deal larger than Margaret Smith. 'I expect my aunt told you all about me. How do you do? Did you have a good journey?'

'It weren't bad, nor I wouldn't call it good,' the girl said in a broad Liverpudlian accent. 'I gorron the train at the crack of bleedin' dawn and had to change two or three times, but at least I gorra seat as soon as folk saw me uniform.' She grinned, showing crooked teeth, and held out a thin, knobbly hand, grasping Nell's with unexpected strength. 'How d'you do, Miss – Miss Jones?'

Nell smiled at the other girl. 'My name's Nell Whitaker, but you must call me Nell and I'll call you Margaret,' she said. 'I expect Auntie Kath told you to call her Mrs Jones, but . . .'

'I told Maggie – she wants to be called Maggie – that the pair of you might as well call me Auntie Kath,' her aunt said quickly. She pointed to the bag slung from the girl's shoulder. 'Put that down, my dear, and wash over the sink. Nell here will take you to your room after we've eaten.'

Maggie's eyes brightened as she looked at the food on the table. 'Wharra wizard spread!' she said reverently. 'Better'n they ever give me in Brompton Avenue.'

Nell was too astounded to be tactful. 'But Brompton Avenue is a real smart part of Liverpool,' she said. 'I know rationing is tougher in the city than in the country, but—'

'I think we've got hold of the wrong end of the stick, Nell,' Auntie Kath said apologetically, giving her niece a glare and nudging her quite painfully in the ribs. 'Maggie worked for a lady who lives in Brompton Avenue, only as soon as she was eighteen she had to leave there to do war work.'

Nell turned to stare at the other girl, who was nodding vigorously. 'I's a foundling,' Maggie said matter-of-factly. 'I were a kitchen maid first off, then when all the rest of the staff left to take war work, I were just about everythin'. Truth to tell, I were downright delighted when I got me call-up, 'cos Miz Avery took me ration book and never fed me proper; bread and scrape and weak tea was what she served up for the kitchen staff.' She laughed mirthlessly. 'That were me, once the others were gone. She tried to say I could stay on, said she'd write a letter sayin' she were an invalid and needed me to nurse her, but no way were I doin' that. I didn't fancy the ATS or the WAAF – I'd had enough of being bossed about in the children's home what brought me up – so I went for the Land Army.' She looked down at her dreadful breeches, the wrinkled socks on her pipe-cleaner legs, and the great clumping shoes. 'It's awright, ain't it? Norra uniform really, more like boys' clobber than girls.'

'I – I see,' Nell said rather feebly. 'Well, I must say, you look very – um – very smart, only you won't stay smart for long once you're working on the farm. Auntie had to buy me overalls and boots and that; I suppose she'll have to do the same for you.' She looked at her aunt, who was straight-faced, but with a twinkle in her eye and a twitch at the corner of her mouth. 'You wouldn't want Maggie to dirty her lovely uniform, would you, Auntie?'

'No indeed, but I think you'll find that Maggie won't need any help as regards suitable clothing,' Auntie Kath said placidly, but still with that lurking twinkle. 'She was telling me, as we drove home, that she has overalls, wellington boots and working shirts in her luggage; the uniform she's wearing is for best.'

'I see . . .' Nell was beginning, when a thought struck her and she clapped a hand to her mouth. 'Oh, Auntie, your homemade lemonade! I completely forgot to bring it through, but at least it will still be beautifully cold since it's standing on the slate slab.' She turned to Maggie, who had put down her bag with a sigh of relief. 'You wash first. There's a piece of soap on the draining board and you can dry on the roller towel. Trains are always dirty.'

Maggie went obediently to the sink and, rather to Nell's surprise, washed with great thoroughness. When she had done, Auntie Kath rinsed her own hands and the three of them were taking their places at the table when the back door opened and Eifion hobbled into the room. Auntie Kath introduced him to Maggie, and the old man immediately broke into a torrent of

Welsh. Auntie Kath began to remonstrate, but Maggie cut across her. 'Don't you go tryin' that on me, old feller, 'cos you'll soon find you've got the wrong cat by the ear,' she said severely. 'I reckon that's this 'ere Welsh language I've been told about, but they said at the agency everyone on the island could speak a bit of English, so I reckon you know enough to say how do you do.' She had already taken her place at the table, but jumped to her feet and held out a hand towards the old man. 'How d'you do? I's Maggie Smith; what's your moniker?'

For a moment, Eifion simply stared, but then he began to shake with laughter. 'You're right, missy, I were teasing you, speaking in Welsh. How d'you do? I'm Eifion Hughes an' I do most of the farm work at Ty Hen.' He turned to Auntie Kath and addressed her in Welsh. 'She may look like a scarecrow, but I reckon she's got all her wits about her. I can see we'll have to stick to English until she begins to pick up God's own language.'

Nell gave a muffled snort, but her aunt shook a reproving head. 'What's so funny?' she asked in English. She was cutting large wedges of pie and sliding each wedge on to a blue and white china plate as she spoke.

'I'm sorry if I seemed rude, Auntie,' Nell said in Welsh, 'but I was just thinking that Maggie will have to learn proper English, because I'm sure Eifion won't understand the Scouse dialect.'

Maggie had been trying to follow the conversation, her eyes darting from one to the other, and now she seized on the only word she understood. 'Scouse?' she said. 'If you think I speak Scouse, you should ha' heared me before I went to Miz Avery's. Scarce a day passed but she, or Cook, or the parlour maid were hauling me over the coals for not talkin' proper.' She looked apprehensively from Nell to Kath. 'Honest to God, missus, I'll do me best, but—'

Nell cast an anxious glance at her aunt, but Kath seemed remarkably calm. 'No one will mind about your accent, Maggie, but folks hereabout are very religious and believe it's wrong to take the name of the Lord in vain. So don't go saying honest to God or anything like that.'

'Got you,' Maggie said at once and Nell saw that the eyes in the pasty little face were bright with intelligence. She's no beauty, but she's quick to catch on, Nell told herself as Auntie Kath began to serve out the potatoes. She'll never try to learn Welsh because she won't think it's necessary, but she'll pick up odd words and phrases without even meaning to and before we know it she'll understand most of what we say. She chuckled to herself. We'll have to go carefully; I often think that if Auntie had known how much Welsh I understood in the early days she would never have said half the things she did.

When the meal was over, Maggie washed up, Nell dried and Kath put away. Then Kath announced that she and Eifion were going to check up on the sheep in Six Acre and advised Nell to take Maggie on a tour of the house, to show her her own room and to explain things generally. Nell was happy to comply, though just as her aunt was about to leave the kitchen she had a sudden thought. 'Hang on a minute, Auntie,' she said urgently. 'Did you ask Mr Mason whether there had been any answer to our advertisement?'

Her aunt paused in the doorway. 'Well, in a way,' she said rather guardedly. 'A boy whose father farms a couple of miles from here says they have a bicycle which no one ever rides. It's in very bad condition, but he thinks if he puts work on it and we buy new tyres, brake blocks and so on, it could be usable. He told Mr Mason that if you cared to go over to his house he'd show you the bicycle and you could see for yourself whether you thought it would be possible to make it good.'

'Oh, I'm sure it will be,' Nell said excitedly. She thought of swimming in the calm blue sea, of going fishing in the little boat, of getting to know the inhabitants of the longhouse. If only she had a bicycle, all these things would be possible. 'Did you tell him yes, Auntie? If so, I'll go over as soon as you can spare me for a few hours. If I were to miss church on Sunday . . .'

Kath grinned. 'Oh aye, and risk losing my good name with the locals? Pull the other one, queen.'

Nell laughed. 'No, but honestly, Auntie, that wouldn't happen. People missed church when we were all haymaking, so why shouldn't I do so in order to get a bicycle? If I have one I'll be able to do every-thing twice as quickly!'

Her aunt gnawed her lip, pretending uncertainty, but Nell had seen the flash in her eyes and said triumphantly: 'You'd make use of the bike as well, wouldn't you, Auntie?' She turned to Maggie, who was beginning to smile delightedly. 'And you of course, Maggie. We could ride and tie – that means take turns – and get everywhere ever so much faster. Don't you agree?'

'Aye, tharr I do,' Maggie said. She turned to Kath. 'If I were you, missus, I'd grab the chance wi' both hands 'cos in Liverpool at any rate, bicycles is rarer'n hens' teeth. I tek it you can both ride a bike?'

'Of course,' Nell said, impatiently if untruthfully. She had never ridden a bicycle in her life, but assumed that since half the urchins in Liverpool careered round on ancient machines it must be simply a matter of jumping on and pedalling fast. 'But if you can't, Maggie, I expect I could teach you in a couple of hours.' She turned an appealing face to her aunt. 'If you agree, I'll go over as soon as evening milking is finished and take a look at the bicycle. I expect Maggie would rather stay here and rest after her long journey, but I've had a quieter day than usual and am raring to go, especially if it means we get a bicycle at the end of it.'

'No, not tonight. Remember the boy's going to do what he can to make it good before we take it. You can go after morning milking on Sunday. Maggie and I will do any jobs you've not had time to tackle. I don't want her handling stock for a while, mind, so you'd best feed the poultry and see to the sows and their piglets. You can turn the cows out and I'll prevail upon Eifion to check that we've no distressed sheep, though the lambs are fine, strong little animals, more than most foxes would dream of tackling.'

'Right. Thanks, Auntie,' Nell said, well satisfied. She turned to Maggie. 'Ready to start the grand tour? Then pick up your bag and follow me. We'll do the bedrooms first, so you can dump your things.'

Maggie was a satisfactory person to show round, Nell decided as her companion oohed and aahed over the size and splendour of the bedrooms. She beamed at her own quarters and went at once to the window, pushing back the pretty floral curtains to admire the view. Nell, whose room was opposite Maggie's, remembered her own fears on her first night and warned Maggie that the sounds she would hear once darkness fell were simply owls, foxes and other wild creatures.

'They won't harm you,' she assured the older girl. 'In fact you may never actually see a fox or a badger because they're wary of people. But you'll hear 'em all right.'

'I won't mind now that I know; ta for tellin' me, chuck,' Maggie said comfortably. She glanced at Nell from under her lashes. 'I oughter mention, mebbe, that I can speak Welsh like a native, so I understood every word.'

Nell gasped, a hand flying to her mouth. 'Oh Lor', what must you have thought of us?' she cried, feeling the hot colour flood her cheeks. 'But you never said . . . we just took it for granted . . .'

Maggie giggled. 'Got you!' she said triumphantly. 'A'course I don't speak Welsh; it's all I can do to under-stand English when it's someone posh speakin'. I were havin' you on, gal!'

'I knew you were,' Nell said loftily, then giggled. 'No, I'll be honest. You had me fooled. And we didn't say anything rude, or I don't think we did.' She frowned thoughtfully for a moment, then her brow cleared. 'We were saying that you'd have to learn Welsh, because though Eifion can speak English, it doesn't come naturally.'

Maggie giggled. 'All right, queen, I believe you, thousands wouldn't.' She unstrapped her bag and put the contents lovingly into the chest of drawers, patting each garment in a proprietorial fashion as she lifted it. 'Coo, fancy bein' give a whole load of lovely clothes what ain't really uniform! I knew I were right to go for the Land Army; what's more, the only person who'll boss me about is your aunt, and mebbe the old feller. If I'd gone for the services there'd be a hundred women tellin' me what to do an' I had enough o' that at the home, to say nothin' of Brompton Avenue.'

'Who says I won't boss you about?' Nell said teasingly. 'Why shouldn't I? After all, I've been bossed about myself. It might be fun to boss someone else.'

Her new friend – for already Nell thought of Maggie as a friend – aimed a playful swipe at her head. 'Don't you try it, chuck,' she advised. 'But I reckon it'll be the two of us agin t'others. What d'you say, pal?'

'I say let's shake on it,' Nell said, holding out a hand. 'Hey, we'd better get a move on, if you're to see the rest of the house and the farm before supper.'

The girls did not take long examining the other bedrooms, then they went downstairs again and popped into the parlour, seldom used, and the study, a small room where Kath did the farm accounts and filled in the forms which plopped through the letter box with increasing frequency these days. After that Nell showed Maggie the dining room with its enormous table and stiffly formal chairs, and the dairy, where the milk was processed. Then the two headed for the farmyard.

Maggie was introduced to the pigs, the poultry and the horses, and shown the cattle grazing in their pasture and the sheep scattered on the distant hillside. She looked at the pigs rather apprehensively and screamed when a hen fluttered up to her, obviously hopeful that it was about to be fed. Nell eyed her anxiously. 'Don't be scared of the farm animals, because feeding them and mucking out is one of our main jobs,' she said. 'You'll just have to get accustomed, I suppose, as I did, but I had one big advantage; I wasn't afraid of them.'

'I'll be all right so long as I don't have to touch 'em,' Maggie said, giving a shudder at the mere thought. 'There were a feather duster at Miz Avery's – chicken feathers they was – and I never could abide it. I were supposed to dust the picture rails and the tops of the paintings with it, but I'd sooner use a duster, even if it did mean cartin' a stepladder all round the house.'

Nell stared at her. 'But Maggie, when you applied for the Land Army you must have known you'd be working with animals,' she pointed out. 'My aunt will expect you to learn to milk and to handle the sheep when the time comes for dipping and shearing. Then there's Feather and Hal; when you're tacking them up you have to touch them, and you can't start having hysterics every time they nuzzle you hoping for a titbit.'

Maggie sighed. 'No, I never give animals a thought,' she admitted. 'I imagined I'd be plantin' cabbages, leadin' the horse mebbe when it were ploughin', cuttin' the hay and the corn; stuff like that.'

'That's arable farming,' Nell said wisely, having recently learned the term. 'We do very little arable farming round here; the land's not suitable. My aunt just has the meadow where we grow our hay. In a good year, it's sufficient to feed the stock through the winter; in a bad year Auntie has to buy in, of course. And then there's a couple of fields – big ones – where we grow wheat and barley, and our vegetable garden, which we all work in because it's lovely to have fresh vegetables and salads for most of the summer. In the winter, the whole of the vegetable garden gets put down to root crops, winter cabbage and sprouts.' She grinned at Maggie. 'When you're cutting cabbage and harvesting sprouts on a freezing winter day, with the field inches deep in mud and icicles hanging from every plant, you'll think wistfully of the nice warm stable, or the shippon, where we milk the cows, and you'll realise there's a lot to be said for looking after stock.'

'Stock?' Maggie said obligingly, as Nell had hoped she would, for she was anxious to pass on the knowledge which she had only recently acquired herself.

'Aye, stock. That covers all the animals on the farm: hens, geese, cows, pigs, sheep, the lot. And when a farm goes up for sale, as a good many did during the

Depression, the ploughs and hay rakes and tractors – if the farmer possessed anything so modern – were called "dead stock", which baffled me when I first heard it.' She chuckled. 'I thought they were selling dead cows and sheep. But it was only what I'd have called farm implements.'

'Blimey, I's goin' to have to learn a whole new language, lerralone Welsh,' Maggie said with a touch of bitterness. She brightened. 'But you and me's pals, ain't we? You'll put me on the right track, see I don't mess up, won't you, Nellie?'

Nell, who hated being called Nellie, nevertheless realised that Maggie was merely following the Liverpool habit of nicknaming, and nodded. 'Course I will. Right now I'll take you over to the pond in the home pasture and introduce you to the geese.'

Maggie said nothing, but gave her a suspicious glance before following her meekly out of the farm-yard and over to the sloping meadow with the big, willow-fringed pond at the far end. Nell smiled to herself. The geese, and Gabriel the gander, could be unpleasant enough to people they knew, let alone to strangers, when they could be really frightening. She would warn Maggie, of course, but thought it would do the other girl no harm to see that, compared to the geese, the other animals were downright friendly.

She swung open the gate and ushered Maggie into the sloping pasture. Half a dozen of the geese were grazing on the rich green grass and took no notice of the new arrivals, but Gabriel and three or four of his wives, who were rooting around in the weeds which bordered the water, came charging up, necks stretched, beaks agape, honking a warning. 'Stand your ground and try to look menacing,' Nell advised. She was beginning to wish she had not decided to introduce Maggie to the geese so soon. She grabbed the other girl's arm and said remorsefully: 'Maybe I shouldn't have brought you here yet, but I wanted to show you that there are vicious animals – birds in this case – on every farm and it's as well to keep clear of the nasty ones and appreciate the friendliness and good manners of the nice ones. Don't turn and run, whatever you do; the only time I did that, Gabriel – he's the big white one – pursued me right to the gate, pecking as we went. I was a mass of bruises next day, which was when my aunt told me I must face them out.'

She was remembering her own disgracefully cowardly behaviour as Gabriel came within a foot of them, neck stretched, hissing like a steam train. To her astonishment, however, Maggie neither flinched nor backed away, but actually stepped forward and punched the gander right between his mean little eyes, with enough force to stop him in his tracks. 'That'll teach you, you nasty bugger,' Maggie said, dealing him another blow, which laid him gasping on the grass.

Nell, doubled up with laughter, grabbed Maggie's arm and began to propel her towards the gate. 'Oh, Maggie, you've certainly settled his hash,' she said breathlessly as they went. 'Eifion was saying the other day that geese have pretty good memories, which is why they never attack the person who feeds them. I reckon they'll never forget the person who punches them between the eyes either.'

They reached the gate, tumbled through it and latched it behind them, both now giggling helplessly. 'Don't you go a-tale clattin' on me to your aunt,' Maggie warned, 'or that old goose won't be the only one to gerra punch. Now where's you goin' to take me next?'

Nell looked at Bryn's wristwatch; she always thought of it as his and was glad to think of him every time she looked at its bright little face. 'We'll go into the kitchen and I'll show you how to mix meal and peelings or scraps of vegetable in the swill bucket, for the hens and pigs,' she said. 'D'you know, it's going to be real fun having someone my own age to chat to.'

As they approached the farmhouse once more, Nell was heading for the back door when Maggie caught hold of her arm. 'Hang on a mo, Nellie. When we come back from the station, me an' Auntie Kath, you looked a bit flustered like. Didn't you like the look o' me, or were it somethin' else, somethin' you'd been doin' which you didn't fancy your aunt gettin' to know about?'

Nell blinked; the older girl was not only quick-witted and fun to be with, she was shrewd as well. But Nell did not intend to let Maggie into any secrets until she knew her a lot better, so she frowned thoughtfully before she spoke. 'I hope I know better than to judge by appearances,' she said rather reproachfully. 'Though you weren't at all as I'd imagined you. In my mind's eye I saw you as not very tall and quite plump. We didn't know how old you were, either, and though I realise now that you had to be older than me to be taken on by the Land Army, I'd not thought of that at the time; I think I expected you to be my age, sixteen. Then there was your address. Remember, we'd been told that you lived in Brompton Avenue, which is very posh, so Auntie, Eifion and I thought you'd be . . . well, a bit snooty, looking down on us, sort of. As for my keeping secrets from my aunt, I don't do that; she's the one who keeps secrets —' Nell stopped speaking; it was all she could do to stop her hand flying to her mouth and a horrified gasp escaping from her lips. The very word 'secrets' had reminded her of something she had completely forgotten. When she had rushed across to the attic window and stuck her head out, then hurried to the stair and begun to descend, her only thought had been to lower the trapdoor soundlessly and hide the books she had borrowed before returning to the kitchen.

Now it occurred to her for the first time that she had not bothered to hide the kaleidoscope when she fled the attic, far less return it to its place deep in the old tea chest. If her aunt should take it into her head to go up the narrow wooden stair and push open the trapdoor, the first thing she would see would be the brightly coloured toy cast down on the horse-hair sofa, the old cane-bottomed chair, or indeed on the dusty floor! But it would never do to tell Maggie that she had been up there, nor that Auntie Kath, without precisely forbidding her to do so, had intimated that the attic was no place for her niece. So she was relieved when the back door opened and her aunt's head appeared round it.

'Come along, you two,' she called. 'I've started mixing the meal with buttermilk, but I want Maggie to see how it's done so she can take a turn at it tomorrow.'

The rest of the day passed uneventfully so far as Nell was concerned, though of course everything was new and strange to Maggie. By the time they made their way up the stairs to their bedrooms, Nell could see the signs of fatigue on her companion's face and realised that the day had been an exhausting one for someone unused to country living. She bade Maggie a cheerful goodnight, however, telling her it would not be necessary to set her alarm since she, Nell, would knock on her door at around six o'clock. 'My aunt serves breakfast between half past six and seven, so we start our day's work on a full stomach,' she explained. 'I filled your jug with water for washing earlier in the day, but I hope you managed to bring some soap with you because that's something which doesn't grow on farms, or on trees for that matter.'

Maggie gave a tired little giggle. 'I nicked a bar of Yardley's off of Miz Avery the day I left,' she said proudly. 'If you're short, we could cut it in two and have half each.'

'Gosh, thanks,' Nell said. 'But don't go telling Auntie Kath you nicked it. She's so perishin' upright she'd probably make you take it back!'

Maggie snorted. 'I reckon that mean old cat owed me a deal more than a tablet of rose-scented soap,' she said. 'Do you know she wouldn't pay me for the last week I worked there? She said as how, since I were goin' to desert her, the Land Army ought to pay me. I began to point out that I'd done me work as usual – got her messages, cooked her meals, cleaned that bloody great house – but she just tightened her lips and said she reckoned I'd ate a week's worth of wages or more and then she marched out of the kitchen and slammed the door behind her.'

'What a horrible woman. No wonder you ate everything but your plate at suppertime,' Nell said, laughing, then realised when she saw the stricken expression on the other girl's face that her words had been tactless to say the least. Quickly, she gave Maggie a playful nudge. 'Only joking; we all eat like starving refugees because farm work is so hard.' She opened her bedroom door. 'See you in the morning, Maggie.' The other girl had entered her own bedroom and was about to close the door behind her when Nell said what she had been longing to say all afternoon. 'Oh, by the way, d'you mind calling me Nell, and not Nellie? I've an aunt called Nellie and every time you say it I look over my shoulder expecting to see a big fat old lady with a red face standing behind me.'

'Sorry, Nell. I'll try to remember,' the other girl said cheerfully. 'I hates it when folks call me Margaret; they always called me that in school when I were in trouble. Goodnight.'

'Goodnight, sweet dreams,' Nell called back as she closed her own door. Then she blew out her candle and rolled up the blackout blind, but did not immediately begin to undress. She meant to wait until the whole household slumbered; then she would sneak up to the attic, find the kaleidoscope and push it to the very bottom of the tea chest, so if her aunt decided to visit there would be no sign of her own presence.

However, the day just past had been a tiring one, and despite sitting close to the window in order that the breeze might keep her awake Nell fell asleep, to awake with a jerk in the early hours. For a moment she could not imagine what had woken her nor why she was lying on her bed, fully clothed and with a nasty taste in her mouth. Then she remembered. She had been going to visit the attic, and a glance at her wristwatch told her that it was two in the morning, which must mean that both her aunt and Maggie were fast asleep and would not hear her ascent.

She had taken off her shoes before sitting down on the bed and now she padded across the room and opened the door. She had never before noticed how the hinges creaked, nor how the boards protested as she trod softly across them. She was halfway to the attic stair when a quavering voice addressed her.

'Nell, is that you? Did I wake you? I'm awful sorry I shruck out, but I heard that awful scream from outside and somethin' tapped on me window . . . I'd only just dropped asleep an' before I thought, I'd yelled.'

Nell stared at Maggie's white face, illumined in the light coming through her own open bedroom door. 'So it *was* you,' she said with an attempt at lightness. 'Actually, I'd only just dropped off myself, but I'm sure we'll both go back to sleep pretty quickly. The wind's got up, so it would be the walnut tree branch tapping against your window. The scream was a vixen – don't you remember me telling you about night noises?'

'I do now,' Maggie mumbled. 'I'm awful sorry I woke you. Goodnight again.'

'Night,' Nell said, retreating into her own room and shutting the door firmly behind her. What rotten luck! But at least Maggie had not noticed that Nell was fully dressed. I'll try the attic later, she decided, but she undressed and got into bed because in her heart she knew she would not make the attempt again tonight. Sure enough, the next time she woke it was broad daylight and her alarm clock was tinkling.

For the next three or four days, Nell was too busy to venture up to the attic, but on the Friday following Maggie's arrival they had an exhausting day chasing sheep. One of the old ewes had managed to barge her way through the hedge and naturally the whole flock had followed her. By the time Eifion had come panting back to the farmhouse with the news of the escape, the flock had spread out and it had taken all four of them, as well as Whisky and Fly, to round them up. Consequently, supper was late, and since Friday was always bath night and Auntie Kath refused to go to bed herself stinking of sheep, or to let the girls skip the weekly ritual, it was three very weary females who eventually climbed the stairs to bed.

Nell, exhausted though she was, glanced at her wristwatch. It was ten o'clock; if she could just keep awake for an hour, surely she should be able to visit the attic secretly? Accordingly, she sat on her bed in her nightie and dressing gown, pinching herself and applying a wet flannel to the back of her neck whenever she felt drowsy. At last her little watch showed eleven o'clock and she found herself gently easing up the trapdoor and entering the forbidden room.

But it seemed all her care had been in vain; the kaleidoscope was nowhere to be seen. It wasn't on the dusty floor, nor on the horsehair sofa, nor on the cane-bottomed chair. Nell frowned; had she returned it to the tea chest after all? She did not think so, but she supposed that in her panic she might have done almost anything. She tiptoed across to the box and began to rummage inside, then received a dreadful shock as a voice spoke behind her. 'And what might you be doing, miss? I seem to recall telling you that the attic wasn't safe.'

Nell turned to face the speaker, feeling the colour drain from her cheeks. 'Auntie Kath, you damn near killed me with fright!' she exclaimed. 'What on earth are you doing up here at this time of night?'

'I've just asked you the same question,' her aunt said grimly. She was standing on the stair, her body only visible from the waist up, but now she completed her climb and looked critically around her. 'Well? I'm waiting for an answer, but I suspect I already know what you'll say, if you're going to tell me the truth, that is. You've come for the kaleidoscope.'

Nell looked up at Auntie Kath and was suddenly afraid. In the pale moonlight her aunt's face looked like the face of a stranger. Her eyes were set in deep black hollows and her hair, which usually fell softly round her face, was pulled back into its bedtime plait. She looked formidable, frightening. When Nell spoke at last, she could hear the tremor in her own voice, but was unable to prevent it from shaking. 'Oh dear, I just *knew* you'd catch me out one day,' she said distractedly. 'I came up here when I had the measles, to find myself something to read. There were lots of books, including some on farming; I've been reading them whenever I've had a chance, and then changing them for others. I'm awful sorry, Auntie, but I was so bored and lonely, particularly after Bryn went. That was why I started rummaging through some of the boxes. I was after games, playing cards, anything to keep me occupied—'

'And you found the kaleidoscope,' her aunt said harshly. 'Did you discover that – that it's not just a toy?'

'If you mean did I find the photograph, yes I did,' Nell said after a moment's agonising thought. She knew her aunt had every right to be angry, but dreaded being thought a snooper. 'But even after I'd seen the photograph, I couldn't see why you wanted the attic kept secret, and I still don't see why. After all, what I really wanted was books. If you'd just nipped up with an old sack or something, filled it with books and brought it down to me, I wouldn't have dreamed of coming up here myself.'

'Wouldn't you? Well you *do* surprise me,' her aunt said sarcastically. 'From what I've seen, you're as curious as a cat. Eifion mentioned that you'd asked him where Owain's photograph might be after I took it off the mantelpiece. That was on the day way back in March when I went to Valley to sell . . . good Lord, I've got it now! That must have been the first time you were alone in the house for a couple of hours.' Suddenly and unexpectedly, she turned towards her niece, giving her a rueful grin. 'I suppose you could say it was all my own fault. I told you that the attic floor was rotten and there were rats, so though I never actually forbade you to come up here I suppose I made it pretty plain that I didn't want you ferreting around. Now I come to think of it, anyone with a bit of gumption would have come up, just to see what the attic was really like. But even after I realised you'd been coming up here fairly often—'

'You realised?' Nell squeaked. 'And you never said a word! Why didn't you tell me off, or at least let me know you knew?'

Auntie Kath shrugged. 'I guess it was because I realised you'd found me out in a lie; the attic floor is as sound as a bell and of course there are no rats. On the other hand, there are a great many books. When I think back I'm ashamed of myself; Owain loved his books and would have been thrilled to know that they gave you pleasure.' She turned back towards the trap-door, beckoning her niece to follow. 'But this is neither the time nor the place to discuss such matters. We'll go down to the kitchen and make a pot of tea and I'll tell you all about the kaleidoscope. Do you want to select some books before we leave? And one thing: I'd rather you didn't bring Maggie up here. I'm sure she's as honest as the day, but she's paid to do farm work, not to come meddling. I'll explain why over that cup of tea.'

It seemed strange, Nell reflected ten minutes later, to be sitting in the kitchen in the middle of the night, clad in nightie, dressing gown and slippers, whilst her aunt bustled about getting out shortbread biscuits, ginger nuts and two large Bakelite mugs. When the tea was made and poured, she and her aunt sat side by side in the creaking old basket chairs, glad of the warmth from the fire, and exchanged quizzical glances.

Nell had eaten her first shortbread biscuit and was starting on a ginger nut when her aunt produced the kaleidoscope from her dressing gown pocket. She smiled at the surprise on her niece's face. 'You know the night Maggie first arrived? We'd all gone to bed, but Maggie woke and yelled out when she heard a vixen scream. Then I heard the two of you talking on the landing outside my bedroom, so I got up and opened the door a crack to see what all the fuss was about. And the first thing I saw, dear Nell, was you in your working clothes and not your nightie. Aha, I thought to myself, the young monkey is off to the attic. So I waited until the two of you had gone back to bed and then went up the stair, opened the trapdoor and had a quick look round. The room was flooded in moonlight and the first thing I saw, lying on the sofa, was the kaleidoscope.' She looked slyly at her niece through the thick curling lashes which had once been the envy of every girl in Liverpool. 'So the little monkey has got her grubby paws on my kaleidoscope, I thought to myself. But she's not had much chance to examine it. Maybe if I take it away now and keep it hidden in my own room, my secret, such as it is, will still be safe. For I knew, Nell, that though you might be curious, you are not the sort of person to enter someone else's own room without an invitation, far less search through their possessions.'

'I thought exactly the same about you,' Nell admitted. 'I knew you wouldn't snoop deliberately in my room; I even knew that if you found the books you might not realise they were from the attic because you know I borrow books from the travelling library when it visits the village.'

'Right. Well, in order that you should understand everything, I'm going to start at the very beginning. And that was a long time ago, towards the end of the Great War. As I'm sure you know, I was nursing at the Stanley Hospital at the time, looking after the wounded soldiers sent back from France. One evening my friend Sarah and I got off early . . .'

Chapter Ten

August 1918

Kath and Sarah emerged from the hospital, glad to be out of the stuffy wards and grateful for the fresh breeze blowing off the Mersey. As they turned along the pavement, Kath let out her breath in a gusty sigh. 'Phew! Do you realise, Sarah, that we've been at war for four years? And everyone was saying it would be over by Christmas. Some hope! I'm beginning to believe it will go on for ever.'

Sarah snorted. She was a pretty, dark-haired girl with a high colour and big dark eyes, and she and Kath were good friends. Now, however, she shook her head chidingly. 'Oh, Kath, don't be so daft. The fellers coming back from the front are sure it's almost over. Both sides are exhausted, and ever since the Yanks came in the Huns have been falling back. A young cavalry officer came on to our ward yesterday and he says it'll be over by Christmas . . . no, don't laugh, he's speaking from experience, not wishful thinking, like they were four years ago. Ah, here comes our tram; we'd better run for it.'

The two girls, cloaks flapping in the breeze of their going, began to hurry, though they were well aware that at the sight of their uniform other passengers would hold back. Anyone in uniform, particularly the soldiers wearing the bright blue which showed they had been wounded in action, was given preferential treatment, so it was no surprise when the girls found themselves being pushed to the front of the queue and given two seats next to one another close to the door.

'Doing anything exciting this evening?' Kath asked as the tram started up. She hugged herself and beamed at her friend. 'I am!'

'I was going to the picture palace with my sister, to see Charlie Chaplin in *The Adventurer*,' Sarah said, settling herself more comfortably in her seat and raising her voice above the rattle and roar of the tram. 'But it's such a lovely evenin' it would be a waste to spend it at the flickers. I'll see if I can persuade Lily to go out to Prince's Park and have a row on the lake.' She sighed gustily. 'Anyway, she ain't that keen on Charlie Chaplin; she'd rather see *Cleopatra*. But she's not stuck in a hot ward all day, tending the wounded; if she was, she'd understand why I'd rather have a good laugh than watch a melodrama, no matter how exciting.' She turned to her friend. 'How about you? I guessed you were off somewhere when you persuaded Bet to swap shifts.'

Kath allowed a small, secret smile to touch her lips. If all went according to plan, she was going to have a marvellous evening because she would be spending it with someone so special that even breathing his name in a whisper too low to be overheard sent butterflies of excitement dancing within her. She cast a quick glance round the tram at her fellow passengers, then leaned so close to Sarah that the other girl's hair tickled her cheek. 'I'm meeting that fellow I told you about. I met him over a year ago . . . do you remember my mentioning him? His name's John.'

Sarah nodded, smiling in her turn. 'Yes, I remember. And no wonder! I take it he's the one you send great long letters to every few days?'

'That's the one,' Kath said. She chuckled. 'He's the reason – or his replies are, rather – that I accost the postman or get my mother to put letters addressed to me under my pillow so my sisters don't see them.' She sighed. 'He writes lovely letters.'

'When you say sisters, you mean Trixie, don't you?' Sarah said. 'I seem to remember you had some daft idea that your youngest sister thinks he's her feller. Only why she should imagine it, I don't know.'

'She does think he's her feller, and in a way I can understand it. After all, it was Trixie who brought him into our family, after she'd met him at a party given by the local ladies at his convalescent home,' Kath explained. 'He'd been wounded and sent back to England for rest and recuperation, and there's no doubt that he did like Trixie; liked her very much. I was in Portsmouth at that time, because there had been a big push and the hospitals down south were desperate for help. You must remember, Sal; you didn't volunteer because you've got lots of family responsibilities, but I knew Mam and the girls could manage, so . . .'

'Of course I remember. So it was then that young

294

Trixie got her claws into your John—' Sarah began, but was immediately interrupted.

'No, it wasn't really like that. Be fair, Sarah! I don't think John ever pretended to be in love with her and Trixie had a heap of young men dancing attendance on her. But I walked into the house the night I came back from Portsmouth, worn out and pretty dirty after the long train journey, and the first thing I saw was a young man in hospital blue. It sounds stupid . . . mad . . . I don't know, but our eyes met and . . . well, it really was love at first sight, and that was that. When he returned to France we wrote almost daily. I knew John and I were made for each other and he felt the same. So you see, if Trixie found out, she could easily cut up rough, say I'd stolen her feller.'

'If John never encouraged her I don't see why she should want to claim him,' Sarah said obstinately. 'Why, whenever I go dancing your Trixie is there, with a different feller each time. You tell her you and John mean to get married and I expect she'll be sensible and wish you happy.'

'My sister Trixie is pretty as a picture and smart as paint, and has a very high opinion of herself,' Kath said, after some thought. 'She flirts with any man who looks at her twice and thinks they're all madly in love with her, but when it comes to the crunch she says she's got a permanent sweetheart who is in France right now but will marry her as soon as the war's over. And if she's pressed, she says he was a rich farmer in civvy street, so since John was a farmer – though I don't think he was rich – I assume she means him. So for the sake of family peace I've kept my own feelings for John to myself. And now he's home on furlough we have to decide whether to tell Trixie – and the rest of the family, of course – that we're serious and mean to marry when the war's over, or whether we should wait until it really is over. Then if there's going to be unpleasantness, at least we can walk away from it.'

'But that's ridiculous. The girl scarcely knows him, so why can't you tell her to fix her interest elsewhere?' Sarah said. 'I've always thought your little sister was spoilt rotten and selfish as they come, and now I'm more convinced than ever. Why, she sounds a right little madam. She wants takin' down a peg or two.'

Kath sighed. 'I don't suppose she can even remember what John looks like,' she admitted. 'Of course, I may be wronging her, but she's always been very posses-sive; always wanted anything I've got, in fact. In a way it's quite touching. If I like a man, then she knows, or thinks she knows, that he's worth liking, if you see what I mean. I suppose I should do what you say and tell her to choose one of the other young men dangling after her, but quite honestly I don't want John's furlough to be ruined by scenes.'

'Well, if you lose him to Trixie you'll only have your-self to blame,' Sarah said. 'I suppose you'll cry into your beer when she calmly makes him buy her an engagement ring and take her off to – to wherever he lives to meet his parents. Really, Kath, you make me cross. Have a bit of courage!'

'Oh, it won't come to that; John would never stand for it. He has plenty of courage even if I'm a bit short in that department. And by the way, I don't drink beer,' Kath said, grinning at her friend. 'Don't worry, John and I will work something out. Perhaps Trixie will decide her latest flirt is the most wonderful man in the world and leave me and John to plight our troth officially, as the saying goes.'

'That kid needs a good hidin', not some poor sucker to boost her opinion of herself,' Sarah said. 'She's nothing but a spoilt baby. Goodness, the way she's been going on at dances she'll end up *havin'* to get married and then how will your mam feel?'

Kath was beginning to reply when the tram drew up at their destination and both girls got to their feet, joining the press of disembarking passengers. On the pavement, Sarah turned to the left and Kath to the right, but Sarah loosed one parting shot before they went their separate ways. 'Tell that Trixie she can't have more'n one feller,' she called. 'Hasn't she ever heard of rationing? One girl, one feller is a rule she don't seem to have took into account.'

Kath laughed. 'See you tomorrow, Sal.'

Her friend waved and Kath set off along the pavement, looking into shop windows as she passed. Not that there was much to look at, she reflected, quickening her pace. Ever since February, rationing had been a reality rather than wishful thinking on the part of the authorities. What one could buy had always been restricted by price, of course, and as prices rose the poor had grown hard-pressed, but at least now that ration books were given to every household shopkeepers had to stump up a certain amount of food for each customer and could not just sell it to the highest bidder. Bacon, cheese, butter and sugar were available in tiny amounts each week, and other goods were doled out monthly. The Ripleys, with everyone earning, were not too badly off, and because Kath and Lou were nursing they often received presents of food from grateful patients; but some women, Kath guessed, scarcely knew how to feed their families.

However, although rationing had made window shopping a thing of the past, today Kath had other, and much nicer, things to think about. John had wanted to come to the house in Kingfisher Court, but Kath had vetoed the suggestion. She had explained that Trixie had somehow got hold of the idea that he, John, was her personal property, and told him she thought they should meet in a small café two minutes' walk from Lime Street station. He had told Kath six months before that Trixie was writing to him and that it was only polite to respond; Kath had replied that perhaps this was not very wise.

But it seemed so ignorant to ignore her letters, and they weren't love letters or anything like that, just chatty little notes, his own reply to Kath had said.

Actually, lots of the fellows get mail from girls they don't really know, so I thought Trixie was just being friendly, keeping in touch, like. Do you think it would be wiser to tell her not to write again? I will if you want me to, but she's only a kid, after all. I expect she likes to boast about knowing an artilleryman out in France, and there's no harm in that, is there?

298

Later, John had told Kath that his letters had got shorter and shorter, and so had Trixie's replies, and eventually it had been she and not he who had ended the correspondence. Kath noted with relief that her sister scarcely mentioned John after that . . . someone called Rodney seemed to have taken his place.

Wending her way along the crowded pavement, Kath reflected now that she was probably worrying unduly. Trixie was spoilt all right, but she had a warm heart; surely when she knew that Kath and John were in love and wanted to marry she would be delighted, for Kath had no doubt that her little sister adored her. Yes, things would work out. If only Rodney had not been called back to his regiment, she was pretty sure that Trixie would have scarcely thought twice about John, for Rodney was an officer and all her girlfriends envied her the tall, fair-haired young man's friendship. Sarah had been very scathing about Trixie, but the kid was young for her age. It will be all right, Kath told herself, entering the corner house and going down the hallway to the kitchen where the family always assembled. Once she had explained how she and John felt about each other, her sister would be pleased for her, would begin to think of John as a brother instead of a possible lover.

Kath pushed open the kitchen door and was warmly greeted by her mother, a couple of aunts, Mrs Bluett from next door, and her mother's crony Mrs O'Halloran, whose husband ran the corner shop. 'Hello, chuck; you're early for a change. Someone pour the lass a nice hot cup o' char, whilst I butter some scones,' Mrs Ripley said. 'You going out this evening?' She turned to the assembled company. 'Nursing's really hard work; Kath and Lou often come home too tired to do aught but seek their beds, whereas our Trixie scarce sets foot in the house before she's off to some dance or party. Eh, she's a lively one is our Trixie.'

Kath sank down on an offered chair and sipped the mug of tea which had been thrust into her hand, then answered her mother's question. 'Yes, I got off early because I am going out this evening. I've just come home to change out of my uniform and then I'll be off. I'm meeting . . .' she hesitated, 'a young man whose furlough starts today. I expect we'll have a lot to talk about since we've not met for over a twelvemonth, so we'll probably get a bite to eat and then go to a theatre or a picture house.'

'Don't you go wasting your money on a meal when there's plenty to spare here,' Mrs Ripley said at once. She was an enormously fat and jolly woman, as golden-haired as her younger daughters, and more easy-going than any of them. Now, she beamed at Kath. 'A new young man, is it? Or do I know him? If I had to hazard a guess . . .'

Kath bit her lip. 'Don't you go hazarding guesses, Mam,' she said quickly. She knew her mother was very shrewd, and might well have read more into Kath's deliberately casual remarks about her correspondent than others would. She was often the only person at home when the post arrived, so she had to be well aware Kath was receiving letters written in the same hand two or three times a week.

But now she was smiling comfortably at her daughter as she placed a buttered scone before her. 'I don't need to hazard guesses because I know right well who you mean,' she said, nodding in a satisfied way. 'Now don't scowl at me, queen, I don't mean to tale clat on you. Just you go off and enjoy yourself, like our Trixie always does. And if you want to bring the young man back here for a bite of supper, he'll be welcome as the flowers in May.'

Kath smiled lovingly at her parent. Sarah was right when she said Mrs Ripley spoiled Trixie, but didn't her mother spoil them all, when you came down to it? Since Kath's father died Mrs Ripley had worked in a large bakery on Everton Road. It was hot and demanding work, especially at this time of year, but nothing ever prevented her mother from coming straight home after work to cook her family a sustaining meal. Yes, Mam is a heroine and we are lucky to have her, Kath thought, jumping to her feet and kissing her mother's round, pink cheek. 'Thanks, Mam. You're the best, and I expect we will come home, though not necessarily this evening.' She glanced round at the assembled company. 'I'm just going to change into my best bib and tucker, then I'll be off.'

She was about to whisk out of the kitchen when her aunt Prue gave a squeak. 'Best bib and tucker, eh? I trust you'll come back to give us a mannyking display afore you bobbies off.'

Kath laughed and made for the stairs. 'Since I'll be wearing the only decent cotton I possess, it won't exactly stun you,' she called. 'But I'll give you a twirl before I go off to meet my pal.'

An hour later, Kath was approaching Lime Street station with her heart bumping in delighted anticipation of the meeting to come. She had not seen John for a year, and then they had only met half a dozen times before he had been recalled to his regiment, but she had no doubt she would recognise him on sight. They had arranged to meet at the Continental Café but Kath felt a strong compulsion to go straight to the station, especially when she saw a number of soldiers emerging from the concourse. And she was right, for she had scarcely reached the station entrance when she saw a sturdy, familiar figure, black hair pushed beneath a rakishly tilted forage cap, and a broad smile lighting his face as their eyes met.

She had meant to be calm but welcoming; instead she found herself in his arms whilst their lips met in a long, hungry kiss. When they broke apart she was trembling, but shook her head disapprovingly at her own behaviour. 'What must you think of me, kissing you in a public place with everyone watching?' she asked him as he slid an arm round her waist and began to lead her out of the crowd spilling on to the pavement. 'I don't know what came over me. I meant to shake your hand.'

John laughed and squeezed her waist. 'If you'd looked around you, Kitty my love, you'd have seen that almost everyone was kissing and hugging, so no shame there was in what we did. Now where's this tea room where you thought you could get away with a handshake?'

Kath giggled, loving the fact that he alone had adopted the nickname Kitty. She reached up and kissed his chin, though he was only a couple of inches taller than she, feeling that it was no sin to show affection but simply natural. 'It's not far, just a hundred yards or so along the pavement, and a very respectable place. If we'd kissed in there they would have turned us out. Honestly, John, even hugging in public is considered not at all the thing.'

John stopped short. 'Isn't there somewhere else we could go?' he asked plaintively. 'I don't fancy being turned out into the cold, cold snow if I so much as squeeze your hand.'

Kath giggled again. 'It's a baking hot day in August and if any snowflake was brave enough to venture out it would sizzle on the pavement,' she declared. 'But the tea room sells some of the best food available in the area and it isn't expensive either. We could have poached eggs on toast, a big pot of tea for two and a cream cake for one and tuppence each. Of course it's not real cream, but you can scarcely tell, honest to God, John.' By this time they had reached the café and she drew her companion to a halt, then looked enquiringly into his kind brown eyes. 'Well? What do you think?'

For answer, John pushed the door open and led her to a secluded table at the back of the room. 'Since we need to talk, one place is as good as another,' he said, beckoning to the waitress. 'I've a plan which I think might solve our problem. I take it that Trixie is still claiming I'm her beau?'

'I'm afraid she might be,' Kath admitted and explained that her sister was at a bit of a loose end since Rodney had returned to the front.

John grimaced. 'Damn!' he said bluntly. 'Still, I've had this idea . . . let me explain . . .'

'Fire ahead,' Kath said cheerfully as the waitress brought a laden tray to their table.

John waited until she had departed, then began to eat, speaking between mouthfuls. 'I say, you were certainly right; this is prime grub. Real eggs, and toast as thick as a tram driver's glove. But I must tell you my idea, see what you think. I've got a pal who's a gunner like me and he's on furlough right now. Normally, he would go home to be with his folks, but he's promised to spend some time in Liverpool with an old uncle who was good to him when he was a youngster. Uncle Emrys – that's the uncle's name – is living with a daughter-in-law who doesn't have much patience with him so my pal means to take him around and so on whilst he's home. He's booked in at a lodging house, but the old feller goes to bed early and rises late, so I suggested he might like to meet Trixie, take her about a bit. Owain is a grand chap, so I thought, if Trixie agrees, we could go about in a foursome.' He grinned shyly at her across the table. 'Once the other two are at ease with each other, you and I can slip off and have some time to ourselves. What do you say? I've arranged to meet him in the buffet on Lime Street station in an hour. If you don't like the idea . . .'

'I do, I do!' Kath cried excitedly. 'It's a wonderful idea and Trixie will love it.' She glanced at the clock which hung on the wall above the door leading to the kitchens. 'I suppose we could go and meet her out of work, but I'm not sure that would be wise. It must seem more casual. Trixie is a great one for dancing, so if I say you and another lad want to make up a foursome and go to the Daulby Hall, I'm sure that will do the trick.' She hesitated. 'Only is this friend of yours very handsome? Because if he isn't something really special, she'll make a dead set for you.'

John laughed. 'He's a bit older than me, but a grand fellow with a nice way with him. Girls go mad for him, Kath. If he doesn't sweep Trixie off her feet, I'm a Dutchman!' He finished off his poached eggs, pushed the plate aside and reached for a cream cake, then glanced up at the clock. 'Glory be, we'd better get our skates on or we'll be late for Owain. Can you eat a cream horn in two minutes flat? I can!'

They finished their meal at a gallop, paid the bill and headed back towards the station. As they entered the buffet, Kath looked round hopefully, but it was impossible to pick out one soldier from amongst the throng of uniforms. John, however, headed straight for a tall man lounging against the wall with a mug of tea in one hand, whilst the other rested on his kitbag. 'This is Owain Jones, a pal from my company,' John said as the stranger held out a strong, tanned hand. 'Owain, this is my girl, Kath, the one I'm always talking about, so don't forget, she's spoken for; it's her sister we want you to charm.'

305

'I don't see myself as a charmer precisely,' the man said, giving Kath an appraising look, and then a somewhat embarrassed smile. 'Down to earth, that's me. Just a simple farmer in civilian life, if the truth be known.' He addressed Kath directly. 'Only I'm going to be in Liverpool for most of my furlough, so when John here said he knew of a pretty girl who would enjoy keeping me company . . .'

'And I've made sure she was respectable, like,' John put in with a lurking grin. 'He's a serious bloke is Gunner Jones, a Welsh Methodist, and he don't believe in strong drink or wicked women. Both being farmers and speaking Welsh has made things easier for us.'

'Nice to meet you, Mr Jones,' Kath said formally. There was no doubt that John's friend was a handsome fellow, but she could see at a glance that he must be in his mid-thirties, a good deal older than Kath herself, let alone her sister. His curly, light brown hair was streaked with grey and he looked as though he took life seriously. Kath knew that Trixie liked her beaux to be young and lively and feared that she would expect her, Kath, to partner Owain. However, she could scarcely say so whilst Owain was present. Instead, she took her courage in both hands and said what was in her mind. 'I'm sure it's very good of you, Mr Jones, to agree to take my sister about, but she *is* only young, and she might find you rather intimidating. What's more, you might find her too frivolous, so don't think John and I won't understand if you'd prefer to give us the go-by. Trixie is very pretty and very sweet, but she's a bit like a little butterfly, fluttering from flower to flower, and—'

'I'm not exactly a flower, Miss Kath, nor am I contemplating marriage, but merely a ten-day friendship,' Owain said mildly, in a deep, heavily Welsh-accented voice. 'If I were after a wife, I'd be looking for a nice little Welsh girl who neither drinks, swears nor smokes, but can bake bread, make butter, milk a cow, plough a field . . .'

'Where I come from, horses plough the fields,' John said, and ducked as Owain aimed a blow at his head. 'Look, Owie, me and Kath have eaten, but you've not had a chance to do so. What say we get fish and chips and go back to Kath's place? Then you can meet Trixie.'

'I thought we'd agreed I'd bring her along to the Daulby Hall,' Kath said, but already it had occurred to her that Owain's looks alone would probably make him acceptable to her sister. Rodney had been a weedy young fellow, a subaltern with his company, and in her heart Kath doubted if Trixie would have looked at him twice had he not been an officer. Owain Jones, however, was considerably more impressive, being tall and well built, with that indefinable air of self-confidence which, Kath thought, made a man doubly attractive.

But John, who had dumped his kitbag on the ground as they talked, slung it over his shoulder once more, tucked Kath's hand into the crook of his arm and beckoned Owain Jones to follow. 'I'll be coolly polite to Trixie and leave my old mate here to charm her,' he said. 'Come along, troops, best foot forward. Left, right, left, right . . .'

When Kath sought her bed that night, it was with the pleasing knowledge that things had indeed worked out as she and John had hoped. Trixie, the self-confident, had been in awe of Owain Jones at first, but from the moment he had walked into the kitchen she had had eyes for no one but him. They had spent a pleasant evening eating the fish and chips which Owain had insisted on paying for and there had been much talk about the war, which both John and his friend were confident was nearing its end. Only when they were drinking a cup of tea and preparing to part did Owain give Trixie his delightful smile and explain that though he would have to spend some time with his uncle during the day, he was as free as a bird in the evenings. 'And I suppose you're working anyway,' he added. 'What time do you finish?'

Blushing brightly, Trixie said she would be free from six o'clock, and Owain promptly suggested that the four of them might visit the theatre together. 'A good show there is at the Playhouse,' he said. 'Nothing too serious, mind. Or we could find a dance.' He smiled at Trixie, and if his smile was avuncular, Trixie did not appear to notice. 'You look like a girl who can dance up a storm, as they say. How about it, cariad?'

Trixie had chosen to go dancing, as Kath had guessed she would, and the next time the sisters met, a couple of days later, Trixie was full of the charms of her new beau. 'An older man knows how to make a girl feel important,' she said. 'I were real cross wi' you at first, our Kath, fixing me up without a word – but I do like Owain, more than any other man I've ever met. Did he tell you he were a rich farmer before the war, and means to be a rich farmer again when it's over?' She hugged herself, shooting her sister a triumphant glance. 'I bet you never thought your little sister would beat you to the altar, eh? But I wouldn't be surprised if Owie popped the question before he returns to France.'

'And would you say yes?' Kath asked curiously. The two sisters were in their room, preparing for bed. The next day was Sunday, and the men had suggested a trip up the Mersey in a pleasure boat, culminating in a meal at a country inn which John knew from his previous visit to Liverpool.

Trixie considered the question, her head on one side and one forefinger pressed against her dimpled chin. 'Marriage is a big step, but I do believe I'd enjoy being a rich farmer's wife,' she said ingenuously. 'And I'd love a big white wedding. I'd have you and Lou as my chief bridesmaids and six or eight of the cousins as ordinary ones. I'd make Dad give me away in top hat and tails if his ship were in port, and cousins Jeff and Albert could be groomsmen. If the cathedral were finished, I'd have the wedding there, but as it is it'll either be the iron church or St Nicholas. Which do you think is the prettier, Kath?'

'Oh, either; but since Mr Jones is a Welsh Methodist, perhaps he'd prefer one of the chapels,' Kath suggested. She could not help smiling at her sister's remarks, which showed all too clearly that she was in love not with her proposed bridegroom but with the romantic idea of a wedding.

Trixie was brushing out her hair, but paused to give the question serious consideration. 'A chapel? Oh, I don't think so. Besides, surely the wedding always takes place in the bride's church? Still, I suppose if Owie insisted, we could marry in a chapel. I say, Kath, Owie's got a huge farm somewhere in Wales; he really is as rich as Croesus – or do I mean Midas? Anyway, he means to buy me a diamond ring before he goes back to France.'

Kath, climbing into bed, turned towards her sister, her eyebrows shooting up. 'A diamond ring! Darling Trixie, does this mean he really has proposed marriage? If so, I think you ought to consider his age before you agree to become engaged. I believe he's thirty-eight, an awful lot older than you. But I can't believe he would ask you to marry him without speaking to Mam and Dad first. Or has he already done that?'

Trixie, who had been staring dreamily at her reflection in the dressing table mirror, put down her hairbrush and took a flying leap on to her bed. After Carrie got married and went to live with her parents-in-law, Lou had enjoyed the luxury of a bed of her own for a while, but when it dawned on Trixie that their shifts meant that her sisters often slept at different times she demanded a bed to herself, saying that Kath and Lou could perfectly well play Box and Cox in the other without disturbing her. Now, she pulled the sheet up to her chin before answering her sister's questions.

'Has he proposed? Well, not exactly. We were looking in the window of that big jeweller on Church Street and I was telling him which ring I thought the prettiest. I like rubies or emeralds; they show up better than diamonds. But Owie said he liked diamonds, because of the sparkle, so I think he means to buy me one before he leaves and of course he'll ask me to marry him first.'

Kath sat up on one elbow and gazed across the moonlit room at her sister's small, fair face. 'Darling Trixie, I think you're taking a lot for granted,' she said gently. 'Owain's a great deal older than you, as I said, and so far he's managed to avoid marriage. Perhaps he simply hasn't had time, because I imagine there's a great deal of work to be done on a successful farm – and then, of course, he joined the army. And if you don't mind my saying so, dearest, you've not so much as mentioned that you love one another. People who marry in haste repent at leisure, especially when there's no affection involved.'

Trixie reared up on her elbow and pointed an accusing finger at her elder sister. 'You're just jealous because I'm going to marry a rich man and your John probably doesn't have two pennies to rub together,' she said hotly. 'And you wouldn't even have him if I hadn't decided I didn't want him. So don't you start—'

At this point the bedroom door opened and Lou, who had been working a double shift, came tiredly into the room. She carried a candle which she set down on the chest of drawers before beginning to undress.

'What on earth are you two doing still awake at this hour? I bet you were quarrelling,' she said accusingly. 'Well, you can both jolly well shut up because I've had the devil of a night and can't wait to get snugged down. Move over, Kath.'

'Sorry, Lou. And it wasn't a real quarrel, it was just a slight disagreement,' Kath said at once. 'Isn't that so, our Trix?'

Her sister looked rebellious, then nodded and pulled the sheet up round her shoulders once more. 'Yes, it weren't nothing,' she mumbled. 'Goodnight both.' She cast a baleful glance at Louise. 'And blow that perishin' candle out or no one will get no sleep.'

Chapter Eleven

'Oh, Kitty, my dearest love, don't cry!' John's arms were tightly wound round Kath, his mouth close to her ear. 'Everyone says it's nearly over; before you know it I'll be back home again and we'll be walking up the aisle together, the two happiest people in the whole world!'

'Oh, John, my darling, I can't bear to let you go,' Kath muttered against the rough serge of his battle-dress. 'I wish I could go with you. A great many nurses do go to France to man the forward dressing stations, but I'm needed here.' A whistle shrilled and men began to head towards the train, which was getting up steam, ready to depart. 'Oh, Johnny, Johnny, I love you with all my heart. Please, please take care of yourself, and write often.'

John released her and ran a gentle hand round her heart-shaped face. 'You must take care too; don't go half killing yourself doing double shifts and missing out on your rest periods,' he said. 'I would have liked to buy you an engagement ring, but you've got the love spoon I carved for you. We don't go in for rings much in Wales, but when a man carves a love spoon for his sweetheart it means they'll marry, so do take care of it.' He tried to smile, but it was a poor effort.

'I shall expect to see it hanging in a place of honour in your mam's parlour when I'm next home.' He turned away, heading with obvious reluctance to where men were pushing and shoving their way into the waiting carriages, and Kath followed him, clutching the back of his tunic whilst tears poured down her cheeks. Reaching the train, he climbed aboard, then turned to lean out of the window. 'I love you, Kitty,' he shouted as the train began to draw out. 'I'll love you till the day I die.'

Kath, hiccuping and sobbing, called back that she would love him for ever . . . and it was not until the train had disappeared round the bend that she pulled out her handkerchief, blew her nose, and began to mop up the tears which were still trickling down her cheeks. Slowly, she began to make her way out of the station, and was just beginning to pull herself together when someone touched her arm. She looked round and it was Owain, his face concerned. 'Oh, my poor girl; I guessed you'd be seeing my old pal off,' he said gently. 'My own train doesn't leave for nearly two hours, so I've time on my hands.' He glanced at the clock. 'I see it's past noon. Can I buy you a meal? I think we ought to talk.'

'It's awfully kind of you—' Kath began, but was quickly interrupted.

'It's not kind, or at least it's kind only to myself; as I said, I think we should talk, and if I'm left all alone for two hours I shall start remembering what awaits me on the other side of the Channel and will probably go AWOL. That means—'

'I know – Absent Without Leave,' Kath said, with a tiny choke of laughter. 'And I'm sure you would do no such thing. But thank you very much; I'd like to share a meal with you, only I think we should go Dutch.'

Her companion laughed. 'I'm sure your charming little sister has told you that I'm a rich farmer; she seems to have told everyone else,' he said ruefully, but with a twinkle. 'We'll go to Lewis's; they have an excellent restaurant on the top floor. And the tables are situated so that one's conversation cannot be overheard.' As they set off he tucked her hand into his arm, smiling down at her, and despite the fact that she was deeply in love with her John, Kath was conscious of the appeal which had attracted her sister.

The thought made her ask him what had happened to Trixie. For the first time his face lightened and he gave her an impish grin. 'She's at work. Oh, she said she wanted to come and see me off but I didn't fancy one of her scenes, so I told her my train left at six this evening.' He chuckled. 'If she remembers, she might even turn up at the station then. But one of the chaps she introduced me to is taking a crowd of pals to a picture palace tonight to celebrate his twenty-first birthday, and then on to the Clevedon Rooms for what he describes as a grand scoff. The film starts at six, so no doubt I'll get a letter explaining that she was held up at work and couldn't come to say good-bye.'

'You don't seem very upset,' Kath said as they entered the big department store and headed for the lift. 'I take it that all Trixie's talk of a possible engagement between the two of you was just wishful thinking.'

Owain Jones gave her a hunted look. 'I told her I wasn't the marrying kind, said if I did get wed it would be to a countrywoman of my own, someone who would help me on the farm. But by golly, your sister's single-minded. She brushed that aside, said she had no doubt she could pick up country ways in a week, and even assured me that though her personal preference was for rubies or emeralds she would accept a diamond engagement ring whenever I felt inclined to bestow it on her.'

Kath was torn between amusement and horror. 'Oh dear,' she said inadequately. 'But she's only a child, Mr Jones. I just hope she didn't ruin your leave.'

'Please call me Owain, since both John and your sister do so; then I shall feel I can call you Kath instead of Miss Ripley.' The lift ground to a halt beside them, and he ushered her inside. 'Red Rose restaurant please,' he said to the smartly uniformed attendant, and neither he nor Kath spoke again until they were seated opposite one another at a secluded table and had ordered a pot of tea and two plates of ham salad.

As soon as the food was before them and the waitress had left, Owain leaned across the table. 'I hope you don't think I'm interfering, Miss Ripley – Kath – but I thought you ought to know that John has put me down as his next of kin and asked me to contact you should he be wounded, or . . . or worse.'

'Oh, but John's grandparents are still alive,' Kath said quickly. 'He's talked about them to me. I know his parents died some time ago, but surely his grand-father must be his next of kin?'

Owain nodded, took a mouthful of ham, chewed and swallowed before he spoke again. 'You're right, of course, but John's grandparents are both in their eighties, and he felt that a telegram announcing he was missing might have a terrible effect on them. His grandmother is very frail and has a heart condition, and his grandfather has already had quite a serious stroke. If John does get killed, we agreed that I would choose my moment and break the news gently.'

'Yes, I understand that, but why are you telling me now?' Kath asked, puzzled.

Her companion gave her a wry smile. 'My dear girl, do think. The army contact the next of kin, and who beside myself would know to inform you if John was posted missing, or seriously wounded? He might have told his pals that he's met the girl he wants to marry, but I'd bet every penny I possess that he never gave anyone beside myself your name or address.' He leaned across the table and patted her hand. 'Don't look so distressed, cariad. Everyone says the war is as good as over, so the chances of his coming a cropper are probably about a thousand to one. Only I thought I ought to tell you.'

'It's awfully good of you and I do appreciate it, honest I do,' Kath said. She looked shyly across the starched white tablecloth at her companion. 'Only I love John so much that I can't bear even the thought of him being hurt. But of course if something does happen, I must know so I can go to him.'

317

Owain nodded gravely. 'Good friends we are, John and myself, though I'm ten years his senior,' he said, and Kath noticed, not for the first time, how his Welsh accent thickened whenever he spoke of his country or countrymen. 'The first time I saw you together I knew you were made for each other, otherwise John would have had competition, I can tell you.'

'Thank you, kind sir,' Kath said automatically, glad of the lightening of the atmosphere, which had been charged with drama only moments before. 'I don't know whether John told you, but he carved me a love spoon whilst he was in France and gave it to me when he came home. He says it's the Welsh equivalent of a betrothal ring.'

'That's right. Keep it safe, and once the war's over and John's home for good, he'll make arrangements for the pair of you to wed.' Owain pulled a gunmetal watch out of his pocket and turned it so that Kath could read its face. 'Well, I've done talking; let's finish our meal and go our separate ways. But remember, if you ever need a friend, I'm your man.'

November 1918

Kath was on her way home from the hospital, reflecting that summer was long gone; a mere memory. She had had a letter from John that very morning, full of hope that he would soon be back with her, and though she had said nothing to Trixie, Lou was now in her confidence and looking forward as much as she did herself

318

to the return of the Allied forces. The two sisters strolled along the pavement, heading for Kingfisher Court. As they passed a newsvendor they saw the headlines painted on the flysheets in bold, black letters: AUSTRIA SIGNS ARMISTICE, they said. HUNS WITHDRAW ACROSS THE MEUSE; VICTORY IN SIGHT.

The two girls stopped to look, then Lou fished around in her cloak pocket and headed for the newsagent's shop. 'I'll just get a copy of the paper,' she called over her shoulder. 'Mebbe my Freddie will be home for Christmas after all. Wait for me, there's a dear.'

'Course I will,' Kath shouted back, then stood gazing dreamily into the distance until Lou emerged from the shop waving a copy of *The Times*.

'We'll read it when we get home,' she said breathlessly as they began to hurry along the pavement. 'It'll give the latest casualties, of course, but judging by what I've read this dreadful flu is claiming more lives than even the war has done. And they say it's just as bad in Germany.'

'Yes. I'm almost glad John is in France, though I suppose even the Frogs are being hit by the influenza,' Kath said as they turned into the court. 'Sister Maddocks is really hot on hygiene, screaming at patients and nurses alike – to say nothing of visitors – to wash their hands twenty times a day, gargle with salt and water and throughly rinse any fruit people bring in before putting so much as a grape into our mouths.'

Lou chuckled. 'The younger nurses call her Mad

Maddocks and you can see why,' she observed. 'But she's right, of course. They're saying this epidemic is airborne so you can't avoid it no matter how careful you are, but not a single nurse or patient has gone down with it on Maddocks's ward, which must mean something.'

'True,' Kath said. 'I've tried to impress the importance of hygiene on Mam and Trixie, and all the aunts and cousins of course, but I don't believe it makes a jot of difference. Mam simply says she's going to start attending church morning and evening on Sundays until the epidemic is over, Trixie giggles and says how can you sterilise kisses, and the aunts and cousins simply look offended, as though I've accused them of something horrible. Oh, except for Auntie Vera of course, who claims the flu is God's way of punishing the wicked and ungodly, which means she won't get it and Auntie Flo will.' She chuckled. 'She's hated Auntie Flo ever since they were girls and both fell in love with Uncle Sam. Only he had the good sense to marry Auntie Flo, so now Vera hates the pair of them.'

'I wonder what Auntie Vera will say if she does get it,' Lou said idly as they turned into the court and approached the house. 'One thing is certain, she won't back down; she'll probably say she hasn't got the flu at all, but some other ailment.'

Both girls were laughing as they entered the house and went down the hallway, but before they opened the kitchen door Kath put a hand on her sister's arm. 'Hang on a minute, queen; what's that funny smell?'

Lou's nose wrinkled. 'It smells like burnt cabbage,'

she remarked distastefully. 'If Mam is making blind scouse then I vote you and me go down the Scottie and get ourselves fish and chips. We need a decent meal after slaving away in the wards all day.'

'It's not like our mam to feed her family on blind scouse whilst she can wheedle some red meat out of the butcher . . .' Lou was beginning, then stopped short as she swung the kitchen door open to reveal Annie Ripley slumped in a chair, whilst a great black pan boiled over on the stove.

Both girls started forward as their mother looked up and tried to smile. 'Tek the pan off the fire, there's a good girl,' she croaked. 'That's smell's enough to turn anyone's stomach. I went into the scullery to bring through some veg, and – oh, God, I felt right queer and had to sit down for a moment.'

Lou rushed across the room, snatched the pan off the flame and peered at the smoking, stinking contents, then carried the pan over to the sink and dumped it on the draining board before returning to her mother's side. Over Mrs Ripley's white-streaked fair head, the sisters' eyes met; Lou looked the question which was in both their minds and Kath nodded. 'It's the flu all right,' she said in a low tone. 'We've got to get her upstairs; bed's the best place for her.' She looked down at her mother's bulk, then went over to the sink and soaked a tea towel in cold water. 'You've got the flu, Mam, in case you haven't already guessed,' she said, mopping the sweat which was now streaming down the older woman's scarlet face. 'Are you game to try to get up the stairs? Only the best place for you is bed and I don't think Lou and myself are strong enough to carry you.'

Ill though she undoubtedly felt, Annie Ripley gave a small, exhausted chuckle. 'You're right there, queen,' she whispered. 'You're right about bed, too, 'cos I aches all over; I feel as if I'd been run over by a coal wagon. But I'll get up them stairs if I have to crawl, and once I'm between the sheets I'll have a nice cup of tea, 'cos one minute I'm burnin' hot and the next freezin' cold. But my old mam always said a cuppa would cure anything.'

Helped by her daughters, she heaved herself to her feet and tottered across the hallway, but when she began to try to climb the stairs Kath stopped her. 'You'll be best going up backwards and sitting down,' she said. 'I'll get behind you, put my arms round you from the back and give you a bit of a heave, whilst Lou will lift your feet and legs. That way, you should arrive on the landing with enough strength to get to your bedroom.' Both girls took up their positions and Kath gave Lou an encouraging smile. 'Off we go then; ready, steady, heave!'

The days that followed were a nightmare. More than half the occupants of Kingfisher Court caught the flu, and those fortunate enough to escape the infection were run off their feet. Kath and Lou worked at the hospital whenever they could until it became more important to nurse relatives, friends and neighbours back to health. In Liverpool, as in the rest of the country, the death toll steadily mounted and one of the first to go was Aunt Flo, who slipped quietly away before the family had realised she was ill.

Mrs Ripley, on the other hand, survived, despite being ill for so long that her daughters were secretly convinced she could not possibly recover. 'Though she'll be a while regaining her strength, and will probably never be as fit as she once was,' the doctor warned the three sisters when he called on them. 'You girls should be thanking your stars that you never got the infection, despite nursing your mother and most of the occupants of Kingfisher Court.' He was an elderly man, but he smiled at them, a twinkle in his eyes. 'Maybe nursing the sick gave you some sort of immunity, I don't know. I'm just grateful for all your help.'

Kath and Lou exchanged a wry glance. Trixie had kept out of the way most of the time, though she had joined wholeheartedly in the rejoicing on Armistice Day. At eleven o'clock on the eleventh day of the eleventh month the war officially ended and Trixie, decked out in red, white and blue, had attended street parties, parades and even church services of thanksgiving. Kath, remembering how Trixie had shot out of the house as soon as it seemed likely she would be asked to help, felt inclined to point this out to Dr Lewis, but held her tongue. No point in tale clatting; no point in antagonising Trixie, either.

As soon as they were able, Kath and Lou returned to the hospital, for they needed their wages and, though no one spoke of it, the girls had tacitly acknowledged that their mother would probably never work again. The bakery would miss her sorely – and she would miss her weekly wage packet – but Mrs Ripley was past sixty and the girls dreaded a recurrence of the infection; if she got it again, they knew it could easily prove fatal.

Now that the war was over and the troops were coming home, however, life would surely begin to return to normal, although rationing would have to continue for a while, even though the convoys carrying essential food from America and Canada need no longer fear the wolves beneath the waves, as the German submarines were called.

'And the post is in a tremendous muddle, what with the flu epidemic and the troops trying to get home,' Lou pointed out. 'I've not had a letter from Fred for weeks, but then you've not heard from John, have you? I dare say the first we'll hear from them will be when they turn up on our doorstep.'

Kath agreed that this was probably so, but nevertheless she began to worry when no correspondence from John came her way, despite the fact that November was half over. John was an excellent correspondent, writing every two or three days, but a soldier returning to the court to be nursed back to health by his family had told her that a good many troops were being sent to Germany, as part of the army of occupation. 'They say the Germans are worse off than us because of the blockade of their ports,' he explained. 'If you think our rationing is severe, you ought to see theirs! Why, even their bread is rationed, and that's when they can get hold of it, which ain't often. They've been so perishin' busy trying to win the war that they've not bothered to grow so much as a field of turnips. They're starving, I tell you, starving to death . . . old folk, little children, even the troops. It'll be the end of them poor bloody Huns, I'm tellin' you.'

Then, one night, shortly after this conversation, Kath had a curious dream. She dreamt that she was sitting in front of her dressing table mirror when she saw a figure reflected in the glass, just behind her shoulder. Her heart gave a great bound, for it was John, and though he looked tired and dirt-streaked he smiled at her lovingly. Immediately she spun round, only to find no one there. When she faced front again there he was, and she realised in the illogical way one does in a dream that he was only visible to her as a reflection and she must not try to touch him unless he told her she could do so. This did not worry her at all, for she was sure that presently he would tell her to turn round and then he would be not just a reflection, but a flesh and blood man, eager to take her in his arms.

'Oh, John, my darling, I've been so worried, imagining dreadful things . . .' Kath said eagerly, but he put a finger to his lips.

'I can't write; not yet at any rate, cariad,' he said slowly, and Kath thrilled to the sound of his deep Welsh voice. 'But I'll be all right; I'll survive. Don't ever leave me . . . leave me . . . leave me . . .'

His reflection was fading and Kath jumped up from the little stool on which she had been sitting, convinced that if she moved fast enough she could catch him before he disappeared. But in rising to her feet she had knocked the stool over and now the clatter woke her and she found that she was standing beside the dressing table, having clearly walked in her sleep from the comfort of her bed to perch on the hard little stool.

Climbing back into bed again and pulling the covers up round her ears, she tried to analyse the dream, but could only conclude that John had been thinking of her and she of him. So that's all right, she told herself drowsily. I *knew* he was all right; if he hadn't been, my dream would have been quite different. And on that thought she fell asleep and slept soundly till morning. Waking, she remembered sleep-walking, but the dream had gone completely.

As November advanced, the weather grew steadily colder, and because Annie Ripley had still not reached anything like her full strength Kath, Lou and Trixie took it in turns to get up early, blow the fire into life, take a cup of tea up to their mother and start breakfast. This meant that when Annie did get up, the porridge would be cooked, the tea brewed and the kitchen pleasantly warm. Knowing her youngest sister of old, Kath, who had suggested the scheme, had been prepared for Trixie to say she could not possibly get up even earlier than she did at present. But though Trixie moaned, she agreed to do her share. 'After all, the nursing you do is a lot harder than standing behind a counter all day,' she had said when Kath and Lou had outlined their plan. 'Only you'll have to give me lessons in making porridge, because the only time I've tried it came out all lumpy.'

Her sisters had laughed but Kath, who was an excellent cook, had watched over Trixie's attempts and very soon the younger girl became more confident. After she had mastered porridge, she learned to bake scones and make pastry and Kath had told her, teasingly, that even if her husband-to-be did not fall for her pretty looks, he would certainly appreciate her cooking.

So the morning after Kath had walked in her sleep, she came into the kitchen to find Trixie pulling the porridge pan off the heat and preparing to carry a large cup of tea to their mother. 'Shall you take the tea up to Mam, Kath, while I toast the bread? Or would you rather do it the other way round?'

Kath peered into the porridge saucepan and nodded appreciatively. 'You're getting to be a really good little cook, queen,' she remarked. 'I'll take the tea, then I can give Mam a hand down the stairs. I don't want to disturb Lou; she's on nights for the whole week and has barely been in bed half an hour. I can manage Mam myself, now she's so much better, but I don't believe you could.'

'Thanks, Kath. I'll pour the porridge out so it can be cooling while you bring Mam down,' Trixie said gratefully. 'Oh, how I wish it was tomorrow! It's my day off and I could perishin' well do with it. I'm on me feet all day and precious little thanks I get, but I've thought for a while I might look about me for another job, something more interesting, like.'

Kath, heading for the hall and stairs, looked doubtful. 'With the troops coming back by the thousands all needing work and a living wage, it's going to be terribly difficult for women to get work,' she observed. 'Still, no harm in looking.'

Her mother beamed at Kath as her daughter entered the room and snuggled her shawl closer to her chin. 'Eh, you girls spoil me and don't I enjoy it?' she said, taking the proffered cup of tea and draining the mug. 'And I smell porridge . . . and toast! Pass me my slippers, there's a good girl.'

Fifteen minutes later, Kath was helping her mother to descend the stairs when someone knocked at the front door. Kath opened her mouth to shout for Trixie, but her sister must have heard the knock, for she erupted from the kitchen and went to the door, whilst Kath and her mother continued their slow progress down the stairs.

'I expect it's the postman . . .' Kath was beginning hopefully when Trixie threw the door open and she saw a tall man in khaki standing on the doorstep. She gasped, whispered, 'John! Oh, Johnny . . .' and then saw Trixie hurl herself into the man's arms with a cry of delight even as she recognised him. It was Owain. Kath clutched the banister, and over Trixie's head she saw his expression and knew why he had come. She gave a little moan and just managed to get her mother down the remaining stairs before she felt the soft rush of cold air from the open front door against her face and fell in a crumpled heap on the hall floor.

Chapter Twelve

September 1940

There was complete silence in the firelit kitchen; you could have heard a pin drop. Nell glanced quickly at her aunt's still, white face, then looked away. Such pain! Kath's blue eyes were tear-filled, her mouth trembled, and in her lap her hands were gripped so tightly that the knuckles gleamed white as bone, yet not a tear fell and presently she resumed her story, her voice steady.

'I expect you guessed, as I did, that Owain had come to tell me that . . .' for the first time, her voice was not quite steady, 'that John was dead. I'd told Mam some time before that John and I meant to marry, and of course Lou knew, but Trixie didn't. She was very sweet to me, because I was ill for several weeks. The doctor said it was exhaustion, but never mind that. I got better, returned to nursing, tried to pick up my life again . . .' She paused, looking thoughtfully at Nell. 'I wonder if you can understand? You're so young . . . you've had so little experience of life . . .'

'I should think you were living in a sort of nightmare,' Nell said rather timidly. 'What are those things called which seem alive but are really dead? Like one of those.'

Kath nodded. 'Zombies,' she said. 'You aren't far out at that. Everyone was very kind, and the kindest of all was Owain. He had to go back to Ty Hen, of course, but he must have spent three days a week there and four in Liverpool for what remained of 1918 and the early months of 1919, and in March he asked me to marry him. You could have knocked me down with a feather, because I knew that everyone, including Trixie herself, thought of him as her beau, even though by the time he proposed I had realised that he was growing very fond of me.'

'And did you return his feelings?' Nell said quietly, when the silence after her aunt's last remark had stretched. 'Well, you must have done, because you married him.'

Kath shook her head. 'No, I'm ashamed to say I didn't; I felt I could never love anyone but John and at least I was honest with Owain. I pointed out that his frequent visits to Kingfisher Court had given rise to false hopes in Trixie's young breast and I said that I'd never love anyone the way I had loved John, but he said he knew all that and it made no difference; it was me he wanted. By this time, incidentally, Trixie had realised that Owain was not interested in her but in me, and she grew very bitter. She accused me of stealing her beaux, first John and now Owain, and in the end I suspect it was this which drove me to consider Owain's proposal seriously. He said in his quiet, thoughtful way that he was sure he could make me happy, that many couples fell in love after marriage, that I would be best away from Liverpool and all the

330

memories of John it evoked. He said he hated to see me so pale and thin, so unhappy, swore that living in the country, on the farm his family had owned for generations, would bring the roses back into my cheeks . . .'

Once more Kath's voice faded into silence, as she stared at the fire and saw . . . what? Nell did not know, but she could guess. After a moment, she said tentatively: 'Auntie? Is – is that why you don't think much of my mam? Because she thought you had stolen Owain from her? Only, if you married in the spring of 1919, and my parents were wed in June, surely Mam can't have borne a grudge.'

Kath laughed. 'Poor little Trixie! I knew I was guilty of stealing her beaux, if one person can be accused of stealing another! It's been my guilt which has made me so bitter towards your mother, and it's taken me all these years to admit it. But now I have, I'll do my best to make amends. I'll write to her, explaining that I had no idea she'd been widowed and telling her how lucky she is to have such a delightful daughter.'

'That's nice,' Nell said, trying to keep the surprise out of her voice. 'So you married Owain and came to live at Ty Hen, and were you happy, Auntie? I remember you telling me once that it took time before you appreciated how beautiful the countryside is.'

Her aunt made an impatient gesture. 'Who's telling this story?' she demanded, quite in her old, sharp fashion. 'I'm sure I don't want to spend the whole night in the kitchen whilst you air your guesses, because that's all they can be.'

'Sorry,' Nell mumbled. 'I won't interrupt again, I promise. So you came to Ty Hen . . .'

Kath nodded. 'So I came to Ty Hen, as you say. When we first arrived, Owain's grandparents, who had brought him up after his parents died, were living here and I promise you I'm not exaggerating when I say his nain took against me from the start. There was a girl the old lady had had her eye on for Owain, a good Welsh girl, brought up on a farm, with whom he had been friendly before the war. Folk marry later in rural communities, and it seems she had considered herself as good as betrothed to Owain, so the grandparents were embarrassed as well as disappointed when their grandson turned up with a bride. Owain had told them over and over that he was courting an English girl, but they chose to believe it was a whim, which would fade and die when he returned home.

'When Owain and I arrived at Ty Hen, both his nain and his taid would speak nothing but Welsh and ignored Owain's requests to use only English when I was present. I tried to understand how they felt, tried to make myself as useful as possible, but I could not conquer the dislike and suspicion with which the old lady viewed me. Indeed, in the first few months, the only person who befriended me was the young woman I had supplanted; but she married an Englishman and moved to Caernarfon. I missed her dreadfully, though I was beginning to learn a little Welsh, which made my life easier.' She smiled rather grimly at her niece. 'The old man, Owain's taid, tried to be friendly, but he could scarcely smile at me or bid me good morning when his wife was around.'

'Gosh!' Nell said. 'Go on, Auntie; saying "gosh" isn't interrupting.'

Kath laughed. 'Very well. You asked if Owain and I were happy. The truth is I was so unhappy at first, so lonely and miserable, that I wanted to die. However, hidden away amongst the few personal possessions I had brought with me was the only photograph of John I ever owned. I valued it more than I can tell you, but had few opportunities to look at it, for either Owain's nain and taid, or one of the farmhands, or even the girl who helped in the dairy, to say nothing of Owain himself, was always around.

'Then, one day, when Owain's grandmother had a tea party for members of her Merched Y Wawr, it occurred to me that I had never visited the attic. I knew I wasn't wanted in the parlour, would be humiliated if I so much as carried a plate of scones into the room, so I scuttled up the wooden stair, pushed open the trapdoor and was immediately enchanted. Old toys, books, clothes, a lovely horsehair sofa . . . well you know yourself that it's full of treasures. I was intrigued and enchanted, especially when I found . . .'

'The kaleidoscope,' Nell breathed, completely forgetting she was not supposed to interrupt. 'And you found how to put the photograph in it, so that you could look at it whenever you pleased, without anyone realising. But I've just thought, wasn't there a telegram that was sent to the families of all the troops who died? And a commemorative coin . . . I remember seeing

333

something of the sort in Mrs Wormington's house in the court. She said it had her son's name on . . . oh, I'm sorry, I forgot; do go on.'

Kath sighed. 'Asking you not to chatter is like asking the tide not to come in,' she said resignedly. 'The coin wasn't a coin, but a plaque which was sent to the next of kin of servicemen who died in the Great War. The fellows called it the Dead Man's Penny or the Widow's Penny and Owain gave John's to me. It's a big, clumsy thing, made of bronze . . . but I'll show you.' She went over to the dresser, produced a disc about five inches in diameter from the bottom drawer, and handed it to her niece, saying as she did so: 'Some folk give them pride of place on their mantelpiece and polish them every week, but to my way of thinking that's idolatry. Daft, too, because it brings back memories which are best forgotten.'

Nell examined the disc with some curiosity. Around the rim were the words *He died for Freedom and Honour*, whilst the figure of Britannia was depicted holding a laurel wreath above a rectangular tablet, upon which was inscribed the name *John Williams*. At Britannia's feet a lion roared, presumably representing Great Britain. Nell tapped the plaque. 'Why the fish?' she said bluntly. 'And what is the thing below the lion's paws? It looks like a bird.'

Kath took the plaque back and walked across the kitchen, replacing it in its drawer. 'One question at a time,' she said. 'The fish aren't fish at all, but dolphins, and they represent British sea power – the Navy, I assume – but the other is a bit more complex. Owain told me it was the German eagle, being torn to pieces by the British lion.' She shut the dresser drawer with a decisive click. 'Well, I suppose it helped some people to come to terms with their grief, but it did nothing for me, nor for Owain either, so it was put away in a drawer and more or less forgotten. As for Owain, he mourned his friend John as faithfully as I did. I honoured him for it.'

She heaved a deep sigh and returned to her chair by the guttering fire. 'However, having told you so much, I had better tell you the rest. As I said, when Owain first brought me back to Ty Hen his mother's parents were living here and though I promise you, Nell, that I did my very best, it was never good enough. Owain told me I should call them Nain and Taid, as he did himself. But since they never answered any question I asked, or indeed spoke to me in any language I could understand, I soon simply stopped addressing them.'

'Gosh, how awful,' Nell breathed. 'But surely they must have known, once you were married, that there was nothing they could do about it? Oh, I know people do get divorced, but I shouldn't have thought it was exactly common in a rural community like this one. Why, even a tiny little swear word horrifies folk, so surely the very idea of divorce . . .'

'To tell you the truth, I really don't know what their aim was, but when I asked Myfanwy she said the old 'uns hoped I would be so miserable that I would simply run away, or perhaps kill myself . . .'

Despite fully intending not to interrupt, this was too

much for Nell. She gave a scandalised gasp and spoke indignantly. 'How wicked, Auntie Kath! But of course I expect they regarded you as a scarlet woman – perhaps not scarlet, but dark pink at any rate – because you weren't Chapel. So in a way I suppose they felt that getting rid of you would be a – a holy act, so to speak.'

Kath laughed, giving a regretful little nod. 'Yes, you've got the right idea. Myfanwy said someone had told the old lady that a perfectly respectable divorce can be obtained by a man if his wife runs off and is gone for seven years. No adultery or misbehaviour from either party is necessary. So I told myself that the old couple thought they were releasing Owain from the worst mistake he'd made in his life. Once free of me, he could turn to some nice young Welsh girl. And the fact that we had no children was another black mark against me.'

'Yes, I can imagine,' Nell said, nodding. 'But didn't they begin to soften towards you as time went on? Things got a great deal easier for me once I began to learn the language. Surely, when you could understand every word they said and could reply in the same tongue, that must have eased matters? It certainly did for me. If you remember, when I first came to Ty Hen, I was in a similar position to your own. But once I conquered the language things got very much easier.' She grinned as her aunt's face grew pink. 'You went on speaking rather too frankly for several weeks until you suddenly realised I understood. I think from that moment we began to get on better.'

Kath put her hands up to her flushed cheeks. 'Oh,

Nell, I'm so ashamed! Having suffered myself at the hands of Owain's grandparents, I should have been a friend to you. But I'm afraid I wasn't even nice. However, that's all behind us now and I promise you, cariad, my behaviour to you was nothing compared to the way I was treated by Nain and Taid. As I said, Taid wasn't nearly as bad as his wife, but she was really dreadful. She was supposed to teach me how to milk, how to make butter and cheese, and to cook and market; Owain thought she was teaching me all her own skills, but she did nothing of the sort. The girl who came up from the village to help in the house, Glenys, did her best to teach me whenever the old lady wasn't about, but Nain got her own back by docking the girl's wages whenever she saw us either working together or chatting. In a way, that was a good thing because it drove me out of the house and on to the farm. I learned all about stock and ploughing, sowing and reaping. I explained to Owain that his grandmother resented me and he tried to make her see how much easier our lives would be if we all pulled together. She pretended to agree, but after a couple of weeks Owain began to realise that his attempts to change her ways would always be fruitless.

'By this time, we had been married for fifteen months and I was beginning to appreciate what a good and loving man Owain was. He had told me that I might consider the attic my own private domain. The old people couldn't manage the steep stair and he told Glenys that the attic was out of bounds. Then, one warm summer day, he told me to pack a picnic

337

because he was going to take me down to the shore, to a place which his family had owned for generations. He explained that it was an ancient farmhouse which the Joneses had used as a sort of dower house; when the parents could no longer manage Ty Hen and the younger generation could manage without them, the old 'uns took over the ancient farmhouse. They could cope with a few hens, a couple of sheep, a pony to put between the shafts of the cart to take them to market . . . you know the kind of thing.'

Nell nodded. 'I expect he was taking you—'

'Hold your tongue,' Kath said at once, but there was a lurking twinkle in her eye. 'What a know-it-all you are, young woman! Yes, as you've guessed, he was going to take me to the Swtan. He had chosen a bright sunny day and we took the pony and trap. Owain had been managing the land and keeping an eye on the cottage ever since the previous occupant had left, and now he wanted to see what needed doing to get the place up and running again. You see, he had finally realised that we would all get on a good deal better apart, so he had decided to move Nain and Taid into the old place, but before he told them of his plan he wanted to make sure that everything was as it should be in the Swtan.'

'Who was the previous occupant, then? What happened to him?' Nell twinkled at her aunt. 'Do go on,' she said graciously.

Kath explained that when he joined the army Owain had employed a manager and the man had lived in the Swtan, since old Mr and Mrs Thomas did not want the bother of his presence at Ty Hen. As soon as peace was declared, however, Owain's manager found far more prestigious and better paid work on the mainland, and by the end of February 1919 the man had departed, which meant that the Swtan had been empty for over a year.

'Owain was proud of the old place and said it could soon be put to rights, but from the outside, the Swtan looked a real mess . . .'

Chapter Thirteen

June 1920

They had tied the pony up to a tethering post near an old mounting block and Kath stood back for a moment, eyeing this cottage, which her husband had told her was called a Welsh longhouse, with very mixed feelings. It was thatched for a start, unlike Ty Hen which was slate roofed, as were most of the properties she had seen on the island. Kath saw that the thatch was in need of attention, and supposed that the strong winds from the sea were responsible for its ragged, weathered appearance.

The cottage was stone built, the great uneven stones roughly cemented together. The whole place had been whitewashed once, but most of this had gone and being, presumably, not necessary for the manager's comfort had never been reapplied. The wooden window frames and door were painted green, but the paint on them was flaked and blistered and the garden, which was enclosed by a wall built of the same stone as the Swtan itself, was a tangle of waist-high weeds. Kath's fingers itched to start work there when she saw gooseberry, black and redcurrant bushes and even raspberry canes strangled by the luxuriant growth of brambles, nettles and couch grass.

However, she said nothing, but followed Owain as he opened the door. 'I wonder where they got the stone from?' she asked idly as they entered the building. 'Was it the shore, do you suppose? How would they get the stones up the cliffs?'

'They couldn't have,' Owain said. 'They would have ploughed them up and put them aside for the building of the very first tiny, one-roomed dwelling. The great advantage of a longhouse is that as family circumstances improve, and children are born, the occupants simply add extra rooms as necessary. Fortunately, the ground here is very stony. In fact, when the Romans built a road on the island, they used local stones to pave it for their legions to march on. Some time after the Romans left, the family then occupying the Swtan – they were Joneses, of course – tore up the bigger, flatter stones and used them to pave their own small yard and the approach to the cottage door.'

By now Owain and Kath were standing in the first room of the Swtan. Above their heads, thick cobwebs swung from the rafters, and Kath chuckled when she saw a tiny bird's head pop through a thin part of the thatch. Owain, oblivious, was still talking. 'This is the dairy, where the woman of the house made butter and cheese. Because the window is very tiny in here it stays cool, so the milk doesn't turn.' Owain glanced swiftly around the room, which was empty save for a large old-fashioned churn, a long wooden table and a couple of benches, though there were a number of stout wooden shelves screwed to the wall. 'The children would have hated this room because they were always the ones who had to churn the milk into butter, a long and tedious business. When I was a boy at Ty Hen I had to take my turn at butter and cheese-making, when I would far rather have been riding my pony, or bird's-nesting, or lying up in the hayloft with a book and a bag of apples.'

Kath laughed with him, then followed him through a narrow doorway into what he told her was the Swtan's main living quarters. This room was larger than the dairy, and it was where the family cooked, ate and slept. Here, the father would mend his fishing nets, sole the family's shoes, read a book or smoke his pipe whilst his wife cooked, patched and darned, spun fleece into yarn and wove the yarn into cloth. There was a blackleaded range, where the fire would have been alight every day, no matter how warm the weather, since it was the only means of cooking. Even the farm manager had eaten here at least once a day, though he would have been up at Ty Hen for the midday meal. In this room the windows, two of them, were very much larger and there was what Owain called a wall-bed, a contraption which folded up into an alcove during the day and was occupied by old grandparents who could not manage the steep ladder up to the croglofft. The croglofft was where a child would sleep until he was twelve or thirteen, when he would be moved down to a small room built on to the main one. Kath peeped through the doorway of that room and saw that it was almost entirely filled by a huge brass bedstead. She turned to Owain. 'It must have been a real treat to have that lovely big bed all to yourself once you were old enough to be moved downstairs,' she commented.

They smiled at one another. 'I expect it was,' Owain agreed. 'You really like it – the Swtan, I mean – don't you? I was afraid you would despise it, not understand why the family love it so, but you don't, do you?'

'No indeed. I think it's delightful, and I wouldn't mind living here myself,' Kath owned cheerfully. 'And all things being equal, I suppose I might easily do just that when you and I are old and can't manage Ty Hen any more.' She looked at Owain from beneath her thick, curling lashes. 'Of course, by then we might have a grosh of kids, all eager to see us retire to the Swtan so that they can try out modern ideas, just like their old dad did when he first came into the property.'

Owain put his arms round her, his face alight with surprise and love. 'Oh, Kath, those are the nicest words I've ever heard,' he said fervently. 'We're going to make a go of it, I know we are.'

For the first time, and completely of her own volition, Kath reached up and kissed him, and did not pull away when he gave a little moan and deepened the kiss. Then he put her away from him and she saw that his tanned cheeks were flushed and his eyes shining. 'I love you, Kath Jones,' he said huskily. 'But we mustn't forget that we came here for a reason. Do you think my grandparents will be happy here?'

Kath laughed. She felt so happy she thought she could have jumped over the moon, but instead she nodded vigorously. 'Of course they'll be happy here, because they'll be away from me. But we must

343

make it beautiful for them; give them no excuse to tell folk we've treated them badly.' A sudden thought struck her and she grabbed Owain's hand in both of hers, raised it to her mouth and kissed his knuckles, kiss, kiss, kiss, kiss. 'Tell you what, Owie, suppose I do the place up myself? You can help with things like mending the thatch, buying stock and provisioning the smallholding, but I'd like to clean it all really thoroughly and then furnish it, right down to bedlinen and blankets, carpets and curtains, pots and pans, china and cutlery. Perhaps if I did that, Nain and Taid might realise that I want to help them, and to love them, for your sake.'

Owain thought this an excellent scheme, though he pointed out that there was plenty of bedlinen and kitchen equipment at Ty Hen which could easily be spared. This made Kath laugh. 'A Welsh tight-wad you are,' she said in Welsh and then, reverting to English: 'They say a Welshman is a Scot shorn of his generosity.' She laughed at Owain's crestfallen expression. 'Only teasing I am; God knows you've given me everything – and more – that I've ever dreamed of having. But your grandparents, when moving to a different home, should have everything crisp and bright and new. And if they know that I've worked for weeks to make it nice for them, perhaps they won't hate me quite so heartily.'

'You're right as always,' Owain said at once. 'And now let me introduce you to the shore. I'm certain you'll love it as I do.'

He took her hand and led her along the cliff path,

putting his arm round her and giving her a squeeze when she grew nervous of the drop from cliff top to sands. 'You're safe with me; I know every inch of Church Bay and the cliffs like the back of my hand,' he told her. 'Here's the little path that will take us down safely. Isn't it a wonderful day, and aren't I glad you agreed to have our picnic on the beach instead of in the Swtan?'

For the rest of that golden afternoon, Owain and Kath forgot they were adults with adult worries and fears and became children once more. Kath looped up her long, heavy skirt, took off her shoes and rolled down her stockings, and Owain shed his own shoes and socks and rolled up the legs of his trousers. Then, as the tide slowly went out, they explored the rock pools, paddled in the little creaming waves and collected shells and long streamers of dark green and brown seaweed. Tired out at last, they sat down on a flat rock to eat the picnic which Kath had prepared and Owain had carried in a knapsack on his back. They had brought a bottle of raspberry syrup and two Bakelite mugs, but since they were both very thirsty and the syrup had to be diluted with water, they were forced to cut their stay short and leave the beach when the sun was still beginning its long descent into the sea.

They had moved the pony from the mounting block to one of the outbuildings once their first examination of the Swtan was done, and now Owain went and fed her with the remains of their picnic, lacking the bundle of hay which would have been available had the Swtan been occupied. Kath, meanwhile, climbed the hill to the well, wound the empty bucket down and brought it back up half full of water. It was hot still, so she made up the two mugs of raspberry drink and then settled back in the shade of the well's thatched roof to wait for Owain to join her.

From here she could see the green-painted door, and when it opened she expected to see Owain. Instead, an elderly, white-haired man wearing a sacking apron over shabby trousers appeared. Kath gasped and leaned forward, blinking against the sunlight, then sank back into her former position with a puzzled frown. It must have been her imagination, for it was Owain himself who was coming out from the shadowed doorway into the sunlight, turning to close the door and giving her a wave as he set off to join her.

On the journey home in the pony trap, Owain kept up a constant stream of suggestions as to their renovation of the Swtan, but though Kath tried very hard to answer him, and indeed to make suggestions of her own, she could not have succeeded too well because, as he swung the pony trap into the yard at Ty Hen and got down to go to Jemima's head, he turned to his wife with a quizzical smile. 'What's up, sweetheart? Several times I asked you something and you answered at random. I thought you liked the Swtan and enjoyed our day out – well, I'm sure you did – so what made you go quiet all of a sudden?'

Kath sighed. 'I didn't want to tell you, because I was afraid you might think I was making it up. And it was awfully hot, so I suppose I might have dreamt it. But just before you came out of the cottage I saw the door swing open and – and a white-haired old man appeared. I blinked because the light was so dazzling, and when I looked again he had gone and it was you emerging from the doorway. But you were all alone down there, weren't you?'

Owain looked uncomfortable, but gave her what he clearly believed to be a reassuring smile. 'Yes, I was alone in there all right,' he said. 'Did you imagine I'd got meself a girlfriend tucked away?' They both laughed before Owain went on: 'But heat can create illusions. I remember once seeing a sort of ghost ship up in the sky, only it wasn't a ghost, it was one of the Irish ferries, and some combination of effects had thrown its reflection up into the clouds. And I've seen a great puddle ahead of me on a tarmacked road, gleaming in the sun, but when I reached it it had gone and the road was dry as a desert.'

Kath nodded. 'I've heard of men almost dying of thirst who see a mirage – a sort of picture of an oasis – when there isn't any water for a hundred miles,' she admitted. 'Only this wasn't a phen . . . phenomenon, but an elderly man. I'm sure it was just a dream, or my imagination.'

'Well, if so, you aren't alone; others have seen such things at the Swtan,' Owain admitted. 'That building was there before the Romans came, you know. I don't believe in ghosts, but maybe folk leave a – a sort of picture of themselves, like a photographic plate, what they call a negative, in the air of a place they have loved.' He looked anxiously up into Kath's face as he

347

helped her out of the trap. 'Would you rather someone else prepared the place for my nain and taid?'

'No indeed; not now I understand,' Kath said stoutly. 'As for ghosts, I don't believe in them – and if there's one listening, I'm just joking!'

Within a week of her first visit to the Swtan, Kath had laid her plans sufficiently well to start work. Without saying a word to anyone, she got up at the crack of dawn, even before the cows were brought in for milking, and went straight to Jemima's stall, where Owain had left all the cleaning materials she thought she would require. For her part, she had packed sandwiches and a bottle of cold tea, as well as a baking of scones and bara brith. She led the pony out of the yard, treading softly and keeping to the big flagstones which made less noise when crossed than the cobbles. As soon as she reached the lane she climbed into the trap, and very soon she was at the Swtan and beginning her work.

When she got home that first night, tired but content with what she had achieved, she asked Owain whether she had been missed, which made him grin. 'Nain looked round at dinnertime, but made no comment, but when the meal was over Taid asked me quietly if you were quite well. I told him you'd gone to help out a friend and he gave me a long look. I don't know what he saw, but it seemed to satisfy him, and of course you're back in good time for supper.'

The conversation took place in the stable where Kath, having unharnessed Jemima and let her into her stall, was brushing her down with a wisp of hay. 'How did you get on?' Owain asked, beginning to work on the pony's fetlocks.

'I think I did all right; the main room, the dairy and what I would call the spare room are now as clean as a new pin. Tomorrow I'm going to put a coat of white-wash on the walls. It will make the place seem very much lighter and will be easier to keep clean than rough stone. After that I'll tackle the croglofft. What about you? Without my help, you must have had to work even harder than usual.'

She was teasing, and smiled when he gave her a playful cuff and shook his head. 'You cheeky young varmint! I managed the farm without you once and can do so again, but in a few days I'll be coming to the Swtan myself to do the things that you can't do, such as mending the thatch, cleaning the chimney, rehanging the front door and making good the outbuild-ings. When we were there I noticed that the hay racks in the cowshed needed attention and the calf house window could do with reglazing. It's in the direct path of the wind off the sea, which wouldn't do the calves any good when they arrive. Then I'd like to get the garden tidied and sown with winter cabbage and so on. And there's a deal of work hedging and ditching, as well as ordering a boat . . .'

'I thought you said you'd been running the Swtan land along with our own,' Kath said. 'And what's this about a new boat? I remember you saying your taid would mend his fishing nets in the winter, so doesn't he have one already?'

'Well, he did,' Owain said as they approached the

back door. 'My manager never bothered with it, never even thought to pull it high up the shore when the autumn gales began, so no doubt the old craft became driftwood long ago. But there's a fellow who builds boats in Bangor; I'll get him to knock up a tidy little craft which Taid will be able to manage, using the mast and sail in a breeze and the oars when the weather is calm.'

At this point they entered the farm kitchen to find old Mr Thomas seated at the table whilst his wife, tight-lipped, glared across the room at the newcomers. 'What sort of time do you call this?' she asked, her very tone a challenge. 'I told you supper was at six o'clock—'

Owain cut in immediately. 'And it's just on six now,' he said, giving his grandmother his most loving smile. 'Oh, Nain, how foolish you are! You never used to be so fond of finding fault. Kath and I will have to give you lessons in treating others the way you would like to be treated yourself.'

Kath, who had never heard Owain enter into direct confrontation with his elderly relative, began to mumble that if they were late it was her fault. But the old man, who had continued solidly munching at the food his wife had set before him, suddenly looked up and, after a cautious glance at his wife, gave Kath a small smile and a large wink.

Immensely heartened by this sign of understanding, Kath winked back, then sat down, not attempting to help when the old woman began to ladle portions of stew on to their plates. Owain's taid pushed the tureen of potatoes towards the young couple, saying as he did so: 'Well, on time or late, no one can beat my good wife's Irish stew. Eat up, for when we have our own place at the Swtan, down by the shore, you'll have to make do with whatever the two of you can produce.'

Owain, solidly munching, raised his brows at that. 'Kath is a grand cook; no one can better her puddings and pies, to say nothing of her beef scouse,' he said supportively, if untruthfully. 'Pass the salt, Taid.'

For the next three or four weeks, Kath and Owain spent some time almost every day working at the Swtan. When Owain was needed at Ty Hen, either one of the farmhands or a girl from the village came to help Kath, and as she told her husband it was a pleasure to see the longhouse gradually return to its former glory.

By the time July was into its stride, the place shone and was fully furnished. Warm woollen curtains graced every window, made to match the deep red carpet with which Kath had covered the floor in the living room. The fire in the range lit up the crockery on the old Welsh dresser, and flickered on the basket of logs and on the grandmother clock, which ticked away the hours on the opposite wall. The long wooden table was covered with cheerfully patterned oilcloth and the dairy contained everything necessary to make butter and cheese, as well as the equipment for bottling and preserving when fruit and vegetables were ripe. There was a large barrel full of salt, and smaller ones which would contain Taid's salted fish. There was a washtub with dolly pegs, and outside a clothes line stretched from the corner of the Swtan to the ty bach at the end of the garden. In the spare bedroom, Owain had driven hooks into the wall to hold the tin bath, which would be taken down and filled with kettlefuls of hot water so that the occupants of the longhouse might bath themselves before the roaring fire.

'I wish I could live here myself, with the sea so near and so little housework needing my attention,' Kath said almost wistfully when she and Owain closed the green-painted door of the Swtan and set off for home once more, having agreed that the little house was as perfect as they could make it. 'Oh, of course I love Ty Hen, wouldn't want to live anywhere else really, but it is a big house and there are acres and acres of farm-land and a great many beasts. We never seem to stop working, though I suppose it will be easier once the old folk leave.'

Owain gave a derisive snort, then looked guiltily at his wife. 'We shall still be responsible for providing them with everything they need,' he reminded her. 'At present, they can still manage most things – milking a couple of cows, feeding the calves, driving the pony and cart to market when they need to buy or to sell. But as they get older they'll have to lean on us because there's no one else.'

'But you've a huge family,' Kath objected. 'I remember you saying that as a boy, though you had no brothers or sisters, you never lacked companions for you had a dozen aunts and uncles and so many cousins they were beyond counting. Wouldn't they help out?'

Owain shook his head. 'It's not that they wouldn't help, but since the war the family have got pretty widely scattered; there's no one living near except us and though Nain and Taid have other grandchildren, I was the only one they actually brought up. As you know, my parents died before I was a year old, my mother shortly after I was born and my father of blood poisoning, so you see I owe it to Nain and Taid to look after them as they once looked after me.'

'I do understand that,' Kath said thoughtfully. 'But tell me, Owain; what did Taid say when you suggested they should move into the Swtan?'

He gave her a conspiratorial grin. 'He said it would be the saving of his marriage.' Satisfied with the effect his words had produced, he went on, 'At first he simply went along with Nain's behaviour towards you because like most men he wanted an easy life, but gradually he began to feel uncomfortable. He tried to make Nain see that what she was doing was hurting not only you and me, but the farm as well, and when I suggested it he realised that the move to the Swtan might well be the answer.'

'But what does Nain herself think of the idea? I don't imagine she can have been too keen.'

'I don't believe she knows yet,' Owain admitted. 'Taid wants to be the one to tell her, and I think he's decided that when the place is absolutely ready he'll drive her over in the pony trap and surprise her with a fait accompli.'

'Oh dear,' Kath said in a hollow voice. 'If she doesn't like it she'll blame me, and if she does like it she'll resent the fact that she has been kept in the dark and blame me for that. Oh well, they tell me daughters-in-law always get the blame for everything and I'm the next best thing to a daughter-in-law, so why should I be different?'

Owain laughed and gave her a quick hug. 'It'll be all right, I'm sure it will,' he said. 'And if it isn't you'll hardly need to know, because once they're settled in the Swtan they'll scarcely ever come up to Ty Hen. When we visit them, it will be to take supplies of some sort. And Taid has promised to stress that the cleaning and furnishing of the Swtan was all your own work. So stop worrying and begin to look forward to being mistress of your own home at last.'

Kath was in the kitchen, taking an apple pie out of the oven, when Owain popped his head round the back door. He sniffed the air, redolent of baking, and came right into the room. He was carrying a large wicker basket, which he set down on the kitchen table with a thump. 'You said you'd clean some of the best and biggest vegetables for the harvest festival service next Sunday,' he said hopefully. Kath pointed to a pile of beautifully clean carrots, onions, swedes and turnips lying at the far end of the table, and with a grateful smile Owain began to transfer them to one end of the wicker basket which, Kath saw, was already laden with fruit from their trees. 'Now all we want is Nain and Taid's contribution, which will be those special pota-toes they promised me last time I saw them.' He grinned at his wife, then indicated the hooks by the kitchen door with a jerk of his head. 'Get your coat on, cariad. It's time you stopped shilly-shallying and making excuses, and came along to the Swtan with me. After all, it's eight or nine weeks since the old folk moved in and every time I go there I think Nain is more mellow, less aggressive. Taid is really happy. I've not had much chance to speak to him privately, but when I took them a sack of that new cattle feed he said he was sure they would both welcome a visit from us – us, mark you, not me – and I promised to bring you with me next time I came.'

Kath sighed, but took down her light jacket, for though September was half over it was still sunny and warm. They had had wonderful crops and a good harvest, and though she had wondered at first how she would get on she had soon fallen into the sort of comfortable routine that had never been possible whilst her in-laws lived at Ty Hen.

Now, eyeing the enormous basket of fruit and vegetables, she wondered aloud where the potatoes would go. Owain laughed and heaved his burden up on one arm. 'I mean to leave this lot on the slate shelf in the dairy, where it's cool,' he explained, heading outside again. 'Knowing Nain, I'm sure she'll have everything ready for us, including a basket lined with hay so the potatoes don't get marked by the wickerwork.'

They entered the dairy and Owain dumped his burden on the slate shelf with a sigh of relief, then looked under his lashes at his wife. 'I thought we might take a couple of pats of butter, some cheese and one of your apple cakes as a present for the old ones, since Nain is bound to offer us a cup of tea,' he said rather diffidently. 'Both she and Taid enjoy apple cake and there are no fruit trees at the Swtan; it's too near the sea for them to flourish.'

'Good idea; I'm sure they won't refuse a gift,' Kath said hopefully, but in fact she wasn't sure at all. Still, if Owain's grandmother claimed to have too much butter and cheese already, and to dislike apple cake, at least she and Owain would have done their best.

Once they were spinning along the lane to the Swtan, however, Kath became increasingly nervous. She had enjoyed the weeks which had followed her in-laws' departure with increasing pleasure; she had always liked cooking and it was nice to see Owain's appreciation of every dish she set before him. Nain was a good cook, but not an inventive one. When Kath had suggested that a glut of eggs and milk might become delicious egg custards, the old lady claimed that there was no such dish and sent the dairymaid home with a basket full of eggs to be given to needy villagers. When Kath had dared a reproach, she had said, sourly, that she would rather see them given to the poor of the village than hand them over to Kath to spoil.

Kath had thought that it was always windy on the island, but today only the gentlest of breezes blew, and as they came within sight of the Swtan she began to feel less apprehensive. After this duty visit was paid and over, she and Owain might go down to the shore and dig up some cockles for their tea, paddle in the pools, and perhaps even bathe, for though Kath had never learned, Owain was a strong swimmer and had offered to teach her.

With this thought in the forefront of her mind, she jumped down as the pony and trap came to a halt alongside the small green gate. Owain handed down the basket containing the goodies they had packed for the old couple, and then tied the pony to the tethering post. Kath approached the door, feeling very like Little Red Riding Hood. 'And Nain is the wolf,' she was telling herself as the door swung open and the old woman's face appeared in the aperture.

Kath pinned a bright smile to her face and approached the door with a lively step. 'How lovely to see you, Nain. Owain and I have called for the potatoes, and we've brought—' She stopped short and stepped back just as the door slammed resoundingly in her face, cutting off the words she was about to speak.

Kath gasped, a hand flying to her mouth. She felt inclined to turn and run, but Owain, coming up behind her, grabbed her arm with fingers of steel. He leaned forward, lifted the latch and kicked the door open, then strode into the room. Kath risked a glance at his face and saw it black with rage. 'Sit down!' he commanded her, then turned to his grandmother, who faced up to him like a little bantam confronting a great cockerel, the fury on her features as plain as that on his.

'This is *my* house, and I shall say who may pass my threshold,' she hissed. 'You are welcome in my home, as are all of my blood, but she—'

'Unless you accept my wife, take the gifts she has brought you and apologise for the way you have treated her today – no, the way you have always treated her – then I shall never visit this house again,' Owain said, and now his voice was cold as ice, though his eyes still blazed. 'Well?'

'How dare you speak to your own nain in such a wicked fashion?' the old woman began, but her husband, who had been sitting on the settle by the fire, laid aside the sail he was patching and got to his feet.

'Mind your words, Eirwen,' he said warningly. 'Our boy means what he says and if he goes, then I go.' The old man's voice for once was firm and his face, when Kath turned to look at him, was set, his chin jutting.

Kath waited as the silence stretched and stretched, but in the end it was she who broke it. 'What a pretty name, Eirwen,' she said musingly. 'If I'm ever lucky enough to have a little girl, I shall call her Eirwen.'

The words, spoken softly, did the trick, broke the ice which had formed almost visibly around the protagonists. Nain sat down abruptly, took a deep breath and spoke stiffly. 'I believe I forgot myself; to turn a visitor away goes against Welsh hospitality. Naturally, as my grandson's wife, I must make you welcome.'

Some of the tension eased and Owain went over to the fire and pulled the kettle over the flame. 'I shall make tea, Nain, whilst you apologise for the words we shall all remember, no matter how hard we try to forget,' he said softly. But Kath could hear the latent threat in his tone and was not surprised when his grandmother actually brought herself to meet Kath's eyes and to mutter that she was sorry if anything she'd said had caused offence.

Taid began to say that since the Swtan was his home as well as his wife's he must share in the apology, but the kettle boiled at this point and in the bustle of brewing the tea, putting the apple cake on a plate and slicing it, the matter of apologising was put aside, much to Kath's relief. She had no desire to humiliate either of the old people, and thought it best that they should now proceed as if the enmity had never existed.

So they ate and drank, the women leaving the burden of conversation to their menfolk, and when Owain wiped his mouth and got to his feet, saying that he was going to take his wife down to the shore to dig some cockles, neither Nain nor Taid begged them to stay.

It had not been an easy half-hour – it had felt more like a week to Kath – and both parties were anxious to part as soon as possible, but with at least the semblance of normality. Owen went out to the shed and fetched a couple of spades and two elderly buckets, and then they set off for the beach. Kath had scarcely realised how tense she had felt until they had left the Swtan behind them, whereupon both she and Owain let out a long sigh of relief, then turned and smiled at one another.

'Oh, Kath, I'm so sorry to put you through that,' Owain said as soon as they were well out of earshot of the cottage. 'Nain was so rude, so hateful! But I honestly believe that we did the right thing by making her aware of her behaviour. I know it was a bit sticky even after she'd apologised, but I'm sure we've put things straight now. In fact next time she wants a lift into Holyhead, you should be the one to take her, instead of me or one of the farmhands. Now that the ice has been broken we mustn't let it form again. You and Nain will doubtless become good friends if you can meet one another on neutral ground. I do believe the trouble was mainly because the old saying is true: two women in one kitchen won't go. Now that you've both got your own place, you'll go on as merrily as a wedding bell.'

Kath looked at him wonderingly; how blind men can be, she thought. Every glance the old woman had shot at her, every word she had spoken, had convinced Kath that the idea of friendship between them was merely wishful thinking. All that existed was a truce, and that would only remain in force while Owain was present. If she took the pony trap down to the Swtan and offered to give Nain a lift into town, or to the Thursday market at Llangefni, then she was sure the old lady would find some excuse not to accompany her. She did not voice these thoughts aloud, however, but merely said, as they reached the long hard stretch of sand left by the receding tide, that she hoped Owain was right. 'By the way, I seem to remember you saying you were going to get a pony and trap for your grand-parents, so that they could have some independence,' she reminded him. 'Wouldn't that be easier than making them reliant on us?'

'It would, but they've nowhere to house either a pony or a trap, and it would just be an added expense,' Owain said. He grinned at his wife's expression. 'And now let's get plenty of cockles, so that we can leave a bucketful with the old 'uns as well as taking home enough for our supper tonight.'

Chapter Fourteen

March 1924

Kath was deeply asleep after a hard day's work lambing when someone touched her shoulder gently and then sat down on the bed, which creaked a protest loud enough, Kath thought crossly, to wake the dead. 'Go away,' she mumbled. 'I'm flaming well asleep.'

Someone laughed gently and a hand smoothed her hair before tugging the covers, which she had hunched round her ears, down to her waist. Kath moaned and tried to follow them, but stopped as the remains of sleep cleared from her mind and a voice she knew and loved spoke in her ear.

'I'm so sorry to wake you, my darling Kath, but we need you desperately in the big barn. We want your small hands to get inside a ewe and turn a lamb so it can be born,' Owain said softly.

Kath scrambled out of bed and flung on her working clothes; no time to wash the sleep from her eyes, or gulp a cup of tea, for Owain had said the situation was already desperate. Swaying with weariness, she followed him to the stairs and clattered down them, across the calm, firelit kitchen and out into the windy dark.

She gasped as the cold wind battered her and the rain lashed across her face, so that she was grateful when Owain's large hand enclosed her small one and hauled her into the lamplit barn. He had shouted something to her as they crossed the yard, but so violent was the wind that she had not heard a word.

'The ewe is an old one, no novice to lambing, which means there really is something wrong, else I'd not have woken you,' he repeated. They were inside the barn now and Owain was pointing, though even in her slightly befuddled state Kath would have known which of the ewes was in trouble. The poor animal stood there, head hanging low, her heavy fleece trembling with every panting breath. It was obvious that Owain had left it until the last possible moment before rousing his wife, knowing that she had had an exhausting day, had not gone to bed until near on midnight. It could not be more than three or four in the morning, and here she was again.

Nevertheless, as she approached the ewe, Kath threw Owain a reproachful look. 'You should have got me earlier. I just hope it's not too late,' she said as she knelt by the stricken beast.

'I know I should, but I kept hoping she'd manage without help,' Owain mumbled. 'I did my best, but my hands are too bloody big; I'm all right when the cows are calving, but sheep are a different matter.' He came to stand beside Kath, idly scratching the ewe's woolly head. 'Do you think you can . . . aah!'

Kath, laying the first little lamb next to its mother so that the ewe could clean it, smiled triumphantly, but remained kneeling. 'There's another one in there, though I doubt it will need any help. I felt the head and a foreleg, so it should come . . .' Even as she spoke, the ewe strained and a second little lamb was neatly fielded by Kath. 'I knew it must be twins . . .' she was beginning when the ewe strained again and instead of the afterbirth, which Kath had been expecting, another lamb was born. Kath gave a squeak of surprise, picked up the tiny animal and put it by its mother, then turned a gleeful smile upon Owain and saw that he was smiling too.

'Another job for you, Kath,' he said, as the ewe began to clean up this small, surprised packet. 'She can't possibly manage three, so this 'un will have to go in the bottle-rearing pen with the other lambs whose mothers can't, or won't, feed them.' He looked affectionately at the ewe. 'She's a grand lass. The old 'uns always make the best mothers, but three is too much for anyone. Here, give me your hands.' He pulled Kath to her feet and gave her a kiss. 'You're worth your weight in gold, Kath Jones! I suppose you know you've saved four lives today? Another half-hour of struggle and the old ewe would have died, and the three lambs with her.'

'Thank you, kind sir, but you'd have done the job yourself if you'd had smaller hands,' Kath said, feeling her cheeks grow hot with pleasure at Owain's praise nevertheless. 'Gosh, I could do with a paned right now. We'll leave her to clean up whilst we do likewise.'

Owain hooked his gunmetal watch out of his pocket and examined it, tilting it so that the lamp's glow fell on its face. 'Goodness, it's five o'clock! Well, I suppose you could go back to bed for a couple of hours, but I don't reckon you will. Eifion will come up from his cottage at seven to do the next shift in the lambing shed and you and I will start our normal day's work.' He grinned at her, slinging a careless arm about her waist and dropping a kiss somewhere in the region of her left ear. 'What a good little wife you are. And you aren't the only one longing for a cup of tea.'

Owain opened the barn door with considerable caution and Kath realised that the storm had grown even more violent whilst they had been dealing with the birth of the triplets. The big old walnut tree screamed and moaned as the wind tore at its branches and Kath was glad of Owain's strong arm round her waist as they struggled across the farmyard and into the warmth and stillness of the kitchen.

'God help all sailors on a night like this,' Kath gasped, sinking into a chair and watching as Owain opened the fire grate and pulled the kettle over the flame. 'I'll make some toast, shall I?'

They were sitting at the kitchen table, drinking the promised cup of tea and eating thick slices of toast, and Kath was just thinking, smugly, how nice it was to hear the gale battering at the stout old walls of Ty Hen, which had weathered many such storms, when the back door burst open. She glanced towards it, expecting to see Eifion or one of the other farmhands, but instead it was Nain, wild-eyed and white-faced. She did not come right into the kitchen, but spoke in a high, trembling voice, ignoring Kath and addressing her grandson. 'Owain, you must come. Taid took the *Valma* out – I told him not to, forbade him to in fact – but he *would* go. He took no heed of the weather warnings . . .'

'Taid took the boat out?' Kath said blankly. 'But it's night-time . . .'

'He would have gone out before the storm started,' Owain said quickly. He turned to his grandmother. 'What weather warnings? What are you talking about, Nain? Have you been sleep-walking?'

His grandmother clenched her bony hands and stepped right into the room. She had left the door open behind her, but the wind seized it and slammed it shut with enough force to make the plates on the dresser rattle. Still ignoring Kath, the old woman crossed the room and, grabbing Owain by the shoulders, shook him feebly. 'Fool, fool! There was no storm last night, but the signs of it were in the sky for anyone to read, and the sea was too still, too calm. But he wouldn't listen; said it was weeks since we'd had fresh fish and he were that sick of salt herring . . . Owain, you must come, you must!'

Owain got to his feet, but only to unbutton his grand-mother's long black mackintosh, hang it on the hook by the door and push her into a chair, whilst Kath, obeying his gesture, topped up the teapot and poured the old lady a fresh cup. 'Drink that, Nain, while I toast you a round of bread,' she said. 'When you're feeling a little calmer, perhaps you can tell Owain what you want him to do.'

The old woman had been leaning back in her chair,

both thin hands curled around the hot cup, and Kath saw that her hair, which had at some stage been confined by a headscarf, was wet with rain and hanging round her face in straggly elf-locks. Her coat was done up on the wrong buttons and the slippers on her feet were thick with mud, as were her bare legs. For the first time, Kath felt deep and sincere pity for the poor little woman and tried to take her hand as she placed the plateful of toast on the table in front of her.

On feeling her touch, Nain's eyes snapped open and she cringed away from Kath as though the younger woman had hit her. Owain, his back to the table, was fetching out his stout boots and did not notice his grandmother's immediate rejection, nor the fact that she had stood down her tea in order to push the toast away, lip curling with distaste.

Kath shrugged and returned to her seat. She sipped her tea, telling herself that the old woman was too distressed to know what she was doing. 'What do you want Owain to do?' she repeated. 'You know he'd do anything in his power to help Taid, but in a storm like this . . .'

'He must saddle up his best horse and ride into Holyhead to call out the lifeboat,' Nain said. 'They'll know what to do.'

Owain had donned his oilskins, and now he turned and gave his grandmother's shoulder a reassuring squeeze. 'I'll do whatever's possible,' he said. He beckoned to Kath. 'Come with me; you can help me saddle up.' As Kath slid into her coat and tied a scarf over

367

her hair he turned back to his grandmother once more. 'Stay here till I return; don't attempt to go out in this awful weather,' he commanded. For the first time he noticed the untouched toast, and jabbed a finger at it. And eat your toast; I'll not leave this room until you've started it. Cut it into fingers and dip it in your tea, that will make it easier to swallow. And do as Kath tells you for once! Tell yourself you're doing it for Taid's sake.'

The old woman mumbled something but obeyed his command, and as she began to eat he and Kath left the room and headed across the yard to the stable. 'I'll take Prince,' Owain said, picking up the lantern which stood by the window embrasure. 'Jed's a grand fellow, but Prince will get me to my destination in half the time.'

Owain had bought Prince only six weeks before at a farm sale, liking the look of him and telling Kath that it would be useful to have a horse broken to riding as well as to the cart and plough. As he lifted the heavy saddle off its peg, Kath adjusted the blanket on the broad black back, then turned to her husband. 'What do you have to tell me that you don't want your gran to hear?' she demanded bluntly. 'You're perfectly capable of saddling up without any help, so you might as well spill the beans.'

'I wanted to say that I heard the maroons go up some time back, which must mean that the lifeboat is already out. Taid might have raised the alarm, firing off a rocket to let them know he's in trouble, or it may be some other craft needing help. But whichever it is, there's no point in my riding hell for leather to Holyhead. I'm going to make my way as fast as I can to Church Bay. Once I get to the cliff top, I should be able to see if there's a boat in the vicinity. If there is, at least I could light up the approach with my lantern, perhaps show him a safe way in. I feel I'd be more use there than in Holyhead. But don't say anything to Nain, there's a good girl.'

'I won't say a word,' Kath promised. 'Oh, I wish I could go with you. Don't forget how slippery the rocks are in rainy weather . . . promise me you'll take no unnecessary risks.'

Owain laughed but promised, and with the tacking up of Prince complete they led the enormous animal out of the stable. He flinched and snorted as the wind and rain lashed him, but stood obediently still whilst Owain swung himself into the saddle. Kath, hanging on to the bridle near the bit, let go and stepped back as Owain turned his mount in the direction of the lane. 'Take care, dearest,' she shouted. As the big horse turned right along the lane, something made Kath run after them. 'Owain, I love you and need you,' she shrieked above the howl of the gale. 'Please, for all our sakes, don't do anything rash.'

She saw the white disc of her husband's face turn towards her, saw his broad grin break out, and knew he had heard, though his reply was carried away by the wind. Kath waited until he was out of sight, then turned and headed back to the farm. She pushed open the kitchen door and went in, relieved to be out of the storm. Nain had disappeared, and for a moment Kath thought she must have gone to her old room in search of dry clothing, or perhaps to the ty bach at the end of the garden. Then she noticed that Nain's mackintosh no longer hung from its hook and her headscarf, which Kath had laid to one side of the stove to dry out, was also missing. Heart thumping, Kath surveyed the room and saw, kicked carelessly amongst the boots which stood close to the door, a pair of tiny, mud-splattered slippers. Kath groaned as she realised that there was a gap in the row of boots; her own were still there, but a pair that one of the farmhands had left behind was missing from its usual place. She tried to tell herself that Nain must have put them on to visit the ty bach, that she would return presently to finish her tea and eat the rest of her toast, but it was no use. She was not convinced.

Hastily, she kicked off her shoes, pushed her feet into her gumboots, tied a scarf round her hair and, with a last wistful look round the warm, well-lit kitchen, set off to investigate the ty bach, though she was already sure she would find it unoccupied. She did, and returned at top speed to the kitchen, cursing Nain beneath her breath and telling herself that no one could blame her if she simply went back to bed. You stupid old woman, she told Nain inside her head. You'd rather die of exposure than spend a few hours with me! Well, though he did not say so, Owain expects me to take care of you, so I'll have to see if I can find where you've gone. Would it be left to Holyhead or right to Church Bay? Which way, which way? She felt like Alice in Wonderland when faced with a similar dilemma; if she ate the right side of the mushroom would she grow smaller or larger?

Kath was about to leave the kitchen once more when she remembered that Eifion and the other farm workers would be arriving quite soon, possibly before she returned. She went over to the dresser, picked up the slate and chalk by means of which she and Owain often left messages and wrote: *Gone to Church Bay, back soon, get your own breakfast.* Then she propped the slate up on the table and let herself out of the kitchen, slamming the door regretfully on the warmth and comfort, and realising as she did so that the storm had eased considerably. The sky was brighter to the east, and though the clouds still hurried across the sky the wind had dropped and the rain fell less steadily. When she led Jemima out into the yard and mounted the little mare, she felt almost cheerful. Now that she could see morning was almost upon them, she was more certain than ever that Nain would have returned to the Swtan. If I hurry, I can be there soon after she arrives, she told herself. She'll go by the fields, of course, which is quicker, but once it's light enough to see any potholes or fallen branches across the lane the pony and I will make even better speed. I must remember to be very conciliatory, tell her I've only come to her home because it was what Owain told me to do, and perhaps she'll realise, at last, that I don't mean to supplant her, but to succour her in her hour of need.

Buoyed up by these thoughts, she urged Jemima into a trot.

* * *

371

Owain reached the Swtan at the height of the storm. Rain was streaming down his neck where the oilskin failed to fit, and when he dismounted water simply cascaded from the big horse. Owain stared around him. Where should he tether Prince? The sheds were all far too small, but if he took him round to the side of the Swtan he would at least be out of the worst of the wind.

Tying him up, Owain glanced at the longhouse, but no light showed. He guessed that his grandmother would have damped down the fire before setting out on her perilous cross-country hike, and went indoors to light his lantern. He was still angry whenever he thought of his nain's mad journey, but his anger was mixed with indulgence, for the old woman had been understandably worried and had turned to him for help. The fact that she had not heard the maroons, or if she had heard them had not understood their meaning, was scarcely her fault. Owain, setting out in the direction of the cliffs, reminded himself that though his grandmother's tongue was still sharp as a knife, her hearing was dulling with age, though she would never admit it . . .

At this point in his musings, Owain had reached the cliff top. He was just wondering, rather apprehensively, whether he would be able to recognise the little path which led down to the beach when a great black cloud which had hidden the moon scudded away and in the brief, temporary light he saw his way clear; saw also the ferocity of the sea. Waves, white-topped and wicked, were hurling themselves at the shore as though they intended to climb the cliffs and snatch him, and anyone else abroad this night, down to a watery grave.

Despite himself, Owain flinched. If his grandfather really was out there in his tiny boat, his only possible chance of survival was to stay out to sea; trying to get any closer to such a rocky coast was certain death. But Owain hoped that Taid would have read the signs before the storm had overtaken him. It was not uncommon for fishermen from this part of the coast to seek shelter as far away as Ireland. Or he might have pulled in to any one of a dozen little bays, all of which would be safe enough to approach whilst the weather was fairly calm, but would have become death traps when waves towered ten or twelve feet high and the wicked teeth of the rocks were hidden in the crash of foam and spray.

Owain sat down on the cliff top and stared out to sea until his eyes ached. Was there a little dot out there? Could it be the *Valma*? Deciding his best course of action was to go down to the beach, he lodged the lamp in a thick clump of grass and began the descent. As he went he clutched at the noses of rocks and clumps of marram, frightened for the first time in his life of the drop beneath him, for the wind tore at his clothing, ripping open his jacket and forcing him to cower against the cliff lest he be hurled down on to the rocks below.

He gained the beach at last and was immediately soaked to the skin and battered by stones and debris as a big comber came crashing inland. He staggered but managed to keep his feet, though the undertow of the wave's retreat was truly frightening. Learning from this, he clung to the bottom of the cliff, making his way towards the ridge of rocks which he could just make out by what light there was from the dark and angry sky. The ridge was in the shelter, if you could call it that, of an arm of the cliff, so though the sea surge was violent enough it did not compare with what was roaring in on the main beach. Owain climbed gingerly on to the highest rock in the ridge and turned to gaze seaward just as a large and extremely heavy piece of wood crashed against his knees. He grabbed for it and caught a glimpse, as it hurtled past his outstretched fingers, of three letters: *Val* . . . The rest of the name was hidden beneath the wave, but Owain had seen enough to turn his blood to ice.

Casting caution to the winds, he tried to hurry towards what he now saw was not just a dark blob of flotsam but a man, being carried by the next wave towards the wicked rocks. Fear lent him strength, and despite the conditions he was reaching out a hand towards the bundle of saturated clothing when a violent movement of the water turned it over and for the first time Owain saw its face, or rather what had once been its face, for now it was unrecognisable, horrible. It might have been his taid or a total stranger; it was impossible to tell. Then for an instant he saw a pale hand, the fingers crooked as though still desperately holding on to something, and on the third finger of that hand Owain saw the big, old-fashioned signet ring which, he knew, his nain had given to her man on their wedding day.

Shock must have made him loosen his hold on the rocks for one instant, but that instant was sufficient for the sea to catch him, drag him down and whirl him away into its dark depths.

Kath had seen the Swtan from afar as she and the pony came fast along the lane and realised at once that it was unoccupied. No light showed, not even the glow of a fire. She was clearly well ahead of the old woman and could go straight to the cliffs, for she was pretty sure that Owain would have made for the beach. She felt she needed to speak to him, to explain that she had done her best, that Nain had fled whilst the two of them were saddling Prince. Glancing at the lightening sky, she decided to tie Jemima's reins up so that the mare could not put a foot in them and leave her to graze until it was time for her to be ridden home.

She was about to set off when she hesitated, then turned towards the Swtan. She would nip in, make up the fire and put the kettle on to boil. Even if the old woman resented what she would no doubt regard as interference, Owain – and Taid too, if he had come safe ashore – would be glad of a decent fire and a hot drink. As soon as she reached the longhouse, however, she saw Prince, tethered against the end wall, and knew for certain that her husband had gone down to the shore. For a moment she was tempted to make straight for the beach, then chided herself. What could she do down there that Owain could not? No, it was her duty to make the Swtan a comfortable refuge from the storm.

Inside the cottage it was the work of a moment to make up the fire until it roared satisfactorily and to hang the filled kettle over it. Then Kath set out, battling against the wind which, though it had eased a good deal, seemed spitefully determined to prevent her from reaching her objective.

As she fought the elements, Kath spared a thought for Nain; she might not like the old woman – could scarcely be expected to do so – but she had to admit that she had courage. I'll just check Owain doesn't need me on the shore and then I'll set off across the fields to see if I can give Nain a hand, Kath told herself. Obstinate old devil that she is, I wouldn't like to think of her in trouble. She's Owain's gran, after all.

When Kath reached the cliff top, the wind still roared and spatterings of rain made it difficult to see what was happening below. But she thought that the tide had turned and guessed that as the waves receded the sea would grow calmer. She dared not go too near the cliff edge but could see no sign of Owain, Taid or the *Valma*. However, if they were close against the cliff she would be unable to see them, though why they should linger in such a dangerous spot she could not imagine. On impulse, she dropped to her knees and began to crawl towards the edge of the cliff. It was not a pleasant journey, for the grass was long and wet and strewn with sharp little pebbles, but then she saw the lamp and knew that Owain had come this way. She made it at last and, peering down, suddenly remembered the caves which she and Owain had once explored. They would, she supposed, offer temporary shelter to two men who needed to rest before tackling the steep cliff path.

She was about to turn away to begin her search for Nain when she saw something in the heaving, restless waves which sent her standing upright, despite the elements, and stumbling towards the cliff path. She had feared the descent in fine weather, but now she almost ran down it, heedless of the drop, the danger and every-thing but the need to see what it was that the waves were casting on the rocks. She reached the shore just as a comber surged around her, soaking her almost to her waist before it began to ebb, but Kath fought against it until she gained the rocks and the figure slumped across them. She had no need to see the face to know that it was Owain, for in the pearly dawn light she recognised the thick guernsey she had knitted for him the previous winter.

Shrieking his name at the top of her voice, she saw the next wave curling in and grabbed his shoulders, and here at last the sea helped her, picking up the pair of them as though they weighed no more than a wisp of hay and carrying them far up the beach before drop-ping them on the hard sand and beginning to retreat. Desperately, Kath hung on to a rock with one hand whilst the other clutched fiercely at Owain's shoul-ders, and somehow, by the grace of God she told herself, she managed to prevent the wave from carrying him out to sea once more.

Dragging him across the hard wet sand called for

every ounce of her strength, but Kath did not even notice the pain, the cracking muscles, buried as they were beneath the fear which dogged her every movement. Suppose she could not get him above the tideline? Suppose – and this was even more likely – she could not carry him up the steep and narrow path? She dared not leave him here whilst she went for help, for she had ascertained that he was only just breathing. Once clear of the water she saw with horror that he was bleeding profusely from a variety of wounds, his mouth, brow and one cheek deeply gashed . . . but he was alive.

Kath put a trembling hand on his brow, and it was cold as ice. She looked around wildly; what in God's name was she to do for the best? She thought she might be able to drag him into the nearest cave whilst she went for help, but the fear of returning to find him dead was too strong.

She began as gently as she could to pull him towards the foot of the cliff, but stopped with a squeak of surprise when another pair of hands seized his shoulders and began to tug. The movement forced a groan from Owain's lips and Kath said sharply: 'Careful! He's badly injured. Can you go for help?'

She looked up at the owner of the hands and it was Nain. Kath could not tell if it was tears or rain pouring down the old woman's cheeks, but it really did not matter. What mattered was that she could send Nain up the cliff again, tell her to mount the pony and fetch help from the nearest village to get Owain to safety.

The old woman began to pull once more, but Kath

plucked her hands away and gestured to the cliffs behind them. 'Go for help,' she said briefly. 'Ride Jemima up to the village and explain. Can you ride the pony?'

'No, so I'll stay with him while you go,' Nain said, her voice coming out as a croak. 'You're younger'n me—'

Kath interrupted her without compunction. 'If we don't get him warm, he'll die of exposure. I'll go up to the Swtan to fetch blankets. If we can roll him up in them, then between us we should be able to carry him into a cave. The tide's on the ebb, so there's no fear that the water will penetrate that far. Once he's safe there, I'll go for help, if you prefer to stay with him.'

The old woman nodded and Kath set out at once, scrambling up the cliff path, wrapping blankets in a piece of rough canvas and returning to Owain's side. It was the work of a very few minutes for the two women to roll Owain gently on to the blankets and carry him carefully into the cave. 'Will you be all right here?' Kath asked the older woman. 'I'll be as quick as I can. Only I don't think he should be moved again because he's broken several bones and his breathing's not too good.' She looked doubtfully at her companion. Nain was soaked to the skin and filthy; her skirt was torn and there were fragments of gorse and bramble embedded in her long mackintosh. She looked a poor little thing, with her white face and draggled hair, but Kath noted with satisfaction the martial gleam in her eyes. Nain would do everything in her power to ensure that her grandson lived and she, Kath, would do everything in *her* power to fetch help with all possible speed.

Satisfied that she was doing the best for her husband, she turned away from the cove and began the climb to the top of the cliffs.

Chapter Fifteen

They took Owain to the Gors Hospital and Kath knew from the look on the doctor's face and from the attitude of the nurses that they did not expect their patient to live. 'Multiple injuries of this sort may mean internal injuries as well,' the doctor in charge said gently. 'The next few days will be crucial. We shall have to operate and then, I hope, we shall know a little more. We'll need to pin and plaster and generally deal with his broken bones and then see what happens when he regains consciousness . . .'

But he did not. For several weeks he lay very still and straight in his hospital bed, arms and legs in plaster, head, neck and shoulder swathed in bandages. Kath scarcely moved from his side, talking to him quietly of how he would soon be well, must not give up, must not dare to leave her who loved and needed him so much.

Nain came in from time to time. She and everyone else still hoped that the *Valma* had been driven ashore somewhere in Ireland and that Taid, perhaps suffering from memory loss, was being nursed back to health by the good people of the Irish coast. That hope was fading fast, however, since a fisherman, setting lobster pots in Church Bay, had found remnants of a once sturdy fishing boat with the letters *'Val'* painted on what was left of its prow.

Many visitors came, hoping to see Owain, but the staff turned them away, all but Nain, who once actually spoke to Kath. 'Get some rest; I'll keep him safe while you're gone,' she said gruffly, and Kath accepted this solitary sign of softening, knowing that it cost the old woman dear. Nain was still convinced that her own man was alive, but though she would not have said so for the world, Kath thought it very unlikely. Taid was an old man and had never learned to swim, saying that a fisherman's place was on top of the water and not in it. But Kath was far too involved in caring for her Owain to worry about Taid, who had had a full and happy life. If he was indeed dead she would miss him, but it was far more important to her that Owain should recover.

It was three long weeks before Owain regained consciousness, and then it was only for a few minutes. Kath had been sitting by his bed, holding his hand and reading him an article from one of his farming magazines, when she felt the fingers, so limp and apparently lifeless in her own, tighten for a moment. She looked up immediately and saw that Owain's dark eyes were half open. Heart thumping, she got carefully to her feet and bent over him. For a moment he looked puzzled, as though he could not focus on a face so near his own. Then he smiled. 'Are you an angel?' he asked in a slurred voice, but before she could reply his eyelids had dropped once more and his fingers slackened.

Kath rang the bell by the bed and gasped out her news when a nurse appeared, almost breathless with excitement. The little nurse ran for a doctor, but though Kath whispered and cajoled and the doctor commanded Owain to speak to them, there was no response. It was another two days before the patient's eyes opened once more and this time he gave Kath an unsteady smile. 'Where am I? What happened?' He groaned. 'I feel as if I've been run over by one of them trams I saw in Liverpool. Is this Liverpool? Kath, for God's sweet's sake, tell me what's been happening.'

Briefly, Kath outlined what had brought Owain to this point. She told of the storm, his attempts to either light his grandfather into the bay or warn him off, she was not sure which. She told of the struggle to get him clear of the waves and the awful damage he had suffered from being pounded against the jagged rocks. She told of Nain's help . . . and at that point his face, which had seemed calm, almost indifferent, sharpened into grief. 'Taid's dead,' he whispered, his voice shaking. 'I tried to bring his body ashore, but the waves snatched it away from me. Does Nain know yet? You must tell her gently. Tell her she can live with us . . . tell her . . .' His voice faded into silence and Kath saw that the effort of both listening and speaking had been too much and consciousness had left him once more.

She dreaded the thought of telling Nain that her husband was dead, but, to her immense relief, she did not have to do so. Leaving the hospital that evening to return to Ty Hen, she met one of Owain's elderly uncles. He had been coming regularly to the hospital to get news of Owain and stopped short when he saw Kath. 'I don't know if you've heard, Mrs Jones, but Owain's taid's body has come ashore,' he said. 'Told Eirwen, I have – Owain's nain, I mean – and promised her I'd tell the lad, if they'll let me in.' He jerked his head towards the hospital's revolving doors.

'He already knows; he saw the body just before he fell into the sea himself,' Kath said. 'He told me so and asked me to break it to his nain.' She gave the old man a tentative smile. 'So you won't have to tell Owain, and I can't tell you how grateful I am that you have saved me from having to convey such dreadful news to my husband's grandmother.'

Anxious not to intrude upon the older woman's grief, yet mindful of Owain's wish that she take care of the old lady, Kath left it a couple of days before setting out in the pony and trap on her visit of condolence. The wind was strong, and when she reached the Swtan she turned Jemima towards the shelter of the row of new stone outbuildings which Owain and his grandfather had built the previous autumn.

Once there, she tethered the little mare and provided her with an armful of hay, then walked across to the longhouse. She was nervous, half expecting a rebuff, telling herself that at worst Nain could only refuse her help. She knocked on the door, softly at first and then more loudly. No one came and Kath put her hand on the latch and pushed, suddenly afraid of what she might find. Suppose Nain was ill, had collapsed . . . but before she could so much as step over the threshold Nain, tidily dressed and with her hair in its accustomed bun, tugged the door fully open, almost precipitating Kath into the room. Kath began to laugh. 'Nain! It's all right, it's only me.'

Nain looked furious, but then her expression changed to a smile which touched her lips but did not reach her eyes. She hesitated, then said, 'Come in. The kettle's on the boil; we'll have a cup of tea. But I haven't much time: a relative is coming presently to give me a lift into town. I need to buy mourning clothes . . . You've heard? My poor darling, the man who meant everything to me . . .' Her voice broke and she turned away, hurrying over to take the kettle from its hook and pour boiling water into the waiting pot. 'There's a little cake in the pantry . . .'

'Oh, Nain, if I'd known you needed to go into town I'd have come for you myself,' Kath said eagerly. 'Is it too late to come in the trap with me? There's something we must discuss – Owain told me to ask you if you would like to move into Ty Hen—'

'No, to change my mind when my brother-in-law has offered to take me to town would give offence,' Nain said immediately. 'As for moving in . . . but I've no time to talk about it now.' She tilted her head and Kath heard the sound of a horse and cart approaching. 'I'll not linger for a paned; you make your own, there's a good girl.' She snatched her coat off its peg, looked quickly round the room, then buttoned the garment and tied a black head square over her thin grey locks. 'Damp down the fire before you leave, would you? And it would be a help if you'd feed the hens and the pig. I've got to go. You'll be gone by the time I return.'

As she spoke she was lifting the latch and letting herself out of the door, and through the window Kath saw the old woman climbing into a cart driven by a man Kath did not know. Before she could so much as go to the door to wave, the equipage had driven off.

Frowning thoughtfully, Kath damped down the fire and made herself a cup of tea, then sat down by the table to drink it. She was puzzled; running the scene through her mind again she realised that none of it made sense. Why had Nain not invited her relative in? She had flown to the door in a fury when Kath herself had arrived . . . but then had come the change of attitude, the smile, the soft words, the invitation to come inside and drink a cup of tea.

I believe I know why she behaved the way she did, Kath decided after some thought. Nain must have known that her brother-in-law would be arriving at any moment and for some reason she didn't want me to meet him. Why, she made certain I wouldn't do so by telling me to feed the poultry and the pig after she left, which would hold me up for some time . . . so that I couldn't overtake them on the road. Now that I've had time to consider, she had a downright crafty look on her face when she was telling me to see to the stock.

Kath went over to the sink and rinsed her cup, stood it on the draining board and headed for the door. She had not taken off her coat, and now, glancing round the kitchen, she checked that all was in order. The clock on the wall showed that noon was approaching, and she decided not to bother feeding the stock, a task which she realised now Nain would have performed several hours ago.

Instead, she left the cottage, went over to Jemima and untied her rope halter, climbed into the trap and turned the pony's head for home. Pointless to wonder why the old woman had behaved so oddly. I must simply accept that grief has made her even more difficult than usual, Kath told herself. I won't mention it to Owain, because what is there to mention, after all? I'll say, truthfully, that she asked me in for a cup of tea, but said she was too busy to talk about what help she might need. She was off into Holyhead to buy mourning clothes, though since she almost always dresses in black that doesn't seem terribly important when compared to discussing her future.

Kath returned to the farm, checked that the workers had done all that was necessary until evening milking, and set off for the hospital. She knew that Owain would be anxious to hear his grandmother's reaction to the suggestion that she might move in with them, but when she entered his small room he looked as much surprised as delighted. 'I didn't expect to see you today,' he said in the thin, creaky voice to which she had become accustomed. 'How did it go?' Kath began to give him the little speech she had prepared about her visit to the Swtan, but Owain frowned and shook his head. 'No, cariad, I was talking about Taid's funeral. I'm surprised you managed to get here – or did you not go to the church hall for the funeral tea? I hope you did, or I'm afraid people will be upset.'

Kath stared at him; she could feel the blood draining

from her face. 'Funeral?' she whispered. 'No one told me the funeral was to be held today. Why didn't you tell me?'

'Because I didn't know myself until my uncle came in last night, after you'd left. I said you'd not know, but he said that was all right, he'd get a message to you somehow, although he was sure Nain would have told you already.'

Kath had been standing, but as the import of his words struck her she dropped down on to the bed, scarcely heeding Owain's gasp of pain. 'My God, that was why your grandmother was so cross this morning,' she said. 'When I went round to the Swtan she told me she was going into town to buy mourning clothes. She said nothing whatever about the funeral, and asked me to do some small jobs for her whilst she was gone. Oh, Owain, how could she be so wicked?'

Owain sighed. 'She's always been a strange woman. Oh, my poor love! When I get out of here I'll do my best to undo the harm she's caused. I'll tell folk that you'd not been informed when the funeral was to take place—'

He stopped speaking as Kath put a gentle hand across his mouth. 'Never mind, dearest Owain,' she said softly. 'It really doesn't matter. What matters is getting you right, and back to Ty Hen. The people who are closest to us, the farmhands and so on, will know me well enough to disbelieve spiteful stories. But I think it would be a waste of breath to suggest that Nain should move back in with us.'

'Don't worry, I shall do no such thing,' Owain said

grimly. 'You must ask the parson to come and see me. I'll explain to him exactly what has happened, and hope he will reprimand the old cythraul and explain to the congregation why you didn't attend the funeral. Then I shall make Nain apologise.'

'I'd rather you didn't,' Kath said. 'If she has to say she's sorry – which I'm sure she isn't – it will simply be another black mark against my name. I'll ask the parson to come and see you, though, and trust in his goodwill to explain to as many people as possible that I didn't know the funeral was today.'

'I hate to think of her getting away with it,' Owain said in a small, tired voice. 'But I suspect you're right; sometimes making waves simply starts a storm.' He gave a weary sigh. 'Come to think of it, the worst punishment I could inflict is to simply not visit the Swtan, because after the way she's behaved she'll not come within a mile of Ty Hen, and I will never cross her threshold again. I'll have to see that one of the men helps out when she needs a hand, but other than that . . .'

Kath thought of the old woman alone in the long-house with memories of her dead husband and no one to talk to, or share in the work, and her heart smote her. Nain hated her, had done her best to ensure that she was shunned by the community, but she was old and her prejudices were immovable. Yet if Owain did go to the Swtan she would consider it a victory and tell folk that Owain was on her side against me. I suppose it would be best to let her go to perdition in her own way, but she's Owain's grandmother . . . oh dear, what to do for the best? If only Taid were alive . . .

Owain must have been thinking along similar lines, for he suddenly put out a heavily bandaged hand and laid it on top of his wife's. 'What about old Bleddyn Jones? He's a cross-grained old fellow, but if I pay him a good weekly wage to work for Nain until her death he'll not refuse.'

'Oh, Owain, that sounds grand. But would your nain accept it?'

'She'll have no choice,' Owain said at once. 'After all, we've been supplying them – her and Taid, I mean – with all sorts, including labour, ever since they moved out of Ty Hen. But so much as put a foot over the threshold I will not, and neither will you.'

'She wouldn't let me near nor by, no matter what,' Kath said ruefully. 'But you've hit upon the ideal solution, I'm sure. When I visit you tomorrow I'll bring a notebook and pencil and you can dictate a letter to this Bleddyn, outlining your offer. But right now, dearest, you must rest; you look worn to the bone.'

September 1940

'And did it work?' Nell asked eagerly, watching her aunt's face in the increasing light. 'That Nain sounds a dreadful old woman. But Owain's plan was a really good one, because though folk might guess Bleddyn was being paid by someone other than Nain they couldn't be sure, so the old woman didn't have to admit she was your pensioner.'

Auntie Kath smiled grimly, then went and pulled

the kettle over the flame once more. 'It's time we had another brew,' she observed. 'And yes, Owain's plan worked well. Nain never attempted to visit Ty Hen, and very soon Owain could not have endured the journey to visit her even if he had wanted to, for chronic rheumatism, arthritis and other such ailments – all the result of the many injuries he had sustained – had crippled him. He tried to make light of his pain and still kept his finger on the pulse of the farm, but it was I and the farmhands who carried out the actual work. Then he slipped coming down the stairs, and though the doctor wanted to send him to hospital he refused to go, insisting that he would rather be nursed in his own bed. The doctor told me privately that he doubted my poor Owain would last until Christmas; he had fractured his hip in the fall and was in a very bad way.

'What with nursing Owain and running the farm I had no spare time, but Eifion was a tower of strength. I sent him over to the Swtan now and again, just to make sure that all was well there, though I would never have dreamed of letting Nain know we were keeping an eye on her. Eifion said that Bleddyn was usually digging the garden or rounding up the cows for milking, whilst Nain was either pottering around seeing to the pig and the poultry or sitting on the bench beside the door, staring at the path which led to Ty Hen.' Auntie Kath sighed. 'I imagine she sat there so that if I suddenly appeared she could either rush inside and lock and bolt the door or simply scream abuse at me, as she had on other occasions.'

Nell opened her mouth to speak, then saw that her

aunt had only paused for breath and might, if she interrupted, refuse to say anything further, so she stayed silent and merely nodded her understanding, though she would have liked to say that Nain might have watched for her in order to put things right. However, Kath was talking again.

'If I'd not been so busy – and so deeply unhappy – I believe I would have dared her wrath and gone to the Swtan to tell her how ill her grandson was, but somehow the opportunity never arose, and though Owain mentioned his grandmother a couple of times, by then he scarcely knew me, let alone her. I knew he was dying, but his death, when it came, was still a dreadful, awful shock.

'I sent word by Eifion to tell her when the funeral would be held and she came to the church, but when I tried to speak to her she turned her back on me, muttering to another old woman that she would always blame me for Owain's death. I think then that the iron entered my soul and my dislike of her turned to something very close to hatred. I vowed that I would never exchange another word with her, never so much as put a foot on her farmland, let alone attempt to cross her threshold. And though I still asked Eifion to check on the Swtan occasionally, I never went within a mile of the place, nor ever shall. Not even now, so many years later. I thought then, and still think, that the long-house should really have belonged to the old woman, but when his will was read Owain had left everything he possessed to me, including the Swtan.

'When Nain died only twelve months after him, I

told Bleddyn he was welcome to move into the long-house and live there rent free whilst he needed to do so, but I think he left after a few months, by which time the place was already so neglected that no one was willing to take it on. The Jones family might have wanted it, though they never said so, but after the way they had behaved towards Owain and me I most certainly did not want them as tenants. So now you know, my dear, why I've never visited the Swtan.'

'But why not now, when the old lady's been dead for so long?' Nell asked reasonably. 'Hywel told me that Toddy isn't a gypsy but a respectable man, trying to make a decent living where he can.'

Kath sniffed. 'I suppose I should speak to the wretched man, tell him he's welcome to continue to live in the Swtan if that's the only way he can keep a roof over his head. But why should I? He's taken over without so much as a by your leave. If I suddenly turn up, he'll probably think I want rent.'

'And if he pays rent, you'll feel you have to spend every penny of it, and more, on rethatching and repairs,' Nell said cheerfully. 'Oh, Auntie, what a humbug you are! You try to pretend you're an old scrooge, when really you're not in the least interested in money.'

Her aunt nodded. 'That's true; money's only money, after all. But Eifion is rare fond of fresh fish or the odd crab or lobster and still goes over there from time to time and takes the boat out. I don't ever question him about his visits, but he tells me this Toddy isn't that old; he was shell-shocked in the Great War and needs a peaceful existence and country living.' The smile that

Kath turned on her niece was suddenly mischievous. 'I'm told he's a quiet man, not at all curious like some I could mention, which is one thing in his favour. And now we'd best get to bed otherwise we shan't have any sleep tonight.'

Nell was happy to obey, especially when Auntie Kath wrote a note for Maggie, telling her to get breakfast for herself and Eifion, and then to start the milking, *by which time*, she had added in her stilted copperplate, *Nell and I should have recovered from our night on the tiles and will be able to tackle the rest of the chores with you.*

When she slid between the sheets, however, Nell's active mind went on working, refusing all suggestion of sleep. So many things which had been a mystery, a closed book, were now clear. The kaleidoscope and the hidden picture of the man her aunt had once loved, the reason for hiding it, even the connection between Ty Hen and the Swtan had been more or less explained, and so romantically, too. She longed to see the inside of the Swtan, the cottage where so many stirring events had taken place. And what of the vague figure she had seen behind the old man on her one and only visit to the longhouse? Hywel had told her it was a ghost in order, she was sure, to chill her blood. Suppose, however, that what she had seen really *was* the ghost of Nain, who had done Auntie Kath so much harm . . .

Nell sighed and reminded herself that she did not believe in ghosts, though she did believe in the 'seeing' of past events, which Hywel had described. But ghosts? Certainly not, Nell told herself, as sleep overcame her.

Chapter Sixteen

Despite Nell's intention, it was not until the spring of 1941 that she actually made arrangements to visit the Swtan. Aunt Kath had tried to keep her promise to see that they all had a day off, but once the cold began to bite Eifion's rheumatism set in with a vengeance, and from Christmas till the end of February he was unable even to hobble the short distance from his cottage to Ty Hen. Maggie, Nell and Auntie Kath called on him to find him bundled up in his warmest clothing and sitting as close as he could to the kitchen fire. He told them that his wife anointed his joints daily with goose grease, which accounted, Nell supposed, for the rather peculiar smell, and though she and Maggie had secret doubts about the efficacy of goose grease, Auntie Kath said that it didn't matter what they thought since both Eifion and his wife had a touching faith in its curative properties.

'Sometimes it's the believing which helps the cure along,' she assured the girls. 'You'll see. When it gets a bit warmer and Eifion comes back to work, he won't put his cure down to better weather, but will claim another success for goose grease.'

So days off had disappeared into the realms of the might have been and were more or less unregretted, though the girls worked incredibly hard from dawn till dusk. But the evenings were their own and they soon began to enjoy a varied social life. Nell was almost always partnered by Hywel, or sometimes by Bryn when he was in port. The fellows would pick the girls up in a borrowed car and take them back to Ty Hen when the dance ended, for like Cinderella they were under orders to be home before midnight.

'You're an odd girl, Nell Whitaker,' Maggie said one evening, as the two of them were in Nell's bedroom getting ready for a dance at a nearby village hall. They both agreed it was more fun to get ready for an evening's entertainment in the same room, which allowed them to help each other try out different hair styles, pin a flower to the shoulder of a dance dress, or simply chat. 'Bryn's the handsomest feller I've ever met and he's nice an' all. What's more, when he comes home on leave he's all over you like a cheap overcoat, but you always push him back. And then you snuggle up to him when you're dancing—'

'I do not!' Nell said indignantly, then softened. 'Well, I suppose I do, because it would be rude and hurtful to poker up and push him away. But as I keep telling everyone, I really don't want a serious relationship and Bryn does. He used to be light-hearted and full of fun, but since Dunkirk he's nagged on about my being his girl and I don't want to be anyone's girl. Why should I?'

Maggie sighed. 'If you feel like that I guess you're probably right, though I don't know how you can resist Bryn. He's so handsome and, if you don't mind my saying so, Hywel's no beauty.'

'Who said anything about Hywel?' Nell squeaked. 'He never tries anything on; he's never even kissed me!'

Maggie laughed derisively. 'But you like him, you know you do. When he's dancing with someone else you hardly take your eyes off him, but poor old Bryn could dance with Ingrid Bergman or Jane Russell and you wouldn't turn a hair. If someone gorgeous danced with Hywel, her perishin' eyes would be scratched out, sure as I'm standin' here.'

'Oh, rubbish,' Nell said, feeling her cheeks flame. If she were honest, she did have a soft spot for Hywel, though she would never have dreamed of admitting it, either to Hywel himself or to Bryn, far less to Maggie. 'And as for liking, you've given yourself away, old Maggie! You're keen on blond and beautiful Bryn. Don't deny it, it's as plain as the nose on your face.'

It pleased her to see Maggie's cheeks go pink, but then she felt ashamed. The other girl didn't have a hope in hell of gaining Bryn's attention. Even if she herself was sensible and firm and told him that she loved him like a brother and would never feel any stronger emotion for him, she was pretty sure he would not turn to Maggie for consolation. He would start to pursue one of the pretty Wrens stationed on HMS *Bee* in Holyhead and never give the land girl a second thought.

Why Bryn was so attracted to Nell herself, however, she really could not say, for when she looked in the mirror all she saw was a large pair of eyes whose greenish-hazel colour she thought nondescript, an elfin face with a small, pointy chin and a mass of

397

chestnut-brown hair she would happily have swapped for black or blonde tresses. She supposed that it had become a habit with Bryn to claim her as his girlfriend. For her part, she had never quite managed to forget how she had dreamed of Bryn the first time she had visited the Swtan. 'If you sleep in the shadow of the well, you'll dream of the man you're going to marry.' Hywel had said. She told herself over and over that it was just a foolish superstition which any girl of character would ignore, yet in a way she felt that, like it or not, her eventual fate would be to marry Bryn. But if I really do have to marry him, I mean to have lots of fun first, she told herself. Oh, if only I hadn't listened to Hywel when he went on about the magic properties of the well; now I feel as though I'm doomed to take Bryn on. But I know it's silly to even think such a thing, because I didn't go to sleep by the well at the time of the full moon on purpose, it was pure accident. And the last thing on my mind was finding out the name of my future husband. So I'll jolly well go out with any bloke who asks me and then I'll choose a husband. I won't have one wished on me.

By this time Auntie Kath had managed to acquire a second bicycle, and for once the girls meant to cycle to the village, where the dance was being held in the Memorial Hall. Neither Bryn nor Hywel was able to attend, Bryn being at sea and Hywel busy on his airfield, so Nell had to admit that the dance would lack a certain something. However, she reminded herself fiercely that she was most definitely not in love with Bryn or Hywel, and would enjoy dancing with any of the young men – or indeed all of them – who came across to her, sketched a salute and asked if he could have the pleasure . . .

March came in like a lion, with winds so strong that Nell and Maggie shuddered for Eifion, because despite every effort the draughts found their way round windows, under doors and down chimneys, and the old man felt constantly chilly.

But around the end of the month the weather suddenly changed, as Auntie Kath told her niece was often the case. 'It's an old country saying that if March comes in like a lion, it will go out like a lamb,' she explained when Nell came bouncing into the kitchen with a handful of yellow catkins and Maggie followed her brandishing a bunch of pussy willow. 'The evenings are drawing out, so when your young men come calling you'll be able to take them on country walks instead of sitting in stuffy cinemas and dance halls.'

'We don't have a regular young man, either of us, do we, Maggie?' Nell said at once. 'I know Bryn and Hywel often call for us, but that's because they've got transport.'

'Transport! Some chance!' Maggie scoffed. They were in the kitchen, arranging their booty in Auntie Kath's big green glass vase, and now Maggie stood back to admire their work. 'Ain't that just glorious? Oh, I know what you mean by transport; Bryn and Hywel share a motorbike and sometimes have the lend of that old banger they call a car, but if you ask me they'd call for young Nell here if they had to carry her on their backs!' She sniffed. 'Why should you have two fellers after you, queen, when I don't have none? You're younger than me an' all.'

'They're pals, that's all,' Nell said. She turned to her aunt. 'Shall I take these through to the parlour, stand them on the windowsill in there? Only it's a bit hot in here for the catkins; they'll drop that yellow powdery stuff all over the show and you won't like that.'

Auntie Kath smiled. 'Good idea. I don't believe I've told you the good news, though. Eifion's coming back to work tomorrow.'

'Gosh, he must be really better,' Nell said, a smile spreading across her face. 'I'm so glad for him; he's had a miserable winter. Oh, Auntie, if he's coming back is there any chance of me having a day off next week? Only Hywel's been on a course – something to do with aircraft engines – and he's got at least one day off coming to him.' She looked hopefully at her aunt. 'You know he's promised to take me over to the Swtan and introduce me to Toddy. He says that if it's a fine day we'll go out in the *Maud* – that's the name of the boat in the bay – and see if we can bag ourselves a crab, or even a lobster. He says Toddy will lend us one of his pots. Or we might just throw out a line and see what we can catch.'

'What a pity I can't spare the pair of you on the same day,' Kath said with what sounded like genuine regret. 'But though most of the ewes have lambed, I still need someone to check up on them.' She turned and smiled at the land girl. 'Perhaps they can take you another time, Maggie.'

'Huh! I'll have me day off to meself, ta very much,' Maggie said loftily. 'Playin' gooseberry ain't never been my idea of fun.' She jerked her thumb at Nell, who was pouring tea into three mugs, ready for their elevenses. 'She may say Hywel's just a pal, but that ain't what he thinks. And Bryn's as bad; makin' sheep's eyes at Nell one minute and gettin' a cob on the next because she don't fall on his neck. I telled him the other day that it's time he growed up; it wouldn't surprise me sometimes if he flung hisself on the floor, drummin' his heels an' howlin' 'cos he'd not gorris own way.'

'He is young for his age, despite the experiences he's been through,' Kath admitted. 'I think it's because as a youngster he was always ailing. But he'll be a fine young man when he's a bit older . . . he's only eighteen after all.'

Nell, who had carried the big vase out of the kitchen and into the parlour, returned in time to hear the last remark. 'Bryn's all right, in fact he's very nice,' she said off-handedly. 'But I get along better with Hywel because he doesn't throw tantrums, or pretend to be dying of love one minute and losing his temper over something unimportant the next.'

Auntie Kath cast her a quick, rather anxious glance, but said nothing, and presently the talk turned to how Nell would find out when Hywel's day off was likely to be. 'I'll bike into the village after evening milking and telephone the airmen's mess. If I leave it until nine o'clock he's bound to be around; he might even answer the phone,' Nell said optimistically.

She was in luck; she made her phone call, spoke to Hywel and arranged to go out with him the following Tuesday. He would pick her up on the motorbike and Nell would provide a picnic. 'I'll get a message to Toddy somehow, telling him I'm bringing a visitor,' Hywel said. 'He's very organised and keeps the place in apple pie order, but of course he's a feller and there's jobs a woman 'ud do what a man don't think necessary.'

Nell giggled. 'Things like washing the crocks and scrubbing the floor?'

Hywel laughed too. 'Oh, he does stuff like that, but he don't polish the brass, nor blacklead the grate . . . but you won't mind that, I dare say?'

'Course I shan't,' Nell said at once. 'Tell him not to worry; if I were trying to keep body and soul together I wouldn't bother fussing over details either.' She laughed again. 'The only time Auntie Kath cleans the brass or blackleads the grate is when the ladies' sewing circle or the WI meet in our kitchen. And even then she spends more time cooking something delicious for their tea than on spit and polishing. Oh, that reminds me. Will Toddy be offended if I get Auntie to let me do a bake? I'm a dab hand now at bara brith . . .'

'Caller, your time is up.' The voice of the operator broke into their conversation. 'Disconnect please!'

Nell just had time to squeak 'See you Tuesday' before the line went dead.

Tuesday dawned bright and fair, and when Hywel arrived all Nell had to do was don her haversack –

now laden with the results of her baking – and go across to the shippon, where her aunt, Eifion and Maggie were cleaning up after the milking. 'Cheerio, all; we'll be back before dark,' she shouted above the roar and splutter of the motorbike's engine. 'Well, we'll try to be back by then, anyway. But you know what motorbikes are.'

'Indeed I do,' Eifion shouted, grinning. 'That old wreck my grandson shares wi' young Hywel is forever lettin' him down. But Hywel's a mechanic, so no doubt he's tuned the engine or whatever they call it and you'll have a trouble-free ride.'

'Some chance,' Maggie bawled cheerfully. 'Have a grand time, queen, and bring me back one of them there lobsters what rich folk have to their dinners.'

'I'll do my best,' Nell said. 'And I'll try to get back for supper, honest I will.'

'And I know what you young people are: never on time anywhere,' Kath shouted, but Nell saw that her aunt, too, was smiling. 'Don't worry, queen. If you decide to see a picture or something we'll understand. It's your day off, remember, and richly deserved.'

Quite overcome by these words, Nell shouted her thanks. Hywel pushed up his visor and turned to smile at her, his dark eyes crinkling with amusement as she tried to climb decorously on to the bike. Not for the first time, she envied Maggie her land girl's breeches.

'Got everything? Good. Then hang on tight. If you want me to stop for some reason tap my shoulder, because once we get going the wind will whip our voices away.'

Nell opened her mouth to remind Hywel that she had ridden on this particular motorbike at least twice before, then closed it again. It really would not do to remind him of Bryn's determined pursuit. Instead, she was going to enjoy this day to the very full.

The motorbike bounced across the cobbles and turned into the lane, and after only a couple of miles Nell realised that Hywel was a much better rider than his friend. The engine purred sweetly and Hywel maintained a steady speed, slowing for corners, stopping at junctions and behaving in a way which showed up Bryn's slapdash and dramatic style.

Presently, the lanes along which they rode were no longer familiar, for Nell always stuck to the fields and meadows when she went walking. Then Hywel turned a corner, slowed and pointed. 'That's my village, down there,' he told her, 'and you can just see the roof of the longhouse. I'll show you my house in a minute. I'd take you in to meet my grandmother, but if I do that we'd never get to see the Swtan because she's a great talker, so we'll give it a miss for today.'

They rode on and Hywel pointed out his house, which looked just like the others to Nell's untutored eye. It was grey and squat, the roof tiled and the walls made of stone. She thought she could see a fair-sized garden at the back, but it fronted on to the road, with only a low stone wall and a wicket gate to separate it from the street.

They began to descend the hill, Hywel throttling back the engine so that its roar became a purr as they reached their destination. Hywel cut the engine, kicked the bike stand, dismounted, and lifted Nell down just as the green-painted door opened and a figure appeared. For a moment, Nell found herself looking past the man who stood in the doorway, half expecting to see a woman's figure behind him, but of course she saw no such thing; only Toddy, tall, straight-backed, white-haired, his face tanned and his smile welcoming.

Nell was so astonished that she let out a squeak of surprise and had to pretend her haversack was coming loose. He wasn't old at all. She knew herself to be a poor judge of age, but thought that he was not yet out of his forties. Indeed, he seemed to be in excellent health, for he pushed open the wicket gate and came quickly towards them, his long, easy stride carrying him swiftly to where they stood. 'Mornin', Hywel; mornin', young miss,' he said, holding out a large, capable-looking hand and seizing Nell's. 'I'm Toddy Williams and I know you're Hywel's friend Nell. How d'you do?'

All Nell's shyness fell away as her eyes met his and read the friendship there. 'I'm very well, thank you, and delighted to meet you at last, Mr Williams,' she said.

'Oh, call me Toddy, everyone does,' he said easily, leading the way to the longhouse. 'I mean to call you Nell.'

'That's fine,' Nell said. They went inside and she looked around her admiringly, for, as Hywel had said, the large kitchen living room was neat as a pin. It was clear that Toddy Williams was more concerned with interior comfort than with exterior show; Nell found it hard to equate this warm, homely room with the

405

peeling whitewash and ragged thatch she had seen from the well. There was a scrubbed wooden table in the centre of the floor, flanked by four ladder-backed chairs and a Welsh dresser, blackened with age, bearing an odd assortment of crockery and cooking pans. The walls were whitewashed and on either side of the fire which burned in the large grate was a comfortable-looking armchair. On the wall in front of her there were several pictures, depicting local scenes; Nell recognised Church Bay on a sunny day when the tide was out and another on a stormy day, when the waves lashed the foot of the cliffs and she could almost hear the howl of the wind. Truly impressed, Nell gestured to the pictures. 'They're beautiful,' she breathed. 'I can't see a signature; who painted them?'

'Me,' her host said. He chuckled. 'They're only daubs really, but they give me pleasure.' He turned to Hywel. 'The kettle's going to boil any minute. You show Nell round the place while I make a pot of tea. I wish I could offer you a scone, but there's biscuits in the tin on the dresser . . .'

Nell clapped a hand to her mouth and unslung the haversack from her shoulder. Smiling, she held it out to her host. 'I expect Hywel told you that I came and stole some of your water last summer, so I've brought you some scones and a bara brith in payment.'

'Well, that's very kind of you,' Toddy said, taking the haversack and pretending to reel at the weight of it. 'And kind of Mrs Jones to give you a day off. I've never met her, you know, but when she heard I was here she sent me a message by Eifion to say she wanted

406

no rent from me.' He chuckled. 'Which at the beginning was just as well, since while I was trying to get this place habitable it was all I could do to feed myself. But now that I'm established, you could say, I've been putting a sum aside every few weeks so that one day quite soon now I shall be able to offer to buy the Swtan from Mrs Jones; regularise the situation, you might say.' As he spoke, he went back into what Hywel told her was called the ty llaeth or milk room – Auntie Kath had called it the dairy, Nell remembered – emptied the haversack on to a long wooden bench and started to butter the scones.

Meanwhile Hywel, clearly at home, had pulled the kettle over the fire, and presently the three of them were sitting round the kitchen table, eating the scones and drinking the tea and chatting like old friends. 'Your aunt's a rare cook, I hear, and I can tell from this scone that you're following in her footsteps,' Toddy told Nell admiringly. 'I've never really mastered baking, though I can manage soda bread and such.' He glanced at their empty cups, then up at the clock over the mantel. 'Want more tea? Only the tide's just right to take the boat out and I know Hywel said he thought you'd like to go fishing.'

Nell looked hesitantly from one to the other. When she and Hywel had planned this day, she had thought of Toddy as an old man, not exactly senile, but definitely too old to enjoy pursuits such as fishing from a small boat or walking miles along the beach collecting driftwood for his fire, or picking mussels from the rocks for his tea. She had imagined him limping along, a hand to the small of his back and a groan on his lips, only too glad of the help offered by either Hywel or the lad from the village. Now she saw that he was a capable and humorous man in the prime of life, who would be glad of their company and, indeed, glad of their help, but who could manage perfectly well without it. She looked at Hywel, trying to gauge whether she should assume Toddy would be coming with them in the boat, but her dilemma was solved by Toddy himself.

'The *Maud* is a grand little craft, but she's built for a crew of two,' he said. 'If you go now, I'll get on with my jobs, and put the spuds on when I see you heading back to the beach.' He smiled at them, getting to his feet as he spoke. 'We'll have your catch for our tea, so make sure it's a good one!'

As Hywel turned the *Maud*'s nose towards Church Bay at the end of their expedition, Nell, seated in the stern, gave a sigh of pure pleasure. She had had a lovely day, possibly the best day of her life. The sun had beamed down upon them and the breeze had allowed Hywel to put up the sail, saving himself the task of rowing. They had pottered along the coast, going in and out of tiny bays and two or three times anchoring the boat in shallow water so that they might go ashore.

On the last of these forays, something occurred which had turned a delightful day into a very special one indeed. The water in which they had anchored proved to be somewhat deeper than either of them had realised. Hywel, going first, had given a shout of dismay as the water reached almost to his thighs. He had begun to warn Nell, too late, and had he not seized her in his arms she would probably have ended up soaked to the waist. 'Oh, oh, oh!' Nell had squeaked, wriggling and trying to climb up Hywel as though he were a ladder, he said later. 'The water's freezing! I never knew anything could be so cold!'

Hywel, gasping and laughing, had begun to wade towards the shore clasping Nell in his arms. As the water grew shallower she had begun to try to pull herself free, but had not been able to do so. She had started to protest, to say that he could stand her down now, but even as she spoke he had let her slide from his grasp . . . and Nell had found herself being soundly kissed. Warmly, and almost without her volition, her hands had crept up his chest, then round his shoulders, meeting at the back of his neck, pulling him closer.

'Mm – mm – mm,' Hywel had breathed against her mouth and for a moment Nell had wanted to laugh, but as Hywel had deepened the kiss she had no longer seen any reason for mirth. In fact, when he had pulled away from her with a long sigh, only her pride had kept her from cuddling closer, demanding that he should not stop.

Pride, however, had come to her aid, though when she spoke her voice had shaken maddeningly. 'Hywel Evans, how dare you! I thought this was a fishing trip, not . . .'

Hywel had cupped her face in both hands and looked deep into her eyes. He had been smiling, but there had been something about his expression which had sent a tingle of excitement racing along Nell's spine. She had tried half-heartedly to disengage herself, but he did not release her. 'Sweet sixteen and never been kissed,' he had murmured. 'And for a complete novice you catch on awfully quickly. Oh, Nell, Nell, what a little darling you are!'

He had kissed her again, and Nell had been fully aware that she was responding far too ardently for someone who, only moments earlier, had pretended to regard Hywel's attentions with shocked amazement. At last he had broken the embrace to hold her back from him so that they could look into one another's eyes. 'Nell? I think I started to fall in love with you when I walked you home after we'd met in the village. At first I was fooled into believing Bryn when he told me you were his girl and asked me to back off. But as time went on I realised it was wishful thinking on his part, and you regarded both of us as pals. You said you were too young for a serious relationship' – he had chuckled – 'but it's pretty clear that you aren't too young any longer. I don't mean to rush you into anything, but I'm telling you straight, Nell Whitaker, you and I were made for one another. And now we'd better do what we came ashore to do, which is to fill that bucket with the prawns that live in the deep rock pools in this particular bay.'

He had slipped his arm round her waist as he spoke, and the two of them had headed for the rock pools, Nell's mind in a turmoil. So this was what other girls were talking about when they spoke of being in love!

She had given Hywel a quick, sideways glance from under lowered lids, and had seen that he was doing the same. They had simultaneously begun to laugh, easing what she now realised had been the almost unbearable tension.

When they had returned to the boat with their bucketful of prawns, he had helped her aboard and then said seriously: 'I haven't asked if you feel the same about me as I do about you, because it's early days and you really are very young. But remember, you're mine.' Then he had given her a brilliant smile and leaned over to squeeze her hand. 'Has the cat got your tongue, cariad? I've never known you so quiet.'

'I'm – I'm speechless,' Nell had admitted in a small voice. 'And as for that sweet sixteen business, I don't know that age is terribly important. But I'd like to be your girl, if that's what you mean.'

'Right,' Hywel had said briskly, pulling up the anchor, which was only an old tin that filled with water when thrown overboard. 'And now we'd better examine Toddy's pots, see if we can bag ourselves a lobster.'

Hywel knew where Toddy laid his pots, but the first three they had pulled to the surface were empty. The fourth, though, contained an extremely angry lobster. It had snapped its claws at them every time they moved and Nell had suggested throwing it back since she had visions of it pursuing her around the boat, but Hywel had laughed, squeezed her hand and said it would do no such thing. 'We've no bait with us, so we'll take it back in the lobster pot. We'll get Toddy to boil it in the outhouse, so you won't have to hear its screams,' he had said ghoulishly. 'Did you know they scream when they're boiled? Well, wouldn't you?'

This remark had so appalled Nell that she had grabbed the pot and tried to throw it overboard. A lively struggle had ensued, during which Hywel tried to silence her with kisses and finally assured her that the lobster would be dead before ever it met the boiling water. 'I was kidding you, honest to God I was,' he had said, sitting down on the lobster pot and drawing a finger across his throat. 'See this wet, see this dry, cut my throat if I tell a lie. There's a spot on its head, just between the eyes; you drive a skewer in and it dies at once. It doesn't know a thing, I swear it doesn't.'

Nell had grudgingly agreed that if this really was the case they would take the lobster back to the Swtan with them. 'Only Maggie's never tasted lobster, so can we ask Toddy for a little bit to take home?' she had asked hopefully. Hywel had agreed and suggested that they should throw out a couple of lines, and by the time they had turned the *Maud* towards what Hywel referred to as her home port, they had a good catch of what Hywel told her were codling flapping in the bottom of the boat.

As the *Maud* grounded, Hywel lifted Nell on to dry land, giving her a quick peck on the back of the neck as he did so. Nell gave a squeak of protest as she saw Toddy descending the cliff, and hoped his attention was on the sharp descent. He was carrying a large reed basket in one hand, which he waved at them as he hurried towards their small craft.

'Saw you coming into the bay as I was getting water from the well,' he shouted. 'Remembered you'd not taken anything to bring your catch home in.' He reached them, threw the basket into the well of the boat and then joined them, straining to pull the *Maud* up the shingle and on to the sand. Then he peered into the boat. 'Ah, I see you've got a lobster; big feller, isn't he? And some codling.' He smacked his lips. 'Which will you have for your tea, then? I've put the spuds on to boil, though meself, I prefer bread and butter wi' lobster.'

'We-ell . . .' Nell began; would it be awfully rude to ask if she might take some of the lobster back to Ty Hen? But once more, Toddy solved the problem for her.

'It's quite a big 'un, but that's a grand lot of codling you've brought in. What say we send the lobster – cooked, of course – back to Ty Hen for the old lady's tea, whilst we have a feast of fish?'

Nell was about to ask which old lady he had in mind when she realised he was referring to Auntie Kath. She repressed an indignant rejection of the phrase and chuckled to herself. What was sauce for the goose was also sauce for the gander; Aunt Kath continually referred to 'the old feller' or 'that old man', so why should not Toddy refer to her as an old lady? If the couple ever met they would be in for a big surprise . . . she only hoped it would be a pleasant one!

Back at the Swtan, the lobster and Hywel disappeared into the cow byre, Hywel armed with a wicked-looking skewer, and Toddy and Nell went to the large stone

413

sink on the outside of the building, which Toddy had already filled with water. They emptied the reed basket into the sink and Toddy produced a gutting knife, then jerked his head at the wooden bench alongside the door. 'You've done all the work of catching our supper, so you can sit quiet and watch me preparing them for the pan,' he said. 'We'll boil the prawns up later; I may leave them till tomorrow since we've so many fish.'

'Do you salt fish down for the winter?' Nell asked, perching herself on the bench. 'I'm not keen on it myself, but I know it's a high treat for some.'

Toddy chuckled. 'Aye, but not this little lot; by the time they're gutted and rolled in flour, they'll make a grand meal for the three of us with not a lot left over. And now you can tell me how you like living on Anglesey.'

The reed basket was beside her on the bench, and Nell moved up as Toddy began to throw the split and gutted fish into it. She started to tell him how she loved the island, but even as she did so she felt a sudden chill, as though the wind had changed direction to blow upon her back. She put up with it for a moment, then shuffled further along the bench, away from the door. Immediately, the little wind – if it had been a little wind – ceased to blow and she and Toddy chatted idly for a while. Nell learned that he not only kept two cows, one of which was always in calf, but had a grand big sow from which he hoped to breed. 'I've not gone in for sheep because I don't have the time to chase after 'em when they go wandering,' he explained.

'And I've no dog as yet, though I mean to get one. The sow's in a sty and the poultry come to the henhouse at nights, which keeps them safe from foxes, but sheep are so empty-headed that if they're not shepherded properly they'll hand their lambs to old Reynard on a plate.' Toddy laughed. 'Unfortunate phrase, but you know what I mean.' He finished the last fish, threw it into the reed basket and gave Nell a quizzical look, raising his brows. 'You've moved, I see.' He picked up the basket and smiled at her. 'That'll give you a bit more room; want to move back again?'

'No thanks,' Nell said promptly. 'Sitting by the door I was in a draught, so that's why I moved. But now you've finished gutting the fish, should we go indoors? I'll help in any way I can, but if you're going to boil the lobster will there be room on the fire to cook the fish?'

'The potatoes are just about ready, so I'll put them in a tureen with a lump of butter and stand 'em on the back of the stove to keep warm. The lobster can cook while we're eating.' He cocked one eyebrow at Nell. 'The fish won't need more than five minutes, so we'll be sitting down to our tea before you know it. I've not asked you how you enjoyed your boat trip; the pair of you were very flushed and bright-eyed when I helped you pull the boat ashore.'

Nell followed Toddy into the milk room, putting a hand to her hot cheeks when she realised that Toddy must have guessed that she and Hywel had been kissing. She wondered if he guessed how her afternoon with Hywel had changed her life, then shrugged

415

and smiled to herself. What did it matter if he guessed that she and Hywel were more than friends and had cemented their new relationship that very day? She was not ashamed that everyone should know she was Hywel's girl; she was proud, in fact, although when folk had assumed that she was Bryn's girl she had objected very much. On the two or three occasions when he had kissed her she had felt embarrassed and annoyed; the tingling rush of pleasure which had assailed her when in Hywel's arms had been a very different sensation from that engendered by Bryn's attentions.

Toddy finished flouring the fish and laid it carefully on a plate, which he handed to Nell, raising his brows as he did so. 'Well, young lady? How did you enjoy your day? I'm rare fond of Hywel; do you feel the same?'

This was frankness with a vengeance! Nell opened her mouth to prevaricate, but her mouth had other ideas. 'Yes, I'm rare fond of him too,' she said baldly. 'And we had a lovely time in the *Maud*.' She hesitated, then said what was on her mind. 'When I felt that draught on the bench . . .'

Toddy turned away from her for a moment to pick up the bara brith she had given him that morning. 'Have you been listening to Hywel's tall tales? It is odd, though, that you can sit on that bench in full sunshine and yet suddenly feel very cold indeed. I decided it was just a freak weather condition. Is that what you were going to ask me?'

'Well, not exactly,' Nell said, following him into the

kitchen and putting the plate of fish down on the table. 'I'd like to know if you think the Swtan is haunted. Or was it just the lads trying to invent a ghost to frighten me? The very first time I came here . . .'

She told him what she thought she had glimpsed, and when she finished he nodded seriously. 'I've seen some strange things – though not what you might call a ghost, not in my time here – but I think that the draught, or cold wind, or whatever you like to call it, is the strangest and needs some explaining.' He grinned at her. 'But since I don't believe in ghosts or similar apparitions, as I say, I decided it was just some quirk of the weather. Hywel has some daft idea that pictures of the past can occasionally be glimpsed, particularly when looking down on the Swtan from the well, but I take no heed of such things.'

Nell giggled. 'I don't blame you; I wouldn't want to share my home with ghosts either,' she said cheerfully. Toddy was cutting the bara brith and she was buttering each slice on a prettily patterned plate. When this was done, Toddy took down the big, blackened frying pan, set it over the flame and tossed a lump of butter into it. The pan began to smoke and Toddy dropped the floured fillets into it and turned to Nell. 'Give the lad a shout,' he commanded. 'Tell him I'm serving up in five minutes.'

When the meal was over, Hywel and Nell went for a walk, for the tide was now out and the beach stretched before them enticingly, lit by the light of a great, golden full moon. They strolled along, arms round each other's waists, avoiding the patches of black shadow which might hide a rock pool, and enjoying their new intimacy. 'We know so little about each other,' Nell said at one point. 'Why, we've not even met each other's relatives. And just when we find we're in love you're off to the mainland to go before a promotion board, and if you pass you say you'll probably be sent to another airfield. What if you're sent abroad? The ship you're on might founder, or the plane might crash . . . oh, Hywel, couldn't you change your mind and stay as you are?'

Hywel gave her a quick squeeze, but shook his head. 'No, cariad; the air force has made up its mind that I'm capable of commanding men. If I pass the board, I'll be promoted to corporal, but hopefully I'll still stay on the same airfield. I wonder what the time is?' He peered at his watch in the moonlight, then gave an exclamation. 'Goodness! Doesn't time fly? We'd better get a move on. Good job we've got the motorbike, so we can be back at Ty Hen before your aunt starts to worry.'

Despite her best intentions, it was nearly midnight when Hywel and Nell arrived back at Ty Hen. She had been more shaken by Toddy's placid assumption that she and Hywel were more than friends than she liked to admit, and she had no desire to see the same knowing gleam in Auntie Kath's eyes, so as soon as they reached the farmyard she begged Hywel to leave.

Hywel chuckled. 'You're afraid your aunt and Maggie will guess you've been kissed,' he said. 'What's wrong with being kissed, eh? I think it clears the mind wonderfully; and it's fun into the bargain, wouldn't you say?'

'No I wouldn't,' Nell said firmly, then gave a little squeak as Hywel pulled her into his arms and nuzzled his face into the hollow of her neck.

'I hope you're not trying to tell me you don't enjoy this!'

Nell giggled. 'Of course I enjoy it, but I don't want people thinking I'm – I'm a bad girl. You know what I mean, like that Waaf – Joyce, isn't it? The one they call the station bicycle because . . .'

Hywel began to laugh, putting his hand across Nell's mouth. 'You don't even know what that means. Now let's just pop into the kitchen so your aunt can see that I've brought you home in one piece. And don't forget to ring me as soon as I'm back to tell me when I can see you again.'

Nell had thought, rather wistfully, that waiting almost a week would be next to unbearable and rang the mess as soon as the time was up, only to be told by an unemotional voice the other end that Corporal Evans's promotion had come through and he had already left for RAF Tern Hill in Shropshire.

Chapter Seventeen

'Well, miss? I know one can pummel dough without ruining the bread, but aren't you taking it to extremes? That loaf will likely come out of the oven flat as a perishin' pancake if you go on beating the living daylights out of it. And don't forget there's a war on and ingredients are either on ration or hard to come by. Why, even Merion wasn't able to find dried fruit on sale last time he was in Dublin. I'd say this bara brith ought to be called Farmhouse Surprise, because if anyone manages as to find a sultana or a currant or even a bit of candied peel in their slice, that's what it'll be.'

Nell looked up from her exertions and gave a breathless laugh, which was echoed by Maggie, though Kath continued to frown across at her niece as she stirred the mixture in her big yellow bowl. 'Sorry, Auntie,' Nell said. 'But I've finished kneading the dough now; it's about ready to put in the tins.'

The three women were in the kitchen, having a baking day. Maggie was making pastry and peeling and slicing apples for a pie, and Nell had been entrusted with the making of the week's supply of bread. Now she picked up the greased loaf tins and began to divide the dough, placing it in the tins and standing them on the hearth to prove before turning back to her aunt.

'Anything else I can do? If Maggie's got some pastry left over I could make a batch of cheese straws, or we could have a fruit cobbler.'

'There ain't goin' to be no pastry left over,' Maggie cut in. She pointed to the large loaf tins, their contents already beginning to puff out. 'Was you pretendin' them loaves were young Hywel? You've been in a rare bate with him for the past week. But on t'other hand, I heared you and Bryn snarlin' an' screechin' at each other like a couple o' wild cats last time he called round, too.'

Nell felt her cheeks begin to glow. 'Don't be daft,' she said gruffly. 'I don't deny I lost my temper when Bryn started saying rude things about Hywel, but it wasn't a real fight.'

'Yeah, maybe, but you've not had a good word to say for Hywel yourself lately,' Maggie pointed out. She turned to the older woman. 'Ain't that true, Auntie Kath? You must have noticed that two weeks ago Nell here were on cloud nine, and Hywel were the only thing she talked about. It were Hywel this and Hywel that, and now she's not got a good word to say for the poor feller.'

Auntie Kath smiled grimly and began to pour her cake mix into a large tin. She addressed her niece, giving Maggie a little nod as she did so. 'It's no good your blaming Hywel because he's been sent to the other side of the country,' she pointed out. 'Once a feller's in the forces, he's no longer his own master. I've heard of young men being dispatched to Scotland one minute and Devonshire the next.'

Nell pouted. 'But he knew if he was promoted he'd probably leave Valley. I asked him not to go before the board, but he wouldn't listen.'

Maggie, tipping sliced apples into the pie dish and pressing down the pastry lid, shook an admonitory finger at the younger girl. 'That was after you decided to fall in love with the feller,' she reminded her. 'You were still dilly-dallyin' betwixt him and Bryn.' She gave Nell a broad grin. 'In fact I reckon Hywel probably decided to move away thinkin' absence might make your heart grow fonder. So it's all your fault!'

Nell snatched up the utensils she had been using and carried them over to the sink. 'It's not my fault that he never even came to tell me he was leaving,' she said crossly. 'One miserable postcard, which he posted when he reached Shropshire, is all I've had *and* he forgot to give me the telephone number of the airmen's mess at Tern Hill. He knows very well we're not on the telephone here and we're far too busy on the farm for me to go into the village and hang around near the phone box in case he rings.' She turned away from the sink to fetch the kettle of hot water steaming on the range. 'I'm so cross with him I could scream.'

'It's hard on you, gal, I admit,' Maggie said, carrying her own utensils over to the sink and dunking them in the hot water. 'But no need to get a cob on wi' us. Think of all the other gals what are away from their fellers, some of 'em wi' no hope of seein' their chaps for weeks . . . no, months; years, even. Beside them, you're bleedin' lucky.'

'Language,' Auntie Kath said automatically. She, too,

carried her mixing bowl over to the sink and plonked it in the water, then gave her niece's arm an encouraging pat. 'If I know Hywel – and I should by now – he'll be in touch as soon as he's able. If he manages to get some leave and comes over here, and you meet him with a sour face . . .'

'He won't get leave for ages,' Nell muttered, swishing the water about with one hand. 'If only the postman would bring a letter . . . oh, Auntie, I'm not just cross because he didn't let me know he was moving away, I'm worried for him. For all I know—'

'What you want is something beside work to occupy your mind,' Aunt Kath interrupted. 'What say you and Maggie take a few hours off? Finish the milking and the chores and go off on the bikes. You can go to the Swtan if you want to. You never know, the old chap might have heard from the lad—'

'If he has . . . if he's written to Toddy and not to me—' Nell began furiously, but got no further.

'If he has it will be because his letter to you has gone astray, or the censor has cut so much out of it that there's nothing left to send,' Auntie Kath said quickly. 'For goodness' sake, Nell, you remind me often enough that there's a war on; do I have to remind you?'

Nell felt her flush deepen and turned away from the sink. Drying her hands hastily on the nearest tea towel, she rushed over and gave her aunt an impulsive hug. 'I'm sorry, I'm sorry, I'm sorry,' she said. 'It's only because I love Hywel so much that I truly need to hear from him. Suppose he's ill, or injured, or—'

'Oh, for God's sake,' Maggie broke in. 'If any of them things had happened, someone would have let you know. For heaven's sake, stop imagining disaster.'

There was a thundering knock on the door and it burst open to reveal Ifor the Post. He grinned widely at them and slung half a dozen letters down in front of Auntie Kath. Then he handed a small yellow envelope to Nell. 'It's from young Hywel, love,' he said ingenuously. 'Wants you to give him a ring. He's give you the number.'

Nell scanned the telegram eagerly. 'Thanks, Ifor,' she said. 'I've been waiting for this.'

'Oh aye? It come in at nine o'clock, but bein' as it weren't important I brung it myself with the rest of the mail.' He glanced hopefully towards the range. 'Something smells good; any chance of a paned?' Without waiting for an invitation, he sat down on the nearest chair and was presently supping tea and eating a buttered scone, whilst Kath flipped through the rest of her post, announcing in a disappointed tone that it was nothing but Ministry forms and a bill for cattle feed.

Naturally, Nell was on fire to contact Hywel, and telephoned that very evening, though the call had, perforce, to be fairly short since as usual there were several people waiting for their turn. Infuriatingly, as soon as she heard Hywel's voice, Nell burst into tears of relief, and quite half their allotted time was taken up with Nell's gulps and sobs and Hywel's comforting words. He had one bit of good news, however, which stopped Nell's tears more effectively than anything else could have done. He was due some time off the following week and it seemed an ideal opportunity for him and Nell to meet up.

'Oh, I'd be so happy if they'd let you stay at Valley,' Nell wailed. 'Oh, Hywel, I worry about you every minute. It wouldn't be so bad if Ty Hen was on the phone—'

'Nell, my love, will you calm down and listen to me?' Hywel said with more than a hint of impatience. 'Will your aunt give you the day off, either next Wednesday or Thursday? If so, I'll catch the milk train and meet you under the clock on Lime Street station, at say lunchtime. We could have a couple of hours together, maybe longer. I daren't come all the way out to Ty Hen. Troop movements mean train times aren't reliable.'

'I'm sure Auntie will let me have a day off,' Nell said at once. 'I'll find out the times of the trains and catch the earliest. I'll ring you tomorrow night . . .'

'I'm real glad you know which tellyphone number to ring,' Maggie observed next day, as they began to clean down the shippon after morning milking. 'But if you go and meet Hywel, d'you think it will mean we shan't get that time off together your aunt talked about? I were lookin' forward to meetin' this old feller, this Toddy, what you've talked about, but will you always be going to this here airfield with the funny name . . . like a seagull, ain't it?'

'Tern Hill, you mean,' Nell said, giggling. 'Oh, I'm sure Auntie will let us have our day out anyway. I wish she'd come to the Swtan with us, but you know how obstinate she can be, and she's quite made up her mind never to visit Toddy. Still, it won't stop you and me going – if she can manage without us, that is. But I want to arrange my meeting with Hywel first, of course.'

That evening, Nell rang the mess at Tern Hill again and spoke almost immediately to Hywel, who must have been, as she told him, practically sitting on the telephone. He was able to tell her that his train should arrive in Lime Street at ten o'clock on Wednesday morning, whilst she herself should be there, trains permitting, a bare twenty minutes later.

'I mean to tell you all about the work we do,' he told her. 'And there's another, very serious subject we ought to discuss.'

'What's that?' Nell asked at once, but Hywel would only say it was not something he intended to talk about over the phone.

'Too many listening ears,' he said. 'Remember the posters: *Be like Dad, keep Mum.*'

'Oh yes, and that other one, the awful one with a hand coming out of a black sea and the words *Someone talked* written above it,' Nell said, shuddering. 'All right, I'll save up my curiosity for Wednesday.' She sighed. 'I wish I had some exciting news for you, but farm work goes on just as usual, apart from the Ministry forms. Oh, Hywel, they're awful; Auntie's terrified of getting them wrong and being in trouble.'

Hywel chuckled. 'She ought to take them to Toddy; he's brilliant at figures and filling in forms,' he told

426

her. 'He gave me no end of help when I was doing the examinations for my promotion . . . oh, and that reminds me, is there any chance of you popping over to the Swtan and letting Toddy know I'm all right? He doesn't have my telephone number and anyway I doubt he'd want to walk all the way to the nearest box, so we'll have to keep in touch by letter. Give him my address, cariad—'

The operator's voice cut across his words. 'Caller, your time is up . . .'

'I'll do my best. See you Wednesday,' Nell screamed, then replaced the receiver, pushed open the door of the box and gestured the next person in the queue to go inside.

Maggie had accompanied her into the village, and as they walked back to where they had left their bicycles she put the question which was obviously much on her mind. 'When will you ask Auntie Kath about our outing to that there Swtan?'

'I'll ask her as soon as we get home,' Nell said at once. She hugged herself, beaming at Maggie. 'Hywel asked me to let Toddy know that he was all right, and said he – Toddy, I mean – was brilliant at filling in government forms, so we've two good reasons for going. I'll ask Auntie if we can do it tomorrow.'

She was as good as her word, and to Maggie's freely expressed surprise and pleasure Kath agreed that if they got the milking and most of their chores out of the way before leaving, they might stay out until four or five in the afternoon. After a few April showers it seemed that sunshine was the order of the day for the time being, and even Auntie Kath intimated that she, too, meant to have a bit of a break from her usual tasks.

As the four of them gathered round the breakfast table next day, Nell suggested to her aunt that they might leave old Eifion in charge for a few hours whilst all three of them visited the Swtan.

'I'm agreeable,' Eifion said at once. He took a large bite from his bacon sandwich, chewed, swallowed, then supped noisily at his mug of tea before wiping his mouth and enlarging on his remark. 'Give me a chance to get on with all sorts, so it will, without no chattering women to put me off my stroke.'

Auntie Kath laughed, but shook her head firmly. 'It's not that I don't trust you, Eifion, but as you've heard me say more than once, that place holds too many memories for me, and I'll not cross the threshold, no matter what.'

'Oh, Auntie, I wish you'd change your mind,' Nell said. 'But you're as obstinate as any mule.'

'That's right,' Auntie Kath said, still smiling. 'But don't let it worry you; the old feller probably doesn't want to meet me any more than I want to meet him.'

'All right, all right, I won't try to persuade you,' Nell said placatingly. 'But I've been meaning to tell you . . . Toddy told me he started to put a bit of money away a while ago, whenever he could afford to do so. He said you wouldn't accept rent from him, so he thought he would try to save up so that he might buy the Swtan. It would regularise things, don't you think, Auntie? Once Toddy owns the Swtan, then neither of you has any reason for avoiding the other. Toddy will be just a neighbour, and—'

She stopped speaking abruptly as her aunt got to her feet and banged both fists on the wooden table. 'The very first thing Owain taught me was that no farmer ever sells so much as an inch of his land,' she said, and Nell saw that her cheeks were flaming scarlet and her eyes sparkling with indignation. 'How dare he even suggest such a thing! I'll have him out of there if it's the last thing I do!'

Chapter Eighteen

Later that same day, when their work was over, Nell and Maggie set off on their trusty bicycles, heading for the Swtan. As soon as they were well clear of Ty Hen, Maggie turned to Nell and blew out her cheeks expressively. 'Phew! I never thought your aunt could be so angry; she fair frightened the life out o' me,' she said. 'What's wrong wi' selling land, anyhow? I thought folk did it all the time. That nasty old woman what I worked for in Brompton Avenue had a brother who owned a big estate on the Wirral, and he were forever buyin' more land.'

'Buying's one thing, selling's another,' Nell informed her. 'That would have been during the Depression, when cheap imports forced many a farmer to sell his land; it's different now.' She smiled at her companion. 'As for being frightened, you should thank your lucky stars you weren't here when *I* first arrived. Auntie Kath was always telling me off, criticising everything I did, talking Welsh before I'd picked up more than a smattering . . . she was horrid to me, honest to God she was.'

'She's usually rare nice to me as a rule, so I guess I shouldn't be scared of her when she shouts,' Maggie admitted. 'But she calmed down pretty quick. What I still don't understand is why she won't go near this here Swtan, nor let that feller come up to Ty Hen. I mean, it don't make sense!'

'It's a long story,' Nell said evasively. She did not much want to go into details about Owain Jones's grandmother and her attempts to drive the young Kath away from the home she had inherited, so she told Maggie what had happened as briefly and succinctly as possible and was relieved when the land girl nodded her understanding.

'I see; what you might call a family feud, I reckon,' she said when Nell had finished. 'But it does seem a bit silly to keep it going, especially since this feller, this Toddy, didn't have no part in it. Why can't she let him either buy the place, if she hates it so much, or pay her rent? When she said she'd have him out of there no matter what, I were shocked, honest to God I were. For a moment her face looked quite different – sharp and spiteful-like.'

Nell nodded. 'Yes, I know what you mean, but she's not a bit like that really. I think it was the shock. When she's thought it over, she'll feel differently, I'm sure.'

For the rest of the ride to the Swtan, the girls chatted on a variety of subjects including, slightly to Nell's surprise, the fact that Bryn had actually asked Maggie to go to the cinema with him. When she had told Bryn, as kindly as she could, that she would not be going out with him again since she and Hywel had discovered they were in love, she had expected him to fly off in a rage and single out one of the many pretty Wrens from HMS *Bee*, more as a gesture of defiance than anything else. Yet he had chosen Maggie; why?

She glanced quickly across at her friend and saw that she was waiting to hear how Nell might greet the news. 'Are you pleased, Maggie?' Nell asked bluntly. 'Bryn's awfully nice, but . . . well, it's a bit sudden, wouldn't you say?'

Maggie laughed. 'Course it is, and Bryn's got a very high opinion of himself, that's what you're thinkin', ain't it? You're thinkin' Bryn likes a looker, which I ain't. But who says I agreed to go, eh? You ain't the only who can play hard to get.'

'You turned him down? Gosh, I bet that rocked him back on his heels,' Nell said. 'What did he say?'

'Norralot. I told him it weren't on to break up with one girl and then to ask her bezzie for a date. He went red as a beetroot and muttered that he hadn't meant to upset me.'

'Well, that was nice of him,' Nell said, just as they reached the top of the hill and began coasting down towards the Swtan. 'He'll find someone else and it won't do him any harm to realise that he's not everyone's cup of tea.' She pointed ahead. 'See that thatched roof? That's the Swtan. The hill's pretty steep, so keep a hold on your brakes and we'll be there in two shakes.'

They reached the longhouse and were about to prop their bicycles up against the cow byre when Maggie put a detaining hand on Nell's arm. 'Hang on a minute,' she hissed. 'Are you going to tell the old feller what Auntie Kath said about not selling him the Swtan?

Surely you aren't going to let him know that she threatened to kick him out of the place altogether?'

'Of course I'm not. For a start, it's none of my business, and anyway, I'm sure Auntie will change her mind when she's thought things over. So I'll pretend I never mentioned the matter; why should I, after all? Toddy didn't ask me to interfere.' She sighed deeply. 'How I wish Hywel was here – he'd know how to persuade Auntie to be reasonable. After all, it's not—'

She stopped speaking abruptly as the door swung open and Toddy came out to meet them, smiling broadly and holding out a hand to Maggie which she immediately took. 'Good morning, Nell. This must be Maggie, of course.' He turned his friendly smile upon the land girl. 'I've heard so much about you that introductions don't seem necessary, because I reckon you've guessed who I am! Come in, come in; the kettle's on the boil and there are some Welsh cakes steaming on the griddle. And I made butter yesterday . . .'

'Wharra lovely feller,' Maggie said as they left, pausing at the top of the hill to wave down at the small figure standing in the doorway of the Swtan. 'And why d'you call him old? I know he's got white hair, but he can't be more than forty or fifty. From the way your aunt talks, I'd have thought he were at least a hundred!'

Nell laughed. They had pushed their bicycles up the hill, but now they mounted and turned their machines towards Ty Hen. 'I know what you mean; I was

433

flabbergasted when I first met him. It's just that when I first spied him from a distance, I saw his white hair and leapt to the conclusion that he was really old. Then Hywel called him "the old feller" and said he had a pension 'cos he'd been injured in the last war.' She sighed. 'Once you get an idea into your head, it's damned difficult to get it out again, but I'm really glad you liked him. What do you think about his offer to take us out fishing next time we go over? He told Hywel and me that the *Maud* – that's the name of the boat – was built for a crew of two, but now I think he only said that because he knew Hywel wanted to be alone with me. The *Maud*'s quite big enough for three, so if you'd enjoy a trip . . .'

'Wouldn't I just!' Maggie said fervently. 'So long as Auntie don't go kickin' him out before then!'

Much as Nell had enjoyed her outing with Maggie, it paled into insignificance beside the excitement devouring her as her meeting with Hywel drew near. They had arranged to meet on Lime Street station between ten and half past on 30 April, and though Nell hoped very much for fine weather she knew that, rain or shine, the day would be a special one.

On the morning in question, she awoke as soon as the alarm went off, got out of bed and lit her candle, for it was still dark. Washing in cold water made her shiver, but the shiver was partly anticipation, and as soon as she had rubbed herself dry and scattered a little of the precious scented talcum powder which she kept for special occasions she crossed to the window and looked up at the sky. It was clear, the stars twinkling brightly, and there was a line of colour on the eastern horizon which seemed to promise another fair day. Nell swung round and examined the garments she had put out the previous evening. She had very few clothes, apart from the working things she wore every day, but she had bought a blue cotton dress from a market stall in Llangefni some weeks earlier and thought it would do very well provided it did not rain. The coat which she had worn on her arrival at the farm eighteen months before had inexplicably shrunk, though when she had said as much to Maggie her friend had guffawed rudely.

'The perishin' coat can't shrink, you halfwit; you've got bigger,' she had said. 'I bet you didn't have no real figure when your mam bought that coat, but now you've got a bust and a waist and that. If it's cold enough for a coat, you'll have to wear it, but it won't be a bit comfortable. Leave it unbuttoned and sort o' flung back . . . but if I was you, I'd risk freezin' rather than wear that old thing.'

So now Nell put on the blue cotton dress and her old white sandals – who looks at feet? – then rooted in her chest of drawers for her navy cardigan. She had darned the holes in the elbows and replaced a missing button, though she had not been able to match the colour. Then she picked up the soft brown crayon which lay on her chest of drawers and tried to draw a line up her calves, to give the illusion that she was wearing stockings. The line, however, was so wobbly that Nell, sighing, gave up, scrubbed it off with her

435

flannel, picked up her old brown shoulder bag and headed for the stairs.

She reached the kitchen, expecting to find it in darkness, and gave a squeak of surprise when she opened the door to find the room lamplit and her aunt, fully dressed, already at the stove. Kath smiled at her niece and jerked a thumb at the frying pan on the range before her. 'Cut a couple of rounds of bread; I'm making you bacon and egg since you oughtn't to set off on an empty stomach,' she said. 'I've boiled the kettle; make us both a paned, there's a good girl.'

Nell set to work, saying as she did so: 'Oh, Auntie, you really shouldn't have . . . you are good! I was going to make do with a cup of tea and some bread and butter; bacon and eggs are a real treat.'

Her aunt ladled the food on to a plate and set it down before her niece. 'And you don't need to hurry because I'm going to drive you to the station in the pony trap,' she said gruffly. 'Can't have you arriving at Valley all of a muck sweat.' She dished up her own breakfast and sat down opposite Nell. 'Give Hywel my regards and tell him to take good care of himself.'

'I will,' Nell said fervently, tucking into her breakfast. 'You may be sure I will, Auntie.'

Nell was waiting under the clock on Lime Street station, more convinced every moment that something awful must have happened, for she had arrived at ten thirty and now it was just past twelve o'clock. She had almost given up when she saw an engine drawing in alongside the platform and doors beginning to open, and she was actually turning away, convinced that she and her lover were destined not to meet, when a voice she knew and loved spoke her name.

'Nell! Oh, thank God you waited! I've been telling myself that you'd think you'd got the day wrong, or I had.'

Warm arms enveloped her and she felt safe and happy for the first time since she had arrived in the city. 'Hywel! Oh, Hywel! I thought you were never coming. I thought something awful must have happened to your train, or that they'd stopped your leave at the last minute! I wanted to telephone the airfield, but I dared not leave the station in case you arrived while I was gone. But now you're here, so everything's fine.' She snuggled against him for a moment, then drew back, linked her arm with his and began to pull him towards the exit. 'Where do you want to go?'

They emerged on to the street and Hywel gave her waist a squeeze. 'Tell me, cariad, is there a Lyon's Corner House round here? I've been travelling since before six this morning and I'm parched. And it was too early for the cookhouse to make breakfast, so I'm quite hungry as well.' He smacked his lips. 'I wouldn't say no to a pot of tea and a meal of some description.'

Nell arrived back at Valley on the last train and to her surprise, for she had not expected to be met, there was Feather, harnessed to the trap, with her aunt at the pony's head. Nell, who had sauntered out of the station, preparing to tackle the long walk home, for she knew no taxi would be available so late, gave a cry of joy and ran over to her aunt. 'Oh, Auntie, you are good! I *do* hope you haven't met every perishin' train.'

Her aunt returned her hug, then gestured to the pony trap. 'Get in, cariad,' she said briskly, then chuckled. 'Fond though I am of you, we've been far too busy for me to go chasing off to the station every hour or so. Besides, I guessed you and young Hywel would want to spend as long as possible together, which meant you'd almost certainly catch the last train. If you'd come earlier, of course, you might have taken Mr Jenkins's taxi, so when you'd not turned up by ten o'clock I decided to give Feather a bit of an airing. Well? Did you have a good day?' She joined Nell in the trap, then clicked to Feather and the equipage moved forward. 'You can tell me all about it as we drive.'

Nell snuggled into her seat and tapped the large brown paper parcel on her lap. 'It was a perfect day,' she said contentedly. 'But I didn't forget the commissions you and Maggie gave me. I bought a length of gingham for Maggie to make up into a summer frock and another length for you, only not gingham, just cotton.' She looked anxiously at her aunt in the faint light afforded by the moon. 'You did say blue, didn't you?'

Aunt Kath nodded. 'That's right. I'm no hand at dressmaking, but Mrs Scissor in the village does a really good job, provided you don't want anything too fancy. And now tell me about your day.' She turned and smiled at her niece. 'I don't want any intimate details, though I don't suppose there was much chance of canoodling with the city jam-packed as usual.'

Nothing loth, Nell began to describe her day until the moment of parting on the station. Then, as the pony and trap turned into the lane which led to Ty Hen, she twisted round to face her companion. 'Do you remember me saying that Hywel had something important to discuss with me? Do you mind if I tell you what it was? It's – it's not exactly a secret, but I don't mean to confide in anyone else. The truth is, I'd like your advice.'

'Fire ahead,' Auntie Kath invited. In the moonlight, Nell could see a little flush creep up her aunt's cheeks and a smile of pleasure tilt the corners of her mouth. 'I won't say a word to a soul, and I'll do my best to help in any way I can.'

'Thanks,' Nell said briefly, then took a deep breath and let it out in a long sigh. 'Oh, Auntie, I just don't know what to do for the best. It seems that Hywel has a friend at the airfield, a young man called Toby. Toby's married and he and his wife rent a cottage halfway between the airfield and Tern Hill village. A week ago, Toby heard he was to go on a course at Church Stretton, to learn to fly bombers instead of fighters. This means he won't be returning to Tern Hill 'cos at the moment, at any rate, there are only fighters on the station. Toby's offered the cottage to Hywel and me. If we got married, Hywel would get a living-out allowance and he says I could easily get a job on one of the surrounding farms, either as a land girl or just as a farm worker. Only I think it's too soon. We've known one another less than a year and we didn't discover we were in love until a month ago. I'm not going to change my mind, there could never be anyone but Hywel for me, but actually marrying . . .'

'It's a big step,' Auntie Kath agreed slowly. 'But war makes a difference, cariad. You won't be seventeen until June, which is awfully young to get married, even in wartime. And if you've doubts . . .'

'Not about Hywel, but about other things,' Nell admitted. 'I've never had to run a house, or cope with rationing, because you've done it all. And then things are easier here – foodwise, I mean – because you grow so much of your own stuff, and keep hens and pigs and cows . . .'

Auntie Kath chuckled. 'You'd learn soon enough how to manage your little house, and you've finally become a fair little cook,' she pointed out. 'As for rationing, that's something that we've all had to learn, old and young alike. What you've got to ask yourself, dearest Nell, is whether you want to spend the rest of your life with Hywel. Are you happy with telephone calls and meetings when you can both be spared, or do you want to be together in the fullest sense of the word?'

Nell put her hands to her flushed cheeks. Auntie Kath clearly understood that part of her reluctance was a fear that marriage was a great deal more intimate than what you might call courtship. Would loving Hywel be enough? Other girls talked of the intimacies they shared with their boyfriends, but Nell had no real

440

idea of what went on between two people once the bedroom door closed behind them. And she was beginning to wonder, she realised guiltily, whether she wanted to know.

She said as much, falteringly, to Auntie Kath, who gave a short bark of laughter and then leaned over and patted her knee. 'I can remember feeling the same when Owain and I first wed,' she told her niece. 'It wasn't something folk talked about then, but though I didn't love Owain, I trusted him and I was right to do so. If you remember, I was still in love with another man, yet very soon my marriage was the best thing that had ever happened to me. Does that answer at least a part of your question?'

'Yes, I suppose it does,' Nell said slowly. 'In fact, if only Hywel were still stationed at Valley, I don't believe I'd hesitate. I'd know heaps of people and I could come back to Ty Hen whenever I wanted. In fact, I could go on working here . . .'

'You're thinking that you and Hywel could have moved into the spare room,' her aunt said, nodding and smiling. 'But believe it or not, cariad, even more problems would have raised their ugly heads. Could you have walked into your bedroom with Hywel and not felt embarrassed? Believe me, two women into one kitchen don't go. I told you how Nain resented any attempt on my part to help in what she regarded as her own home. I dare say I wouldn't make such difficulties for you, but I expect I'd interfere. I wouldn't mean to, but if I saw you doing something wrong I wouldn't be able to resist telling you so.'

Nell heaved another sigh as her aunt drove the pony into the farmyard and drew to a halt. She climbed down and went to the pony's head, and once her aunt was on firm ground she began to lead Feather towards the stable, saying over her shoulder, 'Then do you advise me to agree to get married by special licence, which is what Hywel wants? Or shall I say I need more time and set the wedding date for autumn – or even next spring?'

'Now there I can't advise you,' Auntie Kath said, beginning to untack the pony. 'It's the one question that only you can answer. I – I was in a similar position once, and now, with hindsight, I believe I took the wrong decision. But I'm sure about one thing: you are very young to get married. Further than that, I dare not go. All I will say is, think long and seriously before you make up your mind.'

Nell agreed to do so, thinking that if her aunt knew what Hywel had suggested she would probably have forbidden him even to visit the house, for Hywel had wanted her to go over to Tern Hill and spend a weekend either at a local pub or at Toby's cottage – as Mr and Mrs Smith, of course. She had been shocked . . . but tempted nevertheless. However, now at home once more the idea seemed downright ridiculous, and she decided to put it out of her mind. I'm not seventeen yet, she reminded herself defensively. We've plenty of time for – for that sort of thing.

A couple of days after Nell's return from her trip to Liverpool, Maggie came in from a visit to the village to order animal feed, a newspaper in one hand and her face very red. She burst into the kitchen and slammed the paper down on the table. 'Them buggers have pretty well flattened Liverpool,' she said breathlessly. 'The bloody Luftwaffe targeted the docks, but . . . well, read it for yourselves. Dai Bread told me it's been on the news, but there's something wrong wi' our set; I reckon our accumulator needs rechargin'.'

'Flattened?' Nell faltered. Her voice wobbled and she could feel the blood draining from her cheeks. 'Oh, Maggie, all my relatives . . . well, not the kids, they've been evacuated, and Mam and Auntie Lou aren't there but the rest . . . Auntie Carrie, Auntie Susan, Grandma Ripley and Great-aunt Vera, my cousins . . .'

'Here, read it,' Maggie said briskly, indicating the paper she had put before Auntie Kath. 'It's real bad, chuck. I know I don't have no family, but I've a grosh o' pals in the city.' She turned to Auntie Kath. 'Can we go back, Auntie? There might be something we could do to help.'

Auntie Kath, however, shook her head. 'It says here that the railway stations have been hit and the phone lines are down,' she said. 'There's no way a couple of girls could do anything to help; in fact you'd be more of a hindrance, because judging from the report in that paper there might well be more raids to come.'

'Oh, but Auntie—' Nell began.

Her aunt cut across her words. '*No*, Nell. I said no and I meant no,' she said firmly. 'For a start, how do you mean to get there, with the railways out of action, and no doubt the buses and trams too? Besides, you know very well that your mother sent you to me to keep you safe, not to let you go hightailing off to the city when it's being deliberately targeted by enemy planes.'

'Oh, but Auntie, suppose Hywel was there? Suppose he – he was injured in one of the raids? I can't bear to think of him needing me, wanting me . . .'

'You can telephone this evening and make sure he's still at Tern Hill. Be grateful that you can still keep in touch, which might not be possible if he were stationed near Liverpool.'

'But what about the aunts, and . . . and everyone?' Nell said frantically. 'Auntie Susan's on the telephone; I don't know her number but I dare say I could find it if I rang the exchange.'

'No point,' Auntie Kath reminded her. 'As I've already said, cariad, the lines are down. But I promise you that as soon as it's safe to do so you and Maggie can go back to the city and check up on your friends. Until then you must just continue to be patient, get on with your work, and wait for news. For a start, I'll get the trap out and fetch the accumulator; then at least we'll be able to listen to the wireless morning and evening.'

It was not until the raids had ceased and the clearing up had begun that Aunt Kath agreed to the girls' taking a long day off to check on their friends and relatives. They set off at the crack of dawn and came back to Ty Hen on the last train, but with quiet minds.

The death toll had been heavy, but though Kingfisher Court had been razed to the ground, and the damage to the docks, warehouses and city centre was almost unbelievable, both Maggie's pals from the children's home and Nell's relatives had been in shelters almost throughout the seven nights of raids. Though many of them were homeless, owning only what they stood up in, they had their lives, and after what they had been through, and what others had suffered, that seemed enough.

Nell and Maggie returned from the city knowing that the destruction was so bad they could do nothing to help. Indeed, as Auntie Kath said, their job was providing food for those unfortunates who were not in a position to grow fruit, vegetables and cereal crops for themselves. Nell rang Tern Hill most nights, but Hywel was up to his eyes in work since so many aircraft had been damaged.

'But I'll probably get a few days off when the damage has been put right,' he said. 'As soon as I know, I'll tell you, and then we can see if . . . well, if we can meet.'

Nell had muttered something to the effect that meeting would be very nice, but she knew that Hywel meant more than just meeting. He still wanted them to book in somewhere as Mr and Mrs Jones, and Nell could not bring herself to agree to such a thing. But meeting, if it was just meeting . . . her mind spiralled off into conjecture, so that when Maggie spoke to her, she answered at random and then had to apologise. Maggie grinned. 'You've been in a dream ever since

Hywel said he'd be gettin' leave and wanted to meet you somewhere quieter than Liverpool.' She turned to Kath. 'But tell your niece not to mek it anywhere in Wales, if she's thinkin' of a dirty weekend, 'cos the Welsh would be shocked out o' their minds.'

'That's enough of that sort of talk,' Auntie Kath said, but not as though she really disapproved. In fact there was a little smile on her lips and Nell wondered, with some dismay, whether her aunt had guessed that it had not just been marriage and a special licence that Hywel had suggested.

She shot a look at her aunt from beneath her lashes, reflecting that Kath and Eifion had had to work twice as hard as usual when she and Maggie had visited Liverpool. The four of them were sitting round the breakfast table, eating porridge and drinking tea, and now Kath cleared her throat and tapped the table to quieten Maggie, who was talking at the top of her voice about the possibility of a date with Bryn in the coming week.

'Dates! That's all you young things think about,' Kath said. 'But today it's my turn to abandon Ty Hen for a few hours; I've some business to transact in Holyhead so I mean to take Feather and the trap down there as soon as I've finished my breakfast and tidied myself up. I may be back in time for evening milking or I may not, but you girls – and you, Eifion, of course – should be able to cope without me just for once.' She stood up, collected the empty porridge bowls, and took them over to the sink. 'It's a lovely day; I'll treat it as a bit of a holiday. A break wouldn't harm me. And I

446

might meet a friend or two whilst I'm in Holyhead. Be a nice change to gossip with someone other than you three.'

Nell, Maggie and Eifion set to work with a will. After milking it was Maggie's turn to work in the house – which included, today, baking shortcakes for their elevenses – whilst Eifion fed the stock and Nell went to check on the youngest lambs. These animals were kept in the small pasture nearest the house, since they were more at risk than the older ones, and having satisfied herself that all was well she was heading across the yard once more when she happened to glance across to the shed where they kept the bicycles, and saw that the door was flung wide. Frowning, she went across to check and discovered that one of the machines was missing.

She was still staring, nonplussed, when a voice spoke behind her. 'What's up, Nell?'

She jumped and turned to face Eifion, who was peering over her shoulder. 'One of the bikes is missing,' she said slowly. 'Surely it can't have been stolen?'

Eifion snorted. 'Is it likely?' he said scornfully. 'Borrowed, mebbe . . . or— Hold you on a moment.'

To Nell's surprise he ambled across the yard to the stable, then turned and grinned at her. 'Feather's still in her stall,' he called. 'Clear as mud it is that your auntie have took the bicycle. I'll let Feather out into the birch pasture, shall I?'

'Yes . . . no . . . I don't understand!' Nell wailed, following Eifion across the yard. 'Why should she decide to cycle all the way to Holyhead? It's all of twelve or fourteen miles. She must have decided to go into the village instead.'

Eifion went into the stable and opened the half-door to grab the pony and put a rope halter round her neck. Then he led her out of the farmyard and across to the birch pasture where Hal was already grazing. 'I don't know about the village,' he said, slipping the halter from Feather's neck and slapping her on the rump. 'If you want to find out where the missus have gone, though, take a look at the dust in the lane. We've not had rain for days and days . . . there should be tyre marks.'

There were. Crossing the lane from the birch pasture to return to the farmyard, Nell and Eifion saw the tyre marks at once and they led, not to the village, nor to Holyhead, but in the opposite direction. Nell's hand flew to her mouth. 'She's gone to the Swtan,' she gasped. 'I bet she's going to tell Toddy that he can't stay. Oh, Eifion, she wouldn't want Maggie or me to know what she was up to because she must have realised we'd be upset. Look, go back to the kitchen, would you, and tell Maggie I shan't be in for elevenses. I'm going to take the other bike and see if I can catch Auntie up before she reaches the Swtan.'

'Well, I don't know as your auntie would turn him out, 'cos that ain't her way,' Eifion said slowly. 'Likely she'll just name a peppercorn rent—'

Nell cut across him. 'No, don't you remember how angry she was when I told her Toddy had suggested buying the place? She seemed to think it was an insult to Owain. She actually said she would have him out.'

'Oh aye, but has she done it?' Eifion asked. 'Course she hasn't! If you ask me, despite what she says, she's curious about the old feller and has gone to take a crafty look.'

Nell raised her brows. 'I s'pose that's possible,' she said grudgingly. 'But I've been meaning to ask you why you call him the old feller. He must be thirty years or more younger than you. Auntie calls him that too, though she's never met him.'

Eifion shrugged. 'I dunno. Before we knew his name was Toddy, everyone referred to him as the old feller and I guess it's stuck; it's a nickname like.'

'Hm. But to go back to what I was saying earlier, people do strange things when they're angry. Oh, I don't know; I hope you're right, but I'd feel a whole lot happier if I knew for certain what she meant to do. I think I will take the other bike and see if I can catch her up, ask her why she pretended she was going into Holyhead.'

She entered the bicycle shed, mounted the remaining bicycle and would have pedalled away had Eifion not grabbed the handlebars.

'Hold you hard, girl,' he said, a trifle breathlessly. 'Your back tyre is as flat as a pancake. You ain't going anywhere until it's mended, 'cos that's a real bad puncture. Here, go and fetch me a bucket of water and I'll mend it for you.'

'Thanks, Eifion, but I don't mean to hang around,' Nell said. 'I'll walk. With a bit of luck I might even arrive soon after she does, since I shall be going across the fields and she'll have to go by road. Tell Maggie where I've gone.'

When Kath got up that morning, she decided that she had put off visiting the old man in the Swtan for quite long enough. She would go this very day, taking Feather and the trap, and confront the trespasser – for that was what he was – and suggest that he use his savings to buy or rent some other property. She did not really know why she should resent the man; perhaps what she really resented was the fact that she herself, the owner of the Swtan, was just about the only person who had never met Toddy. In a way, she had brought this upon herself by her determination never to cross the threshold of what had once been the home of the woman who had hated her so heartily.

You were a fool, Kath Jones, to tell everyone that you didn't care who had taken over the longhouse, she reminded herself. Now, by being so stubborn, you've made it impossible to pay an ordinary visit. However, there's no reason why you shouldn't leave the pony and trap in Llanrhyddlad whilst you have a stealthy look round . . . Her mind did a double take. Of *course* there was a good reason for not leaving the trap in the village. If she did so, everyone would know that she had gone to the Swtan to spy on the old feller, so, since she had no desire for folk to think ill of her, she had chosen to go on the bicycle instead of taking Feather.

Pedalling slowly along in the sunshine, she thought

she would hide her machine in the little copse just behind the well and then take a look at the Swtan. Then it occurred to her that there was a good chance the man would be out in his boat, for the tide was right and the sea smooth as silk. She decided that, provided she did not see him pottering around outside the longhouse, she would make her way to the cliff top. If his boat was not on the beach, then she would be safe to really look into things: to examine the outhouses, the vegetable garden, the state of the land upon which he trespassed, maybe even the longhouse itself. She remembered belatedly how she had once loved the cottage, been truly proud of the way she and Owain had made it good, lavishing not only time and material goods but also love on this odd little dwelling perched high above the sea shore.

By the time she reached the little copse by the well, she was very thirsty. She was tempted to lower the bucket into the water and take a drink, but chided herself for her impatience. How embarrassing to be caught helping herself when she had not even had the courtesy to knock at the Swtan door. There was a stream, of course, where the animals drank, but she knew that the water was not fit for human consumption, so instead she settled herself in a little hollow from where she could watch the cottage.

After about ten minutes she grew restive. Hadn't Nell said something about a dog? She could see no kennel and she knew enough about farm dogs to be sure that any resident collie would have given warning of her approach as soon as she had left the lane and walked across to the well. Deciding she had waited long enough, she got to her feet, returned to the lane, and followed it until she reached the cliffs. She went to the edge and looked down on the spot where she remembered the *Maud* was usually pulled up. Indeed, with the tide at this stage, there was only one spot where she could have been beached, and she was not there. Kath put her hand above her eyes to shield them from the sun and peered out to sea. Was that dark smudge on the shining blue water a boat? It certainly looked like one, and as her eyes adjusted to the brightness she saw that it was indeed a small craft, with a solitary rower at the oars, for on such a calm day it would have been wasted effort to have raised the sail.

Kath stood watching for a moment or two longer and was able to ascertain that the boat was moving away from the shore and not towards it. Good! The old feller was off on a day's fishing, which would give her time to have a really good look, not only at the byres and outbuildings, but at the stock and at the Swtan itself.

As she retraced her steps, instead of passing by the wicket gate which led to the Swtan and its garden, she went through it, pausing to look with approval at the neatly laid out bed of herbs. She wondered if the old feller used the herbs when preparing food; if so, he was a better cook than most men. No dog had leapt out barking at the squeak of the wicket gate; clearly, if the man had once owned such an animal, he did so no longer.

Her hand was out, towards the door, when it occurred to her that though she knew the place was empty she should at least knock. However, she was already holding the latch, so she rattled it, then pushed the door open. She stepped inside, not because she wanted to – she had quite made up her mind not to enter the Swtan but merely to look around – but because she felt impelled, almost as though someone behind her had given her a push. And instead of the empty room she had expected, to her horror she saw a man, sitting with his back to her, holding out a slice of bread on a toasting fork towards the fire. She registered that this was certainly not the gypsy she had half expected to find here, for the man who had moved into the Swtan four or five years ago had been short and squat, black-haired and swarthy. This man was tall . . . taller than Kath herself, and fair-skinned, with dark brown eyes, and though his hair was grey he was much younger than she had thought, downright youthful compared to what she had imagined.

Kath began to apologise for entering without knocking and then stopped short, a hand flying to her mouth. Who did he remind her of? Somewhere, in the back of her mind . . . but then he dropped the toasting fork and came towards her. 'Kitty?' he said huskily. 'Oh, Kitty, can it really be you?'

Kath had only time for one disbelieving cry of: 'John! Oh, my dearest . . . but they told me you were dead!' before she found herself in his arms. They clung together, unable to believe what was happening to them until Kath broke free with a shaken little laugh.

'Oh, John, for a moment I thought you were a ghost, but you've certainly proved you're flesh and blood. But I don't understand . . . Owain told me that you were dead, and he would never lie. Oh, John, I've a million questions . . .'

'Come to that, so have I,' he said, an anxious look crossing his face. He sat down on the oak settle and pulled her down beside him. 'Darling Kitty, are you married?'

When Kath shook her head, he gave her an exuberant hug, then settled back with his arm firmly round her shoulders. 'We've a great deal of talking to do. I want to know how you ended up here, and I dare say you'll want to know the same about me. Did you know I was here? Is that why you came?'

Kath, secure in the circle of his arm, gave a breathless little laugh and reached up to stroke his cheek. 'No, I had no idea. I'm your landlady, Mrs Jones, the one who refused to let you pay rent, and was outraged when she heard you'd suggested buying the Swtan. Oh, John, if only I'd not been so pig-headed! If I'd behaved properly, we could have met when you first came here, but you see I thought you were the same as a gypsy who simply made himself at home in the Swtan five years ago. He seemed to believe that if he took possession he could either make me pay to get it back or steal anything worth stealing, or both. When that didn't work he all but wrecked the place, so when my niece said there was a man talking about buying the Swtan I came here full of righteous fury to turn him out . . . oh, John, John, what a fool I've been! I've thought of you every day and never known you were so close.'

'Me too,' John said, and his voice was a low hum, like a contented bee. 'If only I'd plucked up my courage and come up to Ty Hen – I take it that is where you live? – we could have had two blissful years . . . oh, my darling!'

They kissed, then drew apart, each one gazing into the face of the other, each one regretting the lost days, weeks, months. Kath was the first to break the silence.

'Well, John? Who's going to start explaining what has happened over the past twenty-odd years?'

'It had better be you,' her lover said, after a moment's thought. 'My story is both lengthy and complicated.'

Kath drew a deep breath. 'After I was told you were dead, I was ill for a long time . . .'

Chapter Nineteen

Kath finished her tale, then got up and pulled the kettle over the fire. 'After all that talking, I need a cup of tea, and so will you,' she said. 'It's your turn now, John; I just hope your story isn't as complicated as mine.'

John smiled at her, then he also drew a deep breath. 'The trouble is, I don't really know what happened to me around October 1918, because I lost my memory. The first thing I can remember now was waking up to find a sloping ceiling, very clean and white, just above my head. I ached all over, I couldn't move my right arm or my right leg, and there were unbearably loud noises in my head. I know now that I was shell-shocked as well as injured, but as soon as I was well enough to take in my surroundings, and see the people who were nursing me, I realised that I was in a small bedroom in a French gîte, which is a little farm, a small-holding perhaps, and the young woman who was looking after me was the farmer's daughter. The trouble was, having lost my memory, it seems that I had lost my command of English too, for I continu-ally addressed my rescuers in Welsh – I suppose you could say I went back to my native tongue. As you can imagine, this added to their confusion, but Maria took to sitting beside my bed for hours at a time, patiently teaching me to speak French, and I must say I took to it like a duck to water.'

'They were good people. When Monsieur Duval – that was the farmer's name – found me, I was a long way from the action. I was all but dead and he thought I must have crawled away from the noise and fighting, injured though I was. He and Maria got a door off its hinges, put me aboard, and carried me to their home, where Maria nursed me devotedly.'

'But surely they must have known you were an English soldier. Didn't they recognise your uniform?'

'By the time they found me my uniform was in rags and filthy with mud; unrecognisable, in fact. They burned it and gave me a striped nightshirt and a pair of big felt slippers of Monsieur Duval's.'

'What good people. I wish I could thank them. Go on, my dearest.'

'As I said, I'd lost my memory. I didn't know who I was, or where for that matter. The Duvals did their best to discover my identity, but Europe was in a ferment, what with the war and the influenza which had decimated the troops in all the countries involved, so they had no luck. As I grew better I was allowed to get up and give a bit of a hand in the house. Marie had christened me Henri for some unknown reason, since they had to call me something.' He chuckled grimly. 'I didn't care what they called me, as you can imagine. I could have wept – sometimes I did – when I tried to remember who I was and came up against a closed door. My injuries healed and I grew strong, but my mind was another matter. There were times when I thought the door which had slammed on my past life would never reopen, yet a little thread of hope kept reminding me that the local doctor, who had examined me when I first arrived at 'La Picurie,' had said he was sure my memory would return some day.'

'My poor darling,' Kath said tenderly. 'After what you'd gone through, to have to suffer such a terrible deprivation . . . So you grew better and continued to call yourself Henri . . . What happened next?'

'Next I had to find work, because I could scarcely expect anyone to pay me for doing nothing and anyway, with every day that passed I was growing stronger. Monisieur Duval was in his seventies, and needed a strong, healthy man to help him on his farm. I was delighted to work for him and could not help hoping that the tasks he set me might bring my past back, because he often did not have to explain what he wanted done; the knowledge of farming was a part of me and came to the surface when needed.

'I was sure, by now, that my memory really was sleeping and had not gone for good. But at first I just enjoyed the work and revelled in simply being out of doors once more. And what caused my memory to begin to function, oddly enough, happened in the most ordinary and unromantic way. I'd gone into the nearest town with Maria, where there was a street market in full swing, and as I was pushing my way towards the stall Maria wanted to visit I saw a saw a small boy playing "The Skye Boat Song" on a wooden whistle.'

458

John put his hand up to his eyes in an involuntary gesture and Kath saw a tear trickle down his cheek. She realised what an emotional moment it must have been and waited to let him recover his composure before saying gently: 'Yes, music can make one remember times past, both happy and sad. Was that how it was for you?'

John nodded, produced a handkerchief and blew his nose, then resumed his story. 'Sorry about that. Well, as soon as I heard the melody, I remembered myself as a small boy, struggling to play it on just such a whistle. I could even see the scene in my head: I was standing in the farmyard, with hens clucking about my feet and my father's dogs in the distance, rounding up the sheep and bringing them down from the hills for shearing. I could actually smell the oil in their fleeces, which was even stronger at that moment than the sweet scent of the pinks which Mother had planted under the cottage windows.

'I turned to Maria and began to speak in Welsh, which caused her eyes to widen with dismay, for I had not used the language for months. Then, for a moment, I spoke in English, hastily switching to French before the poor girl grew too confused.

'She, bless her, took one look at my face and immediately grasped my hand, leading me away from the hustle and bustle of the market to a quiet little lane. "You've remembered! That's wonderful," she cried, putting he hands behind my head and pulling it down until our eyes were on a level. She stared very hard at me for a moment, and at that moment she looked beautiful to me. "What's your name? Quick, tell me, before something distracts your attention."

'Her gaze was almost hypnotic and I replied at once that I was John Williams. Then, I have to admit, we both shed a few tears and I gave her a hug. She had been the best of friends, but as we returned to the market I think we both knew that our friendship would have to end. I would go to the authorities, tell them who I was – remember, I had no idea I'd been posted first missing, and then dead – and after that I would return to England.

'A few days later, however, I learned to my horror that everyone had been told I was dead; everyone in this case, my love, being my "next of kin" Owain – and therefore yourself. It seems that there had been a huge explosion virtually on the gun I commanded and what remained of the crew was pretty well unrecognisable. But there had been a sniper shooting at us from the shelter of a nearby hayloft and I'd waved my pay book to distaract him; when they found it, it had two bullet holes clear through it, so naturally enough they thought I was one of the unidentified dead. Anyway, as soon as I possibly could, I left the Duvals, and the farm and set out for England, meaning to find you.'

'When was that?' Kath asked eagerly. 'Why didn't you come to Kingfisher Court? I was there until the spring of 1919.'

'It was in the spring of 1920 and that's exactly what I did do. But I never reached Kingfisher Court. I was heading for the Scottie, because I knew the court was off one of the side streets somewhere, when a voice shouted my name. It was Reggie Jackson; d'you remember him?'

Kath nodded. Reggie, though a good-tempered and jovial man, was a heavy drinker and most definitely not on the Ripleys' visiting list. 'What did he tell you?' she asked bluntly. 'He knew I was married, of course. '

'Yes, he told me that, but he had no idea where you were living, though he thought it was somewhere in Wales. He said you'd married a chap called Tom Whitaker and gone away with him . . . there had been bad feeling, he said, between the sisters, but he could tell me nothing more.'

'Oh, how typical of Reggie!' Kath cried. 'And to think that if only he hadn't muddled me up with. Trivie, you might have searched for me. Yes, Owain and I were married, but just to know you were still alive would have thrilled us both.'

John shook his head. 'No; what was the point? Once I knew you were married – it didn't matten who to – I felt strongly that to turn up on your doorstep would only give us both pain. If I could have discovered your doorstep, that is. I decided that my best course would be to return to France. Maria had cried when I left, though even through her tears she was wishing me luck and praying that we would meet again one day. So I returned to the smallholding, told the Duvals that I had sorted things out with the authorities in England, and asked Maria to marry me. Together, we toiled on the farm; her father died after half a dozen years, and though the work was incredibly hard, it served to keep my mind off what might have been.

'As for Maria and myself, our marriage lasted until her premature death in 1937, just after her sixtieth birthday, and it was then that I decided to sell the gîte and come home.'

'Then she was quite a bit older than you?' Kath said, rather timidly. 'Was she very beautiful? I know I shouldn't ask but . . .'

John frowned, but his eyes were twinkling. 'Oh, Kitty, she was a dear, worthy woman, but she would have been the first to tell you that she was no beauty. Well, I'm no beauty myself.'

'And you had no children? Though you were married for so long?' Kath said, unable to resist asking the question which had leapt into her mind. 'Owain and I would have loved a family, but it was not to be.'

'We had no children either,' John said quietly. 'She was a grand woman, my Maria, but I've not finished my story yet. You must be prepared to listen for a bit longer.'

Kath pulled a face, feeling her cheeks go hot at what had sounded like a reprimand. John saw it and cupped her face in his hands, then dropped a kiss on her nose and released her. 'Little goose,' he said tenderly. 'As I was saying, with Maria gone, I had no reason for remaining in France. The Depression meant I got a ludicrously small sum for the gîte, but I didn't care. All I wanted now was my own country; I found myself longing for lush Welsh pastures, woods carpeted with bluebells in the spring, and gentle hills dotted with sheep, and the mountains of Snowdonia rearing behind them.'

He tapped Kath playfully on the nose, making her blink. 'You've never asked me where I came from; well, it was a tiny cottage in the Ogwen valley. My grandparents farmed mountain sheep and had had to struggle hard just to make a living. They both died soon after the end of the war – they never knew I hadn't been killed in 1918.'

Wordlessly, Kath squeezed his hand, and neither of them said anything for a moment. Then she gave herself a little shake, and pressed his hand again. 'So you came home in '37,' she prompted. But how did you end up here?'

'Well, as I said, I was growing homesick for Britain, but I might have stayed in France, believing you to be happily married and beyond my reach, but for the political situation. I could read it all so clearly! I'd met Germans in France, and thought them proud and arrogant. Furthermore, they were building an immense war machine: huge tanks, great battleships and a well-trained and efficient army. Others were saying "if war comes", but I said 'when war comes' and of course I was right.

'Once I was back in England I tried to enrol in the air force, because I thought, judging from what had happened in the Spanish Civil War, that what was coming would be largely an air battle. But they wouldn't have me, so I tried the army and then the Navy, with the same result. I decided that if I couldn't fight for my country – I was forty-seven after all – then

I would buy myself a few acres of land and grow the food which I knew a country at war badly needs.' But discovered that there was a good deal I didn't know about modern British farming methods. Then, though the price of land was lower than it had ever been and farmers were going broke left, right and centre, most of the good places were either too big or to expensive for my purse. I knew a lot about sheep from the old days, but I wanted a mixed farm and for that I needed experience. So I signed on to work for as long as I was needed on a farm in Norfolk. And when I'd been there about a year Mr Maddocks, the farmer, said, regretfully, that he no longer needed me as his son was coming home. However, he paid me a month's wages in lien of notice so that I might have something to live on whilst I searched for another billet and suggested I should go on a walking holiday, keeping my eyes open for properties to rent as I went. I thought it an excellent idea and decided to walk in Wales because, in my heart, that was where I wanted to be. I was born and bred here after all. I meant to go by train as far as Bangor and follow the coast from there, but believe it or not I fell asleep and didn't wake until the train reached its terminus in Holyhead.'

Kath chuckled. 'You must have been on the boat train; what a bit of luck that you didn't decide to go on to Ireland! Why didn't you make your way back to Bangor?'

John grinned. 'Because the moment I realised I was on Anglesey I remembered that Owain had come from round here; he'd often said how beautiful the island

464

was. So I humped my haversack into Holyhead, got myself a night's lodging, and set off the next day. I stuck to the coastal path, so of course I found the Swtan and fell in love with it. It was almost derelict; a good half of the thatch had blown away, I imagine, in the previous autumn's gales. The end wall of the cow byre needed repointing – the wind whistled through the gaps in the stones hard enough to blow a fellow over – and the garden was waist high in weeds, brambles and huge clumps of gorse, as were the nearest meadows. It was plain it had been abandoned for a good many years, but I thought it had immense possibilities. It was small enough for one man to manage, yet big enough if he farmed wisely to reward him with a good living. There was no question of buying it then, for every penny I owned would have to be spent on putting both the cottage and the land into working order once more, but I could rent. Having gone round it really carefully, making notes as I went, I walked up the hill to the nearest village and asked at the post office whether they could tell me who owned the longhouse above Church Bay. They said it belongs to a Mrs Jones, who hated the place. "There was a family feud, I reckon", the postmaster went on, "because she won't even hear it talked of. I tell you what, though, if you moved in there, worked hard to make it good so that she could charge you a rent worth having, she'd maybe put things on a proper footing. After all, the Swtan was a thriving little place fifteen or twenty years ago, so I'm told, and could be again."'

'So you came upon the Swtan by chance,' Kath

breathed. She looked around her at the comfortable kitchen, the fire roaring in the range, the gleaming windows through which she could see the tidy rows of vegetables, the new young apple tree and the stone wall that guarded the garden from the depredations of the beasts which grazed on the turf beyond. 'You've done all this in such a short space of time – it's unbelievable!' She got to her feet. 'Will you show me round, dearest?'

She took due note of the work that still needed to be done to the outside of the Swtan, appreciating the fact that John had put his energies into making good the outbuildings that housed his stock, and his neat vegetable patch. But when they were about to go back inside something seemed to strike him and he put a detaining hand on her arm. He pointed to the bench.

'Sit down for a minute, my love. Just there, by the door, and tell me . . . tell me what you can see.'

Puzzled, Kath took the seat he indicated, then stared before her at the gentle hills, the gorse and the rocks and the little winding path which, she knew, would lead eventually to Ty Hen. Then she turned to John, seated beside her. 'I can't see anything unusual.'

'But can you *feel* something?' he asked. 'A cold wind round your back, a sort of uneasiness? I've felt it myself, and wondered whether I should move the bench to get it out of the draught, but it's been here a long time, a lot longer than I have. I admit I don't understand why one should feel chilled when sitting in full sun, but I tell myself it may have a meaning for somebody else. Let's change places for a moment.'

They did so and John beamed at his companion. 'It's gone!' he said triumphantly. 'I can feel a breeze on my cheek and the sun on my head, but neither the cold draught nor the feeling of unease. You've known the Swtan for years; is there any explanation, do you think?'

Kath looked at him seriously. 'I think there may be. Once, long ago, a woman who hated me and wished me harm spent a great deal of time sitting on this bench. I thought she sat here to repel me if I ever tried to visit her, because after Owain died she forbade me to cross her threshold. But I didn't feel a cold draught, or a sensation of uneasiness. Could it be possible, do you think, that she's been waiting to see me all these years, and now that I'm here she's been able to leave at last?'

'Perhaps she wanted to ask your forgiveness for the way she behaved,' John said quietly. 'People can change. I think it's quite possible that she needed to make her peace with you before she went . . . home. But now I'm sure of one thing: this bench will never be moved while I'm alive.'

He stood up, took hold of Kath's hands, and pulled her to her feet. 'Well, you won't be able to live here once we're married,' Kath said as they re-entered the longhouse. 'Oh, John, finding you again is the answer to every wish I've ever wished, and every prayer I've ever prayed. We must be two of the luckiest—'

She stopped speaking as the door burst open and Nell appeared. She was pink-cheeked and breathless, already talking as she entered. 'Oh, Auntie, please don't make Toddy leave! You've seen how he's looked after the Swtan, which just proves that he'd be a very good tenant. I know how you feel about selling . . .' She stopped speaking, staring from one face to the other, and slowly, very slowly, a broad smile spread across her face and lit her eyes. 'You're not angry with each other,' she announced. 'In fact, you're . . . you're . . .'

'In fact we're old friends,' John said, smiling at Nell. 'I'm John Williams. We met long ago, during the Great War, but we lost touch, and it's taken us more than twenty years to find each other. But we won't lose touch again because we're going to get married.' He turned to Kath. 'Isn't that so, my darling?'

Nell was staring so hard at John that she scarcely heeded his words. 'You're the man in the kaleidoscope,' she said slowly. 'Or rather you're the photograph in the kaleidoscope. Oh, you're older, and your hair is grey instead of black . . . now why didn't I realise that you were him when we first met?'

John looked puzzled, as well he might, but Kath gently disengaged herself from the arm which John had slung round her waist and went over to give her niece a kiss. 'Wish us happy, Nell,' she murmured. 'We've waited a long time for this. I only thank God that it's not come too late.'

Nell returned her aunt's kiss with warmth, then abruptly turned back towards the door and pulled it open. She was just slipping through when her aunt spoke again. 'Where are you going, queen? You've not said you're pleased with our news.'

Nell turned round and Kath saw that she was pink-cheeked and starry-eyed. 'Oh, I'm sorry, Auntie. I'm really, really glad for both of you,' she said quickly. 'I can see how happy you are and you've made up my mind for me. I won't make the mistake of waiting. I'm going to go into the village and ring Hywel, and I shall tell him yes.'